Elias in Love

GRACE BURROWES

Published by Grace Burrowes Publishing, 21 Summit Avenue, Hagerstown, MD 21740.

Cover design by Wax Creative, Inc.

ISBN: 194141950X
ISBN-13: 978-1941419502

To the members of the Scotland With Grace 2016 Tour, and to our hosts in Scotland, Jim and Susie Malcolm

CHAPTER ONE

"If Zebedee weren't already dead, I'd have to kill him for this." Elias Brodie meant every disrespectful, dismayed word of that threat too.

"Your uncle was a generous man," Angus Whyte replied, pushing more papers across a desk so large, it had probably been built in the office it dominated. "He held mortgages for half the family, assisted with the educations of any niece or nephew who showed the initiative to better themselves, and spent a fair bit of coin entertaining and housing you, Elias Brodie."

Elias sat back rather than rip the papers to confetti.

"These investments are pipe dreams and unicorn flatulence, Angus. Emu farms and lavender crops? Organic flowers and solar canal covers? It's not as if Uncle refurbished the lodge solely to keep me out of the wet."

Angus pushed to his feet and leaned over his desk, which only underscored how short Uncle's solicitor had become, or perhaps how tall Elias was in comparison.

"You young fellows," Angus began in the broad accents of the native Aberdonian. "You think you'll live forever, and never stop to consider maybe the old fellows don't exactly plan on having a coronary. Zebedee was as fit as any man his age, and he'd brought the earldom back from ruin twice in the last fifty years. These investments are sound, and you'd be smart to hold onto them. Organic flowers aren't simply profitable, if the bee die-off isn't to—"

Elias rose to his full height, for the petty pleasure of looking down on the person who might have warned him the family finances had flatlined five years ago.

"Spare me the green sermon, Angus. You should have let me know Zeb was frittering away a fortune, and you bloody well had a duty to mitigate the worst of his queer starts. I was supposed to be in Italy this afternoon, making some new friends."

Angus sat with an unceremonious *plop*, followed by the wheeze of the chair cushion as it conformed to his slight weight.

"New friends, bah. You're more like Zebedee than you want to admit. He loved the ladies, and they loved him."

Elias donned his reading glasses, then took the nearest list of figures to the window where natural light made deciphering the numbers easier. On the street below, every stoop and window box was festooned with flowers that could never out-cheer the grimness of native Scottish building stone.

Though Zeb had loved those flowers and the hard granite from which so much of Scotland's enduring architecture was built.

"I have learned to avoid the ladies," Elias said. "Both of my former fiancées were ladies, lest you forget. I am fond of *women*, though from the looks of your balance sheet, the women won't be half so fond of me by this time Monday."

"Then they were never really fond of you, were they, lad?" Angus withdrew a pipe from the pocket of a coat that had gone shiny at the elbows decades ago. Harris Tweed, doubtless, for Angus favored durable goods. "Not too many genuine earls left these days. Can't blame the women for wanting to be your countess."

Elias wouldn't mind having a countess, provided she was also interested in being his wife. "What is this golf course halfway down the page?"

"Your cousin Niall's property in Perthshire. Zeb took a fifteen percent share to help Niall get started. Niall is gradually buying it back."

If there was one thing Scotland did not need, it was another golf course. "Tell Niall the payment schedule just accelerated. He had sponsors on the pro tour once upon a time. Let them help him get started."

Elias had crossed paths with Niall on that tour, shared a few beers, wished his cousin luck, and left him to his golf groupies. That had been… a while ago.

"Niall finally got himself a wife, Elias, and being a Cromarty, that means there will soon be children. He's also recently finalized plans to expand the golf course to eighteen holes and that necessitated taking on another partner of sorts—a MacPherson of all the dodgy characters. You can't accelerate the note on Niall now."

Well, shite. Elias recalled choosing the obligatory bottle of wedding whisky from Zeb's cellar only a few months ago, though lately, the Cromarty branch of the family was enjoying an epidemic of weddings.

"What about these townhouses?" Elias asked. "One in Edinburgh and one in Glasgow. They're forty-five minutes apart if the roads are dry, and we have apartments in both cities. Can't these be sold?"

Angus used a square nail to clean out his pipe, tapping the bowl ever-so-patiently on an ash tray made of a lathe-turned curling stone.

"Those properties house your cousin Morag's pottery shop, and your cousin

Elspeth's book shop. Your great aunt Helga lives in the one in Edinburgh, and her sister Heidi lives in the Glasgow property."

Helga had a recipe for tablet that could make little boys sit still and say grace by the hour. Heidi had taught Elias how to smoke a cigar without inhaling when he was fourteen.

"Then the whisky has to go, Angus."

"Not the whisky, Elias," Angus replied in scandalized tones. "If we auction Zeb's collection, the value of every asset you hold will halve overnight and your property taxes will mysteriously climb when next it's time for an appraisal."

As the Aberdeenshire sun drifted into the long, slow hours of late afternoon, Elias went down the short list of assets, and the endless list of liabilities. Obligations to family cut off the quickest sources of cash, and common sense precluded others, until Elias had gone through two drams of Glenmorangie Quinta Ruban.

And his entire store of optimism.

No significant assets were left that didn't involve breaking a trust, triggering complicated tax ramifications, or taking a significant loss over the longer term.

"Next you'll be telling me I have to marry for money, like some damned Englishman," Elias said. The figures on the page had started to blur, not because of the whisky, but because this wake for the earldom's finances had inspired the beginnings of a migraine.

"Can't you find an Italian baroness with a weakness for whisky and wool, lad?"

"They tend to prefer Italian barons, silk, and excellent wines. I can lease the lodge—put it on one of those fancy 'rent a castle in the Highlands' websites, and let golf-mad trust fund babies wreck it weekly for an exorbitant sum."

"You'd rent the lodge?"

The lodge was Elias's home, the place Zeb had taken him the first summer after the accident. A fellow could contort himself into a hundred comfortable postures in any one of the lodge's two dozen padded window seats. He could read away entire seasons, impress his friends, or hide from them, and even—when travel, keeping up with Zeb, or chasing clients and baronesses grew wearying—hide from his own life there.

"Better to rent the lodge than lose the castle." Elias pinched the bridge of his nose, which set up a peculiar tingling behind his eyes. "We'll have to call it a day, Angus, or I'll be useless for the rest of the week."

"You young people have no stamina."

"You old people have coronaries at the most inconvenient times. Does one of the aunties have room for me?"

Angus stopped shuffling papers, squeaking about in his chair, and fussing with his pipe.

"You'd move in with one of those two? Helga MacQuiston tried to enter the caber toss at Braemar when she was nineteen years old, and Heidi MacGregor put her up to it. They're daft, the pair of them, and they'll wheedle all the good Speysides from you before Christmas."

Angus, of course, favored the milder, more complex Speyside whiskies to the peaty kind. He and Uncle Zeb had spent the last fifty years arguing over which distilleries produced the best single malts. Elias had advocated for variety in one's pleasures, and neither old man had spoken to him for weeks.

"I'll pay my rent in single malts," Elias said. "Spend half the year with each auntie." Except the cities were too loud, too busy, and too gray. If Helga and Heidi didn't drive him daft, city life would.

"Ye canna let those two old harpies have the Speyside," Angus said, coming to his feet. "Your grandfather bought some of those bottles, and that collection is the envy of half the royal families still standing."

"If I don't get somewhere quiet and dark, I won't be standing," Elias said. "We can continue this tomorrow morning."

"Tomorrow I have pipe band rehearsal," Angus shot back. "Maybe you should go to Italy and sit around in a conspicuous location swilling expensive wine and wearing silk. You've the Brodie good looks, and they're worth something."

Elias had spent many a pleasant afternoon sitting around some Italian countess's swimming pool, swilling expensive wine under the Tuscan sun, and wearing nothing but a smile.

Foolish of him, in hindsight, but lovely memories nonetheless.

"The Speyside can be auctioned," Elias said. "I'll rent out the lodge. Tell the charities I'll no longer waive my director's dividends, and find me a few more boards to sit on. Zeb donated enough to his friends' pet causes that I ought to have some value as a fundraiser on behalf of hermaphroditic okapis, or whatever the latest eleemosynary fad is."

Angus wrapped a black watch plaid scarf around his neck, though spring was giving way to summer.

"Are ye drunk, lad?"

"Not even close. Working on a migraine." Also grieving.

"There aren't any okapis in Scotland that I know of," Angus said, tugging a green Harris Tweed newsboy's cap over his head. "I'm not even sure I know what an okapi is."

"They're a sept of clan giraffe." Maybe Elias was a bit toodled, though two drams over the course of an afternoon wasn't nearly enough to get him tipsy. "Apparently, there isn't any Strathdee wealth in Scotland, either. Maybe we should auction the Campbeltown whiskies too."

"Cease your blaspheming, Elias Brodie, or Zebedee will have no choice but to haunt your dreams."

Elias hoisted his rucksack to his shoulder, passed Angus a black watch plaid umbrella, and surveyed the documents, folders, and curling lengths of calculator paper strewn about the desk.

"You'll just leave your office like this? A full scale model of the massacre of clan Brodie's finances?"

The massacre of Elias's freedom, his home, his life?

"Spare me your Scottish drama," Angus said, tossing the end of his scarf over his shoulder. "This isn't the potato famine."

"I'll not lose the castle, Angus. If I have to marry a damned octogenarian duchess, or audition for margarine commercials, the castle stays in our hands."

"Margarine is bad for you," Angus said, leading the way from the office. "You'd marry an English duchess to keep the castle?"

Zeb had, fifty years ago, and he'd recalled her fondly once she'd left him her fortune.

"I'd sponsor Helga in the Over-Sixty caber toss, lend her my kilt to compete in, and flash the queen, but that won't raise much cash." Might be fun, though.

Angus used a key that could easily have doubled as a bottle opener to lock his office. "Did I mention that you own a wee farm in Maryland?"

A *wee* farm could not pay the taxes on a grand old castle, much less finance its refurbishment.

"Zeb never mentioned a Maryland property." Maryland was in the eastern United States. Hot and humid, probably as a result of proximity to the American seat of government, which source of overheated air bore the entire responsibility for global warming, according to Zeb.

"Inherited it from some golf-mad spice heiress about ten years ago," Angus said, leaving the key atop the lintel. "No accounting for Americans, though this farm usually makes money."

So of course, Angus had waited half the day to disclose its existence. Elias paused at the bottom of the steps and braced himself for the torture of bright sunshine.

"How much money?"

"You raise alpacas on this property, I think, or llamas." Angus marched out onto the sidewalk, into brilliant afternoon light that drove daggers into Elias's eyeballs.

"Some sort of runty camel," Angus went on. "The fur is worth a fair bit, something like $10 an ounce finished, and a breeding pair can bring a pretty penny."

A pair of refugees from Clan Camel would not a castle rescue. "You think living with runty camels preferable to living with Heidi or Helga?" And in the great swamp of the American seaboard? America had mosquitoes with measurable wingspans.

Angus paused on the street corner. "I think anything is preferable to selling the whisky, my boy. Zeb would agree." He jaunted along, an old man with a young man's stride.

Angus was wrong though. Zeb would have excused Elias for selling the whisky, for flashing HRM, for selling his very body, if that meant the castle stayed in Brodie hands.

Elias's temples had begun to throb, and even his vintage Vuarnets didn't help with the pain. A memory niggled beneath the gathering weight of his headache.

"Zeb owned that farm free and clear," Elias said. "Eight-hundred-forty-three acres of excellent farm land less than 70 miles from Washington D.C. Seventy miles is nothing to an American, a hop, skip and a toddle."

"Proving the lot of them are daft," Angus said, touching his hat brim to a pair of teenage girls walking a white terrier. "You don't have to live with your aunties. You can live in your farmhouse, and rent the estate properties, and in a few years, when the market has re-aligned and interest rates—"

"We're selling the damned farm, Angus. Not in a few years, now. If it's within commuting distance of the Washington suburbs, then it's going to waste growing corn and potatoes. Email me the particulars, and we'll get it on the market within the week."

The terrier trotted over to sniff at Elias's jeans. Elias waited rather than make the dog choose between obeying its masters or its instincts.

"The arable land is farmed by the locals," Angus said, "and Zeb had some caretaker living in the house and minding the livestock. Should be a fairly nice dwelling, based on the appraisal."

At least the property wasn't devoted to organic pansies or rain resistant lavender. "The farm will be the first asset to go."

The terrier finished its inspection and returned to the girls, who were smiling bashfully at Elias. He smiled back, which sent them giggling on their way.

"Stop your damned flirting, Elias. Somebody should take a look before we sell it, and you'll have to sign all the paperwork to get the real estate people off the mark. I hear you can work on your tan in Maryland this time of year."

"I wasn't flirting, I merely smiled." At a pair of schoolgirls. "I'll not be flying across the ocean to make the acquaintance of a herd of American camels, old man. You go. Overnight whatever documents I have to sign, and I'll sell only half the Speysides."

Angus came to an abrupt halt. "Not even for your arrogant ungrateful *lordship* would I miss the pipe band competition. You own that farm, you should have a look, and while you're larking about I'll hide the whisky so you can't sell it. Just have a wee dram or three before you board the plane and you'll be fine."

All the whisky in Scotland could not make a trans-Atlantic flight "fine" for Elias Brodie, Earl of Strathdee and a damned lot of frozen assets.

"Find me those charities, Angus. Start with half a dozen. I'll sell my titled soul in addition to my camel park and my whisky."

"Your charm has apparently deserted you, but then, Zeb always said you took after the Cromarty side of your family more than the Brodie's."

"Zeb said a lot, most of it utter, blethering nonsense. Get me the information on the farm, and I'll arrange the travel. Best of luck with the pipe band competition."

Angus's old face creased into a fierce smile. "We were runner up last year, and we've been practicing. Those damned MacDonalds won't know what hit them."

Elias stuck out a hand, for he needed to find darkness and a dose of painkiller. "Save me a CD of the final round."

Angus shook, a good, firm grip. "I'll send it to your camel plantation. Don't fret about the flight, Elias. Catch a wee nap, watch a few movies, flirt with the flight attendants, and you're safe on the ground."

Then Angus was off, whistling an off-key version of "Scotland the Brave."

Brave didn't come into it. Elias was angry, but he'd fly over the Atlantic every day, sell the farm, sell his father's sunglasses, the salmon fishing at the lodge, the apartments in Paris and London, the whisky and his soul, if necessary.

He'd be god-damned if he'd be the Brodie who lost the castle that had protected his family's fortunes for more than a thousand years.

* * *

Dogs were like crying babies. They had cranky barks, worried barks, feed-me barks, and furious barks. Violet couldn't decipher the message behind the racket Sarge and Murphy were making, and that in itself was cause for worry.

She closed her blog post file and peered over the porch railing at the Hedstrom place, where a big black pick-up sat in the lane before the farm house. Big black pick-ups were common in rural Maryland, but activity at the Hedstrom farm had become a novelty. The two cats who'd been hanging out there over the winter had gradually migrated to Violet's summer kitchen, leaving the neighboring property to deer, rabbits, raccoons, possums, and the occasional teenage couple in need of a barn to park behind.

Two guys got out of the truck, men not boys. One was dark-haired and wore a black kilt, and the other was… dark. All over dark. Dark hair, dark suit, dark backpack hanging casually off one broad shoulder, dark glasses.

Sharp-dressed, like a god-damned, no good, parasitic, profit-sucking, land-violating developer. Violet shut down her computer, and whistled for the dogs to get back in the house. She ran upstairs, threw on a bra and a clean T-shirt, decided the yoga pants were OK, and slid into her garden clogs.

The two guys were still standing around in the driveway across the lane, Kilt pointing to the barn, while Suit lifted luggage from the back of the pick-up.

If these guys were the bellwethers for a land developer, the surveyors would come next, leaving odd little piles of dirt around the property, making sure the soil would percolate water at an adequate rate. Then would come a test well or two, and surveying stakes.

Anxiety, anger, and fatigue grabbed at Violet as she crossed her yard and traveled on down the lane. In the middle of Kilt's gesturing toward the ridge across the valley, Suit caught sight of her.

He was big, with the elegant proportions of a men's magazine model, and his teeth were bright white against a tan no local would have before high summer. The suit looked hand-tailored, and—surely a sign of the agricultural end times for the Hedstrom property—a gold ring winked on his pinkie.

Then he smiled, and for that gorgeous, charming smile alone, Violet decided not to trust him.

* * *

"Cease bletherin', Dunstan. My neighbor has come calling."

Dunstan Cromarty had up and gone for a lawyer, which transgression Uncle Zeb had paid for. Worse, Cousin Dunstan now lived in the States, in the same valley where Uncle's property lay.

Elias's property now.

"Damn it, Elias, the woman's not even introduced herself and you're flirting."

"You can flirt too," Elias said, as five feet and possibly two inches of soft curves and bright red hair came striding down the drive across the lane. "Women like flirting with old married men like you, because all you can do is flirt."

"Jane would beg to differ," Dunstan said. "I've no idea who this is."

This was a female, a fine place to start. She moved with the easy grace of a woman at home in her body, wearing nothing more than a lavender T-shirt and black yoga pants. Elias liked a lady who knew how to make the most of her assets, but he loved a lady who didn't wear too many clothes.

Less to take off that way.

Her footwear dimmed his smile. They were a pragmatic choice, and Elias had lately had a bellyful of pragmatism.

"Hello," the woman said, walking right up to them. "I'm Violet Hughes. I live across the road."

"Dunstan Cromarty," Elias's cousin said, sticking out a hand. "Pleased to make your acquaintance. My wife Jane and I live about two miles up the valley in the old Yoder farmhouse. This is my cousin, Elias Brodie."

Elias shook hands, the woman's grip businesslike and… *calloused?*

"Mr. Cromarty, Mr. Brodie, may I ask what your business is here? The guy living on the property hasn't been around for several months. I haven't seen any sign of foul play, but his leaving was odd."

I will kill Angus Whyte. "Odd, how?" Elias asked.

"Here one day, gone the next," Miss Hughes shot back. "Left his cats without a word, and didn't bother to spay the female either."

"That explains why Angus's letters have gone unanswered," Dunstan muttered.

"As my question has," Miss Hughes retorted.

Part of Elias wanted to march her right back across the lane, because this was his property, and what he did with it was none of her business, but he'd been raised in Scotland. Taking an interest in the neighbor's situation was simply prudent, and often well-intentioned.

"I now own this farm," Elias said. "Inherited from my uncle, and Dunstan and his missus own a law practice in Damson Valley."

A fat marmalade cat strutted out from under a yew bush and stropped itself against Miss Hughes's ankles.

"Zeb's gone?" she asked, as orange cat hairs collected apace on her clothes.

"Heart attack," Dunstan said, sparing Elias the necessity. "Quick, and apparently inevitable."

Miss Hughes had a lovely mouth—wide, lush, full—made for smiling, though she positively glowered down at the cat.

"Zebedee Brodie wouldn't have said anything if he'd suspected a heart problem," she said, "because he was a stubborn old Scotsman who thought himself indestructible. Dammit to hell. I'm sorry."

She picked up the cat and buried her face against its furry nape. A feline rumbling ensued and more orange cat hairs cascaded onto Miss Hughes's T-shirt.

Elias shifted to stand upwind of her and her cat hair factory. "Thank you for your condolences. I've inherited the property, and was under the impression we had a fellow living here, minding the buildings and dealing with the livestock. You say he ran off?"

Elias wanted to run clear back to Scotland. Dunstan wasn't even sweating, and Miss Hughes appeared perfectly comfortable, while the afternoon sun and an empty belly were broiling up a headache at the base of Elias's skull.

He could go two years without a bad headache, but they'd come with ferocious frequency since Zeb's death.

"Haven't seen your tenant for nearly three months," Miss Hughes said, "possibly longer. I gather you're both Scottish?"

"Aye," Dunstan replied. "I've been in the States for many years, Elias landed at Dulles earlier today, though he's visited before. Is that one of the orphaned cats?"

"Bruno. He's friendly. Worst watch cat in the valley, and he's a soon-to-be father." She held the cat up at eye level, though the beast just kept rumbling. "Though he won't be making any more contributions to the gene pool. Bruno and I went for a little ride to see Doc Garcia about a month ago."

More dependents and another debt to be repaid—just what every impoverished earl dreamed of.

"Would you know how to gain access to the premises?" Elias asked. The alternative was to muck in with Dunstan and Jane, though Elias had only met

Jane an hour ago. She and Dunstan gave off the newlywed vibe, and were in the middle of renovating their farmhouse.

For a few days, Elias could manage on his own, in what was the only house he owned free and clear. The farmhouse was pretty, in a rural way. Made of gray fieldstone, with a big, white porch on the front and a few oak trees providing shade. They had that filmy green, new foliage look, and Elias spotted a squirrel's nest amid the branches.

Zeb would have wanted flowers for this place. Elias only wanted a good price for it.

"You don't have a key to the house?" Miss Hughes asked, putting the cat down.

"We had a caretaker," Elias said. "He had the key or keys." Surely the concept of a caretaker wasn't uniquely British?

The woman's gaze went from Elias to Dunstan. Dunstan had the family coloring—dark hair, blue eyes, solid muscular build, and height. Elias was an inch or two taller, had the same blue eyes, but some perverse genetic imp had added enough red that his hair was Titian, at least in strong sunlight.

Which this was. Also godawful humidity.

"Your wife is Jane De Luca, isn't she?" Miss Hughes asked, peering at Dunstan. "She was in a birdwatching class I took a couple years ago, though she didn't come very often. I'd heard she'd married a Scot."

"Jane and I married over the winter holidays," Dunstan said, smiling at his boots. "She kept her maiden name for professional purposes, and we've merged our law offices."

Though like Dunstan, Jane apparently knew bugger-all about the local real estate laws. She knew how to make Dunstan smile though, so Elias forgave her for stealing Dunstan from Scotland once and for all.

"Congratulations," Miss Hughes said, returning Dunstan's smile. "Lovely isn't it, when a business can be kept in the family?"

They shared a beaming, smiling moment, while a trickle of sweat formed between Elias's shoulder blades.

"About that key?" he said.

The cat strolled off in the direction of Dunstan's truck, backed up to a hubcap, and twitched its upright tail. A distinct *zang* sounded as the cat did what male cats did.

"He smells my cat Wallace," Dunstan said.

"You named your cat for William Wallace?" Elias asked. "A cat, Dunstan, for one of Scotland's greatest heroes?"

"My Wallace is independent, never backs down, never submits to authority. The name suits him."

"Bruno is a name for a cat. Felix, Waldo, even Geeves, but Wallace? Would you name a canary for Rabbie Burns? A dog for old Conan Doyle?"

Twenty years ago, this might have been a matter for fists, but Dunstan only fought with words now, and Elias was desperate to get out of the sun and into the company of a roaring air conditioner.

"I can't make out your words when you argue with each other," Miss Hughes said. "It's kind of cute."

This smile she didn't merely flash at Dunstan, but allowed to settle over Elias for a moment as well. Shy, a hint of mischief, and a surprising warmth. Not the smothering warmth of Maryland as summer approached, but the warmth of a good whisky on a cold night.

"I have never been called cute before," Elias said. "Though arguing with family is something of a Scottish tradition. About that key?"

Bruno had made a thorough sniffing inspection of the visible truck tires. He strutted over as if to sniff next at the last pair of bespoke dress pants Elias might buy, ever, so Elias shifted his suitcase to keep it between himself and the cat.

"As it happens, you're in luck," Miss Hughes said. "In the country, you generally let the neighbors know how to get into the house, and your caretaker was no exception. Fred was a quiet guy, though I think he played the ponies at the track in Charles Town. Come along, your spare key shouldn't be hard to locate."

She marched off—in this stifling, cloying heat, she marched—and Dunstan fell in step beside her. Elias did not trust the cat so he picked up his suitcase and followed, lest every piece of clothing he'd brought with him end up smelling like cat piss.

CHAPTER TWO

Thank heavens, Elias MacSuit wasn't a developer. He was the new owner and had settled family in the area. Violet's emotional battle pennants luffed and then drooped against her mental flagpoles.

Zebedee Brodie would not have left the most beautiful patch of Damson Valley to an indifferent heir.

"Sod this," Mr. Brodie muttered, hoisting the suitcase to his shoulder rather than try to wheel it through the long grass. "Did the yard service also run off to join the circus?"

"I can bring my riding mower over," Dunstan said as they clomped up the porch stairs.

"And how much will you charge me for that?" Mr. Brodie replied, setting the suitcase down. The leather looked butter-soft, and the name embossed on the metal logo was French. Violet made a note to google it, though she suspected the price of that one bag would have paid a landscape crew for many hours of work.

"I'll bill you a pack of Fraoch," Dunstan replied. "Jane fancies it, except when she doesn't."

"What's Fraoch?" Violet asked, stretching up to run her fingers along the top of a window sill. She couldn't quite reach, but neither man seemed inclined to help.

"Heather ale," Mr. Brodie said. "You'll get filthy doing that."

Violet's fingers encountered a key. She held it under Mr. Brodie's nose. "I'll get into your castle, unless you'd like to do the honors?"

An odd expression flickered across Mr. Brodie's face, while Dunstan snatched the key out of Violet's hand.

"Allow me. I've a way with an old lock, according to my wife."

Mr. Brodie snorted. "You fall for that? Have you a way with dirty laundry? A sink full of dishes? A vacuum cleaner?"

"Where uppity cousins are concerned, I have a way with a closed fist," Dunstan muttered, wiggling the key in the lock.

"*Uppity?* I'm *uppity*, am I now? You've gone Yank on me, Dunstan Cromarty, and as head of your family, I'll be having a word with your missus about corruption of your vocabulary."

Dunstan jiggled the key harder and pushed a meaty shoulder against the door. "The humidity gets to these old buildings."

Violet would have let him mutter and push and get nowhere for another few moments, but Mr. Brodie was enjoying Dunstan's failure a little too much.

"Mr. Cromarty?"

"A wee push," he said, ramming his shoulder against the door again.

"Might need some oil on the mechanism," Mr. Brodie said, shrugging out of his suit jacket. His shirt stuck to the middle of his back, though it had to be the whitest shirt Violet had ever seen. "Or perhaps you're turning it the wrong way. Americans drive on the wrong side of the road, put the steering wheel on the wrong side of the car. You cannot trust them to do anything in a predictable fashion."

"Mr. Cromarty?"

Both men looked at Violet as if she'd just led a heifer up the porch steps.

"That's the key to the back door."

* * *

The house was a metaphor for Elias's circumstances—once fine, still blessed with many good qualities, but at risk for a rapid decline.

"Your caretaker left in a hurry," Dunstan said, picking up a newspaper folded on the kitchen counter. "You say the man gambled, Miss Hughes?"

"That's according to the guys at the feed store, and their gossip is considered the best in the valley," Miss Hughes said, wrinkling her nose. "Let's open some windows, shall we?"

The kitchen was stifling and stale. A coffee cup and spoon sat in the sink along with a chipped blue plate. A dingy white towel had been crammed through the refrigerator door handle, and the windows were dim with dust. Elias hung his backpack on a chair rather than set it amid the dust.

"I hope you brought jeans and a work kilt," Dunstan said. "This place is a disgrace."

"It's the only disgrace I own in fee simple absolute, according to Angus Whyte. Let me do that," Elias said, as Miss Hughes tried to wrestle with a window sash.

She gave it one more shove and the window scraped open. Air moved—hot, humid air.

"I'll leave you two guys to admire the property," she said, dusting her hands.

"Come on over if you need anything, Mr. Brodie. We're decent neighbors around here, for the most part. You might see my dogs sniffing around your barn—Sarge and Murphy. They're friendly but Murphy has been known to get too interested in a bag of fresh garbage. Good luck with the place."

She stuck out a hand to Dunstan, then Elias, and with a bang of the screen door, was on her way.

"I suppose you'd best buy some cat food," Dunstan said, using the towel to wipe the dust from the kitchen table.

"I don't care for cat food," Elias said. "And I need to watch my pennies these days, or I'd be staying in a hotel."

"Don't make me thrash sense into you, Elias. You'll not be staying at a hotel when you've family in the valley. The cat food is for Bruno."

"Shite." Bruno, who was at that moment, insinuating himself against Elias's shins, leaving a fine coating of cat hair over a beautiful pair of charcoal wool trousers.

"You can stay with me and Jane, though with some hard work, you'll soon have this place ready to put on the market. Nobody will care what the house looks like."

Elias cared what the house looked like. "It's a fine old home, and should be properly maintained." He wrestled another window up, while Dunstan did battle with the window over the double sink. "Some soap and water, a bit of yard work, a few flowers on the porch, and it will show well enough."

The window over the sink gave with a screech. "If you're selling to a developer, they'll probably scrape the house and the barn, rip up the fences, bury the stone walls. You have some nice views here."

Elias put the cat out, holding it a distance from his body. "They'll scrape a stone house and stone barn? Are Americans truly so disrespectful of the past?"

"Americans are respectful of their coin and pragmatic. An empty barn serves no one, and what do you care? You'll be back in Scotland using your free golf privileges on Niall Cromarty's back nine. Let's find you a bedroom."

A stone barn was a work of art, and a stone house was the personal version of a castle, built to withstand centuries of weather, love, and loss.

"Maybe we can turn the barn into some sort of community center," Elias said, hoisting his suitcase, though he was more interested in finding a shower than a bed.

"There won't be any we about it." Dunstan wiped his hands on the dusty towel. "You'll get your money, and the purchaser will do as he pleases. The land comes under the jurisdiction of a zoning board, but it's not like Scotland where the local council keeps an eye on everything. Bedrooms will be upstairs."

"Let's find the air conditioning controls," Elias rejoined, following Dunstan up a narrow, turning set of steps. "Angus assured me all American houses have air conditioning."

"Angus lied, of course. Though most houses in Maryland have at least a few window units."

The upstairs was even hotter, and because only one window opened on the main hallway, dark as well. Dunstan opened a door revealing a bedroom, the bed unmade but the appointments commodious in a rural fashion. A small fireplace was flanked with worn armchairs, the rug a faded pattern of cabbage roses. A porcelain wash basin sat on top of a heavy bureau, and more cabbage roses adorned the curtains.

"You'll want to sleep on the other side of the house," Dunstan said. "The sun won't wake you as early."

Elias followed him across the hall. "Since when do lawyers concern themselves with sleeping late?"

"I'm a happily married lawyer," Dunstan said, his smile smug. "Sleeping late goes with the territory when Jane gets in a particular mood. Now this is lovely."

They'd found the master bedroom. The bed was an enormous brass article under a fluffy white eyelet coverlet, a door to the left led off to a full bath. A pair of white wicker chairs faced French doors that opened onto a balcony, and a dead fern sat in a brass pot in a spacious fireplace. The rugs were pale green on polished hardwood, a dusty cheval mirror reflected afternoon sunlight against the far wall.

"And there's your window unit," Dunstan said. "What more could a belted earl want?"

Elias was too grateful for the sight of the air conditioner to object to Dunstan's taunt. "That claw foot tub looks good right about now, so I'll see you on your way."

They trooped downstairs, which was relatively cooler, but still filthy with dust. The neglect bothered Elias but so did something else.

"Where are my camels?" he asked.

"Your what?"

"I know the land is mostly farmed by lease, but Angus told me there was significant profit resulting from alpacas or llamas or something of that sort. I don't see them, I don't hear them."

"And I don't smell them," Dunstan said, leading the way out the back door.

Across the driveway, the barnyard was deserted. No livestock to be seen, though Bruno sat on a fence post like a feline vulture.

"The bastard sold my livestock before he took off, Dunstan. Angus told me those animals were worth twenty thousand dollars a breeding pair."

"Then somebody owes you a quarter of a million dollars for receiving stolen goods," Dunstan said. "I can help you swear out a complaint against the caretaker."

If Elias had had a fine bottle of single malt at hand, he'd have drained the contents at one go, and bashed Dunstan's hard head with the empty bottle.

"I'm hot, I'm tired, I flew over the *Atlantic Ocean* this afternoon, and I'm preparing to share a manky old farmhouse with a shedding frenzy of a cat, Dunstan Cromarty. Spare me your lawyerly posturing. Miss Hughes said the caretaker gambled, and that means my quarter of a million is long gone. Thank a merciful Deity that eight hundred developable acres will be worth many times that amount."

And thank the same benevolent God that Elias would soon have privacy, because Angus Whyte was overdue for a sound verbal beating.

"A few hairy beasts more or less won't make a difference once the farm is sold," Dunstan said, as the cat hopped off its fence post. "Make sure you have cell service before I leave. This end of the valley can get a bit dodgy, especially when the weather acts up."

Elias swiped his phone on. "Three bars, though I've roamed enough that I'm about out of battery. See you Monday, and my thanks to you and Jane."

That was Dunstan's cue to shove Elias's shoulder or punch his arm in parting. Instead, Elias was pulled in a hug, thumped on the back, and squeezed hard.

"The Atlantic's a wee ocean," Dunstan said, "as oceans go, but I'm glad you're here."

In the next moment, Dunstan grabbed the bag of groceries from behind the truck seat, shoved it into Elias's arms, and drove the big black truck down the drive.

The quiet was different from Scottish quiet, but it was still country-quiet. The birds in the hedgerow across the road sang different songs, the scent was more freshly cut hay and less turned earth, but it was still the scent of open fields. The Appalachian Mountains weren't the Highlands, but they sheltered Damson Valley with the same geological dignity that characterized the Highlands.

"I lied to my cousin," Elias informed the cat who appeared to be once again contemplating abuse of Elias's tailoring. "I'm not sharing my house with you. You get more than eight hundred acres to enjoy, and I'll bide without your company at the house."

The cat went on ahead toward the back door, though the beast was in for a rude surprise. Elias let himself into the house and shut the door in the cat's disgruntled face.

A fellow learned to live with life's little disappointments, like an entire herd of valuable animals being liquidated by a thieving rotter.

"Nothing to do about that now," Elias said, setting the bag of groceries on the counter. First order of business was to charge up the cell phone, grab a shower, eat something and take a damned nap. Tomorrow was a day to rest and recover, but then Dunstan had scheduled a meeting with a real estate attorney for Monday morning, and by then Jane's car—in the shop for brake work—would be available to borrow for the balance of Elias's visit.

"And then I'm home," Elias said to the empty kitchen. The thought gave him a pang, because generations of Scots had gone forth to new lands, never to return home. This sortie to buggy, hot, humid, thief-infested Maryland would have loomed like a penal sentence had Elias's ticket been one way.

Home would be another transatlantic flight, but a red-eye, so perhaps he'd be able to sleep through part of it.

Elias fished his adapter and power cord from his backpack, jammed the adapter into an outlet above the counter, and attached the phone and cord to it.

Nothing, not a cheery little beep, not a chirp, not the charging icon. He tried another outlet, flipped a light switch, opened the fridge.

No power, which meant no air conditioning, no water, no lights… no *shower*.

"Probably just a fuse," Elias muttered, except that a trip to the fuse box on the back porch, some flipping of breakers, and a lot of vigorous swearing produced no evidence of electrical current.

Elias went back into the house, ready to call Dunstan, except… Dunstan and Jane were newly wed, and their house was in an uproar.

Miss Hughes had invited him to prevail on her for neighborly consideration, after all. Elias had done his share of camping as a youth, and Monday was soon enough to get an electrician out to the property.

He went upstairs to retrieve an item from his suitcase—he would not arrive to Miss Hughes' front door empty-handed—then came back down to the kitchen.

"I'm overdue for some good luck," he reminded his reflection in a dusty kitchen window. "Scots are resourceful, and we're determined. What's a little heat, a little dust and inconvenience, when a man has his wits, determination, the legendary Brodie charm, and a ticket home?"

He headed for the back door, as a torpedo of orange fur came hurtling through an open window.

Perhaps American felines had wit and determination too. "Guard the castle," Elias said, as the cat hopped onto the table. "If you're a Brodie, then guarding the castle is what you do best."

Elias left the cat on the table, snatched up his backpack, phone, adapter and power cord, and prepared to charm his neighbor.

* * *

"What brings you into the office on this fine Saturday afternoon?" Maxwell Maitland asked.

Bonnie Shifler didn't even look up. She'd been able to type 110 words per minute before Max had learned to crawl, and mere conversation with an attorney wouldn't slow her down.

"Derek needed his transcript by Monday morning, I needed to go out dancing last night. Ergo, I'm in the office on Saturday."

Wrecking Max's solitude. He'd heard her lacquered nails clicking away on the keyboard, and that had been the end of his ability to concentrate on the new real estate listings.

"Do you ever consider telling Derek to go to hell when he makes these last-minute demands?"

Bonnie was a shared resource, meaning Max paid half her salary. She looked well put together even in jeans and a Terrapins T-shirt, and the staff at the courthouse liked her. Derek Hendershot, the other attorney in the office, was responsible for all of her overtime and most of her complaints.

"I curse Derek Hendershot nightly," Bonnie said, clicking away, "but I need my paycheck."

Stop whining. If Max couldn't find a good-sized chunk of developable land in the next six weeks, Bonnie's paycheck would be cut in half, assuming the newly divorced Hendershot didn't trade her in for a pair of twenties.

"I'll leave you to your transcript," Max said, heading down the hallway to his office. The building was a converted row house in the historic part of town—meaning a leaking roof, creaking floors, and stuck windows came at a premium.

Bonnie's typing paused. "Oh, Maaaaax."

He didn't turn around. "Bonnie?"

"Saw something interesting as I drove in here today."

Bonnie lived out in the valley, among the farms and fields west of town. "A loose horse qualifies as interesting to you." A guy in cowboy boots who could boot-scoot his belt-buckle off interested her more. Bonnie never wanted for lunch dates, which was fine with Max. He got more done when he had the office to himself.

"So be a shit," Bonnie said, "and I won't tell you what I saw. I drive right by the Hedstrom farm though."

In country fashion, the locals still referred to the property by the name of the family that had owned it for more than a century. The present owner's name was Zebedee Brodie—or had been. The old guy had passed away a few weeks ago, and while Max had liked him, he hadn't liked having his good faith offers for the property tossed back in his face.

Hadn't liked that at all.

Max turned and held his ground twelve feet from Bonnie's work station. "I can drive by the Hedstrom farm myself." Though why torment himself? The farm was a developer's wet dream, in terms of size and location, but not for sale meant not for sale.

"I saw a guy in a kilt standing around in the driveway," Bonnie said, flipping over a page of her steno pad. "Saw two guys, actually. Turns out the guy in the kilt was Dunstan Cromarty. He's married."

And thus, even in a kilt, he only registered on Bonnie's radar because he was an attorney, and legal assistants tended to know the attorneys in a small jurisdiction. Moreover, Cromarty was married to another lawyer, Jane De Luca, and God Almighty probably didn't turn his back on Ms. De Luca when she was on cross-examination.

"Cromarty is Scottish," Max said, propping a shoulder against the wall. "Zeb Brodie was Scottish, and I seem to recall a connection there."

Max kept his tone casual, but current was zinging around his mental circuit board. The Hedstrom property had been on his watch list, but the prospect of squabbling heirs, probate, and the pernicious influence of Violet Hughes right next door had made the watching a pessimistic undertaking.

"Zeb Brodie was hot, for an old guy. That accent, you know." She winked at Max, and she had a cute wink. He did not wink back.

"What else did you see beside Cromarty's knees, Bonnie?"

"The other guy was very well dressed, tall, had that look, you know?"

Damn all manipulative women, and the men who disempowered them into being that way.

"What look?" If she told him the guy looked like a developer, Max would drive his fist through the wall.

"He looked around as if he owned the place, as if he owned the whole valley. I'd like to see that guy in a kilt, or out of one."

"Hostile workplace, Bonnie," Max said, lest she think he wanted the details of her love life. "So you saw Cromarty and another guy on the Hedstrom property. Thanks for sharing. Unless a drill rig was in the driveway, or you saw perc tests in the hay fields, I'll get back to work."

Bonnie rose and put her hands on her hips. "Why are you such a bastard, Max? In the first place, nobody will do perc tests until the first cutting of hay comes off in the next couple weeks. In the second place, you need to get out more. You're not ugly, but you sure as hell lack for charm."

"Charm," Max muttered, wrinkling a nose that nobody had ever called handsome. He was six foot two, dark-haired, and prone to working out his frustrations at the gym. Violet Hughes had called him a monster.

"Charm," Bonnie said, "is when you take an interest in people. Even Derek has pretensions to charm, though he's about as transparent as a four-year-old boy eyeing the cookie jar."

Charm would not create a project to wave at the board of directors for New Horizons, Inc. Charm would not put the Hedstrom place on the market or give Max more time. The deadline for presenting a new project was July Fourth, and Peter Sutherland did not grant extensions.

"Derek is a manipulative SOB whose former wife should have dumped him at the altar," Max said. "What else did you see at the Hedstrom place, Bonnie? We both have work to do."

She sat back down, pulled up her document—Bonnie would never leave her chair without closing her file first—and resumed typing.

"He had a suitcase. The GQ guy with the movie-star shades had a nice big suitcase, and he did not look in the least like a farmer."

Bonnie would know. Her people had been working the land for generations, and about all there was to do in Damson Valley was farm—and frustrate developers who might have brought some civilization to the place.

"You're suggesting the new owner might have come to see his property," Max said, his mood shifting from frustrated to… determined. Cautiously determined.

"Yeah, that's what I'm suggesting. Now, will you go dancing with me?"

She was almost old enough to be Max's mom. "Why? Are your cougar creds slipping?"

"You are an asshole. Derek can't help himself, but you… I'd go dancing with you, Max, because it's fun, because you need to get out, because I might be able to introduce you to a sweet young thing you'd like to slow dance with. Forget I offered. You're hopeless, and I wash my hands of you."

Bonnie washed her hands of him at least once a pay period, but the prospect of sharing a dance floor with a bunch of half-drunk, sweaty, horny fools had no appeal. Closing a deal on the Hedstrom property, now that had eight-hundred-forty-three acres of appeal.

"Sorry to disappoint, Bonnie, but if the new owner is out at the Hedstrom property, then my evening is spoken for. Thanks."

"You're welcome. You're still hopeless, but you're welcome."

No, Max was not hopeless. He would get to the Brodie heir—if that's who this guy was—and whisper in his ear convincingly about large sums of money. Then he would plan the most impressive, beautiful, extensive development central Maryland had ever seen.

Max would also pound the crap out of Derek if Bonnie had to put in any more unnecessary overtime. The woman earned her weekends, and the added expense was just plain stupid.

* * *

Summer nights in western Maryland had to be among the sweetest on the planet, but the nights of late spring were sweeter—before the heat and humidity became oppressive, before the annual bacchanal of spring flowers wound down, and the hardwoods were quite finished leafing out.

Before the brutal hard work of high summer turned life into one sweaty, exhausted slog after another.

Violet did her best thinking in the lee of the day, when the work was through, or her energy wrecked, and time on the porch swing beckoned. She'd run out of juice early today, having been up too late the previous night working on a blog.

"C'mon guys," she called to Sarge and Murphy. Their toenails scrabbled against the pine floors of the dining room Violet used as one of her work spaces. "Don't you ever tire of nosing around the same old yard?"

The dogs replied by charging up to the screen door, their tails wagging furiously. Murphy had needed two years to learn that bolting through the door was not allowed, so he got an extra pat on the head for being a good boy.

"Sit, please," Violet said.

Two doggy bottoms hit the floor, Murphy's tail still wagging when he sat.

"Good boys. Out you go," Violet said, the spoken cue for leaving the house.

They exploded off the porch as if freed from years of captivity, the same as they exploded off the porch at least eight times a day. Violet grabbed a knife and a bowl of strawberries from the table and followed.

"Who in their right mind would live anywhere else, if they had the choice?" she asked the empty porch. At this time of year, the honeysuckle was perfuming the air, the last of the lilacs were blooming on the north side of the barn. Nobody was making hay yet, but the scent of mown grass wafted beneath the floral fragrances. The valley boasted infinitely many shades of green and gorgeous, and the roll of the cultivated fields was the signature of a land of plenty.

High wispy clouds promised glory to the sunset, and for a moment, all was right with Violet's world. Late mortgage payments, a hay crop that could be destroyed by a passing shower, and the constant threat of development faded as she sat on her porch steps and got to work capping strawberries.

She'd snitched several excellent specimens and capped about half the bowl when something attracted Sarge's notice. He stared across the road, his posture not anxious, but interested. Murphy left off rooting beneath the forsythia and came to attention as well.

Elias Brodie emerged from the back of the farmhouse, his backpack slung over one shoulder. Not another guy in all of Damson Valley could have pulled off that look—three-piece suit and a leather rucksack—but on him it came across as… confident, natural, just what a well-dressed, well-heeled Scotsman would wear.

Sexy too, damn him.

Violet waved, because neighbors did, and Mr. Brodie crossed the road, evidently intent on stopping by. Well, fine, because she had some questions for her new neighbor.

"Good evening," Mr. Brodie said, letting his backpack slide from his shoulder. He held his pack by a strap, while the dogs came over and gave him the whiff test. He let each dog sniff his free hand, patted their heads, and tugged on Murphy's ears.

Murph loved to have his ears tugged, and predictably, he was on his back, paws in the air, begging for more.

"Have you no dignity, dog?" Mr. Brodie asked. "May I sit, Miss Hughes?" He had the sense not to encourage Murphy, a bellyrub-ho without shame.

"Of course," Violet said. "Are you getting settled in?"

He came down beside her, right there on the wooden porch steps. "Aye.

It's very pretty here, reminds me of home. Did you grow those strawberries yourself?"

Men and food, food and men. At least he'd complimented the valley. "I trade with another farm up the road. I get their soft fruit, they get my apples and pears as part of an organic produce co-op. Murph, get lost."

Murphy had remained at the foot of the steps, rooching around on his back, trying to look adorable, and mostly looking like a hundred pounds of idiot dog.

"I admire persistence in a fellow. Have you lived here long?"

This was what neighbors were supposed to do—to visit, to take an interest in each other, to stop by of a pretty evening. Violet had gone so long without a real neighbor, she was out of practice socializing—not that a single suitcase suggested Elias Brodie intended to stay in the area.

Or maybe she was out of practice socializing with good-looking guys who purred their way across the English language. Elias Brodie caressed his vowels, and snapped off his t's and d's, like verbally snipping fresh green beans.

"I've lived here all my life," Violet said. "My dad farmed this property, his dad before him, back five generations."

"So this is home for you."

Murphy cast Violet his best hopeful-doggy look, then gave up, wiggled to his feet, shook, and trotted off after Sarge, who was sniffing around the mailboxes at the foot of Violet's driveway.

"This is home," Violet said. "Where is home for you?" She wanted desperately to know what Mr. Brodie had planned for the Hedstrom farm, but she also wanted to know about him.

No harm in a little neighborly curiosity, after all.

"I live in Perthshire for the most part, at the foot of the Highland line. You've never seen such beauty, Violet Hughes. Every season takes your breath away, the fishing is the best in the world, and yet, you can be in Paris or London by early afternoon. And then there's the whisky."

He spoke of whisky as some men spoke of the first woman who'd stolen their heart.

"Have a strawberry." Violet held out the bowl.

He chose a small specimen, which was smart. The largest berries often lacked flavor.

He tore off the leaves, pitched them among the pansies, and popped the berry into his mouth. In the spirit of neighborly visiting, Violet helped herself to a strawberry as well.

"These are excellent," he said. "I'm more of a raspberry man, myself, but that is delectable fruit."

A raspberry man, though not razzberry, as an American would have pronounced it. Rasp-bury.

Violet had been around all manner of attractive guys. Her hay dealer was six-foot-three, roped with muscle, and had a smile as wide as Nebraska. The Knightley brothers were three fine specimens of local manhood, and Niels Haddonfield, manager at the therapeutic riding stable, had more Saxon-warrior handsome going than was decent—and he was a nice guy.

But he wasn't a rasp-bury man.

"Have another," Violet said. "They taste better when they're snitched." They tasted best of all when sun-warmed, fresh from the vine.

"Forbidden fruit is the most delicious." Mr. Brodie helped himself to a second small berry. He paused before eating, sending Violet a smile that was…

Trouble. That smile was pure, sweet, succulent trouble, and yet, it had nothing of pandering in it. Elias Brodie's smile was conspiratorial, a little self-conscious, and even a touch naughty, but it was naughtiness shared among fellow snitchers of berries, not a man flaunting his wares *at* a woman.

"What will you do with your farm?" Violet asked, selecting another berry for herself. "It's a terrific property, has plenty of arable land, good pasture, solid structures, fences are in good repair, and not too much deadfall on your wooded acres."

"Would you like to buy it?" He lounged back so his elbows rested on the top step.

She'd *adore* owning the Hedstrom property. "I can barely afford my own place, but then, a competent farmer seldom turns a profit. Aren't you hot in that jacket?"

Elias Brodie wore beautiful clothing, probably hand-tailored. But even lightweight wool was wool, and the temperature still hovered near eighty.

He sat forward and shrugged out of his coat, hanging it tidily over the porch rail. Next he slipped gold cufflinks into his pants pocket and turned back his cuffs.

"The last time I saw French cuffs was at a funeral," Violet said, then crammed another strawberry into her mouth—one she'd neglected to denude of leaves.

"We wear our kilts for send-offs," Mr. Brodie replied. "Also for weddings and celebrations. So what would you do with my property, if you'd inherited it?"

His gaze as he surveyed the rolling fields and lovely barn across the road was bleak. Of course, he missed his uncle, and Violet had been an idiot for mentioning funerals.

"With the land that isn't under leased cultivation, I'd take off as much hay as I could, though a lot of it's only suited for round bales. I can put you in touch with an excellent hay dealer up in Thurmont who might be able to find you somebody to make up your first cutting on short notice. You can do a summer wheat crop, there's still time for corn if July doesn't get too hot, and you are ideally situated to start a co-op garden."

Violet's corn had gone in two weeks ago, and thank God no late hard frost had come along to ruin it.

Mr. Brodie crossed long legs at the ankle, as if lounging on farmhouse porches was what Scottish businessmen did best.

"That's twice you've mentioned cooperatives, Violet. Are they popular in this area?"

As the sun sank toward the Blue Ridge off to the west, Violet waxed eloquent about co-operative farming, community gardens, fresh produce, children getting outside, and how to teach simple gardening techniques. Without intending to, she'd soon circled around to the topic of which she never, ever tired, the backbone of American agriculture, family farms.

And Elias Brodie let her talk. He stole the occasional strawberry, slipped in a request to charge his cell on the porch outlet, ambled back to the steps, and let Violet talk some more.

By the time she was tossing out the url for her blog and website, both dogs were dozing at Elias's feet, and Violet was mentally thanking Zebedee Brodie for having such a lovely nephew. Maybe all Scots were good listeners, maybe neighboring was something that came naturally to them.

The strawberries were capped, the crickets had started to chirp, and a pitcher of icy lemonade had been consumed. Elias had tossed his ice cubes into the grass before swilling his lemonade, and the afternoon had given way to evening by the time Violet wound down.

"You're passionate about your agriculture." Elias rose and extended a hand to Violet. She accepted the help because her butt was numb.

He picked up the bowl of strawberries and the knife. "Should the berries be put in the refrigerator? One doesn't want them to spoil."

Unlike raspberries, strawberries did not mold in mere hours, but yes, the produce ought to be chilled.

"Have you had dinner?" Violet asked, taking the berries and knife from him.

He gathered up his jacket and his backpack. Both dogs came to their feet. "I'm off-kilter if you must know. I left Scotland somewhat precipitously, and I do not enjoy air travel. I'm fairly certain if you put food in front of me, I'd be ravenous."

"Come into my kitchen. I can feed you, and you can tell me about farming in Scotland."

"You needn't go to any trouble," he said, stuffing his cell phone in a pocket, and collecting the empty glasses. "I don't want to impose and I honestly know very little about farming in Scotland—or anywhere."

Well, damn. Chances were he wouldn't be moving in next door. "We're neighbors. Sarge and Murphy like you, otherwise you would not get past my front door."

In other words, Violet knew she was being stupid, admitting a strange man to her house. Except what guy intent on bad behavior would lounge on the front porch for more than an hour first, pet the dogs, snitch strawberries, and listen to endless raptures about vintage tomatoes?

"You ought not to allow me into your home, Violet. We've just met, and you're isolated here."

Violet snitched one last strawberry, trying to label her feelings. The hint of a scold in Elias's words rankled—she'd been taking care of herself more or less since childhood—but he wasn't exactly chastising her.

Maybe he was being—she rummaged around for the right word—*protective*?

"You are among strangers," she said, "far from home, and you're hungry. If you don't mind plain fare, I'd like to share a meal with you."

"You have a hay crop coming off soon. Will you let me help you with that?"

Violet understood the fine line between charity and hospitality, between pride and arrogance. "You'll hate me if I let you make hay. Dirtiest, hardest, most back-breaking, curse-inducing work there is."

"I enjoy hard work, what little I've done of it. We'll share a meal, and you'll introduce me to the business end of a hay wagon."

"Assuming it doesn't rain." Violet gestured Elias into her house, but paused a moment to study the property across the road. For the third time in an hour, a dark blue SUV drove slowly past. She knew that vehicle from somewhere, and she didn't like—

Recognition struck, with equal parts anger and anxiety.

God rot Maxwell Maitland to the foulest manure pit. Abruptly, Violet wished she were holding her shotgun, and not half a bowl of fresh, succulent strawberries.

CHAPTER THREE

The Brodie charm was as much legend as fact, just like much of Scotland's history. Auld Michael, Elias's many-times great grandfather, had toddled off to the Napoleonic wars for nearly a decade, and had come home to his lady with a barony in hand. Brenna Brodie had apparently required some charming before she welcomed her soldier back to the castle—stories abounded about their reunion—but Michael had managed to win the fair lady's heart and many children had resulted.

Some years later, Queen Victoria had taken a shine to her Highland neighbor, deeming Michael the dearest old flirt ever to strut about in a kilt. His strutting had seen the family title elevated to an earldom, and exporting Aberdeen Angus breeding bulls had similarly elevated the family's fortunes.

Zebedee Brodie had certainly commanded a great deal of genuine charm. By comparison, Elias rated his own appeal of the counterfeit variety. He was a pleasant escort, he looked good in a kilt, he wasn't difficult to get out of that kilt.

Not much of a resume for a man who'd celebrated his thirtieth birthday.

Sitting on Violet's steps, watching the sun set, fatigue had hit Elias like a gale-force wind. Fatigue of the body, for he'd gone short of sleep in recent weeks dealing with Zebedee's estate; fatigue of the nerves, because flying did that to him; and fatigue of the spirit.

And now he found himself in a woman's kitchen, anticipating—of all things—a home cooked meal.

"Just set the glasses in the sink," Violet said, putting the strawberries in the fridge. "Unless you'd like more lemonade?"

The lemonade had been ambrosial—cold, sweet, tart, fresh. Elias could not recall having had better.

"Water is probably a good idea," he said. "Flying can result in dehydration." Also in death. He filled his glass at the sink, drank it down, then refilled the glass. "I would not have known this was a log cabin from the outside."

Violet's farmhouse had a sort of pioneer chic. The walls of her living room were the exposed interior of a log cabin, while the kitchen appeared to be a later addition. Her furniture was pine, possibly handmade. Sturdy and unassuming, but comfortable-looking. Pillows, quilts, afghans, dried flowers… a woodstove that looked more functional than high-tech.

Not at all like the baronial opulence of the castle's lodge, but inviting in its way.

"Most of the old farmhouses in this valley are log cabins," she said, "but the log structure is hidden under drywall and siding. Some are 'out and up' stone houses—take the rocks out of the field and use them to put up the walls. If you look around, you'll see that on many farm properties, there's still a tiny homestead cottage."

Violet was at ease in her kitchen, opening cupboards; getting down bowls, measuring cups, ingredients; and making a domestic racket that soothed the part of Elias's soul that had never wanted to leave Scotland again.

She ran the hot water, testing its temperature with her fingers, then filling a measuring cup—non-metric units—and adding a teaspoon of sugar.

Elias propped a shoulder against a doorjamb because the lady hadn't invited him to take a seat. "What's a homestead cottage?"

"Look out that window," Violet said, dumping a floury mixture into a glass bowl. "That log-cabin-type shed is where people lived the first winter they settled here. They'd get it built over the summer, or cut the wood one year, come back and build the cabin the next. They'd have shelter for winter and a dwelling on the property for homesteading purposes, and then they'd build a proper house as time allowed."

Violet was making bread. Elias had seen his aunts and cousins make enough bread to know the rhythm and sequence of the task. Never before had he found the activity of much interest, but he liked watching Violet Hughes in her kitchen.

She was competent, efficient, and… feminine. Her hair was bound in a braided bun that held itself together through invisible means, but this late in the day, entropy had made progress over order. Wisps of auburn hair brushed against her nape—a tender, vulnerable spot, and kissable too.

"Can I do something to help?" Elias's aunts had smacked some manners into him, when they'd had the chance, and having a task would help keep him awake.

"Wash your hands. Then you can start on the salad. Bathroom's down the hallway to your right."

How to ask. Elias had come here in search of a shower, then ended up sprawled on the porch steps. He'd been felled by jet-lag, the delight of sitting in sight of the mountains and fields, and the pleasure of listening to a woman wax eloquent about eggplant—whatever that was.

He remained in the doorway, not sure how to ask for the use of the facilities, knowing he had clean clothes in his backpack.

Violet pulled a small step-stool over to the counter and stood on it to knead the dough. "Better leverage this way," she said. "Conserves energy."

Elias snagged his backpack and headed down the hallway rather than let it appear he'd spent two hours with Violet, and listened to her pour out her agrarian heart just so he could have access to hot running water.

* * *

Maybe Bonnie had simply wanted the office to herself.

Max gave up on casually introducing himself to the Brodie heir—or whatever minion the estate had sent to look over the Hedstrom property—when darkness encroached, and not a light went on in the house. He'd tried knocking on the front door, then the back door—Damson Valley was *rural*—and even poking around the dusty, cobwebby barn.

No sign of life save for a fat orange cat that had hissed and arched its back while following Max all over the property. Damned feline was probably spying for Violet Hughes, a porcupine of a female who'd spent too much time riding her tractor in the summer sun. Three years ago, she'd stopped one of Max's projects north of town—ten miles from her farm—and Max had spent the next twelve months freezing his balls off on a job out in Garrett—godforsaken snow capital of the Appalachians—County.

The Hedstrom property by contrast, was beautiful. The land rolled just enough to create a sense of cul-de-sacs and neighborhoods, the class four rural stream would make a couple of nice water features. Jogging trails nearly laid themselves out, and never had a parcel of land begged so eloquently for development.

Max drove back to town at the hour when deer in their red summer coats foraged at the edges of hay fields, and bats swooped across a darkening sky. Damson Valley was only half-civilized by his standards. Needed a decent grocery store so people didn't have to drive into town for a loaf of bread. A gas station or two would help, maybe a liquor store, and a smattering of—

The phone rang, so Max punched the controls for hands-free discussion, but too late realized who was calling.

"It's Saturday night," Pete Sutherland said. "Why isn't a good looking young guy like you out painting the town red?"

"It's early," Max replied, putting a smile he did not feel into the words. Then too, young was a relative term. "What can I do for you, Pete?" Besides make the man several million dollars Pete would do nothing to earn.

"I have some news. Don't know if it's good news or bad news."

Peter Sutherland had been born in West Stump, New York, a municipality so small, it was technically a hamlet rather than a town. At some point, Pete had decided that his station in life required a Southern accent, though Max had been unable to divine exactly how this linguistic transformation had occurred—sometime after Pete had acquired a degree in business from Dartmouth (no mention of honors), and before acquiring the first of several Mrs. Sutherlands.

"I'm always happy to listen to news," Max said as a rabbit darted across the road. Another rabbit followed immediately, necessitating a sudden application of the brakes.

Spring in the countryside. Love made everybody stupid, and rabbits probably weren't that bright to begin with.

"I can't tell you how I came by this particular information," Pete said, his tone conspiratorial. "Not a word to anybody, Max. I mean it."

"I can keep my mouth shut." Max could also put up with all this posturing and self-importance because Pete was chair of the New Horizons board of directors. Max found the projects, and Pete decided whether to spend money on them.

"This is entirely on the DL, Max. I mean not a peep to your honey."

Whatever a honey was. "Not a syllable." Max didn't roll his eyes, because Pete was canny as hell, like an old dog. In possession of all his teeth and not to be underestimated no matter how much he napped or how often he farted. Pete had lately decided that New Horizons was ready to take on bigger, more prestigious projects, to "step up and be counted."

In a half-crap economy, with regulatory lunacy running rampant on even the smallest zoning boards, and banks more neurotic than ever.

"As long as I have your word," Pete said. "I have contacts in the UK, and they tell me old Zebedee Brodie has gone to his reward. He owned a sizeable parcel out in Damson Valley. I believe I've mentioned it to you more than once."

Well, no. Max had mentioned the Hedstrom Farm to Pete more than once, but the fine art of sucking up required a flexible grasp of the truth.

"One of the largest intact parcels in the county," Max said. "I forget the name of the place. Most of it's under leased cultivation."

Five hundred and twenty-three acres in hay and crops, about another 150 in woods, the rest in pasture, right of way, water features, lanes and residential ground. Max had checked his files before leaving town.

"The Hedley Farm," Pete said. "I want that parcel, Max, and here's the thing. Zeb's nephew is a useless sort, old European money. Likes to drive fast cars and run around with models and actresses. He'll be coming through to look at the property, and we are just the outfit to tell him what to do with it. A genuine Scottish earl doesn't need a pesky, run-down farm creating tax liabilities when he could be shagging some super model. You get my drift?"

"Sure, Pete. Do the guy a favor, take the farm off his hands." Insult him for the company he keeps and the tradition he represents, underestimate his business acumen though his people have likely been handling fortunes for centuries, and if the poor bastard does part with the farm, pretend the deal would never have gone through but for Pete Sutherland's finessing behind the scenes.

"You got it," Pete said. "Take the farm off his hands. Money's not a problem. These European snobs are a bunch of lazy, pansy-assed, greedy bastards who depend on flunkies to keep their heads above water. We'll be Elias Brodie's flunky, and even name the damned development after him. The Earl's Acres—has a nice ring to it, dontcha think?"

No, Max did not think. A bunch of overworked, middle-class families should not plunk down their life savings and go into decades of debt to move into a development named for foreign aristocracy.

"This earl might want to keep the land in cultivation, Pete. Zeb Brodie was adamantly against selling that farm." Selling it to Pete Sutherland and his gang of rogue trust fund babies, anyway.

The lights of the town—also named Damson Valley—appeared as Max crested Holbeck Hill—Holstein Hill, in the parlance of the local youth. The Lutheran Church steeple was illuminated against the night sky, a picturesque white square spire that marked the center of town. Damson Valley had a number of other churches, and the river winding through town had green space on either bank. Festivals abounded, as did farmers markets, municipal concerts, and craft shows.

The schools were good, and the cost of living reasonable. The valley was screaming for development, if only the damned farmers would turn loose of a few acres.

"Now, Max, you just didn't know how to approach Zebedee Brodie," Pete said, for maybe the hundredth time. "My wife is Scottish, and once a Scot gets his back up, there's no reasoning with 'em. You have to make them think everything is their idea, and that they're getting away with something. They like their whisky too."

Max liked whisky, and he'd give the present Mrs. Sutherland credit for tenacity. Her predecessors had all lasted about five years. She'd passed the ten year mark with no sign of turning loose of Pete or his money—even if she did have to make him think every worthy idea was his.

"So what do you want me to do, Pete?"

"When this guy shows up, you be hospitable, drop some numbers on him, and for God's sake keep him away from that Hughes woman. Why the hell you haven't gotten into her knickers yet is beyond me. She looks like she might clean up half decent. If Fiona wasn't the kind to take exception—"

Now there was a cheering prospect—Violet Hughes eviscerating Pete

Sutherland for his sexist, condescending, suicidal pandering.

"Violet Hughes will be too busy working her farm to bother with visiting dignitaries. If we're lucky, nobody will list the place, and the title will be flipped before Ms. Hughes can scrape the manure off her paddock boots."

Though when confronting a zoning board, Violet Hughes generally wore a stunning smile, and left the boots in her pick-up.

"Just get me that parcel, Max. July is coming, and I don't see much else out there that fits what New Horizons needs. Fiona's calling me. We'll talk more later."

Max disconnected, mildly comforted to think that Fiona Sutherland had Pete's balls in a vise. Violet Hughes was a problem though. When Max had tried to be cordial—without even knowing much about her—she'd laughed in his face and climbed right back on her tractor.

That, of course, had nothing to do with why he'd be happy to see her farm foreclosed on. A guy could dream, after all.

* * *

Violet was strongly temped to barricade Elias Brodie in the woodshed, where nosy developers couldn't wave their check books under his handsome Scottish nose. Maxwell Maitland was nothing if not persistent, and he had the damnedest habit of turning up exactly where Violet least wanted to see him. Had Elias not wandered across the road, Maitland would doubtless have already started whispering in his ear.

Children, Max would say, should be raised in the bucolic splendor of Damson Valley, safe from city crime and crowding… as if the people buying McMansions in Maitland's developments would otherwise have been crowded into rat-infested slums?

"Has that batch of dough offended you?" Elias asked, hanging his backpack on the coatrack near the back door. "I don't know when I've seen yeast, flour, and water endure such a pummeling."

"And sugar," Violet said, folding the dough over one last time. "Bread won't rise without a little sugar. Are those your play clothes?"

Gone was the three-piece hand-tailored suit, and in its place Elias wore jeans and a black V-neck T-shirt. Wore them scandalously well.

"I always pack clean clothes and basic necessities in my carry on, because there are two varieties of luggage."

His uncle had said the same thing. "Carry-on and lost," Violet concluded. "I don't get away from here much, but when I go see my mom I never check a bag."

A farm was a jealous mistress, and Violet paid for spending even a few days off the property.

"You assigned me to making the salad," Elias said. "I'm guessing that means tearing up the lettuce?"

Well, no. Violet typically chopped the lettuce with any handy knife, because what mattered a few brown edges on the leftovers?

She gestured toward a sealed bag of organic greens. "Tear away, it's already washed."

Elias had damp-combed his hair back, setting off his profile more cleanly. The resemblance to Zebedee was clearer, in the angle of his jaw, high cheekbones, and defined brows. Zeb had been a fierce, merry old man.

If the fate of the lettuce was any indication, Elias had a start on the fierce part, though Violet didn't see much evidence of the merriment.

"Tomatoes are in the fridge," she said, sprinkling flour over a portion of the kitchen counter. "I like black olives, but toss in whatever appeals to you. A hard-boiled egg or two will add some protein."

This was more fuss than Violet would have gone to normally—a grilled cheese sandwich or a cheese omelet would have sufficed—but she wanted time to study Elias, and to interrogate him.

Kinda mean to interrogate a guy on the verge of exhaustion though. Kinda sneaky.

"How do you feel about peppers?" Elias asked, extracting a fine red bell from the crisper and tossing it into the air. He caught it and set it on the counter, along with the tomatoes, half a green pepper, and a package of mushrooms.

"Bell peppers have nearly twice the vitamin C of oranges," Violet replied, "and they're full of carotenoids and other anti-oxidants." A good dose of vitamins E and A, plenty of phytonutrients, and some fiber too.

"More to the point, they're pretty, and they taste good."

Was he joking? *Flirting?*

Violet got out the rolling pin and began flattening the dough. "So get chopping, Elias. We're burning daylight and I still have night chores to do. There's a bottle of White Zin behind the milk."

He zipped the lettuce bag closed and stashed it in the fridge. "What are night chores?"

"Make sure the buildings are secure—one possum loose in the feed room can wreck your whole month—close up the chicken coop, make sure I didn't leave the keys in the tractor." Take a minute to stare at the stars and say a prayer the farm would still be hers by the end of the season.

Why did nobody warn a gal that a man who knew how to conduct himself around fresh veggies was a sexy creature?

"You're the bailiff of an agricultural castle." Elias passed over a slice of crisp red pepper. "I need a bailiff for my castle. For the right person, it's a fine occupation."

The pepper was perfectly ripe, nearly sweet. "You own a castle?"

"I inherited the family seat, though parts of it are more ruin than dwelling. The property includes a lodge that's quite commodious, but the castle itself is badly in need of repairs. Stone masons don't come cheap. Enough?" he asked, holding out the salad bowl.

He was so casual about owning *a castle*. "Enough peppers. Don't spare the olives. Monounsaturated fat and vitamin E are good for you."

A silence rose, punctuated by the chirping of crickets and a dog barking down the valley. The oven beeped, apparently having reached a temperature of 350 degrees.

"A glass of wine is usually a fine idea, too," Elias said.

"Cork screw is in the drawer below the microwave." Violet busied herself brushing the dough with olive oil, then sprinkling on shredded cheese—cheddar, mozzarella, parmesan, and asiago because support your local dairy farm—and chopped ham. "It needs something."

Elias paused in the middle of wrapping a towel around the wine bottle and peered at the dough.

"Capers?"

Capers? Violet grabbed a handful of the undressed salad—greens, olives, peppers, mushrooms, some chopped egg—and sprinkled the whole over the ham and cheese.

"Excellent choice," Elias said. "Salad Nicoise, American style."

Violet finished with oregano and freshly ground black pepper, while Elias opened the wine. He looked sexy doing that too—arm muscles bunching and flexing, easing the cork from the bottle.

Good God, she needed to get off the property for something besides the weekly run to the feed store and the supermarket. Violet got down two jelly glasses, the closest she could come to the crystal Elias was probably used to.

"What do you plan to do with the property you've inherited, Elias?"

He poured two servings, passed one to Violet, and touched his glass to hers. "I'm not sure. Here's to journeys safely concluded."

Not a bad toast. Violet tipped up her glass. "To journeys safely concluded."

"Why don't we tend to those chores you mentioned while our dinner is baking?"

He was dodging her question, and that was a relief. If Elias intended to sell his property, he could convey that tragedy as well after dinner as before.

Violet rolled up the ham and cheese loaf, put it in the oven, and set the timer for twenty-five minutes, while Elias scraped the salad mess into the compost bucket and scrubbed off the counter. He had a natural sense of work flow in a kitchen, or maybe he was just hungry.

"We can eat on the back porch," Violet said. "No point cleaning off the table."

The back porch had no view of Elias's farmhouse, so if Max Maitland was still cruising the neighborhood, Violet could at least have one more meal in peace.

"You should post your property," Violet suggested as she led Elias out the back door and across the yard. "Your house has been unoccupied for too long, and we have bored teenagers in Damson Valley the same as anywhere else." They also had nosy developers who weren't above doing some informal perc testing without an owner's permission.

"Bored, horny teenagers? I don't begrudge them a peaceful place to kiss and cuddle."

The night was lovely—cool, starry, a half-moon casting enough light to navigate by. A good night for kissing and cuddling, as it happened.

"What about teenagers who need a place to smoke dope and toss around a few burning matches? A place to get drunk and turn up destructive?"

"Has somebody vandalized your property, Violet?" Elias's question was quiet, but not casual. Somebody by the name of Max Maitland was trying to vandalize her livelihood, her dreams, her future and also—very likely—her property.

"A few months ago someone set fire to my wood pile. The homestead cottage could have caught fire, and who knows what else might have gone up in smoke. I'm on the board of directors for one of the farmers markets, and I should have been at a meeting that morning."

Elias stopped half way across the back yard. In the dark, Violet caught the scent of the lavender soap she kept in the powder room. He'd washed up then, not merely washed his hands.

"You were home?" Elias asked.

"I had a miserable cold. I'd cleaned out a loafing shed for Hiram Inskip two days before—his farm is down the road about a mile—and that meant hours on the tractor in stinky weather. I was home working on my taxes when I smelled the smoke." How symbolic was that?

"In the middle of a school day?"

"Yes." Which only suggested more strongly that Max Maitland had been behind the maliciousness.

"Let's check on your chickens," Elias said, as the lone dog began barking again. "In Scotland, we have a right to roam. Anybody's welcome to wander anywhere as long as they do so responsibly. You'd better explain this posting business to me."

He laid a companionable arm across Violet's shoulders, and began walking with her toward the looming shadow of her barn. His gesture was mere friendliness, nothing presuming about it. Violet chattered happily about Rhode Island Reds, Appenzellers, and Hamburgs, all the while battling the urge to turn that casual arm around her shoulders into an embrace between two people who were closer to strangers than friends.

* * *

Violet had bent over to put the loaf into the oven and Elias had had to look away. She had a lovely *shape*, and he had a farm to sell. He'd sat with Violet on her porch, and looked out across pastures and fields that were his—*his*—and he was planning to part with them before he'd even walked their bounds.

The notion rankled. The idea that somebody had set a fire on a property owned by a lone woman rankled even more. Old-fashioned of him, but he came from an old-fashioned lineage.

"Posting your land," Violet said, "means anybody on your farm without your permission can be charged with trespassing."

Beneath his arm, Violet's shoulders were slender, though her gait as she moved through the darkness was confident. Elias endured a wayward urge to slow her down, to make her stop, stand still, and simply admire the stars.

Sleep deprivation and homesickness were making him daft.

Floodlights came on as they approached the barn, and Elias dropped his arm. "How old is this barn?"

"The property dates from the 1830s, and the barn's foundation probably goes back almost that far. No telling how many times it's been re-sided, and when my father was a boy, they were still cutting saplings on the mountain each spring to use for the floors of the hay mows."

What Elias knew about hay wasn't half what he knew about whisky. "Better air circulation?"

"And better circulation of the air means less chance of spontaneous combustion if the hay isn't properly cured before it's baled."

Violet had a routine, checking locks, gates, and water buckets. Her livestock included a herd of fat, fluffy sheep, one fawn-gray burro who roomed with the sheep, and chickens.

"You count your chickens?" And did Violet wander around out here in the dark night after night? Winters in this part of the United States could be fierce, and the summers didn't exactly recommend the place either.

"Have to count them," Violet said. "They're supposed to come home to roost each night, but chickens can be contrary. We have foxes here, loose dogs, bobcats, the occasional cougar, and I'm convinced coyotes have moved into the valley."

Violet could count and converse at the same time—at least when the topic was farming.

"I thought coyotes were creatures of the western prairies?"

"There's an established coyote population in every one of the lower forty-eight states. Around here, we have coyotes and some hybrids that have wolf and dog DNA. We're missing Brunhilda."

The prodigal pullet merited some concern, based on Violet's tone. "Does she often evade curfew?"

"She's shy," Violet said, scanning the barnyard. "The other girls are mean to her, but she's a sweet little lady, and she's—there you are."

Violet marched across the barnyard and retrieved a large red chicken from beneath an empty feed trough. The trough was a single tree trunk about thirty feet long, carved out to resemble a rough, rectangular canoe.

"Time for nighty-night," Violet said, carrying Brunhilda into the end of the barn that served as the chicken dormitory. The hen made bird-purring noises, and got a good-night hug before being deposited on a straw-lined shelf.

Lucky bird, to be the object of Violet Hughes's affection.

Elias issued a stern warning to his imagination—Violet Hughes did not need him tucking her in—but who knew a woman cradling a chicken could look both fierce and adorable?

"Are your chores complete for the evening?" Elias asked as the chickens were secured for the night. The evening air smelled different near the barn—earthier, more grain and livestock, not simply cut grass and countryside.

Still fresh, still peaceful.

"I might do a night check," Violet said. "The shearer has yet to come through, and as the temperatures go up, the sheep drink more. It's cool enough tonight they should manage."

The relentlessness of the responsibility she bore reminded Elias of Zebedee, who'd never complained about being head of the family. Cousins, nieces, nephews, in-laws… they hadn't hesitated to turn to Zeb for help, and Zeb had come through for them. After a time, he'd begun to delegate family matters to Elias, and of family matters, there had never been a shortage.

Which had left the castle in disgraceful condition.

"How about you bring the wine and we can start on the salad?" Violet said as they approached the house. "By the time the table's set, the bread should be done."

Full of plans, she was, while Elias's mind had slowed down to the point of merely registering impressions. Violet's hair was coming undone, for example. The end of her braid had escaped from her bun.

"You are a natural caretaker," he said, one of those thoughts that came out of his mouth without benefit of review by his brain. "Don't you get lonely here, Violet?"

"You work hard enough, you don't have time for loneliness," she said, tromping up the porch steps. "This is the busiest time of year, the time when you do the next necessary thing no matter what, because it could rain—or stop raining—next week. The tractor and baler can go on the fritz when you need them most. The sheep will get out right before the shearer comes, and they'll head straight for the damned burdock patch."

Oh, so busy, and yet, she *was* lonely. Elias knew this the same way he knew he was lonely, but had remained blissfully ignorant of his own affliction until that moment.

"The jet lag is threatening to drop me in my tracks," he said. "Let's eat, and you can tell me how you came up with the name Brunhilda for a shy hen."

* * *

Tomorrow was Sunday, though for Violet, it would be a day on the tractor. She'd cut her first fields of hay on Thursday, and once the dew evaporated in the morning, she'd rake what she'd mowed. If the weather remained fair and dry, she could bale her first crop on Monday afternoon, and then—only then—breathe an enormous sigh of relief.

Until the second cutting later in the summer required the same combination of meteorological good luck, backbreaking hard work, and reliably functioning equipment.

Having Elias Brodie for a dinner companion was tiring, but also a comfort. On her own property, Violet was safe, of course, but having Elias at her side made the final chores more of an evening stroll.

The hens had liked him, always an encouraging sign.

"Our timing is good," Violet said, because the oven clock showed the bread would be done in about five minutes.

"The scent of cooking bread is… How can I be homesick when I can smell fresh bread?" Elias replied.

"You're homesick?"

"The Scots have a propensity for homesickness. Makes for some excellent weepy ballads. In my lifetime, most of the castle my family considers home hasn't been habitable, but after I turned eleven, that pile of rocks up the hill from the lodge was what gave me a sense of home."

That, and the feel of Zebedee Brodie's welcoming hug. Maybe Elias hadn't the Brodie charm in any great quantity, but he did have an affectionate nature. If the epidemic of weddings among his cousins was any indication, that was a family trait too.

"Grab the wine," Violet said, drawing a pair of salad tongs from a drawer. "I'll get the silverware, and we can put the hurt to the chow."

Her idea of "putting the hurt to the chow" was a quiet meal on the back porch. The fresh salad and ham-and-cheese bread was as good as anything Elias had enjoyed at five-star restaurants, and the white zin, while humble, nevertheless added the mellow glow of the grape to the end of the day. Violet served a vanilla mousse with fresh strawberries for dessert, the perfect complement to an informal meal.

Elias set aside a glazed bowl that had held a quantity of dessert.

"Thank you for a delightful meal, Violet Hughes. I will do my part with the dishes, and then take myself across the road. You've made a stranger feel very welcome. Perhaps you're part Scottish."

She was a redhead, and the Scots were the most redheaded nation on earth.

His hostess ate the last bite of strawberries and cream, then scraped an additional half a spoonful from the serving bowl. Violet was not shy about satisfying her appetite, and Elias had learned to appreciate a woman who enjoyed a good meal.

"I'm mostly Irish," she said, "with the occasional German gene for extra stubbornness. My great-grandmother was the wild child from a fine, upstanding Mennonite family that's still farming closer to the Pennsylvania line. You don't have to hang around to do dishes. I'll wrap you up some leftovers, and you can be on your way. If you like, I can pick up some no trespassing signs the next time I'm in town."

Guarding his farm mattered to her, but then, she might have lost her buildings to arson.

"I doubt I'll be here long enough to find any miscreants on my property, Violet." That needed to be said, because the part of Elias that had noticed Violet's fine shape, that had presumed to put an arm around her shoulders, had also noticed how attractive her hands were.

Those hands would feel lovely stroking over Elias's bare back. Instincts honed in the company of women from Rome, to Budapest, to Copenhagen, to Edinburgh told Elias that Violet was speculating about his wares too.

Some things were the same, regardless of the continent a man found himself on.

"You have a castle to fix up," Violet said, rising. "Having a castle must be like owning a farm. The damned place never gives you a moment's rest, but you love it. You love what it stands for, and that means it owns you, owns your heart, owns everything you have to give."

Her summary wasn't far off, but it wasn't a happy recitation either.

Elias piled the plates and salad bowl in a stack and followed Violet into the kitchen. "I wish I could show you my castle when it's been put to rights. We use the great hall for weddings and the occasional *ceilidh* now—the main structure is sound—but the wiring and piping, the interior finish, need updating. The fireplace in the great hall is 27 feet across—takes up the entire north wall and provides radiant heat for the laird's chamber above it."

"Sounds like the renovations will cost a fortune." Violet took the plates from him, and stacked them in the sink.

"While I'm here, one of my cousins back home has started gathering bids from the trades. The project will take years, but I refuse to leave that mess for another Brodie heir to deal with."

Violet turned on the tap. "That was my father and our barn. Had to have the whole thing repointed and parged, replaced the siding, all the hardware. That man loved his barn. Said a barn was like a church."

Elias reached around her and shut off the water, then turned her by the shoulders, and put his arms about her. He'd been honest—he was just passing through. If they spent the night together, the encounter would be casual, sweet, enjoyable, and a nice memory—a very nice memory.

He had many such memories, he suspected Violet had all too few.

She took her time making up her mind, which suited Elias just fine. For a moment, she simply stood in his embrace, her arms at her sides. A gentleman never rushed a lady, and he never coerced her decision.

"You're leaving in a few days," she said, dropping her forehead to his chest.

Elias got his fingers into what remained of her bun, and massaged the muscles above her nape. She was fit, trim, and too tense for a woman who'd just shared a moonlit meal on a fine evening.

"I'll leave in a few weeks at most. I have matters at home to attend to. You can send me on my way, Violet. In fact, you probably should."

Her arms stole about his waist. "Why send you on your way? Are you trouble?"

"I'm a good time, I suppose, nothing more—also nothing less."

She relaxed against him, though Elias could still feel her mental gears whirring. "I haven't had a good time since Hector was a pup. I'm not that kind of woman."

Oh, that was just societal judgment, foolishness, and fatigue talking, also a lack of confidence Elias found intolerable in a woman as competent and passionate as Violet Hughes.

No sense arguing gender politics though.

He gathered her close and kissed her.

CHAPTER FOUR

Farmers developed a sense of time rooted in the seasons and the progress of the sun across the sky. Not for them, the arbitrary movement of hands around a clock face, not when ripening crops and shifting temperatures marked the passing days according to the rhythms of creation.

Elias Brodie's kisses held a hundred generations worth of patience, centuries of tenderness, and eternities of passion. Violet might have been an exotic garden, one Elias explored as if every nuance of her kisses—her sighs, the texture of her hair, the exact contour of her eyebrows and jaw—fascinated him.

He made it easy to be fascinated in return. Elias was built on beautiful physical proportions that Violet measured in caresses and embraces. He offered her gentle, relentless overtures and counterpointed them with an obvious and unapologetic rising of desire.

So this was seduction… This was what it felt like to be coaxed closer and closer to pleasure, and lured away from lists, schedules, and oughts.

"You're good at this," Violet said, as her braid went slipping down the center of her back.

"I'm enthusiastic about shared pleasures. You are too."

His smile said he approved of Violet for enjoying his kisses, he applauded her accepting the challenge he offered.

"I'm not… I don't get out much, Elias," she said, drawing back. "A farmer needs every available hour of sleep, every spare dime, every free moment to keep the land happy and prospering. I'm a fifth-generation farmer. I don't socialize often."

Elias let her go, and damned if he didn't start doing the dishes. "You're also a woman, Violet. I'm not proposing a three-day bacchanal, and I don't kiss and tell."

That he'd exercise a little discretion mattered to her, though she wasn't likely to cross paths with him ever again—another reason to indulge in what he offered. Violet unwrapped the dish towel from the wine bottle and accepted a clean plate from Elias.

"I doubt I'm your type," she said.

He used his thumbnail to scrape a spot of cheese from the second plate. "You should be more concerned with whether I'm your type, assuming you have a type for a friendly encounter. These plates look hand-made."

He did a thorough job washing dishes, not merely a rinse and a promise.

"My mother made them. I have only the two left." Blue and white glaze with a flower-and-vine pattern around the rim. The plates were heavy, and didn't really go with anything else Violet owned. "She made them the year I was born. Took a class when she got too pregnant to do much manual labor. I'll sleep with you, Elias, but don't expect much."

He tackled the mousse bowls next. "Why will you sleep with me?"

Violet's decision had been made in those moments when Elias had simply held her. He'd offered her time to consider options, and given her excellent reasons to trust him. He didn't push. He didn't wheedle. He didn't bargain or make false promises.

"You respect me," Violet said, the words effecting a sort of sunrise where her flagging energy had been. "And you want me. Both."

She felt as if she'd solved a riddle, though maybe ten years later than she should have.

"I respect the hell out of you," Elias said, passing her a squeaky clean bowl. "You work hard, take your responsibilities seriously, and genuinely care for your property. Respect is not the only reason I'm attracted to you."

This foreplay without touching was enjoyable, but also more serious than it should have been. "I went to college, Elias. Had my share of rodeos. You don't have to draw me pictures."

"Will you dry that bowl or rub the glaze off? What is your degree in?"

Violet set the bowl in the cupboard. "Sociology, undergrad and a master's. What about you?"

And why else did he want to spend the night in her bed? Thank God she'd changed the sheets earlier in the day.

Thank God the bed was made for once.

"I studied business at uni, and am considered well informed regarding the organization and operation of charitable establishments. I detect the patter of little paws on your back porch."

"Good Lord, I nearly forgot to feed the pups. Silverware can go in the drain rack. Guys, I'm coming!"

Murphy woofed softly. And the next few minutes were absorbed with more of the odd domesticity she'd been sharing with Elias throughout the evening. He put away the leftovers while she fixed the dogs their dinners—some wet, some dry, some leftovers—and took their bowls to the fenced side yard off the sun room.

When she got back to the kitchen, Elias was checking his phone.

"Everything OK?"

"It's the middle of the night back home. I was just scrolling through my email, of which there is plenty, but it can all wait until morning. Shall we to bed, my dear?"

With his burr, he could carry off that question—quaint, vintage, old-fashioned—and still make Violet's insides dance.

"C'mon," she said, taking his hand. "There are two bathrooms upstairs."

Elias grabbed his backpack and came along peaceably. "I could do with a shower."

The image of him wet, naked, and slick with soap had Violet nearly jogging up the steps. "Separate showers, I think. Quick showers. Three minutes, tops."

Elias came to a halt outside the bedroom door. "Are you nervous, Violet?" The idea seemed to genuinely puzzle him.

"A little, but mostly…I don't want to lose my nerve. A friendly encounter, you called it. A roll in the hay by any other name. A part of me still thinks I ought to know a guy better before I—"

Elias kissed her, a little smacker that let him snatch the conversation ball. "A friendly encounter can be memorable, and you'll know me a whole lot better by morning."

She wanted to know him better, which was stupid. He'd be back in Scotland before strawberry season was over, and then she'd miss him, which was stupider still.

"Bathroom is down the hall to the left, help yourself to anything. Last one in bed's a rotten egg."

He sauntered off, backpack hanging off one shoulder. Violet took a minute to admire the view, then darted into her room, and shucked out of her clothes. The shower she took was more than three minutes, but not much more, and because she owned exactly one summer nightgown, her what-to-wear debate lasted only a moment.

Elias knocked on her door—she really would miss this guy—which gave Violet time to grab her hair brush and take up a place sitting cross-legged against the bed's headboard. He wore his jeans, nothing else.

Not even a smile.

"I can brush out your hair for you," he said, hanging his backpack on the bedpost.

"I have other jobs in mind for you. What do we do about protection?"

He rummaged in his knapsack then tossed a box of condoms on the night table. "And yes, they're well within their expiry date. Any other questions, because if not, I have a few for you."

Gracious days, he was a fine specimen. Broad shoulders, clean musculature, just the right dusting of hair across his chest. Oh, yes, Violet would miss him for a long, long time.

"We're not talking about tabs and slots," Violet said, unraveling her braid and angling her head to shield her face. "Parts is parts, Mr. Brodie. Please lock the door."

This was why college students got drunk, because conversation under these circumstances was an exercise in inanity.

Violet finger-combed her hair free of the plait she'd put in sixteen hours earlier. The shower had left her hair damp enough to brush out without creating that oh-so-stylish porcupine-meets-light-socket coiffure.

"Who or what am I locking in or out?" Elias asked.

Violet hit a snarl as the sound of jeans being unzipped ripped across her composure. She wanted to look, and she wanted to dive under the covers.

I'm being an idiot. "The dogs sometimes come in here, especially if there's a thunderstorm."

Elias prowled closer, his fly undone. He sat on the bed at Violet's hip, brushed her hair back over her shoulder, and leaned in for a sweet, soft, nearly chaste kiss.

"The dogs are outside at their dinners," he said. "Should I let them in?"

What dogs? "Please."

"Violet?"

The kissing part was so easy, so lovely. Violet left off indulging herself to pull back an entire inch. "Elias?"

"I have a suggestion," he said, fingering the neckline of her nightgown and scattering her last coherent thought. "I'll tend to the dogs, and you can turn out the lights and scoot under the covers. You might consider taking off this fetching bit of pup tent, but you should know one thing about me first."

Violet knew she liked him, respected him, and wanted him. Then too, he'd soon get on a plane, and what law said a hardworking farmer wasn't entitled to a little frolic in spring?

"What should I know, Elias?"

He kissed her nose and pushed off the bed, shutting out the lights when he reached the door. "I'll tell the dogs you wished them sweet dreams. I've recently discovered that a shy woman makes me hot, that's what you should know."

* * *

Violet's arms were freckled, but the tops of her breasts were not. Elias wanted to kiss his way across the transition between the two parts of her—farmer and lady, and he wanted to throw his phone out the nearest window.

Jeannie had left two messages and sent three emails, all under the subject line, "Castle renovation," and the last one marked urgent. Not good news.

Angus Whyte detested email, but then, he detested the telephone as well, preferring snail mail, of all the quaint eccentricities. His call was likely bad news as well.

Niall Cromarty, the cousin who'd thought opening the fourteen-thousandth golf course in Scotland was a fine idea, had also sent an email, as had Dunstan.

It could all wait until morning—preferably late morning.

Elias set the phone on mute then used it to light his way through the darkened house. He called the dogs in—why were dogs such relentlessly cheerful beasts?—and closed up for the night. On impulse, he filled a glass of water and took it with him upstairs.

Outside Violet's room, Elias took emotional inventory, knowing he was running on false energy. Casual sex had become a rarity at some point in the last few years, in part because Elias's tastes had become more… refined?

Finicky? Or maybe he'd grown tired of being kilted arm candy. Violet was a departure from his usual encounter, and he was doubtless a few yards from her beaten path as well. Novelty had an appeal for them both, apparently.

He rapped on the door again, and waited for Violet's permission to enter. Moonlight streamed in the window, and she was still sitting up in bed, her hair arranged in a long, loose braid over one shoulder.

Elias set the glass of water beside the box of condoms then crossed to stand in the moonbeams.

"I had an idea," he said, unzipping his jeans the rest of the way. He turned to step out of them, which left him in black briefs. "I wondered if even a shy woman might enjoy the sight of her lover unclothed."

Maybe that was Violet's appeal. She was reserved, unlike the women Elias usually consorted with, and yet, Violet was both confident and competent in her own world. She knew chicken breeds by personality, coloring, egg production… practical information that Elias found charming.

He slid his briefs off and laid them with his jeans on a chair, then faced the bed.

"Moses in the bulrushes, Elias Brodie." Violet might be blushing, but she was definitely looking. Elias stretched, his hands bracing flat on the bedroom ceiling. He was pleasantly aroused, and yet Violet had forbidden him to enter into the usual, "tell me what you like," discussion. No tabs and slots, she'd said.

"I have rules," he said, climbing on the bed. "Maybe you do too?"

"Protection," Violet replied, scooting to one side. "Every time, no matter what."

Elias stretched out on his back, which was a moment of sheer bliss in itself. "Protection, of course, but in the event the protection fails, I'd like to be a part of any subsequent discussions."

"Of course."

The bed bore the fragrance of lavender, the sheets were cool, and Violet had put aside her pup tent, though she'd tucked the covers up nearly to her chin.

All was by no means right with the world, but the evening was off to a lovely start.

"My other rule is unenforceable," Elias said. "I suppose that makes it more of a request."

Violet slid down next to him, got an arm under his neck, and tucked her cheek against his shoulder.

"Let's get the public service announcements over with. I have plans for you, Mr. Brodie."

Elias was actually Lord Strathdee, when the occasion was formal. He'd pass that tidbit along some time when his cock wasn't trying to steal all the blood flow from his brain.

"My request is that you don't… that you give me honest responses. Don't fake, Violet. A passing encounter this might be, but it can be a genuine passing encounter."

"No faking," she said, wrapping her fingers around his erection in an exquisitely snug hold. "I like that request, provided it goes both ways. Any more edicts, pronouncements, negotiating points, or final requests?"

How lovely her calloused grip felt. "Just one more request: Make love with me, Violet."

She did better than that. She stroked Elias to a raging arousal, then kissed him as if she'd recently invented the undertaking and was trying to perfect her craft. Sweet, teasing, searing… all the while, Elias lay on his back feeling oddly unmoored from himself.

He was thirty-odd years old, had, to use Zebedee's terms, *frolicked* with women on four continents—five now—and other than handsomely framed academic degrees, his sole accomplishment was looking good in a kilt.

Violet bit his earlobe. "Jet lag catching up with you?"

Years of it. He wrapped his arms around her. "Holding you feels lovely, Violet. You are a talented kisser."

She was, in fact, a talented lover. Her touch had a presence, a sensitivity that made Elias want to roar and purr at the same time, made him want to lie still lest he do anything to distract her from her plundering, but also to rise over her and join his body to hers.

Perhaps hours of flying over water had turned him daft, but it needn't have made him lazy.

Elias went exploring. With both hands, he learned the contour of Violet's back, the flare of her hips, the muscular fullness of her backside. She was just the right combination of sturdy and shapely, fit and feminine.

All woman, all the time, everywhere. Her breasts were surprisingly full, and she liked—very much—having them caressed.

"Elias, about that protection?"

Hell, yes. "The protection sitting on the night table?"

"The protection I'm ready for you to put on—right now—that protection."

He got his mouth on her nipple, and she took to sliding her lady bits over his gentleman bits, until the boundary between plunderer and plundered blurred wonderfully.

"Now, Elias. Please."

He reached for a condom without taking his mouth from her, not as a display of any particular skill, but because Violet was delectable, and he didn't want to let any part of her go, ever.

She took the condom from him and sat back. "I can do this part, if you want me to."

She wanted to. Elias's shy, temporary neighbor was as passionate about her lovemaking as she was about her chickens and strawberries and vegetables. The secret to her touch, he realized, was that she enjoyed getting her hands on him.

"I want you to," Elias said. "But take your time."

Who knew if they'd end up in bed again? Tomorrow, Elias would be mired in emails and phone calls, and then Monday began a round of meetings with real estate attorneys. At some point an electrician would have to be fitted into the schedule, and—

A combination of resentment and sadness filled him. All that busyness and productivity could not possibly be as important or precious as making love with Violet, and yet, a castle that had been crumbling for centuries did not repair itself.

"You're dressed for the party," Violet said, tossing the torn foil onto the nightstand. "Now what?"

She had no artifices, no technique—only passion and honesty. Elias nearly loved her for that.

"You've been in the driver's seat enough for the present," he said, sitting up. "Get comfortable, Violet. The wild rumpus is about to begin."

She wiggled onto her back, her smile approving and shy in the moonlight. "That's from a children's story."

"It's from the bottom of my heart, too," Elias said, positioning himself over her on all fours. "You seem to enjoy a bit of kissing."

If she'd been enthusiastic before, she was positively fiendish now. Her ankles locked at the small of Elias's back, and her hands went a-Viking over every inch of him.

"And here, I thought you were shy," he muttered, nudging his way into bliss.

"I'm reserved. That's dif—oh, Elias Brodie. I can't... That's...." A great, eloquent sigh went out of her, and Elias knew from what she didn't say that joining their bodies pleased her as much as it pleased him. Some part of him rejoiced to be with her this way, not simply to get his ashes hauled, but to be intimate with Violet Hughes.

"You all right?" Elias whispered, pushing deeper.

"I'm…" Another soft exhalation breezed past Elias's ear. "Talk later."

He spoke to her in easy rhythms and soft kisses, in occasional pauses to marvel at the pleasure, and to catch his breath. Violet let go with all the glory of a healthy female yielding to nature's greatest joy, and she held Elias so tightly his own satisfaction threatened to swamp his self-restraint.

All three times.

"I'll be sore if I don't stop being so greedy," Violet said, brushing her hand over Elias's flank.

He felt that caress in wonderful, too-long-neglected places. "You sound pleased." She sounded smug, satisfied, and happy—with herself, with him, with life.

"I'm acres past pleased. I forgot how good lovemaking can feel, or maybe it hasn't felt like this before. I'm babbling. I'm happy-babbling. Yum."

She kissed him witless, then kissed him beyond witless, until the pleasure took him, tossed him high, and left him in a panting, contented heap at her figurative feet.

"Lovely," she said, kissing his cheek. "Lovely, lovely, lovely. No wonder Scotsmen wear nothing under their kilts. Your womenfolk probably won't hear of it."

Elias did not want to move, but being a gentleman wasn't entirely a matter of holding doors. He extricated himself from Violet's embrace, tended to the practicalities, then returned to the bed and spooned himself around her.

"Thank you," he said, kissing her shoulder. "I can take myself back across the road if you'd like to sleep in peace for the rest of the night."

"Don't you dare run off now, Elias Brodie. The fun and games are delightful, but the cuddling matters too."

Mattered a great deal, in the right company. Elias drifted off, happy to oblige a woman who had her priorities in such fine order. His last thought was a wish that Violet could buy his property from him. She might not be able to offer as much as a developer could, but with her own farm as security, she might be able to pay enough to cover the castle renovations.

He liked that idea. Liked the notion that a property of his could pass into her capable hands rather than be turned into cookie cutter yards separated by privacy fences and privet hedges.

Maybe Violet would like the idea too.

* * *

Elias Brodie was a perilously generous and talented lover. Had Violet met him ten years earlier, she would have been ruined for most of those self-important college boys and their equally clueless grad school successors. She'd awoken to the caroling of the robins in the pre-dawn gloom, and to Elias kissing her nape.

What a lovely way to start the day, and then Violet's morning had grown lovelier still.

She was dozing blissfully when Elias returned carrying a tray with three steaming mugs. His hair was damp and he smelled of lavender soap, suggesting he'd grabbed a shower while the coffee brewed.

"I didn't know if you took tea or coffee in the morning," he said, nudging the door closed with his foot. "I brought both. The dogs are fed and sniffing around the side yard. I didn't see any cats."

Violet struggled to sitting, though her hair wasn't cooperating. At some point in the middle of the night, Elias had unraveled her braid and teased her with—

Maybe she'd dreamed that part?

"Good morning," Violet said, tucking the sheets under her arms. Elias wore a pair of blue turquoise board shorts.

Violet wore an idiot grin.

"I'm a tea drinker in the morning," Elias said, sitting on what had been Violet's side of the bed before she'd scooted over to wallow in sheets warmed by his body heat. "Black first thing in the day, green tea in the afternoon, herb concoctions in the evening. I didn't know how you preferred yours."

For a man who'd been God's gift to a single lady farmer an hour ago, he was studying a plain mug of tea almost bashfully.

Violet added milk and sugar to hers, and wished she had the next eternity to get to know Elias Brodie better.

"I don't care for coffee," she said, "but I'll resort to it during lambing season, or when the tractor has turned up contrary the day before the combine is supposed to come through. Needs must when the devil drives."

Elias set his mug on the nightstand, among the foil wrappers left over from their lovemaking. "How are you, Violet Hughes?"

Dandy came to mind.

"Half in love with you," Violet said, setting her tea aside and curling along his side. "Don't get your manly commitment phobias in a bunch. I can fall half in love with a seed catalog or a freshly stacked mow full of first-cutting hay." She hadn't though, not for a long time.

Elias's arm settled around her shoulders, the embrace so natural Violet would have started purring if she'd been able.

"Only half in love? My technique is in want of polish, apparently. I can claim a similar affliction where you're concerned. You are a wondrously passionate woman."

If Elias Brodie had manly phobias about anything, they were apparently kept in check by a roundtrip plane ticket, damn the luck.

"What are you passionate about?" Under no circumstances would Violet pass up an opportunity to cuddle with a man who'd brought her hot tea and fed her dogs without being asked. Her mood was beyond rosy, and thank God and the Farmer's Almanac, the hay needed another day to dry.

The day's plans included changing the oil in the tractor, scrubbing out the sheep's water trough, sweeping the hay mow in preparation for the wagonloads coming off the field…

And eighteen other pressing, important, demanding chores Violet couldn't recall when Elias was tracing her eyebrows with one finger.

"You ask about my passions, but I haven't many. I'm decent at any number of peculiar sports—skeet shooting, for example, polo, shinty, curling—and I like fast cars and the smell of engines. I enjoy seeing a charitable institution thrive if it has a true sense of vocation—many don't—and I'm competent in several languages. That's not unusual where I come from. I'd have to say Brodie Castle is about all that qualifies as a passion."

He sounded as if this was a recent realization and not a particularly happy one.

"My dad was the same way," Violet said. "He could fix anything with his hands, played a mean harmonica, knew Beatles trivia inside out, could shear the most ornery sheep without a nick, and could predict the weather ten days out with 90 percent accuracy, but all he cared about was this farm."

And his family. Violet had taken years to figure out that for her father, caring for the farm amounted to caring for the family and for humanity as a species.

Elias pulled her closer, close enough to kiss her temple. "This was your father's castle. I wish Zebedee had been a bit more respectful of the family seat, and not quite as avid about collecting his single malts. I suppose every one of the earls of Strathdee has inherited something of a work in progress."

Violet sat up to take a sip of her tea, though she didn't want to leave the bed. This was what a morning after ought to be like—a lovely, cuddly, extension of the previous night's intimacies, not an awkward parting that both parties intended to be permanent.

She paused, the mug half way to her mouth. "Did you just tell me you're an *earl*?"

"Elias, Earl of Strathdee, at your service, not that that title means anything."

The sun was clearing the ridge to the east, bright streaks banding the white coverlet. The light was clear, suggesting the humidity would stay low for the rest of the day, which was a gift to every farmer in the valley who had hay down.

"The title is part of you," Violet said, rather than admit to a goofy pleasure at having gone to bed with what had to be one of very few earls on the face of the earth. "I suspect the title is wrapped up in your castle too. I own only part of this farm. My mom owns the rest."

Elias stretched out his arm, a silent invitation for Violet to resume her place at his side. She complied, reveling in the sheer bliss of a day starting out with affection and companionship rather than hard work and worry.

And loneliness. Mustn't forget the loneliness that no chickens, dogs, or quilting projects could ever address.

"Where is this mother of yours, Violet?"

"In Florida with husband number three. He's a big improvement over husband number two, but if I want to see my mother, I go there. She loved my father, she did not love this farm."

"That was Zebedee. He loved the family, right down to the drooling babies and contrary aunties, but not so much the family seat. He loved me, too, so I won't criticize him for leaving me a castle to put to rights."

How many men spoke this easily of love? "You loved him," Violet said, thinking of her father. God-damned lousy business when a farmer dropped over from a heart attack. "He raised you?"

"The Brodie heir is traditionally sent off to a properly snobbish public school—boarding school, you'd call it—so off to boarding school I did go. Headmaster called me into his office one day and said I was to leave school a few weeks ahead of the other boys. I was overjoyed. Most of the other lads were English, and I hadn't really made friends among them. Then Headmaster told me my uncle was waiting for me in the chapel. One look at Zeb's face and I was certain nothing in my life would ever be the same."

Elias's voice held compassion for that young boy, and also for the man who'd ended up raising him.

"No wonder you're attached to your castle. It stood for security and stability when you needed them most."

He wrinkled his nose. "Possibly, but castles are also magic, if you have any imagination. I used to lie in the great hall on my back, hoping to hear the voices of the ghosts. Zebedee claimed he saw the first earl and his lady in a passionate embrace upon the parapets one night last summer. He said the lady's smile put the stars to shame. Zeb was very fond of his wee dram, mind, and we've had many a wedding at the castle of late."

And Elias had been very fond of his uncle.

"Tell me about this castle." Violet could picture him in his great hall, tricked out in his kilt for some cousin's wedding.

"A properly maintained castle is bloody expensive," Elias said, his finger wandering along Violet's collarbone. "Thank the heavenly powers the roof is mostly sound, or there'd be no limit to the cost of the repairs. As it is, I was wondering if you'd like to buy my farm. All proceeds of sale will go toward keeping Clan Brodie out of the wet for the next two hundred years."

Violet had been considering whether the remaining condoms on the night table ought to be consigned to a happy fate when something in Elias's tone caught her attention.

"So you came here with intent to sell the Hedstrom property?" He hadn't exactly said, had he?

"I came here to see if it can be sold, and if so, how. I'm not competent to manage a farm in these latitudes, and neither was Zebedee. Did you know our alpacas were stolen?"

Unease trickled through Violet's rosy mood. "You can't sell that farm to just anybody, Elias."

"Of course not," he said, kissing her temple. "I'll only sell it to somebody with a vast fortune and a pressing need for a tax dodge. It's a pretty patch of ground. I was honestly hoping you might make an offer."

He sounded… *hopeful.* Not even apologetic.

Violet was off the bed and across the room. "Do you always talk business in bed, Elias?" she asked, pulling a green cotton sundress over her head. She'd plucked from her closet the sort of comfy dress every woman ought to have for lazy summer mornings at home.

This morning had just lost its quotient of comfy.

"You're upset." Elias had sense enough to leave the bed himself, and even to scoop up the detritus of their *protection* and pitch it in the waste basket.

"I'm… I was hoping you weren't here to sell that pretty patch of ground. I was hoping you might see that it's worth keeping."

Max Maitland would be all over that farm by sundown if he knew Elias was short of cash.

Elias stepped out of his shorts and fished a pair of black briefs from his backpack. "Zebedee kept it, though why I'm not sure. He was no kind of farmer, and neither am I. Won't you enjoy having some neighbors for a change?"

Unease escalated to dread, even as Violet grieved to watch Elias preparing to dress for the day. She'd never see his like again, and almost wished she never had.

"What do you mean, Elias? Neighbors—plural?"

"You're across the road from eight hundred arable acres and not a soul dwells there," Elias said, facing her without a stitch on. "Wouldn't a sign of human life every once in a while be some comfort, Violet? Somebody to visit with at the mail boxes?"

"I visit plenty." Every two weeks at the Feed and Seed, also at the fire hall's quarterly pot lucks.

Unless the tractor was on the fritz, some ewe was ailing, or the accounting was behind again.

"What aren't you telling me, Violet?"

Elias was absolutely unselfconscious about being naked in the morning sun, suggesting he'd been in a state of undress around more than a few women. The briefs went on, followed by his jeans, though he didn't bother to fasten the snap.

"I'm telling you, Elias Brodie, that your farm has some of the best ground in the county, if not the state. You have nothing less than class two soil over there, and most of it's class one. You have two surveying oaks in your woods—

virgin trees hundreds of years old. You won't find two surveying oaks on the same property anywhere else in Maryland—I'd bet my sheep on it. You said it yourself, a farm is a castle, and that makes you its steward. Don't sell that property. I can manage it for you, make it turn a profit even."

Elias came closer, his expression solemn. "If you had to choose, between my property and yours, which one would you protect?"

Abruptly, he was not the affectionate, generous lover from the previous night, but a man who spoke several languages, drove fast cars, and played sports Violet had never heard of. He was out of her league—an earl—a wealthy man who tinkered with charitable corporations in his spare time.

"What sort of question is that, Elias? It's not like the English are going to come sailing up the Potomac to reprise the battle of Bladensburg."

"When was the last time you took a vacation, Violet? When was the last time you drove away from this place without worrying about your sheep, your chickens, your profits, your fences?"

Her blog, her produce swap, her wood pile, her cats, her finicky tractor, her everything.

And her valley, when Max Maitland was loose without supervision. "I'm not saying I'd manage your place for free."

Elias passed Violet her mug of tea, cold now.

She wanted to toss it in his face. "Thank you."

"I'm in a cash squeeze, Violet. Paying a manager to look after the place, waiting on rents, sinking money into the buildings, purchasing another herd of alpacas or goats or sheep or whatever doesn't make business sense."

Violet sank to the bed. "How bad is your cash squeeze?"

Elias sat beside her, though he'd be within his rights to keep his finances entirely to himself.

"Very bad," Elias said. "The castle will get what I can spare it, but Zebedee also invested in family businesses. One cousin owns some sort of art dealership, and Zeb had open contracts with him. Another cousin owns a golf course of all the albatrosses, and now he's expanding it. Yet another is a potter, and her business has good and bad years. Jeannie's husband walked out on her leaving her with a new baby and a newer mortgage. They all leaned on Zeb, and he never let them down or expected them to pay him back."

"And they're family," Violet said, an enemy she could not combat. "You can't turn your back on family. Let's get some breakfast."

Elias remained on the bed, while Violet pushed to her feet. She smoothed his hair back—god damn, she would miss him—and would have bolted for the door except he took her hand.

"I wish I could give you that farm," he said, kissing her knuckles. "Property should be held by people who care about it."

Violet wanted out of the bedroom, where she'd been so foolishly happy.

"Promise me you won't sell that farm to a developer, Elias. It's good ground, and you'll get a fine price for it if you keep it under cultivation. You think I'm passionate about this farm, but I'm passionate about all farms."

He dropped her hand and rose. "I can't promise you not to sell to a developer, Violet. I haven't the luxury of waiting for an agricultural buyer to come along. I'm sorry."

He kissed her forehead and snagged his backpack. Violet beat him out the door.

CHAPTER FIVE

Zebedee had claimed the Scots had a talent for grief, but then, Zeb had claimed a lot of things—including an intention to live for 90 years at least.

Elias didn't feel grief, so much as he endured a sense of déjà vu, of being again in Headmaster's office, anticipating unforeseen joys, when instead disappointment and sorrow had lurked in the chapel. He followed Violet down the steps, the feeling in his gut akin to what he'd experienced 38,000 feet above miles of cold, pitiless ocean.

Queasy, resentful, frustrated. Trapped in a bad situation.

"Are eggs OK?" Violet asked.

"You needn't cook for me," Elias said. "I'll collect my things and be gone. I'll look for an agricultural buyer, Violet. I'm not making any promises."

She was beautiful in the morning light, auburn hair rioting down her back, nothing but a simple cotton dress between Elias and his sweetest dreams.

And she was furious.

"Do you know Elias, in one five-year period, this country lost a space nearly the size of Maryland to development? By some estimates we lose nearly 10 acres of farmland every minute, a square mile every hour."

Elias knew better than to argue—Violet was merely revving her engines on this topic. She retrieved a bowl of eggs from the fridge—not a package, a bowl that included both white and brown eggs.

"The developers don't go fifty miles into the wilderness to turn some random hillside into a housing development," she went on. "That would be too costly, of course. Instead, they snatch up the land close to the cities and towns, the land ripe for growing a crop of commuters who will only add to our carbon footprint, while they destroy our ability to produce food."

She cracked eggs against the side of the bowl with a practiced expertise. "A farm takes generations to bring to full production, and once it's been turned into a tot lot, agriculture will never get that land back. And don't think the farmer can take his business out into the hills, either. What it costs to clear land and get it under cultivation is more than any farmer has in his back pocket."

Out in the yard, a chicken yodeled, or whatever chickens did that woke everybody up.

"God dammit," Violet said, glowering in the direction of the barn. "It's not even 7 a.m."

"Let me make breakfast," Elias suggested. "You can see to the chickens, and I'll get some food on the table."

Violet's expression suggested she didn't trust him not to poison her, and that… that would make it easier to get on a plane in two weeks.

Ten days, at the most, possibly sooner.

"Don't bring the dogs in until we've eaten," Violet said, shoving the bowl of eggs at him. She slid on her ugly shoes and was out the door with a parting scowl.

Elias put together an omelet, toasted a few slices of last night's ham and cheese bread, and put the last of the strawberries on the table on the back porch. He was tempted to look at his phone, but instead sat on the top step and waited for Violet to resume her rant.

She came stomping across the back yard, a few wisps of hay in her hair which Elias did his best to ignore.

"This looks good," she said, taking the same chair she'd occupied last night. "If you sell your farm to a developer, I will hate it."

"You will hate me, though I am not responsible for land use problems throughout the United States, Violet."

She speared a forkful of eggs. "It's happening all over the world, Elias. China has lost forty percent of its arable land while its population is increasing. Asians, who number in the billions, are also consuming more meat than ever before, and growing livestock takes a ton more resources—I can't eat this."

Elias could eat, because the alternative was stale energy bars and airplane peanuts. "I thought the American real estate economy was sluggish, and vacant houses were the blight of nearly every city."

"I don't know about the U.S. economy. I just know people would rather steal my farmland than gentrify some part of D.C. I won't hate you."

Magnanimous of her, when he hadn't done anything wrong. "I won't hate you either."

Violet fell silent, which was worse than her ranting, and Elias's breakfast lost its appeal. He'd been wrong about her.

She was not passionate about her chickens or sheep or seed catalogs—whatever a seed catalog was. She was *enthusiastic* about those things and in some regard, she enjoyed them.

About preservation of the American farm, she was evangelical. Passionate to the point of irrationality. People had to live somewhere, and America was a huge place.

"Pass the salt," Violet said. "Please."

"I put salt in the eggs," Elias replied, reaching for the salt shaker, a plain white ceramic article in the center of the table. He knocked the salt over by accident, and out of habit, shook a bit into his right hand and pitched it over his left shoulder.

"What was that about?" Violet asked, taking the salt cellar from his hand.

"Spilling salt is bad luck, so you toss a pinch over your left shoulder, into the face of the devil who might lurk there."

Violet set the salt down and rose, going to the steps and gazing across the yard at her barnyard. "I'll wrap you up some food to take with you, Elias, but I think you'd better leave."

"Because I throw salt over my shoulder?"

She nodded, and instincts honed on four continents—five now—told Elias she was crying. He stood behind her, wishing he was back in Scotland, and wishing he could give her the damned farm.

"Wait here," she said, whirling past him.

Elias finished his breakfast, equal parts angry with Violet, and disgusted with himself. Nobody had lied, nobody had misrepresented, not on purpose anyway, and yet, feelings were hurt.

Feelings were badly hurt, and it felt as if that was his fault.

Violet emerged from the kitchen carrying Elias's backpack, and a brown paper bag. "Some ham and cheese bread, a couple oranges, the leftover mousse," she said. "I know you haven't had a chance to get to the store."

He was being run off the property, because the Chinese were eating beef. "Thank you. I don't suppose you'd spare me a bottle of water?"

"I don't have any bottled water. The plastics alone—"

Elias rummaged in the backpack and extracted a nearly empty refillable water bottle. "I haven't any power across the way, and thus no water. If you'd fill this for me, I'd appreciate it."

She took the water bottle without touching his fingers. "You don't have power or water?"

Too late, Elias realized what dots her female mind was connecting. "You think I spent the evening with you because my own accommodations were wanting."

Though to be honest, he'd come over here hoping to charge his phone, and.... well, hoping. Admitting that would hardly grant him a pardon from the disappointment in Violet's eyes.

"You spent the night, Elias, not simply the evening. Try to sell the farm to somebody besides Max Maitland." Violet's voice was an arctic breeze on a summer morning. "He's a scoundrel and he won't pay you what the land is worth."

She disappeared into the kitchen again and re-emerged with a full water bottle. "Before you sell to anybody, get a decent lawyer to explain the agricultural conservancy easement to you. Post your property now, or there will be perc tests in your front yard by Monday." She shoved the water bottle at him. "Good-bye, Elias. Best of luck."

Elias stashed the water in his pack, and ignored the urge to wrap his arms around Violet and babble useless apologies.

He was sorry, and he was selling the farm to whomever offered him fast cash for it.

"Good-bye, Violet. Take care."

He walked around to the front yard, in the mood to kick something solid—perhaps his own backside. Perhaps Zebedee's headstone.

Women liked Elias Brodie, and they knew what to expect from him—a good time, exactly as he'd said. Fond memories, good sex. Not the salvation of Damson Valley's food production goals, for God's sake. Not dreams come true.

The day would be scorching hot, of course, and when Elias's one bottle of water ran out, he'd have to call Dunstan and Jane to put him up until a damned electrician could be located. Violet might turn him off her property, and Elias would retreat from the lists like a gentleman, but he'd be damned if he'd be banished from his own land.

He was comforting himself with similarly useless righteousness when a truly cheering thought popped into his head.

His best suit of traveling finery was hanging on the back of the door to Violet's downstairs bathroom. At some point before leaving Damson Valley, Violet would probably return his clothing.

Or maybe… maybe he'd fetch it himself.

* * *

"You lose," Dunstan said. "Hand me that level."

Jane passed over the level, which was like a yardstick with a tube in the middle of it, and in that tube was liquid containing an air bubble. When the air bubble sat in the exact middle of the tube, whatever the yardstick was sitting on was level.

All of which Jane had pretended to find fascinating when Dunstan had patiently explained it to her as they'd embarked on home renovations. Mostly, she found the sight of Dunstan in his work kilt fascinating.

"Which bet did I lose?" Jane asked, passing over the requisite tool.

"The laird texted me while you were cutting irises. Mind you, Elias didn't call me. He texted me, asking that I call him at my convenience."

Clearly that bit of consideration had struck Dunstan as imperiousness. In the courtroom, Jane saw guys going toe-to-toe with each other verbally every day, but this cousinly blend of affection and combativeness between Dunstan and Elias left her uneasy.

"You want me to return the call?" Jane asked, smoothing her hand along the mantel. Dunstan was creating what an interior decorator would call a great room, and Dunstan called a wee project. His farmhouse was a work in progress, formerly the bachelor abode of one hardworking lawyer and a shamelessly lazy cat.

Jane had moved in after the wedding and the house was undergoing a transformation.

Wallace remained a feline monument to *noblesse oblige*, with Wallace in charge of the nobility, and his humans in charge of tending to all obligations.

Dunstan set the level on the mantel, a handsome span of oak at which he'd been cursing and crooning for most of the weekend.

"I'll call himself when this blasted mantel… by God, it's level. You are married to a genius, Mrs. Cromarty. The damned thing only needed a day or two to settle. This room will be done by Independence Day, see if it isn't."

The morning was lovely—a mild Sunday leaning toward summer, and Jane's mood was lovelier. Before marrying Dunstan the previous winter, she'd spent most of her Sundays in the office, wrangling legal files, plotting litigation strategy.

Now, she lost bets with her husband, and rejoiced.

"What do you suppose Elias wants?" Jane asked, taking a sip of lemonade. Dunstan had sawdust in his dark hair, a tool belt slung around his work kilt, and whatever Elias wanted, Jane wanted an hour up in bed with her husband more.

She'd expected desire to ebb after holy matrimony, particularly when she and Dunstan also shared a law practice. Never had a highly competitive attorney been so glad to be so wrong.

"Whatever Elias wants," Dunstan replied, "he might have left a message, or simply used the telephone in the conventional manner. He dials, I pick up, communication ensues."

Jane held the lemonade up to Dunstan's lips, and he sipped. He watched Jane over the rim of the glass, his blue eyes sending a particularly husbandly message.

"Are ye pining for a nap, wee Jane?"

"Stop it with the burr, Dunstan Cromarty. Is it possible Elias's phone doesn't work right here?"

Dunstan took one more gander at the level, as if the mantel might have moved while he'd flirted with his wife.

"Elias likes functional equipment. He's a mechanical sort, and his phone wouldn't have the audacity to cut out on him simply because he's nipped off a few thousand miles from home. Shall we put some flowers in here? Give the room a few airs?"

The plank floor had yet to be stained, but the walls had been painted a soft green that went well with the woodwork. The room still needed rugs, a few comfy reading chairs, and the little touches, but the couch was well cushioned, and pictures of family adorned the walls and the piano.

Did Dunstan want to spruce up the room because for the first time in years, family was in town?

"I have enough irises to fill every vase we own," Jane said, ruffling the sawdust from Dunstan's hair. "Call your cousin, Dunstan."

What sort of family relations required that Dunstan pick his cousin up at the airport, swing by the house for introductions, then dump said cousin at some neglected farmhouse five miles away?

Dunstan left off admiring his mantel. "Elias is a bit imperious, if you must know. He was never quite one of the cousins, he was always off at a polo camp in Italy as a boy, or apprenticing in some obscure trade. We were never really sure what Elias Brodie was doing, other than riding on Zebedee's coattails."

This vibe had come rolling off Dunstan the day he'd received the email announcing Elias's impending visit. Dunstan had been quietly ecstatic that a member of the family was finally coming to see Damson Valley, and even more quietly resentful that a business transaction rather than familial fondness had inspired the travel. Elias had sent along two bottles of what was apparently very good whisky to the wedding celebration, but he'd failed to attend.

He apparently regularly failed to attend family gatherings.

And yet, Jane had liked Elias. Had liked how tightly he'd hugged Dunstan on sight, despite Dunstan's inherent reserve. Had liked how Elias had not wanted to impose on "newlyweds," had liked how he'd carried his own bag, and presented Dunstan with yet another excellent bottle of whisky.

Dunstan's phone rang, and he stared at the screen. "His lordship again."

Jane snatched the phone and swiped into the call. "Jane here. Hello, Elias."

"Jane? Well, yes, of course Jane. I'm sorry to be a bother but is Dunstan there?"

"He's nose down with power tools in his hand. I'm temporarily widowed. Can we kidnap you for dinner?"

Dunstan's brows rose. Jane stuck her tongue out at him. He fluttered the hem of his kilt, but the tool belt prevented him from displaying anything truly interesting.

"Well, yes," Elias said. "I'd enjoy that, in fact, if it wouldn't be any trouble."

Something was wrong. Jane could hear it in Elias's voice, the way she could hear prevarication from a squirrely witness.

"I'll come get you around 5:30. The master builder will be lounging in the tub with a beer by then, and we mustn't begrudge him a chance to relax. Pack up your suitcase while you're at it. I've changed the sheets in the guestroom and they are calling your name."

"I can call a cab, if there are any that serve the area."

"We're not like Scotland," Jane said. "Virtually no public transportation here outside of town, so brace yourself for a dose of getting to know me. My charm is subtle, but I'll grow on you. See you soon!"

Dunstan accepted the phone back after Jane had ended the call. "Your charms are about as subtle as a freight train on a downhill incline, Jane Evangeline. Are you up to something?"

"I'm up to lasagna with garlic bread, and maybe Italian cream cake for dessert. Do we have any decent wine?"

Dunstan took up a broom that had been leaning against the mantel and went after the sawdust on the hearth bricks.

"You're getting out the wine for Elias? His tastes are somewhat refined, I'm guessing."

"We usually have wine with dinner on weekends. Something is amiss with your cousin, and he's family. Either tell me what you're strutting and pawing about, or put it aside, Dunstan. None of your family has been here to see you since Zeb came through a few years back, and yet you were perfectly friendly with them this winter. Elias can't help it that his parents died."

Dunstan was by nature thorough in all he did, but the sawdust was in a tidy pile, and he was still sweeping.

"Elias never talks about it. He was eleven. How could that not leave an impression on a boy?"

Dunstan was honestly bewildered by his cousin, in other words.

"You've been in this country for many years, Dunstan. Do you miss your cousins?"

"Terribly," he said. "The whole time I was in law school, I was nearly ill with homesickness. Went home every chance I got, saved up all my pennies, and tried to entice every one of them into coming over here to go into practice with me."

And yet, not a single cousin had gone into law, much less practicing in the New World.

"You never *say* you miss them. I'm *your wife*, and I've never heard you say you miss them. If you, a grown man with wickedly accomplished language skills, the courage of a lion, and the most loving wife in the world can't admit you miss your family, why do you assume Elias's silence is indifference on his part?"

Jane kissed her husband to soften the sting of her closing argument. "Elias is Scottish, you know. They can be proud, stubborn, and shy."

"We're also affectionate and loyal," Dunstan said, unfastening his tool belt. "Are the irises in water?"

"Yes, and the meat's in the fridge so Wallace can't make off with it while we're arguing about your cousin."

In the next instant, Jane was scooped off her feet and cradled against

Dunstan's chest. "We're no' arguing, Jane, my love. We're having a wee discussion, and it's one I'd like to continue upstairs, if you've no objection."

Jane kissed his cheek. "No objection, your honor. My husband truly is a genius."

* * *

"I'd forgotten your neighbor is my egg lady," Jane said as Elias hefted his suitcase into the back of the truck. From the porch, Bruno watched him with an inscrutably feline gaze that nevertheless conveyed a scold.

"I'll be back," Elias said to the cat, who commenced casually licking a front paw. "Why don't you go home?"

"Dunstan does the same thing," Jane said. "Talks to Wallace as if the damned cat had a mind that considers more than food, sleep, and random acts of mayhem. Do you mind if I stop over at Violet's and get some eggs?"

Elias's mind was full of dire emails from Jeannie, two rounds of missed calls with Niall Cromarty, a spreadsheet that promised ruin in the next year if the worst cases all lined up, and some incomprehensible websites pertaining to Maryland zoning laws.

"I'm sorry?" Elias said, as Jane gave Bruno a scratch. And where was the great litigating wonder of Clan Cromarty, that Elias was cast on Jane's mercy for a ride?

"Eggs," Jane said, rising and closing her hands in an egg shape. "I'm almost out of eggs. Violet Hughes sells eggs at the farmers market. May I stop next door and buy a few eggs?"

God, no. "Of course. I'll wait here." Elias flashed what Zebedee had called his Côte d'Azur smile. "The heat has left me not quite presentable for company."

"Dunstan still isn't too keen on our summers," Jane said, hopping up into the truck and slamming the door. "Climb in, your lordship. I'll get my eggs some other day."

The truck had marvelous AC, but Elias wasn't sure of the etiquette of adjusting AC in another person's vehicle. He had learned not to rise to the "your lordship" bait when his cousins had started teasing him within weeks of his parents' memorial service. Protocol meant Elias had not become a lord by title until Zebedee had died, though his cousins probably hadn't grasped that as children.

"Go ahead and crank the AC," Jane said. "I always do, and I turn on the seat heater at the same time. Dunstan doesn't get it. Maybe it's a woman thing."

Or a contrary American thing. "How well do you know Violet Hughes?"

Now where on earth had that question come from? Jane gave Elias a side-eye, confirming that his casual tone hadn't fooled her.

"Not well enough that you should be worried," she said, maneuvering the truck onto the road. "Violet's a farmer, and they tend to be married to their land. I'm married to your cousin."

Elias was jet-lagged, possibly coming down with a cold, and probably dehydrated. Subtlety was beyond him.

"I'm familiar with your marital status. If Dunstan were any more in love, he'd be singing maudlin ballads beneath your window." Which was… sweet. Lovely. Wonderful, in fact.

"You jealous, Elias?"

What a question. Though Elias wasn't entirely sure of the answer. "You don't back down, do you?"

Jane patted his knee. "I'm a litigating buzzsaw, Elias Brodie, but you're family, so I will back down if you tell me to. Dunstan will back down if I tell him to, too."

Good God, she was a terror. "Where did Dunstan find you?"

"I found him in the law library on the opposite side of a stinky little marital misunderstanding which we managed to settle to the satisfaction of all concerned. I notice you put your suitcase in the back of the truck."

The damned thing weighed a ton. "My accommodations, while splendidly bucolic, are somewhat lacking in amenities, and you did offer a guest room."

Jane drove her husband's truck with a natural feel for the engine, braking and accelerating smoothly, easing the vehicle down the road when others might have made a statement with their driving. Trucks like this were rare in Scotland, in part because gas prices were so much higher.

The air conditioning, the rumble of the engine, and the relief of being away from That Place eased some of Elias's bad mood.

"Lacking amenities," Jane said. "Did you have to use the two-seater?"

Elias had to think a moment to translate the term. "The electricity is in need of repair. Earls don't use two-seaters." Though he'd insulted the vines growing up one side of the barn. Tam O'Shanter's witch could not have driven him back across the road to beg a favor from Violet.

"I won't use an outhouse either. Spiders and I have an understanding. I see them, and Dunstan kills them."

Violet wouldn't kill a spider just for being a spider. She'd know what sort of spider it was, how it benefited the ecosystem, and how its life cycle unfolded.

"Dunstan has become an assassin for hire," Elias said. Though wasn't that pretty much how a lawyer expected to earn a living?

The houses were closer together as the route approached town, and church spires poked up into the summer sky at artistically irregular intervals. Though the terrain—a green valley spreading between low mountains—wasn't that different from Perthshire or parts of Aberdeenshire, Elias was hit with a queasy sense of being far, far from home.

"Dunstan claims he's killed the spiders," Jane said. "I think he mostly takes them outside. Snakes know better than to come in the house."

Did Violet's dogs keep snakes away from the house? "You're afraid of spiders?"

"I'm respectful of them, Elias. We have the black widow and brown recluse, as well as copperheads and rattlesnakes. A bite from any one of them calls for immediate medical intervention and around here, that means a half-hour drive into Frederick, at least. Then there's poison oak, poison ivy, poison sumac, stinging nettles, deer ticks and dog ticks, both of which carry diseases, to say nothing of the lowly mosquito which can—"

"Enough, Jane. I'll take my chances with Scotland's 200 distilleries."

But ye thundering gods, Jane's recitation left Elias wanting to turn the truck around, so he could ask Violet how she dealt with all those hazards. Scotland had no venomous spiders that Elias knew of, and no venomous snakes. As for those disease-bearing insects…

Only a mad woman would farm in this climate. Or a mad man, and Elias had no intention of misplacing his sanity any time soon. Misplacing it *again.*

"We take precautions," Jane said, "and no place is completely safe. What's it like, being an earl?"

Castles were safe. Castles stood for centuries against wars, weather, and wanton pillaging. Elias wasn't sure what force of nature could withstand Jane's cross-examination.

"Being an earl is like being a person," Elias said, "except other people ask you a lot of irrelevant questions. I have only been an earl for a short time, though, so feel free to check back with me as I muddle along. What do you know of a man named Maxwell Maitland?"

"Elias," Jane said gently as they came to the first stop light. "I'm family. You can tell me to back the hell off, and I will. As for Max Maitland, he's a real estate attorney who works for land developers. My real estate practice is limited mostly to residential loan settlements and quitclaim deeds, but I haven't heard anything particularly bad about Max."

None of the houses in this town were built with good old quarried granite, and the window boxes were all in want of flowers.

"You haven't heard anything good about Maitland, either?"

"Developers always face resistance from the locals," Jane said. "This is the longest light in town."

Even the stop lights were different in America. They didn't turn yellow between red and green, they simply flipped from stop to go without giving the driver any warning.

"Did you get any sleep last night?" Jane asked. "Dunstan says the jet lag isn't so bad coming this direction, but I beg to differ. I was wrecked for three days, coming and going."

"I slept adequately, thank you."

Jane gave him a look that suggested she knew when a man was lying, then she smoothly accelerated into the intersection. Driving calmed Elias, especially driving well-maintained, powerful vehicles.

"I'm sorry," he said. "I'm not used to the heat, and I'm a nervous passenger." Then too, Jeannie's emails had been nothing but bad news.

"So am I, but I trust Dunstan behind the wheel. I trust him pretty much everywhere. It's a nice feeling. He trusts me too."

"You are making a point," Elias said. "I don't claim to know you well, but I have a full complement of female cousins, and I was engaged twice. My every instinct suggests you are making a point."

And his every instinct further insisted, he would not like the conclusion she was about to bludgeon him with.

"Dunstan and I got married in Scotland."

"I'm sorry I wasn't available to attend," Elias began, though he still had no clue what the woman was babbling about.

"You didn't attend," Jane went on, "because if you came to our wedding, you'd have to go to all of them, and the picnics, christenings, and graduations. I get that. I did maid of honor duty three times before I learned to say no."

Elias hated saying no, but he hated more the idea that feelings would be hurt if he said no some of the time, and yes the rest. Zebedee had warned him about that, at least.

"I gave my cousin Jeannie away—Zeb was off at some polo association conference in Argentina—and I knew in my bones that bastard she married would make her miserable."

"And you haven't been to a wedding since," Jane said. "Dunstan and I could have gotten married here, where my family is. I was the bride, and traditionally, the wedding is the bride's shindig. We got married in Scotland, and half the de Lucas in Maryland came over. There are a lot of de Lucas."

Elias's mental lightbulb came on with all the glare of an interrogation lamp. "Dunstan's family would not have come here, not in any significant numbers." They might have if Zebedee had bought them all tickets, which was the sort of thing he'd done regularly.

More's the pity.

"Dunstan has been in Maryland pretty much his whole adult life, Elias, and you and Zeb are the only ones to come see him. The planes fly both ways."

Jane took a left, and soon the truck was again rolling by pastures, hay fields, and greening stands of wheat. Corn was barely sprouted, and the foliage along the mountaintops was still gauzy emerald, much as it would have been in Scotland.

Homesickness assailed Elias again, and also worry. Violet Hughes lived in the rural valley alone, working around livestock and heavy equipment all day, out in all kinds of weather. Elias resented the worry even as he knew it was justified.

Violet needed help, and Elias knew how that felt.

"I hope I haven't spoken out of turn," Jane said, as she drove along the winding lane that led to Dunstan's property. "Dunstan and I are glad to have you as our guest, and I think he was honestly a little puzzled that you'd want to stay somewhere else."

"I didn't want to crowd you. I'll explain that to Dunstan." *Again.*

"We have tons of room," Jane said. "And we have AC, heather ale, and bug spray. If you need anything—from lawyering, to spider extermination, to fresh shortbread—we're your family." She'd made that point several times now, and still Elias wasn't sure what she was getting at.

They tooled along in silence, across a valley that to appearances was lovely, despite its spiders, snakes, and noxious plants.

"Dunstan wants to get this right." Jane didn't need to explain what *this* was. Family was family in any language.

"Dunstan is lucky to have married you," Elias said, and yet, that was a platitude, and the moment called for something more honest. "What I meant was, I want to get this right too."

Jane offered him a brilliant, benevolent smile. She'd make a formidable adversary, and she was a wonderful addition to the family.

And yet, as Elias left the cool comfort of the truck for the hot afternoon, his thoughts were focused on Violet Hughes. She'd be making hay tomorrow in this awful heat, and Elias had offered to help her. A Brodie always kept his word, no matter how inconvenient that might be for the lady involved.

CHAPTER SIX

"So how's my favorite farm girl?" James Knightley asked, climbing out of his pick-up. He was drop-dead gorgeous, had the smile to prove it, and the law degree to whip out in case some fool thought he was just another handsome face.

"I'm not a girl, James," Violet said as she endured a one-armed hug. "These are not your haymaking duds."

James took up a lean against the truck's hood, and he looked good doing it, but then, James Knightley, Esquire, looked good pretty much all the time. He was a shade over six feet, blond, blue-eyed, and one of those men who truly, madly, deeply, liked women.

When he wore a three-piece suit to go with his smile, any sighted female would have been hard put not to like him right back.

"I stopped by to let you know I have to go into the courthouse for an emergency hearing," James said. "I'm sorry. You still planning on baling this afternoon?"

Violet ran through a mental litany of very bad words. "No, James. I just mowed forty acres of timothy and alfalfa last week because I like to numb my butt on a tractor seat every chance I get. Then I raked it because the deer prefer it that way, and I'm going to drive around on my tractor some more now because it's the only way to guarantee the baler will break before sundown."

She was being ungracious, which she blamed on Elias. James's offer to help with the haying was in return for some tools he'd borrowed, rather than time and effort on Violet's part. Charity, in other words, but charity she'd relied on.

James had the grace to look uncomfortable. "I had planned to send Luis to help you out in my place, but he's sprained his wrist. Mac has court, and Trent's in depositions."

"I don't know what depositions are," Violet said, as Bruno came strutting across the road. "But thanks for dropping by. Do you need any eggs?"

"Damn, I'd forgotten. Vera said to pick up a dozen. Twyla likes the brown ones."

"C'mon, sharp-dressed man. I've just put the day's haul in the fridge. How are your brothers?"

Violet asked out of basic manners—she'd been a few years behind James in school, but she knew his older brothers Trent and Mac reasonably well too. The Knightley brothers, like their uncles and grandfathers before them, would be "local boys" until the day they were buried in a Damson Valley churchyard.

"Mac and Trent are busy," James said, following her into the kitchen. "It's nice to see them happy-busy rather than just billable-busy. I've cleared the decks for tomorrow, if you want to bale what you have down and leave it in the field."

The suggestion was reasonable—if it didn't rain. Whatever hay Violet made into square bales could simply sit in the field overnight, then be tossed onto a wagon and loaded into the mows in the morning. The more efficient alternative was for the hay to go straight from baler to wagon to mow, though that worked much better if somebody was on the wagon to stack the bales as they emerged from the baler.

"I have only two wagons with sides," Violet said. "I'll fill those." Which would leave most of the crop in the field, and that made any farmer nervous. If hay was rained on at any point in the process—when it was down, after it was raked into windrows, even after it was baled—the nutritional quality suffered and its value dropped.

She picked out twelve brown eggs—hurray for species diversity—and arranged them into a plain biodegradable cardboard carton while James lounged against the kitchen counter looking delectable.

"How are things going, Violet?"

She closed the door to the fridge. "Are you asking as my lawyer or as my neighbor?"

"As your friend," James said. "Though I can put on my lawyer hat if you need me to."

A farm was a large, complicated business, subject to regulatory oversight from a dozen different angles. Wetlands, forestry, soil conservation, federal subsidies, livestock maintenance, zoning, fencing, building codes, wildlife conservation… they all impacted even a small farm in any given year. James had been raised on the farm where his brother MacKenzie now lived, and he knew agribusiness like Violet knew the contours of her arable fields.

James had gone over Violet's tax returns, both the personal and the business, not six weeks earlier. His question was not *quite* casual.

"I'm still here," Violet said. "What time do you have to be in court?"

"Eleven, which means we have time for you to put on the coffee."

Any other Monday, Violet would have been happy to catch up with James, to update him on the not very encouraging life and times of Violet Hughes. To whine a little, and maybe get a short pep talk from somebody to whom tax liens were not a theoretical misery.

Bruno, who seldom came into the house in mild weather, batted a paw at the screen door.

"Maybe some other time, James. I have three fields of hay down. You know what they say…"

"They say if you bale hay before the dew has dried off of it, you're more likely to burn down your barn." He let the cat in, though Bruno was capable of opening the screen door himself. "This guy looks like he's put away a few mice."

To Violet, the cat looked accusing, as if it was her fault Elias Brodie had left the neighborhood.

"Bruno's an easy keeper. My mom has been after me lately, James." A beat of silence went by, while more bad words piled up in Violet's mind. "She called last night to scold me for not going down to see her over spring break, as if planting can just wait until July. She says all the other ladies in her cul-de-sac have daughters who visit them."

Mama was a *lady*. She never raised her voice, never cursed, and had never complained in Violet's hearing about marriage to a man who'd seldom been on time for dinner, and often tracked mud into the house.

Mama hadn't forgiven Daddy for giving his life to a farm that had never made him rich. To Mama's credit, even a sizeable life insurance settlement hadn't mollified her indignation with her late spouse.

"You could move down to Florida. You have a master's degree," James said—carefully. "You're a hard worker, and you'd be an asset to any organization."

"I told her I'd visit once the hay's in." A white flag which wouldn't resolve the basic issue. Mama hated the farm, Violet loved it.

Which made Violet want to cry all over again. She'd watched from her bedroom window as Elias had tossed his suitcase into the black pick-up yesterday, and the tears had ambushed her. Then she'd cried after her mother's sneak attack, and now… now she had hay to bale.

"Shall I look for a buyer, Violet?" James asked. "You own a beautiful little farm."

Bruno hopped up on the windowsill, nearly toppling the African violets.

"James, you know better." Violet extricated the cat from the flower pots, put him on the floor, and wedged a chair beneath the window.

James *knew* Violet technically owned only half the farm.

"I know that options are a good thing," he said. "I know that farming any property is a lot for one person, no matter how hard-working or competent they are. I know farming is an extremely hazardous occupation."

A farmer was more likely to die on the job than a police officer, firefighter, or construction worker—not as likely as a logger or fisherman though. That was something.

"I liked you better when you were everybody's favorite flirt, James."

"I didn't like me better," James said, scrubbing a hand across the back of his neck. "I didn't like me very much at all. What if I drew up some leases, nosed around, maybe found somebody to rent a few acres from you?"

Bruno hopped up on the chair, his air that of a feline bent on destruction.

"Dammit cat, not today," Violet said, picking him up and holding him at eye level. "I'll lock you in with the hens if you don't behave."

He gave Violet a bored stare then yawned cat breath at her.

"No leases," Violet said, putting the cat down. "Not because I can't pay you to draft them, but because tenants are as much a hassle as anything else." Then too, if word got around that Elias was selling, the tenants on his property would jump ship in a heartbeat. No need to give them a handy place to jump to, because developers typically had honor the terms of any existing crop leases.

Bruno stropped himself against Violet's calves. The idiot beast was purring like a street rod.

"Violet, you can sell this place for enough to comfortably invest." James's tone was excruciatingly reasonable. "Then you could take your time deciding your next move. Developers typically take two to five years dealing with the permitting, planning, and re-zoning, and during that time—"

During that time, Violet could farm land that was doomed to become parking lots, sidewalks, paved jogging trails, and pesticide-drenched yards.

No, thank you. "James, put on your friend hat and leave," Violet said. "I know you mean well, but…"

"But you have farming in your DNA," James said. "So I can just take my eggs and get while the getting is good."

Bruno gently bit Violet's ankle—gently for him.

"Cat, you have a death wish," Violet said, nudging him away with her foot.

He leapt onto the table, scattering a stack of bills.

"Living dangerously, fella," James said, patting Bruno's head, then picking up the eggs. "I'll be on my way, but expect me before sundown with a couple extra wagons." He stopped by the door, gaze going to the deserted property across the road. "Didn't you used to have alpacas or llamas for neighbors?"

Violet left the bills for some other time—Bruno would probably just scatter them again in his present mood.

"The guy who lived over there apparently sold off the herd without the late owner's permission, then ran off with the proceeds. The present owner isn't too happy about that, but he has more pressing problems to deal with."

And they were valid problems, at least from Elias's perspective. He was head of his family in a way Violet did not understand, while she was…

She was angry with *the situation.*

"That has to be the most arrogant cat I have ever encountered," James said, as Bruno prowled to the door. "Somebody should file a police report if valuable property was stolen, Violet. Insurance companies won't pay restitution otherwise. If you'll be out in the heat all day, remember to hydrate."

"Yes, James, and I'll see you and your wagons—"

Bruno had got hold of the laces of Violet's right paddock boot. He tugged, the laces between his teeth, and glowered up at Violet, as if she was supposed to play a game with him.

"This is how nice kitties get their pictures on pet-shaming social media pages," Violet said, shaking her boot free. "Or I could sell you as a—"

Bruno stared up at her, the shoe lace hanging from his mouth like spaghetti.

"Violet?" James asked, hand on the doorknob.

A cautious trickle of hope dripped through Violet's lousy day. "You asked if you should look for a buyer for my farm. I assume you meant an agricultural buyer?"

"This side of the road is mostly zoned agricultural preservation, so yes. I'd be looking for somebody who wants to own a farm."

"Start looking," Violet said, opening the door and putting Bruno on the porch. "I'll walk you to your truck. I want you to find me a rich, ambitious farmer or farmers, and find them as fast as you can."

* * *

The electrician couldn't fit Elias in until Tuesday, and Dunstan and Jane both had court on Monday, which meant… Once Elias had spent the morning answering emails and phone calls, he was at loose ends, and he had Jane's car at his disposal.

The compact hybrid was a marvel of design and engineering, a significant step forward from an environmental standpoint, and—in Elias's opinion—absolutely pathetic as a driving experience. Acceleration was foreign to its nature, and the relationship between the suspension and the road surface was far from genteel.

The car did, however, have air conditioning.

Elias tossed several bottles of water into his knapsack and headed out to his property. When he parked in his driveway, Sarge and Murphy came bounding over, ears and tongues flapping.

"It's hot," Elias said, patting each dog's head. "Nobody should run in this weather. Have you no sense?" They panted happily, while on Violet's porch, the orange cat sat looking smug and overfed. "Where's Violet?"

The dogs capered around, though they didn't jump up and they didn't bark. The only sound was the whine of an engine—diesel, heavy, and the pitch was wrong for a truck.

"In this heat," Elias muttered, striding across the road. "She's out in this heat, and probably not wearing so much as a hat for protection."

Behind Violet's barn stretched a fairly level field, the tall grass having been cut and raked into fluffy rows. Violet drove a green tractor straight down one of those raked rows, the tractor pulling a machine that converted the cut grass into bales which were ejected into a slat-sided wagon.

The whole business was ponderous, noisy, and showed every potential for making a day already hot and increasingly humid outright miserable.

Elias waved, but the tractor continued chugging along. He left his pack in the shade of a maple and marched across the baled part of the field. When Violet spotted him, she shut the clattering baler down and halted the tractor, leaving the engine wheezing and thumping.

"The timing on your tractor needs adjustment," Elias said.

"Needs an oil change, too," Violet replied, wiping her temple with her forearm. "I was supposed to get to it yesterday, but the day got away from me. Hello."

The tractor was an inelegant, old powerhouse that would probably outlive Elias, but it was sorely in need of maintenance. Violet looked entirely at home on her tractor, a straw hat her only protection from the sun.

"Hello, Violet Hughes. I'm here to help with the haying."

"I'm mad at you, Elias."

He loved her honesty, loved how fearless she was whether making love or airing an opinion.

"You're being polite. You hate me because I'm selling arable land to the highest bidder, or I'll try to."

A weak breeze fluttered a damp curl against Violet's neck. Her hair was back in its bun, which was a relief. Heavy machinery and long braids made Elias nervous.

She took a drink from a metal water bottle, then capped it and stuffed it into a box beside the seat.

"Would you sell the farm to an agricultural buyer?"

"Depends on the price, and the situation with my castle. How does one make hay?"

Violet studied the sky, and if Elias lived to be ninety, he'd not forget the look of her. She wore only a white V-necked, short-sleeved T-shirt, thin with age. Her jeans were equally worn and her boots were dusty. She was hot, the breeze bore the scent of diesel fuel and new hay, and Elias wanted her on her back in the grass beneath him.

Damned prickly business, though, in more ways than one.

"You want to help me bring the hay in?" she asked, squinting at the clouds.

"I said I would, and you appear to be alone with the task."

She fired a pair of wrinkled work gloves at his midriff, then snatched a straw hat from behind the tractor seat and frisbee'd it at his head.

"My stacker had to cancel," she said, "and I can't be choosy. Those clouds are not supposed to be collecting anywhere near my valley. When I got up this morning, the forecast was clear until Wednesday. When I checked twenty minutes ago, this evening has a twenty percent chance of showers. I hate showers when I have hay down."

Elias would have loved a shower right about then, though not in the sense she alluded to. The hat fit him, thank the kind powers.

"I gather the haying exercise has acquired some urgency."

Violet's smile was not exactly benign, but it was pretty, and aimed at him. Elias chose to be encouraged.

"If it rains on my hay, Elias, I lose thousands of dollars in the space of an hour, and that's just in the price the hay will bring. If I'm feeding it to my sheep, then I'll have to feed more because the quality of the crop suffers for being rained on, and if the nutrient content is diminished—"

Elias let her natter on, though stacking hay bales did not require a PhD in economics. Climbing onto the wagon was an undignified undertaking, but he managed while Violet watched.

"Lay three bales across the long way for one layer," she said, "then five across the short way in the next layer up. Use the gloves unless you want to die of blisters on your blisters to go with your sunburn and your blisters."

Elias tugged the gloves on, and the afternoon went straight to noisy, broiling, itchy, blistered hell.

* * *

If Violet hadn't forced Elias to stop and drink, he'd have worked without a pause. He was damned fit, and it didn't take him long to get the hang of stacking a wagon. In the barn, he insisted on handling the end of the job that meant tromping around in the hay mow, dealing with the worst of the heat, dust, and sheer effort.

All Violet had to do was toss the hay bales onto the elevator, and that was exhausting enough. The crop was perfect though—lovely fodder, cut at the peak time, dried to perfection. The sheep would love it, and come winter, the horse owners would pay dearly for every bale.

Wagonload after wagonload went into the mow, and with each one, an anxiety known only to hay farmers eased for Violet. So much depended on getting the hay in, and the first cutting was the largest and most valuable.

"It's a shame you're selling your farm," Violet said, when she'd backed the last wagon into the barn's center aisle. "You have an aptitude for haying."

"Don't badger me when every part of me itches like the devil, Violet Hughes. Aren't you going to start the elevator?"

"No. The last wagonload can just sit here in the barn, to be unloaded some fine day when you aren't at risk for heat exhaustion. I'm in your debt, Elias. Thank you."

He climbed off the wagon, his movements lithe. For a Scottish earl, he did a mighty fine impression of a Maryland farm hand, right down to the way he slapped his gloves against his jeans.

"Must you be so honorable?" he said, accepting a water bottle from Violet, and draining half the contents. "I said I'd help. How often do you do this?"

"A third cutting isn't unusual, though fall hay isn't as valuable. I've made hay in December, when the conditions were right. Pretty stuff. Wasn't worth much. I have one more first cutting field to do, but it sits low and the alfalfa has been a little slow. I'll probably cut it next week, if the weather cooperates."

Or if it didn't. Hay that grew old and stemmy was as hard to sell as hay that got rained on.

Elias dumped the rest of the water over his face and head, shook, and slicked his hair back, then used the hem of his T-shirt to scrub his face.

"Do you never rest, Violet?"

She'd rested in his arms. "I'll rest after the first hard frost. My dad used to say he'd rest when he was dead."

"You'll have a lang sleep when ye're deid," Elias murmured. "I'm nearly dead. You must not tell Dunstan that a few hours on a wagon has me nearly undone."

He was rumpled, had chaff all over his T-shirt, and water ran in rivulets down his neck, but he wasn't nearly undone enough.

"Let's refill the water bottles," Violet said. "Do you have a clean T-shirt with you?"

"In my worst nightmares, I could not imagine being this hot and dirty, but I have a clean T-shirt in my backpack because I came intending to do manual labor."

He'd come offering an olive branch. Violet let the distinction pass, because her barn was full of beautiful hay, among other reasons.

"Are you expected anywhere for dinner?" she asked.

"I am not. I left a note for Dunstan and Jane saying not to expect me. Jane made rather a grand meal last evening, and I didn't want to put her to the trouble again."

What would Elias Brodie consider a grand meal? "I'm not cooking after the day I put in, but neither will I hit the shower in my present state. Meet me at the truck and bring your backpack."

She liked giving him orders—liked it plenty, because he took them. He didn't give her lip or sass or mansplaining or *reasoning*, for God's sake. He passed Violet the empty water bottle and sauntered off in the direction of the truck.

He was downing more water when she met him there ten minutes later, and that was smart. Haying had to be the hottest, sweatiest, most dehydrating, back-breaking, satisfying work in the world, and Elias was new to it.

"What's in the hamper, Violet?"

A jug of wine, a loaf of bread… She tossed him the truck keys. "Bug spray.

Hop in, unless you want to leave hay mess all over that nice little car."

Elias hauled himself up into the truck, though of course, he had to adjust the steering wheel and the seat.

"That nice little car is an abomination against all who take pleasure in driving. Where is the—?" He slid the key into the ignition. "Where are we going and why am I driving?"

Violet simply wanted to see him behind the wheel of her truck. "I drove that tractor all afternoon. We're going that-a-way." Violet pointed off behind the barn, to the tree line along the hedgerow at the far end of the third field. Even that gesture twinged the ache in her arms from wrestling the tractor all afternoon. "No hot dogging, Elias. This truck is paid off, and we don't have the health care system you guys do."

"Somebody keeps your vehicle tuned up," he said, letting the truck idle for a moment. "Your tractor is another matter." He drove down the lane, which was reasonably smooth. Raspberry bushes lined Violet's side—no fruit yet, profuse blossoms, and the poison ivy beneath the raspberries was thriving, too.

Elias drove the truck with none of the awkward misjudgment of people accustomed to smaller vehicles. Had Violet been asked, she might have said the truck liked him—or he liked the truck.

I've missed you, Elias Brodie. Violet couldn't say that, but she could admit it to herself. Had she never seen Elias with hay in his hair, his arms burnished by the sun, and his jeans creased with dust, she might have missed him less.

"Aim half way to the sycamore," she said. "Groundhog hole on the right as we pass the wishing oak."

"Do you have fairy mounds?" Elias asked easing the truck past the groundhog burrow.

I have memories of you. "Not that I know of. Try to get us some shade."

He tucked the truck under a spreading maple as sweetly as Bruno ensconced himself in a patch of sunlight.

"I neglected to use the air conditioning," Elias said, cutting the engine. "Perhaps I'm acclimating to Dunstan's inferno."

"Perhaps you're too tired to think. Haying does that. Second cutting is the worst. Ninety-five degrees, humidity you need a machete to cut, and bugs everywhere you least want bugs to be."

Elias climbed out of the truck, and while Violet rummaged for the wicker hamper, he came around to open her door.

"I know this is home to you," he said, "but can you entertain the notion that there are other places on earth more congenial to agricultural endeavors?"

Violet looked past his shoulder, back the way they'd come, to her barn, snuggled up against the rise of the land. Animals could shelter below, feed and fodder were stored above.

"My mother wanted to paint that barn," she said. "Tremendous expense and effort, but she said a weathered barn was shabby."

Elias brushed his thumb over Violet's brow. "A smudge," he said, repeating the gesture then dropping his hand. "Your mother's wishes didn't prevail, I take it."

"My father did the research, and wouldn't you know it, somebody has taken the time to compare what happens when raw wood weathers for twenty-five years versus when painted wood endures the same twenty-five years under the same conditions. The raw wood weathers better."

"So your father did the practical thing, and left his barn unpainted."

Violet wanted Elias to touch her again, and she wanted to shout at him that selling his farm would be an act of unforgivable betrayal.

Which was unfair and inaccurate. She passed Elias the hamper and climbed out of the truck. "My mother called last night."

"Is all well with her?"

The sound of water running over rocks should have been soothing. The sight of the barn so majestic and peaceful should have pleased Violet. The hay in the barn was like money in the bank, and yet, her heart was breaking.

"Mom wants me to sell, Elias. She came right out and said so last night. My own mother wants me to sell this place, and she might be able to make me do it, too."

Elias set the hamper down, wrapped Violet in his arms, and cursed in a language she'd never heard before.

CHAPTER SEVEN

Family was the most mixed of mixed blessings. Elias held Violet loosely in deference to the heat, but the sheer misery of her admission—to him, her virtual adversary—made him want to howl.

"Violet Hughes," he said softly, directly at her ear, "if I were to choose one person on the face of the earth who could not be coerced into behaving contrary to her principles, it's you. Perhaps your mother was having a bad moment and needs a placatory visit."

Violet eased away and picked up the hamper. "I should not be dumping my woes on you."

Elias collected his pack and followed her beneath a tall row of trees to a stream flowing over pale rocks. The opposite bank was covered with ferns that gave way to woods, while on the near side the bank was grassy.

"This is lovely," he said, as Violet opened the hamper and extracted an old quilt. The material was a faded blue and white patchwork—the same colors as the Scottish saltire, as it happened.

"Later in the season, the bugs can be a problem, especially at dusk, but for today, this is perfect. I come here when I'm too dirty to take a shower. Ever been skinny dipping?"

Despite grinding fatigue, myriad aches, and stinging blisters, some of Elias's exhaustion fell away. "I'm familiar with the concept, though the lochs in Scotland tend to be quite chilly."

Violet sat on the blanket and unlaced her boots. "I'll go for a swim first. If I start with the cold beer, I'm often asleep before I know it on a day like this. I do enjoy hard work, but I enjoy getting clean too."

Cold beer? Elias peered into the hamper and on top of a folded towel, saw the answer to unspoken prayers.

"Do I understand this libation is available for consumption?"

Violet yanked off both boots and set them in the grass beside the blanket. "You are hilarious, Elias Brodie. Yes, you may have a beer. Sandwiches are on the bottom. Last one in the water is a rotten egg, and I can tell you, from personal and regrettable experience, you do not want to be a rotten egg."

She stood and pulled her T-shirt over her head, then shucked out of her jeans. She wore a two-piece bathing suit, deep pink, on the modest side, but still…

Violet Hughes in a bathing suit was another answer to unspoken prayers.

"The deepest water is in the center," she said, striding to the bank. "There's soap tucked inside the towel, if you're so inclined."

Elias was inclined to watch Violet when she was driving a tractor, ranting about preserving farm land, or scolding her cat. To see her nearly naked, the perfect blend of curves, muscles and, hollows…

He forgot the beer, he forgot he was filthy, he forgot ravenous hunger, he forgot—well, he didn't forget his castle. Instead he pictured Violet there, looking just like this. Eager, determined, happily anticipating a simple pleasure.

She waded in, shivered, splashed water on her arms and belly, and grinned at him over her shoulder.

"You can swim, right?"

The last time he'd gone swimming had been in Italy, and he'd mostly been obliging his hostess's desire to add him to her collection of poolside decorations.

"I'm competent in the water," he said, pulling his T-shirt off. He turned it right-side out, and shook it hard. Boots, socks, and jeans followed, until he was wearing only wrinkled cotton boxers. He found the soap—not lavender, rosemary maybe, and peppermint—and crossed to the stream.

"Water's damned cold," Violet said, wading out. "Mind you don't get a cramp."

A cramp was the least of Elias's worries. "Is it deep enough to dive?"

"Eight feet or so in the middle," Violet said, pushing off in a breaststroke. "Holy bejesus, this stream gets colder every year."

Elias scaled a likely rock, positioned the soap within reach, and dove for the center of the stream. The shock was ghastly and invigorating, a welcome torment to blistered hands, lacerated arms, and sore everything.

The water was also cold enough to thwart nascent arousal—some.

"Shall I use the soap first?" Elias asked. "You seem content to paddle about."

"I like to swim. Go ahead and get clean."

The water was too cold to truly enjoy for any length of time, so Elias scrubbed off, passed Violet the soap, and left her to her ablutions. By the time Violet climbed out, Elias was in a T-shirt and board shorts, and half a beer had met its fate. The moment was lovely, but like all lovely moments, it would pass.

"You waited until my back was turned to change your clothes," Violet said, appropriating a sip of his beer. "Not like I haven't seen the goods before, Elias."

Elias passed her the towel. "You're getting gooseflesh, and I'm opening another beer. You're angry with me, remember? You should also be angry with your mother."

Elias was angry with Violet's mother. Violet did not need betrayal from the only parent she had left. Not now.

She wrapped the towel around her shoulders, and fortunately for Elias, it was a large towel.

"Mama has her reasons. Husband number three isn't much help. He's the protective sort."

In defense of his ability to argue coherently, Elias settled on the blanket, beyond touching range.

"Woe to any man who develops protective fancies where his womenfolk are concerned," he said, fishing for the sandwiches. "My first fiancée explained that commandment to me a month before the wedding."

The three p's, she'd termed it. Protective, paternalistic, and philanthropic. Any one of them was troublesome, but a prospective spouse who'd turned out to be three for three… Maria had had plans for the Brodie wealth that did not include looking after Elias's extended family, or donating regularly to any charities. She'd been equally clear that paying the nonrefundable wedding expenses didn't interest her either.

Violet cracked open the second beer. "You've had more than one fiancée?"

"Only two. The second numbers among my friends. Would you like a sandwich?" Ham and cheese on sourdough with yellow mustard—food for the gods, in Elias's present mood.

Violet's expression suggested passing mention of former fiancées—plural—had not gone unremarked.

"I'll take a half," she said, coming down beside him. "The water felt divine."

They ate in relative quiet, though not silence. The water lapped over the rocks, a sheep occasionally bleated from the direction of the barn, some small creature scurried through the ferns on the opposite bank.

"What will you do about your mother?" Elias asked, when he'd demolished both halves of his sandwich.

"Husband number three is protective of Mama, but that's a polite way to say he's protective of her money. I detect his guiding hand agitating her worries regarding the farm."

"Can you negotiate a buyout?"

Violet tossed a bit of her bread crust into the bushes. "For the squirrels. I hadn't thought about a buy-out, because I'm so busy trying not to show a profit so the tax man doesn't put me out of business, not that there's been much profit lately."

"I'm descended from one of the few Scottish families to claim some wealth," he said, around a mouthful of sandwich. "The blood of a hundred generations of accountants flows in my veins. Here's how you structure the buy-out. You make sure title passes to you as quickly and completely as possible, so that in effect, your mother is holding a private mortgage with the land as security. She escapes liability, you gain ownership. Have you a competent attorney?"

"Yes, when I can afford him. I do send him business from my blog, too."

Elias's second fiancée had become quite the blogger. "You make your mother pay the legal fees as part of the closing on the transaction. Does husband number three expect to inherit her portion of the farm?"

Violet chewed the last of her sandwich. "He's five years younger than she is, and takes care of himself, but I don't like to think… Elias, I don't know. He's more or less a stranger to me. He seems devoted to Mama, but a little charm can hide a lot of self-interest."

Elias crushed his empty beer can and pitched it back into the hamper. Violet's observation had not been casual.

"Would it help if I apologized, Violet?"

"For?"

"For selling my property. Every time you look out your front window and see a development where fields were, your heart will break all over again." Just as Elias's heart broke to see the mortar crumbling from the castle walls, the lichens working their insidious damage year by year, the grounds left to errant sheep and nesting birds.

Fatigue hit him on a beer-assisted wave. Everything ached, from his blistered palms, to his sunburned arms, to his lower back.

To his heart. The lovely moment was over.

"You have a castle to save," Violet said, "or an earldom, or a legacy of some sort. I want to hate you, and I might yet see my way clear to a burning resentment, but my family has been on this property for five generations. I think about turning my back on this, and I can't, which means I can't judge you too harshly for defending your castle. This is my home. What I do here matters…"

That Violet could be left in peace on her farm mattered to Elias, too, which was damned inconvenient. They'd spent a night together, and in a week or so, Elias would return to Scotland, there to stay for a good long while.

Sometimes, life was unfair, sad, and lonely. He'd learned that as an eleven-year-old boy, the lesson held true two decades later.

"So come up with that buy-out plan," Elias said. "You will sleep better if you know your farm is in your hands, regardless of what transpires across the road." Elias would sleep better as well. Because he'd had enough of problems, worries, and woes, he passed Violet the second half of her sandwich and put a question to her. "What is this blog you write?"

"How can I work up a burning resentment when you know exactly when to change the subject?"

Elias closed his eyes, and felt again the sense of plunging loss that had assailed him as a boy. Zebedee hadn't sugarcoated anything, orphaned was orphaned. The only thing worse might have been to be orphaned and lied to.

"Violet, I'm meeting with Maxwell Maitland on Wednesday."

Violet tossed the entire half of the sandwich into the bushes. "Dang it, Elias. One burning resentment, coming right up. That's fast work."

"If Maitland intimidates you, he must be formidable, so why not start with him?"

The rest of her beer watered the good earth of Damson Valley. She shook the can, hard, so it was empty to the last drop.

"Keep it up, Elias, and that resentment might yet blossom into loathing. Maitland doesn't intimidate me, he scares the holy living peedywaddles out of me. He won't settle for half your farm. His backers love him, because he thinks big and plays hardball. He'll want the whole property, his own little fiefdom, with fire control ponds that look like they were landscaped for five-star golf courses, maybe even a supermarket, bank branch, and drug store."

The trifecta of high traffic magnets, right across the road from Violet's chickens.

"Violet, I'm sorry."

She fired her empty beer can into the hamper. "Yes, Elias Brodie, you are sorry indeed. Let's get back to the house."

She ignored his hand when he tried to help her up, and when he gathered up his effects, she shook the hell out of the old quilt before stuffing it into the hamper. Violet also drove them back to the house in silence, while Elias resisted the urge to check his phone.

No email or text would have arrived from Scotland making everything all better, no codicil to Zebedee's will would pop up revealing some huge buried trust.

And yet, the silence tore at him. "If I'd told you earlier that I was meeting with Maitland, you would not have allowed me to stack those wagons of hay."

"I would have managed, Elias. I always manage."

Alone. She always managed alone. "I didn't lie to you, Violet. I won't ever lie to you."

The truck bumped along, across a trio of lush fields temporarily enjoying a manicured, tidy appearance. Elias did take out his phone, but he used it to take a photo, the mountains green and stately behind rolling fields and hardwood hedgerows.

"Why take a picture?" Violet asked, as she pulled into her driveway.

Self-torment, of course. "I have good memories of this place, and it's beautiful. Why wouldn't I take a photo?"

She cut the engine, and Elias waited—for a rant, a curse, an explosion.

"I'm trying to find you an agricultural buyer, Elias. My attorney knows everybody in the valley—he was born and raised on a farm not two miles west of here. It might take subdividing, might take a consortium. If there's a buyer out there anywhere in the four-state area, James will find them."

Oh, not this. Not her dogged persistence turned on his problems too.

"Violet, I've had news from Scotland."

The keys remained in the ignition, and she apparently didn't intend to remove them. Country people took that risk—left the keys in the vehicle, so they wouldn't get lost.

"Not good news," she said.

"Not convenient news." Awful news, really. "My cousin Jeannie has taken on management of the renovation project. She's a single mum, very organized, and she needed work. She contacted the master mason I'd apprenticed under years ago, a man who's worked on more castles than there are hay bales in that barn. I'd told Jeannie to start gathering estimates. Nick was surprised to hear from her."

"Drop the other shoe, Elias. Your idea of not lying hasn't gone very well on this end."

He deserved that, mostly. "Nick Aiken is the best, and he's already under contract to start the major repairs. Seems Zebedee had signed a contract, paid an advance, and approved a crew and schedule. By the end of this week, my castle will be swarming with certified master craftsmen, and every one of them will expect to be paid handsomely and regularly for their labors."

She opened the truck door, and the dogs bounded off the porch. "You want sympathy, Elias?"

He wanted to kick something, wanted the damned world to cut them a break, wanted to hold Violet and make wild promises to her and even wilder love.

"I want you to have the truth, though my timing in that regard seems ever to be wanting."

The dogs must have sensed the mood, and rather than capering around Violet's feet when she climbed out of the truck, they both sat, panting and silent, in the grass.

"I have a blog to write. Thank you for your help with the hay, but in the future…"

"Right. Back to Scotland with me, soonest. I'm working on it." He got out of the truck, and started down the driveway, but Violet's voice halted him.

"I'm sorry, too, Elias. Good-bye and take care. Best of luck with your castle." She slipped into the house, the dogs trotting at her heels.

* * *

Dunstan stared at his laptop screen, Gaelic curses dancing through his head. A fine way to start a Tuesday at home, exercising rusty language skills.

"That expression does not bode well for somebody," Jane said. "Is Aaron

Glover giving you fits on the Holmes case?"

"Mr. Glover's client is pure as the freshly fallen snow on Christmas morning in Bethlehem," Dunstan replied, "while my client—at least in Mrs. Holmes's eyes—is a lying, cheating scoundrel who has hidden what assets he hasn't squandered. But no, this email isn't from Glover, it's from Jeannie."

Jane set aside her book—she was a diehard print reader—and scooted out of the recliner to peer over Dunstan's shoulder. They were in the study, Dunstan's favorite room of the house after the bedroom. Two desks rescued from the law library's rummage sale sat face to face by the windows. A fieldstone fireplace with a small woodstove took up the opposite wall. Braided rugs covered the hardwood floors and in the far corner sat the recliner in which Dunstan had spent too many hours of his bachelorhood.

Jane had added the touches—a fern by the window, a blue and green afghan on the recliner, antique apothecary jars on the mantel full of dried lavender, statice, and eucalyptus leaves. A single iris graced an aquamarine antique glass bottle beside her computer.

Jane had transformed Dunstan's house from a campsite with wifi and a resident cat to a home.

"Did Jeannie send any pictures of Henry?" Jane asked.

Wee Henry was less than a year old, and as the youngest Cromarty—for now—he enjoyed great popularity among the extended family.

"Not this time. She's checking on Elias."

"Remind me not to cross that woman," Jane said, draping an arm around Dunstan's shoulders. "That is some intuition, if it works at this distance."

"What are you reading, wee Jane?" Dunstan had dipped into some of her fiction, and gained insight into why Jane was an avid reader.

"A Carolyn Brown." She slid around and straddled Dunstan's lap. "I'm in a cowboy mood."

"Cowboys are a fine American cultural icon," Dunstan replied, wrapping his arms around his wife. They had the house to themselves. Elias was off meeting with an electrician, and Tuesday was the day Dunstan and Jane either worked at home, or at least scheduled no client appointments if they had to go into the office.

The courthouse sometimes interfered with that schedule, but even two or three Tuesdays a month at home had made a difference to Dunstan's outlook on life. Marriage had given both him and Jane the motivation to do something other than work and rest enough to work some more.

Then too, marriage had introduced such a steady flow of pure affection into Dunstan's days, he pitied the single man he'd been for so long.

Jane cuddled close, a lovely lapful of wife, best friend, legal partner, and lover. "Elias is in trouble."

Elias *was* trouble. Since boyhood, Elias had been the cousin who hadn't fit in, though it was hardly his fault. Every other child had arrived to family gatherings with siblings, parents, a dog or two. Elias had been delivered by a driver, when he'd attended at all.

"Elias will sort out the Brodie finances," Dunstan said. "He's well qualified to handle the load he's carrying." Elias was the only person Dunstan knew personally who had a PhD in economics, in fact.

Jane sat up and regarded Dunstan with a gaze more legal partner than lover. "Where do you suppose he spent Saturday night, Dunstan?"

"In a bed. His farmhouse is furnished."

"You assume he stayed there even though the place has no electricity?"

Jane was regarded as one of the best trial attorneys in the jurisdiction, and Dunstan knew at some point, she could well be considered for a judgeship. She was twiddling the hair at Dunstan's nape, while she angled around to a conclusion Dunstan could only guess at.

"The power often goes out around here," he said, "as you well know. Elias could manage to sleep without the lights on." And probably look like a fashion model while he did, poor bastard.

"But no electricity means no water, no refrigeration, and he was on that property for more than 24-hours."

Dunstan rose with Jane barnacled to his chest and settled in the recliner. "Dry camping is inconvenient, but Elias probably had a few necessities with him. He's a seasoned traveler." And for Elias, self-sufficiency was a commandment.

"I asked if I could buy some eggs while I was out that way, just to see how the witness would respond," Jane said, getting comfortable against Dunstan's side. They'd spent many an hour cuddling in this recliner, hours when Dunstan had wallowed in the sheer pleasure of proximity to his beloved.

His beloved had an agenda other than wallowing at the moment. Dunstan forced himself to pick up the thread of the discussion, something about…

"Eggs?"

"From chickens. Violet Hughes lives across the road from Elias's farm. I get my eggs from her at the farmers market sometimes, and we took a birdwatching class together a couple years ago. One of my failed attempts to get out more. You smell good, like yard work—freshly cut grass and summer morning with a dash of manly-man."

He'd mowed the grass before the day had grown too hot. "About the eggs?"

"I suspect Violet and Elias have taken notice of each other, Dunstan. Your cousin was mighty spruce for a guy who'd overnighted in a hot, dusty old farmhouse with no running water, and he most assuredly did not want me chatting Violet up while he was in the vicinity."

Jane's instincts were never to be dismissed. Not ever.

"Elias is something of a tom cat, Jane, though I suppose he can afford to be. He's been engaged twice, and almost made it to the altar both times. The ladies seem to like him, at least for a short time."

Jane rose up on her elbow to peer at Dunstan. "Do *you* like him?"

God help all husbands married to litigating attorneys. "I hardly know him, Jane. He was educated at boarding schools, and then I moved here. I suppose I like him, but it's hard to respect a man who in the normal course is shagging the neighbor the same day he meets her."

Jane patted his chest and tucked herself against his side. "You can take the Presbyterian out of Scotland, but he'll still be a Scottish Presbyterian."

"What's that supposed to mean?"

"Your cousin lost both parents suddenly when he was eleven. He was cast into the care of an old guy who liked to live large and probably knew squat about kids. When Elias should have been kept close by his family he was sent off to some snooty school, or probably a progression of snooty schools. Two women dump him at the altar and then his closest family member dies."

Jane scooted around while Dunstan felt an uneasy welling of shame.

"Instead of worrying about your cousin," she went on, "you're worried he might have lifted his kilt for a woman who'd probably welcome the diversion. That's bullcrap, Dunstan. Elias is a good man in a tough situation, he's family, and if he needs our help, we will help him."

Oh, how he loved her. "You told him as much?"

"I tried to be subtle. He still looked like he wanted to jump out of the truck."

"How fast were you going?"

Jane smacked him, then kissed his cheek. "I wish you could come with us to meet with Max Maitland tomorrow."

So did Dunstan, for the sheer pleasure of watching Jane in her professional role. Then too, Jane's scold bore consideration. Elias *was* a good man, and he was facing worse problems than even he knew.

"I wish I could come along as well," Dunstan said. "Alas for me, Mr. Glover and I have a date in Courtroom Three. Pistols, swords, violins, and drumrolls. Mr. and Mrs. Holmes have paid good money to bludgeon each other in the halls of justice, and counsel must provide zealous representation within the bounds of the law. Common sense offered at no extra charge, to no avail thus far. Glover and I have agreed, the winning attorney buys lunch with all the trimmings, if the case ever ends."

"The clients aren't ready to settle yet, then," Jane said. "Timing is everything. What did Jeannie want?"

"Jeannie exhorted me to keep a close eye on Elias, much as you have. She said Zebedee had apparently contracted for work to start on the castle without telling Elias. The master mason is on site, and expecting a crew any day. Elias is not happy that expenses are accruing faster than revenue."

"It's a lovely old castle," Jane said. "I will never forget our wedding reception, Dunstan. Fairytales do come true."

The great hall had been freezing, as usual. All the whisky in Scotland couldn't make tons of granite cozy in winter, though the laughter of family had echoed wonderfully from the vaulted ceiling.

"It's an expensive old castle," Dunstan said. "The head mason is fairly certain Zebedee also hired carpenters, glazers, and landscapers. For all Jeannie knows, tapestries are being woven in some Flemish studio using gold thread, and Elias will have to find a way to pay for it all."

"Ruh-roh. That could cost a bundle, couldn't it?"

A fortune, if the renovation was done properly. "Elias knows about the masons, but not about the rest of it. Jeannie wants me to tell him."

"I gather Scottish tradesmen frown on broken contracts?"

"Of course not. If the tradesmen are good at what they do, a broken contract simply means remuneration without having to do the work."

One moment Jane was tucked against Dunstan's side, the next she was straddling his lap. "So I was right," she said, undoing his belt. "Elias is in trouble."

"You are frequently right," Dunstan said. "You are also possessed of significant manual dexterity when it comes to undressing your husband."

"I never realized how much I take our privacy for granted," Jane said, unzipping his fly. "I think Elias is trying to leave us in peace as much as he can. Why Mr. Cromarty, what have we here?"

"Evidence of impending bliss, Mrs. Cromarty." And then, because a husband was entitled to tease his wife: "I should answer Jeannie's email."

"Later," Jane said, pulling her T-shirt over her head. "Before you hit Elias with more bad news, let Jeannie do some investigating. The mason might be wrong, and you'd be worrying Elias for nothing. He has enough on his plate."

Sound reasoning, but within two minutes, Dunstan was too busy loving his wife to bother with reasoning on any terms at all.

CHAPTER EIGHT

Elias extricated himself from Jane's hybrid, though the process was painful. He'd arisen aching in every joint and muscle, and he'd slept miserably. Sunburned forearms were a painful novelty he hoped never to experience again. His palms were blistered despite his conscientious use of work gloves the previous day, and his heart…

He'd disappointed Violet with his honesty, and she'd sent him on his way.

Smart woman. Smart, stubborn woman.

She was on her porch, intent on her laptop when Elias pulled into his driveway. The dogs looked up but didn't bother to greet him, and the cat sitting sentinel on Violet's porch railing ignored him.

Which was for the best. He fetched the tools he'd borrowed from Dunstan from the back of the car, and prepared to spend more hours sweating under the Maryland sun. The weather today was worse than yesterday—more humid, hotter.

Lonelier.

The electrician hadn't given a specific arrival time, so Elias started on the overgrown beds nearest the house. He'd pulled weeds, pruned what rosebushes he'd found, and practiced his Gaelic curses at length before a white van pulled in bearing the logo for Tri-County Electrical Services.

The electrician was a well-fed specimen with wheat-blond hair, a ruddy complexion, and crooked front teeth. His blue-and-white striped work shirt bore the name "Marvin Eby" embroidered in red on the pocket.

"You Mr. Brodie?" Marvin asked, propping a clipboard against his ample midriff.

"I am he. Glad you could come by. The fuse box is on the back porch." Elias led him around the back of the house, the sound of Marvin cracking his gum punctuating the morning quiet.

"I did wonder who owned this place," Marvin said, as he clomped up the porch stairs. "Nice property, but kinda going to seed, know what I mean? Needs somebody to live here, a few cows, maybe some goats. I like goats. Goats are smart."

Nothing in Elias's education or world travels had prepared him to hold forth knowledgably on the subject of goats.

"I'm sure the lowly caprine is quite clever," Elias replied. "With respect to the power, I couldn't find a problem with the fuses, so the challenge is one of diagnosis rather than simple repair."

Marvin did not inspect the fuse box, which Elias had kindly opened for him. He instead squinted at his clipboard.

"Where'd you say you were from, Mr. Brodie?"

"Aberdeen."

"Over by Baltimore?"

The company of goats must have addled the poor man. "Scotland. I'll be in the front yard if you need anything. The house is open. As far as I know, nobody has lived here for at least the past 90 days."

Marvin's gaze took in the house, the barn, the fields spreading off to the south. "Pretty place you got here, Mr. Brodie. You're the owner?"

Hadn't they established as much? "I have that honor." *For now.*

"But you don't know how long the place has been sitting empty?"

"I travel a great deal, mostly in Europe." Mostly in first class, mostly in the company of people who'd never known a goat by name, much less a hen.

"If I had a place like this, I'd sure as hell be living here. Know what I mean? That is one sweet view, and the wife loves her a nice big garden. The kids aren't so keen on the vegetables, but they like playing in the dirt."

Elias did not mistake Marvin for a fool—the view *was* lovely—but tradesmen worked by the hour, and time was money.

"I hope the view will be enjoyed by the subsequent owners, and I'll leave you to the electrical repairs."

Marvin turned over a page on his clipboard and stuck his pen behind his ear. "Aberdeen, you say. In Scotland. The wife will want to hear about this. Do you know that Jamie fellah from the TV show?"

"I have been introduced." At a very successful charity gathering to benefit testicular cancer.

"Now that is a right marvel. You don't say. Small world. Let me see if I can at least make it a small world with a few more lights on when the sun goes down, Mr. Brodie."

Marvin peered at the fuse box, and Elias left him to work his magic. The front of the house looked marginally more presentable for the morning's labors, but half of the north wall of the barn was still covered in green vines growing to nearly fifteen feet.

Stone walls that had withstood centuries of Viking raids could be brought down by vigorous ivy, given enough time, and Violet would never forgive Elias for neglecting his barn.

But then, Violet might not ever forgive him on general principles. Elias picked up shears and a rake, pulled on gloves, and prepared to do battle with Maryland's vegetation anyway.

* * *

James Knightley had come by Violet's farm the previous evening, wagons in tow behind his tractor. Violet had explained that her hay had all been put up, and James had insisted on helping her unload the last wagon. She'd broached the topic of a buy-out when the last bale had been tucked in place, and James had given her an hour of his time to discuss it.

The problem, of course, was cash. Buy-outs worked best if there was cash on hand to do the buying with.

Lots of cash. Violet had spent half the morning playing with the numbers, trading emails with the state's agricultural conservancy office, and trying not to stare across the road.

Elias's farm was beautiful in so many regards. The eight hundred acres encompassed pastures, hayfields, cropland, woods, streams, and that gorgeous stone barn. Soon, all of it would be contoured, paved, cut up, and turned into cul-de-sacs if Max Maitland had his way.

"And Max Maitland usually gets his way," Violet muttered.

The blue compact hybrid pulled in, and Violet went back to answering comments on the week's blog. The topic, as it happened, once again dealt with the conservancy easement Maryland farmers could apply for if they were willing to keep their land permanently out of development. Nearly 300,000 acres of farmland had been protected since the program had started in the late 1970s, but that was millions of acres too few in Violet's estimation.

Elias was in his jeans again, and his T-shirt was blue. He took an old-fashioned wooden tool box from the back of the car and was soon attacking the flower beds at the front of the house.

"What are you staring at?" Violet asked Bruno. The dogs were at her feet, Bruno had migrated from the porch railing to the arm of the glide-a-rocker Violet occupied. "One of these summers I'm going to shear you when we do the sheep. You'll be a lot happier."

Talking to domestic animals was probably a sign of some mental aberration. Violet tried to focus on her blog comments, but Elias....

He was thorough, leaving each bed chopped, weeded, tidied, and ready for mulch. A pile of yard trash was growing on the walk as he worked his way across the front of the house.

"He'd better have brought water with him. Heat exhaustion is cumulative."

Infatuation was apparently cumulative too. Saying good-bye, and meaning it, apparently did nothing to stop the heart from aching, or the imagination from speculating. An agricultural buyer for eight hundred acres was a long shot, and Elias's problems back home were mounting.

"A swing and a miss, cat," Violet said.

A white van pulled in with Tri-County Electrician's logo on the side, and Elias and the electrician soon disappeared around the back of the house.

"I will miss Elias Brodie for the rest of my damned life." Which made no sense. He was a skilled lover, attractive, and honorable in his way, the kind of guy who made hooking up look mighty tempting.

"But a hook up has to come unhooked in the morning."

Elias emerged from the back of the house, pulled on gloves—must he look so sexy simply pulling on gloves?—and picked up a set of long-handled pruning shears and a rake. Violet sensed his intention between one heartbeat and the next, and came off the porch at a dead run.

* * *

"Elias, stop! Stop right now, just please—what in the Sam Damned Hill do you think—*will you please stop*!"

Violet Hughes had pelted across the road, yelling all the way, while Elias watched, his gloved hands full of greenery. The vines had been growing long enough to develop thick branches near the barn's foundation and a secure hold on the barn wall.

"Violet. Hello."

"Drop that stuff, Elias," she panted. "Are you out of your stubborn Scottish mind?"

She was upset—he apparently had the knack of upsetting her. "I am attempting to tidy up my property in anticipation of sale. Dunstan and Jane work at home on Tuesdays, which I believe is a euphemism for activities generally considered normal between the newly married. I had to wait here for the electrician, so I've kept busy as best—"

"That is poison ivy," Violet yelled.

"I don't intend to eat it."

"Elias, that plant will give you the mother of all rashes, and make you itch within an inch of your sanity. Go over to my house. Get your clothes off and leave them in a heap on the floor. Scrub off your arms using the rubbing alcohol that's under the bathroom sink, and then take a cool shower—cool, not hot. Use the soft soap on anything the ivy might have touched. Any part of the plant—the leaves, the roots, the stems—can cause a reaction and the oil can get on your clothes as well as your skin."

Elias dropped the bundle of vines he was holding, and yet he was torn by conflicting urges. The first was to stay and argue with Violet, because arguing was a form of conversation and he'd resigned himself to never conversing with her again.

"I'm not prone to allergies, Violet. I've only started on the wall five minutes past."

And she'd been tearing across the yard almost immediately.

"Go," she said, shoving at his shoulder. "You pulled down enough poison ivy in two minutes to keep you itching for three weeks, Elias. Go, and I'll deal with your electrician."

He went, pausing to snag his backpack. He jogged across the road, up Violet's drive, and straight into her house, the dogs woofing him a greeting as he passed them on the porch. He was in the shower off Violet's bedroom a few minutes later—cool, not hot, which felt wonderful—and then using his spare toothbrush and comb to make himself presentable.

"Elias Brodie you had better get in that shower in the next—" Violet came to a halt in the doorway to the bedroom.

Elias set his comb on the dresser. "You were saying?"

"I'll put your clothes in the wash."

"My clothes, all of which have been dutifully left in a heap on your floor, thus explaining my current state of complete undress."

Violet's expression was an exquisite blend of yearning, appreciation, and frustration. After staring at Elias for the space of three slow heartbeats, she whipped around, giving him her back.

"You seem to carry a change of clothes with you everywhere," she said.

Elias sauntered up behind her. "My state of undress is a matter of practicalities. My state of arousal is a function of proximity to present company, and the memories made in that bed. I am attracted to you, Violet. I'll not apologize for that."

Violet was passionate, complicated, determined, and many other things, but she was not a hypocrite or a prude. She was, undeniably, the inspiration for his arousal, and she was clearly determined to keep her back to him.

"You are meeting with Maxwell Maitland tomorrow," she said, hands fisting at her sides. "Elias, it won't help to go to bed with you. We did that already."

Not nearly enough, they hadn't. He yanked his board shorts out of his pack and stepped into them.

"I am not in the habit of having intimate relations with women on the verge of hating me," he said. "In the very near future, I will likely commit an unpardonable act of ecological treason in your eyes. I understand that. You can turn around now."

Violet turned, slowly. "If I went to bed with you, I'd regret it. I can give myself a pass for Saturday night, because I didn't... because it was a hook up."

"No, it was not," Elias said, stepping closer. "I've done my share of hooking up, Violet, more than my share, and whatever else is true, we did not *hook up*."

She smelled of lavender, and Elias wanted to touch her so badly, the aches from yesterday's exertions were nothing compared to the longing he battled. He'd load ten wagons of hay in the broiling heat every day for a week if she'd only take his hand.

Instead, she patted his chest. "*We didna huke opp*. You are almost unintelligible when you're fierce. I like it, which proves I'm losing my damned mind. You muddle me something awful, which I do not like. How about we take this discussion somewhere without a bed?"

Elias could probably coax, wheedle, kiss, and cuddle her onto the bed. He was good—princesses, billionaire heiresses, and one fiancée, had told him so, as had any number of casual partners in graduate school and elsewhere.

"I *muddle* you?"

Elias didn't see the kiss coming. One moment, he was trying to content himself with a sop to his dignity—he muddled her—and the next, Violet was in his arms, a winsome, fiendish lover whose kisses sent hope skittering well south of Elias's heart.

She made her point thoroughly, reminding him how well their bodies fit together, how luscious her kisses were, how generous and passionate her loving.

Then she stepped back, walked around him, and patted his bum. She stuffed his comb in his backpack, and handed the pack to him, all the while ignoring an erection that should have come equipped with a complimentary windsock.

"You haunt my dreams, Elias Brodie. Someday, I might forgive you for wrecking my valley, but for haunting my dreams… I'll never forgive you for that."

She patted his chest again and walked out.

* * *

"Are those for *me*?" Bonnie asked.

Max shifted the flowers and for once found his admin smiling at him. "No, but you're welcome to put some of them on your desk."

He'd chosen flowers that consisted of a series of blossoms all in the same bright color on one long stem. They'd been on sale, and looked office-chic to him—not like damned daisies.

"So, you just stopped and bought yourself a gladiolus bouquet because the Grinch's heart periodically grows to the size of ten men plus two?"

Gladiolus. Max made a note of the name, in case Elias Brodie liked flowers. The internet described Brodie as newly wealthy, connected to all the right charities, and frequently in the company of gorgeous, rich women. A guy like that might know one flower from another, but he certainly did not need ownership of a chunk of the Maryland countryside complicating his busy schedule.

"This office is a dump," Max said. "It's a historic dump, but it doesn't need to be an ugly dump."

Bonnie came around her desk and took the flowers from him. "Our office is quaint, and I keep it presentable. You got these for tomorrow's meeting, didn't you?"

Bonnie was petite, and the flowers dwarfed her.

"Do you think they're too much?" The colors were bold—magenta, lemon, scarlet—but to somebody with sophisticated tastes, they might be gaudy. "I thought an orchid would be overdoing it."

"You don't have the patience for orchids," Bonnie said, laying the flowers on her blotter. "Are you nervous?"

Max was desperate, not the same thing as nervous. "This project has the potential to… Development moves in waves, Bonnie, and both D.C. and Baltimore are ready for another wave. For both cities, the buildout can go either north or west, and if it goes west of Baltimore and north of D.C., then Damson Valley sits at the end of two rainbows."

Bonnie took the stems one by one, held them over the trash can, and snipped off several inches, always cutting at an angle. Her movements, like everything else about her, were competent and economical.

"So you'll be set up for life, right? One sale, and you become the Maryland development czar. Is that what you want?"

"Why do you cut them like that?" At the same sharp angle, stem after stem.

"So they can drink as much water as they need, and you should—what am I saying? *I'll* trim them up regularly so they last as long as possible. A lot of people around here won't like to see Damson Valley turned into a bedroom community."

Bonnie among them, based on her expression.

"They'll like the growth they see in their businesses, they'll like having a larger tax base for the schools and infrastructure, they'll like having a place to live that's convenient, pretty, safe, and affordable. I build the American dream, Bonnie, not the crap houses put up by half the outfits around the Beltway."

Pete Sutherland would have cheerfully built crap and had in the past. Max suspected Pete wanted to build crap again, because in a shaky economy, cut corners and fudged specs could generate most of a project's profits.

"You're the white knight of Maryland's dual-income families," Bonnie said, gathering up the flowers. "Though don't turn your back on my brother-in-law or his herd of Holstein heifers. If your tires ever end up slashed, don't say I didn't warn you."

No smile, no wink. Was she warning him?

"Let's put half of those in the conference room, three of them in my office and a couple in Derek's," Max said. "If you wouldn't mind tidying up Derek's desk, I'd appreciate it."

"I do not touch His Majesty's desk, Max. I've taken to putting my phone on record every time I walk into his office, because he accuses me regularly of not remembering his instructions, not hearing him correctly, or confusing what he's told me."

Well, crap. "He's getting worse?"

"He was awful to begin with. Divorce and a falling out with his father have only revealed Derek's true, utterly disgusting colors. I'll make sure his office door is closed tomorrow morning."

Bonnie marched off toward the kitchen, flowers in hand. Max had the unpleasant thought that she could find another job at any point, though it might mean commuting to either D.C. or Baltimore.

"Hey, Bonnie?"

She disappeared into the kitchen. "I'm busy."

And she was his admin, not his mother, so Max followed her into the kitchen. "Don't bother putting any of those flowers in Derek's office. Half in the conference room, three for me, and three for you."

She hunkered down to open the cupboard under the sink. "Sure, and an assortment of pastries, and fresh coffee. I know the drill. Plenty of napkins, conference room tidy, but a few convincingly legal references scattered artfully around the room."

Artfully? "Where do you get pastries around here?"

"Never mind. Pastries are carbs, and they might sweeten your disposition. You're better off not knowing."

He was being dismissed, and he wasn't sure why. "Brodie is supposed to be here at 9:30 a.m., and he didn't mention bringing anybody else. The flowers are gladiolus, right?"

Bonnie set a tall green vase on the counter with a definite *thunk*. "The plural is either gladioli or gladioluses, depending on how hifalutin you want to sound. The flowers are pretty, Max, and you are hopeless. How about we leave it at that?"

He brought flowers to the office, and the result was a pissed off administrative assistant. "Does Derek have court tomorrow morning?"

"You're in luck. Two DUIs, and they're both contested. Spring break did him some favors this year. Or maybe he met them at AA."

Derek attended AA meetings, not because he had a drinking problem, though he probably did, but because he trolled for business while impersonating an alcoholic—DUIs, divorces, landlord tenant problems, disorderly conduct, all manner of miseries congregated at Bill W's house. The behavior was despicable, of course, but when Max had consulted the bar association's ethics hotline, expert counsel had been unable to find a requirement that Max report Derek for it.

"You'll keep the meeting quiet?" Max asked as Bonnie set a blue vase next to the green one.

"Yes, Max, I will keep your important, super-intense, deal-of-a-lifetime meeting quiet. Don't you have some spreadsheets to tweak?"

As a matter of fact, he did. "Where did we get those vases?"

"You are an idiot. I work for idiots. What does that make me?"

"It makes you employed and solvent. Solvent is good, Bonnie."

She set a third vase on the counter, a slender tube of curving raspberry-colored glass. "My friends send me flowers, Max. On my birthday, on Willie Nelson's birthday, when the Terps win, for the hell of it, or when I've introduced them to somebody they take a shine to. That's what flowers are for, not for impressing some Scottish playboy who'll trash half the valley so he can afford the maintenance on his private jet."

"I'll see about my spreadsheets, and the verb is develop, not trash."

"Leave, Max, before the verb is I quit."

"Quit if you must, but please not until Thursday."

"You said please. That's a crumb, but for you, it's progress. I'll be here tomorrow, now get out of my kitchen."

* * *

Why in the name of all that was sensible had Violet put Elias's clothes in the wash? She ought to have tossed them in a plastic bag and warned him not to touch them until they'd been thoroughly laundered. Now she faced a choice of sending him on his way immediately—nobody would object to Elias Brodie clad only in board shorts on a hot day—or returning his laundry to him later in the week.

Slow footsteps descended the stairs. Elias's footsteps—Violet knew his tread already.

"Shall I leave, Violet?" He stood on the bottom step, his backpack dangling from his hand, his board shorts riding low on his hips.

"You can't leave," she retorted. "Your jeans, T-shirt, socks, and skivvies are in my washing machine. I'd just as soon not have to send them to you." Or leave them on his porch, then watch to see if he retrieved them before he flew home.

"I am held hostage by my *skivvies*," he said. "Perhaps this is why men wear nothing under their kilts. Less chance of being taken prisoner. What did Marvin have to say?"

Violet ached to whip out her cell phone, as Elias had the previous day. She wanted a picture of him like this—casually half-naked in her kitchen, fresh from the shower, a little grouchy, a lot scrumptious.

"Who's Marvin?"

"Marvin," Elias said, tapping a finger over his heart. "His wife likes a big garden, the children aren't fond of vegetables. He's repairing my wiring."

"There's nothing wrong with your wiring, Elias."

His lashes lowered. "Why, thank you. You're parsimonious with compliments, you know. My second fiancée had quite a way with them. Then I realized she never accepted compliments, she only passed them out."

Whoever Fiancée No. 2 she was, she'd been an idiot to let Elias Brodie slip through her grasp. Which made Violet…

"I left my computer on the porch."

"Then let's sit on your porch and pretend to answer emails, shall we? The business day will soon be over in Scotland, and I'm sure all manner of dire epistles are clamoring for my attention."

The farther away from the bedroom, the better. "If you want something to drink, help yourself. I noticed you didn't bother to hydrate much this morning."

"Another compliment—you noticed me." He poured himself a glass of water from the tap, downed it, rinsed the glass, then set it in the drain rack. "Please excuse my testiness. You don't deserve rudeness simply because you are honest and sensible."

The line of his back was anatomical perfection, the breadth of his shoulders the embodiment of ideal male geometry, and yet, those shoulders were tense.

"On second thought, let's work in the sun room. From there, I can hear the laundry timers, while I might not on the porch."

His expression suggested he didn't want to be anywhere near her, but he took out his phone and was swiping and jabbing at the screen before he'd left the kitchen. When Violet found him in the sunroom, he'd stretched out on the sofa, and his phone was playing… bagpipes?

"If you like music when you work, Elias, can we agree on something a little less boisterous?" The tune was jaunty and vaguely familiar, but strident as only bagpipes could be.

"I'm honor-bound to listen to this," Elias said, propping an arm behind his head. "My solicitor's pipe band finally won the championship, and Angus will quiz me about every bar and drumbeat. Tell me about your business, Violet, and about whatever keeps you so enthralled with your laptop when a handsome neighbor is hard at work across the road."

The pipe music droned on, and maybe the tune had restored Elias's brand of good cheer.

"Your property has been quiet for so long, any activity over there draws my notice. Marvin won't be back though."

Elias reduced the volume of the pipe march. "I have power, then?"

Oh, he had tons of power. "The problem, as best Marvin and I can diagnose it, is that your account got into significant arrears, and the power was simply shut off." Violet got comfy in her papasan chair, but didn't open her laptop. "That's a long song."

"Scotland the Brave. It's actually fairly brief. Pipe marches tend to come in sets, and this one is extraordinarily popular. Even I can play it, but Angus's crew is doing a right proper job. He'll be insufferably proud for six months, and then he'll be insufferably anxious about defending the championship title as the next competition approaches."

"You like this guy." Violet liked simply visiting with Elias. She liked seeing him relaxed and casual, liked watching his moods shift.

"I love Angus Whyte, but I don't dare tell him that, at least not before the third dram. He and my uncle didn't always get along, and I needed to see that, to see somebody could stand up to Zebedee, call his bluffs, and take him down a peg on occasion. Angus is the reason I did graduate work in business and economics, and he's the reason I have some money of my own now."

Insight niggled beneath all the emotions Violet juggled where Elias was concerned: He'd lost both parents, and had no siblings to soften that blow. Jeopardizing his uncle's regard in any sense would have been not only difficult for him, but frightening.

"You have a master's degree?" Violet had resisted googling Elias, unwilling to see one photo after another of him in kilted formal attire, escorting some lovely woman whose jewels were worth more than Violet's half of the farm.

"I blush to admit I have a doctorate. They're not that hard to come by, if you have funds and ample free time to apply yourself to scholarship. I'm something of a specialist in charitable organizations, which are peculiar business entities, part eleemosynary institution and part pirate ship. They interest me."

The music came to a throbbing, screeching end, and the day took on a deeper quiet for the contrast.

"And I loathe the business aspects of running a farm. My mother handled the books and assumed I'd happily take on that as well as the rest of the farming, if I was so dead set on keeping the place going."

Elias stuffed his phone in his pocket, jammed a pillow behind his head, and crossed his arms over his chest.

"Tell me about your business, Violet."

"It's boring. Taxes and more taxes, and loans, and inspections. I'm on the board of the farmers market, and there's more squabbling there than among my hens."

"Then get off the board," Elias said. "You are one person trying to run an entire farm. Marvin's wife probably has more time and enthusiasm for the farmers market, and she needs a break from those filthy children."

He was half serious. "What was Marvin's last name?"

"Eby."

"That narrows it down to half the valley." Though Elias had noticed the man's name, and not everybody would have bothered. "I never expected a monthly board meeting would be so time-consuming."

"Who prepares the agenda?"

"We don't really have an agenda. We have a list of action items and discussion topics."

Elias launched into a checklist of everything wrong with the farmers market board, sight unseen. People with no experience in a traditional business environment trying to run the most traditional aspect of what was actually a corporation. Volunteers who should have brought enthusiasm and energy to their duties instead bringing a sense of entitlement. A director unskilled with either meeting facilitation or—when all else failed—Robert's Rules of Order.

"And nobody with any expertise is responsible for fundraising or public relations," he concluded. "I write this memo a half dozen times a year, and am generally paid too much for it, but if I don't charge my clients, they don't take me seriously. Am I boring you?"

"What sort of clients?"

"Bothersome ones. Give the board a ninety-day notice, in writing, and graciously allude to giving somebody else a turn to benefit the organization. Tell me about your blog, Violet."

Her own mother never asked about her blog. "The Violet Patch is my way of advocating for farms, for farm life. One week, I'll do a piece on composting, the next, I'll take a look at different breeds of chickens."

Elias sat up. "Show me."

One moment, he'd been lounging on his back, a testament to the male in his prime at rest. The next he was fishing glasses from his backpack, and perching them on his nose.

"You want to see my blog?"

"Yes. Bring your laptop here and give me a tour."

Half an hour later, he was still prosing on about first browser loads, responsive code, native advertising, affiliate links, and social media reach.

"As much traffic as you have, you should be monetizing," he said. "And for pity's sake take the time to use your analytics. If you're ever to sell advertising on this site, you'll want that information, and it can show you what's working, and what's not. Accountability and evaluation aren't optional if your business is to run well."

He managed to sound professorial wearing nothing more than board shorts and glasses.

"You've given me a lot of ideas," Violet said, and half of those ideas were about how to make money with her blog, and spend less time on the heavy lifting of generating original copy. Guest posts, round ups, post swaps, open forums, frequently asked Fridays….

"Offer a virtual internship," Elias said. "The right person will be grateful for the education, have ideas that aren't limited by prior experience, and become a marketing resource when the internship is over. They'll carry your standard forward for the next forty years of their career. You should also incorporate a separate business entity to handle the blog revenue and any liability resulting from your posts."

He was endlessly knowledgeable about how a business ought to be run, and he was endlessly helpful. James Knightley could execute some of these ideas—setting up a corporation, for example—but no one had ever *talked* with Violet about how she spent her time, and how to make her dreams grow.

Elias powered down the laptop and passed it to her. "The first Earl of Strathdee was a soldier by training, but I think that made him determined to assure peace and prosperity for his progeny. He was keen on exporting Aberdeen cattle all over the globe—bulls especially—and he had the good fortune to hold property near Balmoral. Queen Victoria became quite fond of him—or of the money he made the royal couple."

Violet had the good fortune to sit next to Elias. His business expertise was unexpected, but his willingness to share what he knew, to offer his insights with no expectation of remuneration....

That was just Elias.

He was an aristocrat by virtue of honor and generosity of spirit, not as a function of wealth and status. He made love generously, his consideration for others was bone deep, and Violet could listen to him evangelize about mission statements all day for the sheer pleasure of hearing him talk.

I am so in love, and he's going back to Scotland as soon as he's ruined my valley.

The washing machine buzzer sounded, as loud as the bagpipes and not half so merry.

"Let me throw your clothes in the dryer, Elias, and then I want to hear about your castle."

He rose and stretched, pressing his palms against the ceiling. "I'll put my clothes in the dryer, and then you'll tell me how to get the power turned on across the road. I'd rather not impose on Dunstan and Jane any longer than I have to."

He prowled off to deal with the laundry, while Violet swallowed back tears, and punched up the website for the power company.

CHAPTER NINE

Elias parked Jane's hybrid and set the brake. "If I bring up Maryland's agricultural conservancy program, act as if you've never heard of it, please."

Jane undid her seatbelt and stashed her sunglasses in her shoulder bag. "Elias, for purposes of this meeting, I am your lawyer. That means you level with me about anything that pertains to legal matters. You don't keep cards up your sleeve so you can whip them out if Maitland wants to play mine's bigger than yours."

No wonder Dunstan had married her. "Jeannie would get on with you famously. Have you met her?"

"Haven't had the pleasure. Henry had recently made his appearance when Dunstan and I were in Scotland, and being a new mom takes precedence over attending weddings. So why are we meeting with Maitland if you're thinking of keeping the farm?"

They were fifteen minutes early, because Elias had no tolerance for people who were habitually late. Money could be replaced—in theory—but time lost was gone forever.

"I cannot afford to keep the farm, Jane. I simply did some research last night in preparation for this meeting." And because Violet had asked him to, though not in so many words.

"I know the general idea with agricultural conservancy: You sell your development rights to the state, more or less, and agree to keep your land in agricultural production."

There was more to it than that—much more—but Jane had the basics in hand.

"Any final words of advice?" Elias asked, checking his tie in the rearview mirror. He'd had to borrow a suit from Dunstan—Violet apparently didn't frequent her own powder room—but the fit and quality of the suit was surprisingly good. The alternative—kilted finery—would not have turned heads in Edinburgh, but surely wasn't the done thing here.

"You want advice? I have some advice. Get drunk with Dunstan. He has a beautiful singing voice, but I don't know any of the songs he does, and now that he's married, his old drinking buddies don't come around much. I'm not sure what he misses more, the buzz or the songs."

Maitland's office was on a narrow street about two blocks from the courthouse. A hundred years ago, the street would have been pretty, with flower boxes on every window, and plenty of sunshine finding its way through the oaks on either side.

Now, those oaks had lifted and cracked the sidewalks, the foliage was dense enough to give the street below a gloomy feel, and the houses were leaning on each other for support, twigs and leaves peeking from the gutters.

"I might not know the songs either, Jane. Why does nobody build with stone here? Nothing else lasts as well."

"We build with stone," Jane said, zipping her bag closed. "Fieldstone, anyway. You have a beautiful stone barn on your property that Max Maitland will probably bulldoze right off the face of the earth."

Violet would hate Elias for that. She'd hate him for a thousand other betrayals too, but the day she had to watch that barn turned to rubble, she'd consign Elias to an eternal case of poison ivy.

"I thought my attorney was supposed to keep my best interests foremost," Elias said, hitting the unlock button.

"Elias, my expertise regarding land development wouldn't fill a shot glass. You know that and I know that, and Maitland will probably figure it out in the first five minutes. I'm your wingman because Dunstan couldn't get out of court on short notice."

A squirrel set out to cross the street by virtue of leaping along a power line overhead.

"Dunstan had court today? He said you knew more property law than he did."

"Holmes v. Holmes. Domestic relations, at which he excels. I know nothing about real estate, he knows about the same. Let's get this over with."

Let's get this over with. A fitting candidate for the Brodie family motto, except Elias was the only Brodie left to spout it.

He would have held Jane's door for her, but she was out of the car and marching down the sidewalk before the squirrel had reached the opposite side of the street. Elias snatched his pack from the backseat and followed.

"I've made the acquaintance of Violet Hughes," Elias said. "She's the one who mentioned the agricultural conservancy business."

"I don't know her well, but what I do know, I like. Is she messing with you?"

Mortally. "In what sense?"

"Violet's rabidly opposed to developing Damson Valley, Elias. Pick up the local newspaper when a controversial zoning variance is being considered, she's the citizen you'll see quoted. Has all sorts of arguments against turning farmland into housing developments. Of all the farms in all the valleys in all of the United States, your farm is right across the road from the person who'll hate you most for selling to Maitland."

They approached a row house painted a hue that might once have had pretensions to bland yellow. Now, the paint was faded to a color Elias had seen in some of Henry's most odoriferous diapers.

"So I'll do my silent, shrewd routine," Jane said. "You be the charming, bon vivant globetrotter whose investment advisors suggested ditching the extraneous provincial real estate."

"Do they teach you how to talk like that in law school?"

"Yes," Jane said, trotting up the front steps, "and how to charge obscene sums for it too. Hold still."

She turned a gimlet eye on Elias, smoothed his lapel, nudged at the Windsor knot in his tie, and punched him on the shoulder.

"Relax, Elias. This guy wants your land like you probably want to get back to Scotland. He's got deep pockets backing him, and you're prepared to be reasonable."

To be fussed at and twitched at by a woman who regarded looking after him as her right… Elias had had to learn to recognize the behavior, because a boy who endured adolescence without a mother had gaps in his vocabulary when it came to women. Jane was not finding fault with his appearance. This was her version of a pep talk before battle.

"I will be relieved to get away from this heat and humidity," Elias said, and he *was* prepared to be reasonable—for a Scotsman talking business.

Reasonable, up to a point.

Jane had her hand on the doorknob, when Elias interceded. "Globetrotting bon vivants pride themselves on their Old World manners when approaching the lion's den."

She let him hold the door for her, but handled the introductions with a receptionist who struck the balance between friendliness and professional decorum on the nose. That boded well for Maitland's chances, as did his handshake.

Firm, brief, not out to prove anything.

The pastries were quaint—the truly high powered financial meetings offered attendees only designer bottled spring water and pretty glasses from which to drink it. The flowers made Elias miss Violet, who would be arranging to visit her mother in Florida, weeding her vegetable garden, and putting up strawberry jam.

While Elias saved his castle.

* * *

Elias Brodie was precious.

Max had never heard such a Hollywood-perfect Scottish accent in real life. Brodie also had a gold ring on his left pinkie, wore a purple plaid tie with his forest green suit, and flashed the self-conscious smile of a man about to endure a meeting that would doubtless bore him. Brodie likely played a mean eighteen holes when he wasn't busy crewing for a friend in the America's Cup.

"Would anybody like coffee?" Max asked.

"Black, please," Jane de Luca said, hefting a shoulder bag onto the table. She extracted a sleek little silver laptop and popped it open. "Elias, anything for you?"

"I'm fine, thanks."

Brodie held Jane's chair, and Jane put up with that. Made no fuss at all, and Jane de Luca was a first rate, bare-knuckle fusser. The county bar association speculated that Dunstan Cromarty had married Jane de Luca just so he wouldn't have to oppose her in the courtroom.

Max fetched the coffee, putting up with Bonnie's smirk from the front desk. He set Jane's coffee in front of her—he'd made sure the pot was fresh before pouring—and cracked open a bottle of water for himself.

"Jane, you're here as counsel for Mr. Brodie?" Max asked, taking the seat before the window.

"I certainly am, while you represent exactly whom?"

"I'm Elias," Brodie interjected. "Formality is fine for occasions of state, but we're discussing a simple business transaction."

Occasions of state. Hooookay. Old money from the Old World. Max had done his homework, and Brodie was actually some sort of nobility, to the extent nobility was still a thing in the United Kingdom.

"I'm representing New Horizons, Inc.," Max said, "and my team is very interested in acquiring a sizeable property in Damson Valley." That was Brodie's cue to smile handsomely, admit his desire to sell, and spend the next hour looking expensive and polite.

Brodie managed the expensive and polite part, but he said nothing.

"Elias owns the largest single, privately held parcel in the county," Jane said, "in fee simple absolute with no liens or encumbrances. What do you have, Max? Elias didn't come all the way from Scotland to play slap and tickle."

Max had an urge to pitch Jane de Luca out the window. "Elias, I mean Jane no insult when I point out that she's a first rate attorney, and much respected, but she doesn't practice a lot of real estate law, not at the level of the transaction I hope you came here to discuss. A certain protocol is typically observed, because an exchange of assets of this magnitude requires trust between the parties. May I tell you a little bit about New Horizons and our community building philosophy?"

"Spare us the dog and pony show, *and* the gratuitous shaming of counsel," Jane shot back. "I do enough real estate—"

"Jane," Brodie said, quietly. "I'd like to hear the man out. I'm somewhat familiar with the field of economics, Mr. Maitland. You needn't oversimplify."

Economics—the dark science, if it was a science at all. "Call me Max, Elias, and I promise not to take up too much of your time."

Max went into the four-color glossy spiel, half a century of commitment to blah, blah, blah, so that Maryland families could prosper in safe, wholesome, blah, blah, while singing the national anthem over the grill every summer and churning out Harvard-bound prodigies in increments of 2.4 tax deductions.

At least half of it was true.

"Very impressive," Brodie said, "and I applaud any business that puts mission before money, though not instead of money, of course."

"Of course." Whatever that meant.

Jane was clicking away on her laptop, her expression disgruntled.

"Jane, do you have any questions?" Max asked.

"How much and when can we see paper?"

Brodie looked pained, but Max mentally saluted him on his choice of attorney. "I can email a redacted draft contract at the conclusion of this meeting, but I've yet to hear Elias admit to an interest in selling. Before I send detailed terms, I'll need you to sign a non-disclosure at least, and a 90-day guarantee of exclusivity. We'll need to run a certification on the title, and do some preliminary tests on ground water quality and environmental—"

"A moment, Max," Brodie said. "Jane, have you had a chance to research that agricultural preservation business yet?"

Max's mood went from cautious elation to queasy dread. "I can tell you about the agricultural conservancy program, Elias. It's a fine feature of the Maryland legislative landscape, and we're justifiably proud of it." *We* being the hayseeds who hated their offspring enough to prevent development of land in perpetuity.

Jane's expression had gone bunny-in-the-headlights, which at any other time would have been reason to gloat.

"Please do enlighten us," Brodie said. "The Scots are quite keen on preservation generally, and I'm no exception. I've only recently learned of these preservation arrangements and would appreciate an expert's explanation of them."

Max hammered on the theme of preservation—preserving the land owner's options, preserving flexibility for future generations, preserving control of private assets free from state easements, and most of all, preserving Elias Brodie's right to squeeze every dime out of a property that a sale to New Horizons could earn him.

"The environmental stuff can get really tedious," Jane said. She held her coffee under her nose, and sniffed before taking a sip. "I've never even seen a forestry plan, Elias, much less soil certifications or wetlands preservation plans. Sounds a little complicated, but I'm sure we could find a firm to subcontract all of that to."

"For a price," Max added. "Unfortunately, the construction season is well underway, and the companies doing seasonal environmental work are usually booked months in advance. If owning a farm is your ambition, you should certainly look into the preservation program at your leisure. I can tell my team you're not interested in pursuing negotiations at this time, and we'll look into other projects."

Jane closed her laptop. "You should consider all of your options, Elias. Max is right."

Why would Jane de Luca advise her client to walk away from a deal that would be enormously lucrative for the client, and probably for Jane as well?

Because she'd found another buyer? Because she'd gone behind Max's back straight to Sutherland, who was ever one to shoot his mouth off at the worst possible time?

"Here's something to consider," Max said. "Two things, actually. First, any deal will come down to a price per acre, and I've done some research on your property." He tossed out a price per acre that Sutherland could easily afford, one that would hold up in appraisals and project financing negotiations. A fair price in other words. Not generous, not scalping, but fair.

"That figure means little," Jane said, "until we negotiate terms. Any transaction will be conditioned on tests and certifications, preliminary wells, water quality evaluations, and permitting, to name a few. You could saddle Elias with all of that, and then walk way. Don't think you'll dazzle us with numbers, Max, though I don't blame you for trying."

"I'm sure Elias knows how complicated a major land transaction can become, and for that reason—"

"The deal will not be complicated," Brodie said. The genial guy with the whisky commercial accent was gone, though a veneer of relaxed cordiality remained.

Had Brodie expected to walk out with a check? "Development is a complex undertaking, Elias. Even the planning and zoning phase can take years, and for all that time, the price of labor, materials, and equipment—"

Brodie held up a hand, the gold ring winking in the morning sun. "You have money, I have land. You buy the land speculatively, assuming all risks pertaining to development; I am compensated a fair price for transferring title to you. My land for your money, and we can do business. Anything more *complex* or protracted, and I'll find another disposition for the property."

Well, damn it all and a half, as Bonnie would have said.

"The price per acre is, of course, affected by the terms," Max said, mentally taking a baseball bat to Violet Hughes' blog posts. He kept track of her rabblerousing, and the demons in SEO-hell had apparently delivered her recent rant about agricultural conservancy easements right onto Brodie's browser.

"One assumes price and terms are interrelated," Brodie said, getting to his feet. "Now that you know my terms, I'll give you the rest of the week to come up with a lump sum offer. Jane is available should you wish to discuss the matter, though I can't imagine a simpler arrangement."

Jane rose as well, and again Brodie held her chair.

"Max, you wanted to make two points," Jane said, stuffing her laptop into her shoulder bag. "Was there something else you wanted to bring up?"

In other words, don't call me until you have a number.

"The second point is the more important," Max said, getting to his feet. "Development around here has a bad name, Elias. Tree huggers and climate change alarmists will tell you all development is bad. The problem is, their concerns have some validity. The environment matters and energy policies should be sustainable and responsible."

Jane tossed her bag over her shoulder, but Brodie was listening. Max hadn't exactly underestimated him, but neither had he read him correctly.

"Go on," Brodie said.

"Some developers will turn a piece of land without regard to ecological concerns, Elias. They won't lay out roads so cross traffic turns are minimized at peak hours, because they don't care how long somebody has to idle at a stop light when taking the kids to school. Some developers stash the moderately priced dwelling units at the back of the development, because low income home owners are less likely to gripe about shoddy upkeep, and if the rest of the development never sees the clogged storm drains and sagging gutters, the maintenance can wait. There are endless dirty tricks that haven't been zoned or regulated out of bounds, and I know them all."

Brodie was studying the glad-somethings in the blue vase on the windowsill. "Are you boasting of this knowledge, Mr. Maitland?"

Mr. Maitland, no longer Brodie's best new good old buddy Max.

"I'm not ashamed of it. Working construction for eight long summers means I've seen a few developments done right, and I've seen a lot of them done wrong, from curb and gutter, sediment and erosion control, to tree-save plans, to electrical grid, home wiring, to everything in between. I don't build crap, Elias. I develop land, and there are costs associated with that, but there are costs to every choice we make. Turn that land over to me, and I'll treat it and the people who make their homes there with respect."

Max had delivered this speech to Elias Brodie only because it was necessary to keep the deal alive. In Max's experience, people with access to great wealth either developed a scrupulous conscience as a function of their privilege or they bent rules on a whim.

Brodie apparently had a conscience and a better grasp of land development than Max had realized.

"I appreciate those sentiments," Brodie said, extending a hand, "and your time. I assume you know how to reach Jane?"

Jane shoved a card at Max, though her office was less than two blocks away. "Thanks for your time, Max. I'll wait to hear from you."

Max escorted them to the door, because a man who held a woman's chair would expect that kind of etiquette. Sutherland would fall all over himself trying to ape Brodie's manners, if the two ever met.

Which they might.

"Well?" Bonnie said, when the office was free of Jane de Luca and her Highland land tycoon.

"Well, what?"

"How did you do?" Bonnie said, enunciating each word. "Should I be looking for a j-o-b or did you just get your dirty dibbles on the prettiest farm in Damson Valley?"

Violet Hughes owned the prettiest farm in Damson Valley. "It was a good news/bad news sort of meeting," Max said. "He's smart and competently represented, which is inconvenient, though manageable. Brodie isn't about to let us vet the land while he holds title. In other words, Sutherland can't have his cake and eat it too, which is also inconvenient, though manageable."

"Kinda like you," Bonnie said. "Inconvenient and manageable. I've been meaning to ask you, where did you get the gladioli? They're the best I've seen this year."

"At the farmers market. I shop there every week."

Bonnie hooted with laughter, and Max had no idea why.

* * *

Elias took a moment to savor the sight of Violet Hughes in her garden. She worked her way on her knees along a row of staked plants, tossing weeds into a bushel basket. Her straw hat hid her expression—and hid Elias from her view—but he could hear her lecturing her vegetables, while he, like a fool, stood two yards away, aching to keep her in his life.

"Worry and work, work and worry," she muttered. "I promised myself I would not turn into my father or my mother." A clump of greenery, dirt clinging to the roots, went sailing into the basket. "I'm worse than they were, and that means I'm awful."

She tore up another plant, peered at it, and patted it back into the soil. "Sorry, buddy. I'm not at my best. Elias met with Maitland this morning."

Eavesdropping was not honorable.

"I'm meeting with Dunstan and Jane's bank tomorrow morning," Elias said. "Do you always talk to your vegetation?"

"Beans are good listeners," Violet replied, sitting back on her heels. "Hello, Elias."

She hadn't ordered him from her property—always a good sign. "Hello, Violet. Have you drafted a resignation from the farmers market board?"

"Mailed it this morning. I thought I'd feel guilty, but I'm bearing up just fine. Give me a hand, Elias. Delayed onset muscle soreness from haying, and not enough stretching have laid me low."

When would she have time to stretch, for pity's sake? Elias offered her his hand, and didn't turn loose of her when she'd gained her feet.

"Maitland is not quite the snake I had anticipated," he said. "We are negotiating."

Violet shook free of his grasp and tossed her hat onto the pile of weeds in the basket. "Elias, you cannot trust that man. If you must sell your farm to him and his sharks-in-seersucker, don't get screwed in the process."

"I've been thinking about our discussion yesterday." Had thought about it for most of the night, and had read every blog post she'd put up for the past year. She missed some weeks, but not many. "I'm gathering information, and considering options, which is simply prudent business."

The sun was beating down, and clouds piling up to the south suggested a storm was building. "Don't mess with me, Elias, and I might let you live. Did you cut a deal or not?"

"I did not. I might not." Before he braced Jane and Dunstan with his ideas, he wanted to talk scenarios through with Violet. Jane and Dunstan were lawyers, and family, but Violet knew what it took to wrest a crop from the earth, to care for livestock.

And she knew Maitland as only dedicated foes could know each other.

"Grab the other handle," Violet said, picking up one side of the basket. "My ewes believe in doing their part for the environment. So what did you and Maitland discuss?"

"I told him I will sell him the land for a lump sum, the title to transfer from me to him at the time of closing. It's not what he or his investors want, but it's what I need."

"Cash," Violet said as they walked across the yard, the basket of greens between them. "Gerald O'Hara only got the lecture half right."

Perhaps she'd been out in the heat too long? "I haven't made Mr. O'Hara's acquaintance."

"'Land, Elias Brodie…'" Violet intoned in a mock baritone. "According to some, land is the only thing that lasts, but the guy who said that never met my mortgage banker. Payments last until hell freezes over. Hello, my wooly darlings."

Her darlings apparently knew what the basket meant, and were bleating and cavorting around in their pen. Violet shook the weeds from the basket in a row on the ground, and the sheep were soon devouring every last leaf and root.

"Have you started to itch yet?" Violet asked.

Elias picked up the empty basket. "No, and I'll thank you not to remind me. Jane laughed uproariously while Dunstan kindly told me where the cortisone cream was. Seems poison ivy ambushes many an unsuspecting Brit new to the wilds of America."

"I love to hear you talk," Violet said, wandering over to a gray metal water tub in the shade of the barn's overhang. "It's not your accent, or not entirely that. It's your eloquence. If you weren't an earl already, somebody would have to earl you."

She lifted the handle of a pump and added water to the metal tub. "They'll drink more if I top it up with the cold stuff. What did you come here to say, Elias?"

I am falling in love with you. Elias had been infatuated many times as a younger man, and when his enthusiasms had run their courses, he'd learned to enjoy attraction, and to settle for that and sincere liking. He'd respected both of his fiancées, and Christina was still a dear friend.

But this aching, relentless desire simply to be with Violet was new and raw. He'd been as happy to spend yesterday afternoon poring over website analytics with her as he'd been to share a night in her bed.

By contrast, he'd dreaded dumping messages and emails at the end of the day, even though some of those communications were from family.

"I came here to gather information," Elias said. "And you can, of course, bid me to leave at any moment. I have a meeting set up with the largest commercial bank in Damson Valley tomorrow, and I will present myself more knowledgeably if I have the benefit of your thinking. I'm to join Dunstan and Jane for dinner this evening, but I'd rather talk to you first."

"You met with Maitland," Violet said, shutting off the water. "I should tell you to go to hell by way of the muck pit and the poison ivy patch." She shaded her eyes with one hand, and scanned the sky. "I do believe summer will soon be here. That is a stinkin' big bank of thunderclouds."

Ah, but she had *not* told him to go to hell—yet. "This isn't summer?"

"This is merely warm. We get stretches of weather over a hundred degrees, and so humid it doesn't cool down at night to speak of. You ever hear the term blizzard babies? They compensate for the fact that few children are conceived around here during the month of July."

"How long have you been out in the sun, Violet?"

"Years. Don't look so worried, Elias. I'm not big enough to throw you off the property, and you didn't sign a deal with Maitland. You're safe for now."

No, he was not, but if a Scot claimed one skill from the moment of his birth, it was the ability to coax a bonfire of hope from a smoky wisp of inspiration.

Violet slapped her hat onto Elias's head, and they returned to the house.

"I'm changing out of my grubbies," she said. "Help yourself to anything."

Violet disappeared up the steps, and Elias forced himself to check his email—Jeannie again, and confirmation that the bottle of single malt he'd sent Angus had been delivered. Niall had left another message, which Elias would return later, and cousin Magnus—newly married to a whisky distiller from Montana—had flagged the most recent email as urgent.

"That is not a happy expression," Violet said, coming down the steps. "But then, I don't know if I've seen you happy." She wore a lavender sundress, and had undone her hair and piled it on her head with a big wooden clip, creating a dewy, summery—*kissable*—picture.

"You've seen me quite happy. I am not happy now. I have two plans to discuss with you, and there might be others. We'll start with two." And who knew where the discussions might lead.

As if offering a celestial retort to Elias's hopes, thunder rumbled in the distance.

"The sun room is my favorite place to listen to the rain." Violet breezed past Elias, giving him a whiff of lavender and a peek at the nape of her neck.

When they reached the sunroom, both dogs were splayed on the floor, though the cat was nowhere to be seen. Violet sat on the sofa, where she and Elias had spent such an agreeable afternoon, and Elias took the place beside her.

"The problem to be solved is that I need money," he said, "a lot of it and fast. The agricultural preservation easement is worth considering, but I don't know enough about it."

"And you don't want to put all your eggs in one basket," Violet said. "Hence, you have more than one plan. Let's start with selling your development rights to the state in perpetuity."

Her analysis of Elias's situation was thorough, balanced, and as disinterested as a woman could be when discussing what was probably her fondest wish.

"Why isn't your farm in this program?" Elias asked, when Violet had answered myriad questions. She got up to close a window, and the dogs lifted their heads to watch her. Outside, the sky was growing overcast, and a breeze stirred the leaves of the trees along the hedgerows.

"My development rights have not been sold to the state for two reasons," Violet said, as thunder sounded again. "First, it's not a simple application process, as you've learned. You have to have the right kind of soils, a forestry plan if you have more than 24 acres of woods—and I do—and there are other costly hoops to jump through. In my case, the bank would probably get the entire sum, so I'd be giving up my heirs' rights for the pleasure of enriching the bank. Kinda like when you sell the back forty acres. The whole amount goes to reduce your principle owed."

"A consummation devoutly to be avoided," Elias said. "What's the second reason?" *And thank you, sincerely for resuming your place beside me.*

"The funds available to the conservancy program are limited. I want that money to go to the farmer who has to choose between development and land preservation. I will never, ever, not if I live to be ninety-five and have only one laying hen to my name, allow this farm to be developed. I'm not the farmer who needs the program."

"You need the money, though." And she needed exactly what she was providing Elias—somebody to thrash through her problems with her, a fair hearing, a fresh take on the endless challenges she faced.

A trusted partner, as Jane and Dunstan were partners.

"I need money," Violet said, tucking a foot up under her, "but I need to be able to look myself in the eye more. What's your second plan?"

Elias had come here hoping for forgiveness, possibly, and—in his wildest, most honest dreams—a renewed exchange of affections. The erotic affections were apparently to remain an unfulfilled wish, but overshadowing that frustration was an odd pleasure.

Violet *listened* to him. She didn't lecture him, as Zebedee and Angus had, and she didn't expect Elias to wave a financial wand and make her wishes come true, as everybody from clients to cousins so often did. Instead, Violet took Elias's concerns to heart, despite his differences with her, and her willingness to share his burdens even theoretically was a precious comfort.

"My second plan," he said, "is not complicated, though I'm not keen on it. I'll simply take out a mortgage on the farm, and use the money to finance my renovations. I'll bank a significant enough sum so the interest covers the mortgage payments, and use the rest as I see fit."

Violet took his hand in a loose grip, as casually as she might have petted her cat, while Elias forgot all about mortgages, lump sums, and interest rates.

"The preservation program is cumbersome," she said, "and time-consuming, and it would tie up your land forever when you're not even a farmer. A loan would be relatively quick, and leave you the option of developing the land later. In your shoes, I'd apply for the loan."

He kissed her knuckles, for her honesty, for her courage. "I don't want to be a farmer, and I don't want to carry a mortgage on a property I'm not sure how to manage. Neither option is a true solution, but I appreciate your hearing me out."

Violet was silent for a moment, while lightning flashed, and Sarge whined.

"Can you sell that castle, Elias?"

"No, I cannot." Which made his decision simpler, and his emotions more complicated. "Scotland has so many historic properties that the public has all the castles they'll ever need, and private buyers have their choice of many properties already renovated. Then too, if I put the castle on the market in its present condition, all of my other assets would lose value."

Violet drew a fingertip along his knuckles, a beguiling caress though she clearly had her mind on business. "Can you put off the renovations?"

Jeannie's emails made it increasing obvious Elias could not. "Delay would be unwise. I suppose it's like looking after the land. If you don't do the weeding, fertilizing, and cultivating at the first opportunity, the job becomes more and more difficult, until you're better off starting over on fresh turf instead of trying to reclaim what's been so badly neglected."

The breeze had become a steady wind, whipping the foliage like so much wheat. The dogs had moved to sit at Violet's feet, while Elias felt a sense of nerves soothed.

Violet had taken his hand, she was tucked close to his side, and that was more than he'd expected.

"This farm was not in good shape when I took over," Violet said. "I'm guessing your predecessors kept kicking the renovation ball down the field, hoping for a pot of gold."

"Your people have been in this valley for five generations, Violet. This is your home, and you'll fight to the last chicken for it. My people have been in that castle for fifty generations. You mentioned being able to look yourself in the eye, and it's my castle to save. I can't turn my back on it, or on the family who expect me to put it to rights. Should the kind powers grant me children someday, I don't want to leave them a legacy of debt and disrepair."

The rain started, a hard spatter against the windows that settled into a steady downpour.

"In other words," Violet said, "you might yet have to go to bed with the devil. I comprehend that, Elias, and I loathe the very thought."

This discussion had settled something for her. Elias could feel the calm in her, and while he wouldn't call her mood accepting, exactly, he was encouraged. They'd rationally discussed options, and while neither choice was a panacea, both were worth considering.

"I love a good storm," Violet said. "It's not the best way to water the crops, because so much runs off instead of soaking into the ground, but it lets me sit still for a while without feeling guilty."

She shifted against him, scooting down to pillow her cheek against his thigh.

Desire leapt, as did tenderness. Elias snagged a quilted throw from the back of the couch and draped it over Violet's legs. When she didn't object to that presumption, he unclipped her hair, and slowly massaged the back of her neck, until her breathing became slow and regular, and she was a sweet, warm weight, sprawled beside him.

CHAPTER TEN

"How was lunch, and do you know anything about agricultural preservation?" Jane asked.

By agreement, Dunstan and his wife tried to keep their demeanor professional during office hours. At home, Jane would likely have greeted him with a hug and a kiss. Now, she remained at her desk, amber glasses perched on her nose, hair in a sleek chignon.

The very picture of a woman whom Dunstan would dearly love to muss and cuddle.

"Lunch was interesting," Dunstan said, hanging his suit coat on the back of his chair. "Did you know Aaron Glover is writing a book?"

"Half the bar association is probably writing boring old legal thrillers, poor fools, while you and I are living a romance. I take it the Holmes hearing went OK?"

How had he practiced law for years without a partner? Jane had been wiser than he, teaming up with a lady who now numbered among Dunstan's cousins by marriage, while Dunstan had slogged along as a solo practitioner. From one year to the next, he'd barely made ends meet—frequent travel back to Scotland cost a pretty penny—and always, he'd promised himself he'd socialize more "soon."

"The hearing was postponed," he said, loosening his tie. "Aaron's star witness, a forensic accountant, came down with some stomach flu last night, and was getting IV fluids at Hopkins when last Aaron spoke to him. The court was overbooked, and we were bumped. Tell me about the meeting with Maitland."

"Bumped can be good, when the clients ought to be talking settlement," Jane said. "Maitland played it cool, but he wants that farm. Elias does not want to sell it to him for reasons that might have to do with Violet Hughes, of the readily available shower."

Dunstan propped his feet on the corner of his desk, something he never did before clients.

"I worried that I should have been at the meeting today, because Elias is my cousin. Then I resented the worry, because a man with an extra 800-acre farm on his hands doesn't need my fretting, and then I felt ashamed of the resentment. If he can blunder into poison ivy, he's worth some fretting over." Dunstan's feelings were more complicated than that, and he'd ponder them at greater length after office hours. "Did you get anything to eat?"

"Stopped at the Stale and Awful," Jane said, assuming the same feet-up posture Dunstan had. She wore a pair of purple high heels of which Dunstan was *exceedingly* fond.

The Steak and Ale was a reliably good meal, contrary to its moniker. Lawyers took humor where they could find it.

"Elias wants you to go with him to meet with the bank tomorrow," Jane said. "I think you should accompany him, if you can."

"I can. Tell me about the meeting with Maitland."

Jane stuck her pen in her chignon, leaned back, and closed her eyes. "Maitland, of course, wants to thoroughly vet the land before he lays down a penny. I suspect he wants to keep it from other developers at least as much as he wants to build there himself. He was honest, I guess is the word. Elias was… Elias has a lot of cool, Dunstan. I don't know what I was expecting, but with very few words and excellent manners, none of them flamboyant, that meeting went exactly as Elias wanted it to go. He reminds me of you."

"Thank you, I think. Where did you leave it with Maitland?"

"Ball is in his court. Elias will entertain an offer for a lump sum, and Maitland can have the land as is, where is. The transaction will be fast and simple or there won't be a transaction. Damson Valley goes straight to hell, and Elias walks with a crap-ton of cash."

"A well-planned development isn't hell, Jane." Dunstan argued not because lawyers argued compulsively, but because Elias was not responsible for the fate of an entire valley—not exactly.

Jane peered at him over her glasses. "I grew up in the burbs, Dunstan. Unless the neighbors had kids in the same classes I was in, I had no idea who my neighbors were. The parents didn't know which kids went with which houses, much less what their names were. Those houses were very nice, plenty of parking, not much crime, but there wasn't much community either. Then too, once you kill a farm, that land is dead forever for any other purpose. A tot lot feeds no one but the Weed and Seed crews, and who knows what poison they're adding to our grandchildren's groundwater."

Jane was effortlessly fierce. Even in repose, her mind seized on logic and data the way a raptor on the wing spotted prey.

"I had no idea I'd married an environmental crusader."

"I like to eat," Jane said. "And I'm not a crusader. If I wanted congestion, higher taxes, lines at the drive through, noise, and lower air quality, I would have stayed closer to either D.C. or Baltimore. I wanted peace and quiet and a small town practice with a handsome, brilliant, hard-working Scotsman."

"You forgot passionate," Dunstan said. "And lucky, and married to the love of his life."

"And so modest," Jane said, grinning. "You still good to leave around four?"

"God forbid I should miss your company cooking, wee Jane. Where do you suppose Elias has got off to this afternoon?"

Jane leaned forward to unhook the straps of her stilettos, then put her feet down. "I sent him on a little errand."

And Elias, like the prudent Scots he'd descended from, had apparently marched out smartly, Jane's orders in his hand.

"The truth, if you please, wee Jane. The whole truth, and nothing but the truth."

"When we met with Maitland, Elias brought up the idea of selling his development rights to the state, so the farm always remains a farm. It wouldn't be anywhere near as much money as Maitland would offer him, and I gather the state runs the program competitively. You figure out what a developer would pay, offer the state a discount, and the greater the discount, the more likely you are to be accepted into the program. Maitland about gave birth to striped kittens."

"Elias is the last person to sink his wealth into something as bothersome as a farm," Dunstan said, though in an honest corner of his mind, he wished at least one other member of the family might develop ties with the Damson Valley.

Cousins should grow up knowing each other, after all.

Jane's cell phone buzzed to the opening theme from the old "Perry Mason" show. She peered at the screen. "Elias wants to bring company to dinner and he won't forget to pick up the eggs."

Eggs? Ah, well. Jane hadn't sent Elias to the supermarket for those eggs.

Jane tapped at her phone screen, then put it away.

"Elias is bringing company to dinner?" Dunstan asked.

"Violet Hughes. I sent Elias to buy eggs, but I also told him to grill Violet about that easement thingie. Real estate law makes my eyes to cross and my teeth to ache. What has put that frown on your handsome face, Mr. Cromarty?"

"Elias isn't about to give up the right to develop that land, Jane. He's a shrewd negotiator, and I'm sure he was merely posturing to intimidate Maitland."

Jane opened her desk drawer, peered inside, then closed it.

"The pen is in your bun."

She extracted the pen from her hair, twisted it to retract the point, and tossed it in the drawer. "Why do you think Elias was posturing? Agriculture is the largest industry in Maryland. He could probably make money at it."

"Some money, but a farm requires management, and he's not a farmer. He was rattling his swords, and he'll get a better price from Maitland because the display was convincing."

Jane crossed her arms, and had Dunstan been on the witness stand, he would have known to fashion his half of the dialogue very carefully.

"Dunstan Cromarty, why are you so unwilling to consider Elias might like it here? He's on jump-in-the-shower terms with Violet Hughes, and his castle will be turned upside down for the next five years, at least. I like having him around, and I suspect you do too."

"I do," Dunstan said. "I like hearing the sound of home, I like… I love you, Jane, but to have no family, none at all, within a thousand miles—Magnus is clear out in Montana, for God's sake. I never saw myself settling down so far from family, and yet, I can promise you, Elias won't be settling down on that farm."

"How can you be so sure?"

"I've known Elias all of our lives, Jane. Did you know he's quite the business turn-around consultant? He specializes in not-for-profits, and he can pick and choose his clients, all over the European Union. I thought he traveled constantly simply for pleasure, but Jeannie says there's plenty of business involved. Elias, who's probably worth the whole rest of the family put together, works for a living."

Which apparently wasn't common knowledge even among the Scottish cousins, because Elias didn't advertise his profession.

"This is the information age," Jane said. "He can do his consulting over the internet. What's your point, Dunstan?"

The point, now that Dunstan had clarified it in his own mind, was sad. "You said it yourself, Jane. Elias will close this deal, make a ton of money, and walk. That's what Elias Brodie does. He takes care of business, and then he walks away. Always."

* * *

Violet drifted off, lulled by the patter of the rain, and the caress of Elias's fingers winnowing through her hair and stroking gently over her nape. The bliss of cuddling next to him was laced with sadness, because this was a stolen pleasure.

Elias might still do business with Maitland—the possibility made Violet ill—but whether he sold the farm, sold the development rights, or borrowed against the land, his time in Maryland grew short.

Rant, rave, and rail against fate later, cuddle now. Had Elias shown any resistance to Violet's presumption, she would have apologized and backed off.

Her pillow shifted, probably getting out his phone. He tapped away for several minutes, the rhythm blending with the rainfall.

"They never leave you alone, do they?" she murmured.

"I'm alone much of the time. I've learned to enjoy solitude."

Had he mastered that lesson because he was an only child, orphaned at an early age? Violet laced her fingers with his.

Why did Scotland have to be so far from Maryland?

The storm was fading, the thunder moving off, but no part of Violet was interested in leaving the couch, much less in being *productive*.

"May I ask a favor of you?" Elias said.

"Of course." He'd asked for her help developing options for his farm, his request more gratifying than he could know.

"Will you join me for dinner with Dunstan and Jane this evening?"

Violet scooted around and sat up, keeping the quilt over her lap. "I expected you to ask me, I don't know, to keep an eye on the house when you leave, or take in the mail."

"Will you come to dinner with me?"

His expression was hard to read—he did hard to read well—but that in itself told Violet this request was important to him.

"Why, Elias? I have a passing acquaintance with Jane, but she and her husband are your family. I'm sure they'd rather not have a stranger gatecrashing supper."

Elias rose and let the dogs out, though a soft drizzle was still falling. He remained by the door, silhouetted against a day turned gloomy and cool.

"I know you have endless obligations, Violet, and your time is valuable. I've taken up too much of it, I know that as well. I also know you need to get away from here for more than the mandatory trips to the feed store and the farmers market. I'd like to have your company this evening, but say no if I'm imposing."

Violet joined him in the doorway and wrapped an arm around his waist. "You're offering an olive branch, a consolation for selling your property to Maitland, because that's still your best option."

Elias's arm settled around her shoulders. "I'm not sure what the best option is. We don't know much more than we did twenty-four hours ago."

And yet, Elias's course had changed significantly. He was looking for options, investigating alternatives, hesitating rather than grabbing the pot of gold right at his feet.

"Yesterday," Violet said. "You wanted… that is, I wasn't prepared. I was surprised yesterday too."

The careful glance he brushed over her suggested Violet had surprised him with her admission.

"Yesterday, I had an erection," Elias said. "As it happens, the same befell me when I awoke this morning, and will likely occur again if we belabor the topic. We needn't discuss—"

Violet kissed him, because he was being too chivalrous for his own good.

She belabored the pleasure of her mouth on his, and further expounded on how well their bodies fit in a close embrace. Then she indulged in a digression focused on insinuating her knee between Elias's legs, the better to summarize for him the arguments in favor of a trip upstairs.

"You mean business," Elias said, feathering his thumbs over her cheeks. "Do you mean to make love with me? I have it on the best authority that *we've already done that*, and *it won't help anything*."

Her rejection yesterday had hurt him, in other words, even though he hadn't really been offering.

"I have it on the best authority we did not hook up the first time we were intimate, Mr. Brodie, but I'm here to tell you, we also didn't make love. Right now, my heart aches, and I expect it will ache again tomorrow. Making love with you won't fix that, but I don't think anything could make it hurt worse."

Elias gave her a lingering kiss—not an apology, more of a consolation. "My heart aches too, Violet. Will you come to dinner?"

So determined and so careful. "Yes, I will come to dinner. Will you come to bed?"

* * *

Elias had read the first earl's journals, kept throughout much of Wellington's march across Spain. Two hundred years ago, war between France and England had proceeded with an odd abundance of civility. The French and English camps would often use the same streams and rivers as a mutual water supply, each patrolling one bank within easy firing distance of the other.

Outside of a pitched battle, however, the rivers were demilitarized zones despite an absence of articles of war or general orders to that effect.

An English officer might confer with his French counterpart on where pickets should be deployed, lest confusion result in unnecessary skirmishes. Under the same circumstances, French officers might trade their brandy for English flour, and military gossip flowed across the lines in many languages.

The first earl had excelled at that peculiar battlefield diplomacy.

Elias felt some kinship with his progenitor that mere assumption of the title hadn't yielded. In the midst of significant differences, Elias and Violet would also acknowledge a significant connection.

As they undressed on opposite sides of the bed, Elias took a moment to appreciate the view from Violet's window: Newly mown hayfields, croplands beyond, sheep grazing contentedly, oblivious to the drizzling rain.

This was worth protecting—this was worth protecting, *too.*

"I wish I could show you my castle," Elias said. "It's not grand, as Scottish castles go, and no great battles were fought outside its walls that we know of, but it's lovely. Special."

Right now, that castle was also a source of sorrow. Elias acknowledged the sorrow in silence, and wedged it aside far enough to admit a shaft of hope.

The numbers might work out, the bank might cooperate, the conservation easement might be lucrative enough. On the basis of more ephemeral hopes, many a Scot had struck out for a new life in a new land and found success.

"I would love to see your castle," Violet said, "and you can tell me all about it—later. For the next hour, Elias, we will not worry over castles or mortgages or crops or easements. We won't worry at all."

A fine plan, if impossible to execute. Elias climbed under the quilt and Violet tucked herself against his side. Desire simmered, not the adult glee that anticipated a passing encounter, but a combination of arousal, tenderness, and loss.

Violet took Elias's hand and placed it over her breast. "No worries, Elias. We are entitled to one hour on our own terms."

When Violet got serious about her loving, Elias lost the ability to focus on anything else. She struck a balance between attentive and demanding that let him know he was intensely desired, but that his needs were important to her too.

"How many condoms do we have?" Violet asked as she wrestled Elias over her.

"Two." To buy more would have tempted fate, to Elias's way of thinking.

"Let's make this count." Everything strong, brave and vital in Violet expressed itself in her passion, but Elias wanted the other parts of her too.

When Violet demanded with her hips, Elias teased with his tongue.

When she fisted a hand in his hair he used a fingertip to gently trace each of her features.

When her kisses grew desperate, Elias paused and simply stroked her cheek until her breathing had slowed.

"Elias, you are slaying me."

Storming her castle walls, that she might take him prisoner. "I mean only to love you," he said, "to bring you pleasure."

"I'll cry if we do it your way."

She referred to both a tender loving and to the sale of the land, and Elias didn't know how to answer her. This time—very likely their last time—he wanted to love her. *No faking*, no pretending he could leave her with a wink and a smile in the morning, no denying she'd haunt him for all the rest of his days.

He reached for the condom, and Violet let him deal with the practicalities. She didn't take charge, hand down rules of engagement, or declare certain subjects off limits. She lay on her back, one hand resting near her head on the pillow.

A lovely, wanton picture, and yet, her gaze reflected worry too.

Elias took her hand in his, cradling her knuckles against his palm. *I will find a way.* Find a way to turn that worry into trust, if not trust in him, then trust in a secure future for her valley.

Violet undulated against him, joining them in one slow, sinuous movement, and Elias answered her with a deep, measured rhythm. He held his pleasure back, even as he drove her up into a silent, shuddering surrender.

I will find a way, to safeguard her dreams, to honor his obligations to family and to a legacy that stretched back for centuries.

Violet subsided beneath him on a soft sigh, her only movement a slow glide of her hand down his back. Elias gathered her close, poised between the desire to ravish, and the longing to cherish. They needed so much more than an hour for all the emotion she stirred in him, all the challenges they faced.

A trickle of damp heat kissed Elias's collarbone.

"Again, Elias. Please, almighty God, again."

Not a command, a plea, and Elias obliged, but first he kissed the tears from Violet's eyes, and silently offered her the only promise he could make:

I will find a way, no matter the cost. I will find a way.

* * *

"Violet, if you'd help me with the dishes, I'd appreciate it." Jane said. "Dunstan, it's your turn to feed Wallace."

"One doesn't feed Wallace," Dunstan said, taking Violet's plate and stacking it on top of his own. "One surrenders placatory offerings to him, in hopes he won't leave dismembered rodents where bare feet are most likely to tread in the dark. Elias, your plate."

"You're turning into Uncle Donald," Elias said, passing his plate. "Donald insists that scraping plates at the table is the most efficient means of clearing a meal. Fewer trips from table to kitchen, however unrefined the guests might find it."

Dunstan picked up Jane's plate. "Uncle Donald likes to remain where he has an audience, and avoid the real work that's done in the kitchen. Come along, Elias. We'll feed the cat, and have a wee dram to finish a fine meal."

"Jane," Elias said, "my thanks for an excellent dinner. I'm available to assist with the dishes, assuming Wallace doesn't have me for a snack."

"Get your own wife," Dunstan said, giving Jane a kiss, "and stop flirting with mine."

"Flirt with me all you like," Jane said, picking up the stack of dirty dishes. "But feed the cat first. Wallace has a fanatic attachment to regular meals. C'mon, Violet. Dunstan, stop worrying. I won't cross-examine her, and she's not a hostile witness."

"Don't turn her into one," Dunstan said. "Violet, take the fifth as much as you need to."

The men left, and Violet gathered up silverware and glasses, then followed Jane into the kitchen. The meal had been delicious—a homemade pizza buried in pepperonis, black olives, mushrooms, and peppers; and a salad of grated cheese, more mushrooms, and chopped celery.

Deceptively hearty fare, particularly when topped off with a warm brownie that shouted, "made from scratch" with every forkful.

"I rarely use the dishwasher," Jane said. "I can make an exception tonight."

"Let's deal with the dishes now so you don't have to unload in the morning. I gather Elias and Dunstan are preparing for tomorrow's meeting with the bankers?"

The local banks had all been bought out by multi-state banks years ago, and Violet's relationship with the bank had become arms' length and perfunctory. Elias would likely merit better treatment than she received, though she was a third-generation customer. Money not only talked, it was addressed in the most polite terms.

"You're here to keep me company," Jane said, piling dishes in a dish tub. "Have a seat. I know how hard farmers work, and you're my guest. That means you get to endure my hospitality, which is a nice way to say that in my kitchen, I'm the boss."

Violet took a barstool at the end of the counter. "I'm not a lawyer, Jane de Luca, so you don't have to be on the offensive with me. Didn't anybody tell you it's OK to be shy? And you do not know how hard farmers work—nobody does, except another farmer. What do I have to do to get some peppermint tea around here?"

Jane's expression went from wary, to bashful, to pleased. "You would have made a fine lawyer, Violet Hughes. Not too late to go to law school, you know. Does wonders for us shy, retiring types. Teas are in the cabinet above the breadbox. Honey and agave nectar on the lazy susan, and my half of that brownie we're splitting should be at least two inches square."

"Being shy burns a lot of calories. What did you really drag me in here to discuss?"

Jane shut off the tap and stared at the dirty dishes. "I'll get to that, but part of my motive for putting you on dish duty is that I want Dunstan and Elias to act like cousins. To watch them, you'd think they were opposing counsel in a high stakes divorce. Maybe it's Scottish family stuff, but I can tell you, the de Lucas aren't like that."

Violet got up to put herself together a cup of tea, rather than admit the greater Hughes family settled for inconsistent Christmas cards.

"You're worried about Elias and Dunstan?"

"Yes, I'm worried about them. They're my family. I'll have a cup of tea too, plain peppermint will do. Has Elias told you about his castle?"

He had, after a loving so thorough and tender Violet had cried—twice. Once in Elias's arms, and again in the privacy of the shower before they'd come here for dinner.

"He loves that castle," Violet said, nudging Jane away from the sink long enough to fill a teakettle. "He loves what it stands for, and what it can mean to future generations. I respect the everlasting aspirations out of a man who cares for his legacy."

"But?"

Violet set the kettle on the burner and cranked the heat up to high. "But I want to throttle him for wrecking my valley. I want to shove statistics at him, about the loss of farmland worldwide, not only to development, but to climate change. We cannot afford to develop too many more Damson Valleys if we want our children to have enough to eat, and now you've gotten me started. I was doing so well, too."

"I happen to agree with you," Jane said, turning her back on the dishes, and leaning against the counter. "In Scotland, there's plenty of green space, and not very many people, relatively. There, they worry about the environment, and about their history, and about looking after each other, but they're not going to run out of land any time soon."

"It's not just a matter of having the space, Jane. We build out hundreds of acres as if we're setting up toys that can all be thrown back in the toy box at naptime. The developers always want the best farmland, not too far from existing population centers, attractively situated in the middle of the countryside, unencumbered by municipal zoning controls, and environmentally clean. I've given this speech so many times, at so many zoning board meetings."

She hadn't given it to Elias, though, not the whole sermon. She'd hummed a few bars, and Elias had probably googled the rest.

"You might have to give it at a few more," Jane said, as the kettle began to whistle. "Weren't we about to fortify ourselves with another dose of brownie?"

"Help yourself, I'll get the tea."

The soothing aroma of peppermint soon filled the kitchen. Violet drizzled honey into hers, gave it a stir, and set Jane's by her plate.

"You're letting the dishes soak?" Violet asked.

"Brownies before dishes," Jane said, taking the other bar stool. "Sitcha down, Violet. Let's talk about the conservation easement, because I get the sense that Elias will go for it if he can make the numbers work."

"The program is one of the oldest and best run in the country," Violet said, sliding onto the barstool. "A lot of the farms around me have either applied or been approved for conservancy zoning, and the state likes that—big, contiguous chunks of farmland, a greenbelt, only more productive."

"Then maybe I'm worrying for nothing," Jane said, picking up her brownie. "I hope I'm worrying for nothing, because for purely selfish reasons, I'd like to see Elias keep his farm."

Violet was desperate for him to keep his farm, for reasons altruistic, selfish, delusional, and everything in between. "The state should consider a property that size very favorably."

Jane gave her a sympathetic look around a mouthful of brownie.

"I know," Violet muttered. "Applying to the program costs money and takes time, if you get all the studies, tests, and certifications done, and Elias has neither time nor money. If I had any spare cash at all, I'd give it to him just so he had some breathing room."

Jane stopped chewing. "My husband will be feeding that cat for the next month."

"I beg your pardon?"

"Dunstan just lost another bet. I think he does it on purpose, to spoil me without me noticing. Let's crash the meeting on the porch. If we come bearing brownies, the guys will act pleased at the interruption. Don't tell anybody, but Dunstan has been known to dunk a brownie in his whisky."

Jane was smiling a marital smile, speaking a marital dialect, and Violet was hopelessly jealous. To enjoy both office and home with the person you loved most in the world, sharing the work, the dreams, the challenges and the triumphs—how sweet was that, and how few couples had it?

Violet put two more brownies on a plate, and followed Jane out of the kitchen. They hadn't started down the hallway before Violet heard the unmistakable—if nearly unintelligible—sound of two Scotsmen in the midst of a roaring difference of opinion.

CHAPTER ELEVEN

"Glaziers, Dunstan! A *team* of glaziers?" Elias spat. "Do you know how many windows that castle has, and how variable the window measurements?"

Elias knew. The family seat boasted thirty-seven different window sizes—everything from arrow slits to Palladian fancies inflicted by improving Victorians, and no two were the same size.

"You should be happy that Zebedee reserved the services of historically astute professionals. Jeannie says their work is backlogged for two years."

"Which means," Elias retorted, "their prices will amount to daylight robbery."

This *discussion* took place on a porch painted white and decorated with potted ferns, wicker chairs, and hanging baskets of red, white, and purple petunias. Hostility crackled across this pretty magazine cover of a porch, not simply a difference of opinion.

"Did you plan to undertake renovations without installing windows?" Dunstan asked. "Is that what passes for Scottish air conditioning these days, your lordship?"

Elias stepped closer to Dunstan, though he knew he was being distracted from the real issue. "Do not call me that, Dunstan Cromarty."

"Why not? You're a bloody earl. Will you banish me from your windowless castle?"

"You wanted them to talk like cousins," somebody—Violet—muttered.

Dunstan clearly hadn't noticed the ladies standing in the doorway any more than Elias had. Violet looked amused, and Jane was holding a brownie an inch from her mouth.

While Elias was holding at least one answer. "I don't have to banish you, Dunstan. You banished yourself when you turned nineteen and upped stakes for the New World. You've no idea how envious I was, or how proud we all are of you."

Dunstan absorbed that blow while he took a sip of a fine Speyside single-malt. "If you're so proud of me, why does nobody ever come visit? Am I the only Cromarty capable of booking a flight?"

He'd made a try for casual grousing, but bewilderment had crept into the question. Bewilderment—and hurt?

Elias loved his cousins, though he hadn't found a way to express that sentiment, other than by handing out advice, ceremonial whisky, and funds in equal measure. Watching the look that passed between Jane and Dunstan—one consuming a brownie, the other Scots whisky—insight struck Elias, like the sun cresting a hill.

Dunstan was soon to be a father. That's what this grousing and snorting was about. Whether the conclusion was the result of instinct, prescience, or keen observation, Elias didn't care. He knew only that Dunstan was asking for support, the only way a proud man could.

"You're the only Cromarty who doesn't expect me to pay for your flights," Elias said. "Or one of the few, and now that I know your marriage can bear the strain of houseguests, I'll send you all the company you like. Helga and Heidi will likely lead the charge."

"They aren't houseguests," Dunstan said. "They're a plague of locusts on a man's liquor cabinet. They'll get along with Jane famously, and be teaching her sword dances in the living room."

"That's the best place to learn the sword dances," Elias said. "I am not happy about your deception, Dunstan."

"Dunstan is honest," Jane interjected, her defense marred by a spot of chocolate on her upper lip.

"Dunstan withheld information from me," Elias said. "I was prepared to be bankrupted by a team of masons I'd never hired. In addition to masons, I now learn—only because the liquor is in the study, and Dunstan had printed out Jeannie's last email—that glaziers, carpenters, landscapers, a veritable army of first-rate artisans, are descending on my castle with signed contracts in hand. When did you plan to tell me, Dunstan?"

Jane stuffed another bite of brownie in her mouth. Violet took up a lean against the doorjamb.

"Sooner begun is sooner done," Violet said. "I thought this whole business of selling the farm was to finance renovations, and now it's a problem that the renovations are under way. What exactly is going on?"

"It's a bad news/bad news situation," Elias began.

"Must you be so Scottish?" Dunstan muttered.

"I *am* Scottish. So, as it happens, are you, and if we're to compete for most stubbornly, pessimistically Scottish, I will concede rather than bloody my knuckles knocking aside your plaid crown."

"This is like watching a pair of lawyers go at it in court," Jane said, passing Violet a brownie. "Though the sniping sounds a lot more impressive with those accents."

"Elias doesn't snipe," Violet said, saluting with her brownie. "Tell us what's going on, guys, and you can get back to playing Robert the Bruce later."

"Braveheart, please," Dunstan said, taking one of the wicker chairs.

"Then you have to be William Wallace," Elias retorted, propping a hip against the porch railing. "Executed by the enemy, but fondly remembered by those whose opinions matter."

Jane took the chair next to Dunstan's. "We were bringing you seconds on the brownies. Guess you might have to get your own."

"I'll get them," Violet said, disappearing back into the house.

So Dunstan missed his family? Elias knew all too well what that was like. He'd been missing his family since he'd turned eleven.

"You know Dunstan, when that plane went down, I lost more than my mother and father." Elias hadn't planned to say that, but then he hadn't planned to fall in love with Violet Hughes either.

"Damned rotten business, losing a parent, much less two," Dunstan said. "If I never said it before, I'm saying it now. You have my condolences."

The sun had set, and the Maryland version of the gloaming was fading. In the woods bordering Dunstan's back yard, darkness had taken hold, though a tiny light glowed momentarily in mid-air.

"Was that a firefly?" Elias asked.

"Or a lightning bug," Jane said. "Same thing. First I've seen this year."

Another little flicker glowed closer to the house then winked out. What a curious creature, the firefly must be.

"None of the cousins expressed condolences," Elias said, getting back to the topic at hand. "What child knows enough to offer sympathy when the greatest imaginable cataclysm has befallen one of their number? Most children can contemplate their own death more calmly than that of a parent."

"Were your cousins cruel to you?" Jane asked.

Violet set a plate of brownies on the wicker coffee table and took the chair closest to Elias. He shifted to sit at her feet, his back resting against her legs.

"Nobody was cruel to me, not on purpose," Elias said. "But whenever I attended family gatherings, awkwardness followed me like a stray dog. If Zeb came along, he deposited me among the children, then wandered off to drink with the men and flirt with the ladies."

"While the rest of us had parents," Dunstan said, "and siblings, which probably broke your stubborn little heart every time you had to watch us take that for granted. I'm fetching a wee dram for the ladies."

Or maybe Dunstan needed a moment to compose himself. Elias should have—but he'd worked these sentiments out for himself years ago.

"So nobody knew what to say to you," Violet said, "and you didn't know how to ask for what you wanted?"

"I wanted my parents back, of course, and nobody could give me that, so then I wanted the awkwardness to stop." And Elias wanted this gloomy conversation to be over, so he could get back to verbally thrashing Dunstan.

"Which, I'm guessing," Jane said around a yawn, "is when your darling little cousins started calling you 'your lordship.'"

"Among other things." School had eventually become a refuge, at least for Elias's intellect.

"I'm sorry for that too," Dunstan said, setting the whisky bottle next to the brownies. "Consider yourself invited to visit here any time, Elias, and I will buy your plane ticket happily."

The offer was sincere, and heartwarming. Violet's silence behind Elias was… not heartwarming.

The talk drifted from there to various topics—the meeting with the bank, the success of Jeannie's holiday cottage, the difference between practicing law in Scotland and in Maryland. When Jane yawned for the second time, Violet patted Elias's shoulder.

"I hear my chickens calling me," Violet said. "Elias, will you take me home?"

Goodnights followed, with Jane hugging Violet hard, and Dunstan bussing her cheek. They liked her, and if the sale to Maitland went through, Elias's family would try to look after Violet when he'd gone back to Scotland.

Not that Violet would allow them to.

They drove back to her house in Dunstan's truck, a smoother ride than the hybrid.

"James said something I wanted to pass along to you," Violet said as they left the lights of the town behind.

James? Ah, the attorney fellow. "Is it bad news or awful news?"

"It's paperwork, which is never good news," Violet said. "File a police report on the stolen livestock. Dunstan can help you do it, and insurance might reimburse you."

Well, likely not. The same caretaker who'd failed to pay the electric bill had also failed to tend to much of anything since the first of the year. The insurance policy was doubtless a casualty of bad management.

"I'll take care of filing a police report after the meeting tomorrow," Elias said. "May I say goodnight to the chickens with you?"

"I'd like that."

While Violet counted her hens, and Elias retrieved Brunhilda from beneath the trough, stars came out. The lightning bugs apparently hadn't hatched this far out in the valley yet, and the peace of the evening was profound.

"How bad is the situation with the castle?" Violet asked, as she walked Elias back to the truck.

He understood why Dunstan had dissembled. The situation had been challenging before, but now…

"It's bloody awful," Elias said. "Zebedee hired the best, and promised them premium wages for putting his project ahead of others. They all have signed contracts, and are eager to commence work on such a large job. Zeb was often foolish like that, or maybe he knew his time was growing short."

"Another reason to be unhappy with your family," Violet said. "Will you be able to sleep tonight, Elias?"

"I'll dream of you."

Dunstan had given Elias a look that promised the door to the house would remain unlocked, and Elias had passed at least one late-night pharmacy on the trip from town, but he hadn't stopped for more condoms.

The afternoon's lovemaking had been lovely, and devastating, and he couldn't ask that of Violet again.

"Are you angry with your uncle, Elias?"

Elias couldn't see her expression, but he could hear the concern in her voice. "Anger is a part of grief. Try not to be too angry with me if the meeting with the banker doesn't go well tomorrow, Violet."

"Let me know how it goes." She kissed him goodnight, then walked through the darkness to her house. Elias waited until the lights went on, then climbed back into the truck.

An honest self-appraisal of Elias' s emotional state revealed surprisingly little ire directed toward his uncle. Zebedee had probably sensed his heart trouble growing worse, and known his time to set the castle to rights had been limited.

A bad feeling, when a man's time grew short, and his heart was increasingly troubled.

* * *

"Let me remind you about how this is supposed to work, Derek," Bonnie said, her words dripping with ire. "When you take the last cup of coffee, and it's all of 9 a.m., you're supposed to make a fresh pot."

The reception area was free of clients, so Max remained at his desk, letting the altercation in the kitchen run its course.

"Don't get your panties in an uproar, Bonbon," Derek Hendershot retorted. "So I drank the last of the coffee. You can make more."

"*You* can make more," Bonnie shot back. "You are of age, and thanks to blind chance and your daddy's money, you survived college and law school, both of which require a passing grade in Java 101. You know how to make a pot of coffee, and if you've forgotten, you are literate, and can read all three lines of instructions some underappreciated, overworked admin kindly posted on the wall."

"Maybe you should read up on perimenopause," Derek suggested. "Makes women irritable and too hard deal with. There are drugs for it, though, hormones and shit that—what are you doing with the coffee pot, Bonnie? We only have the one, and if you—"

"It's my coffeemaker," Bonnie said, "because neither of my bigshot attorney bosses could be troubled to replace the cheap-tastic one that died at Christmas. Possession being nine-tenths of the office policy around here, I'm revoking your caffeine privileges."

In the ominous beat of silence that followed Bonnie's decree, Max pushed away from his desk. He picked up the vase of flowers—happy somethings—and marched down the hall to the kitchen.

"Derek, if you have a minute, I'd like to bounce something off of you." A few quick lefts to the solar plexus, a boot to the rear, and a rabbit punch, for starters.

"I'll be across the street grabbing a cup of coffee," Derek said, shooting Bonnie the women-are-crazy look that had been getting men in trouble for eons. "Better company and better coffee."

He slouched out of the kitchen, hands jammed in his pockets in what was doubtless intended as a blond, blue-eyed, Great Gatsby exit. When the front door had slammed in his wake, Bonnie took the flowers from Max.

"He's spawn, Max. You are a hardass, entirely lacking in clues, and you'll be the ruin of this valley, but somebody ought to put Derek in the witness protection program and lose his file."

She poured the water from the vase, got a knife from a drawer, and cut the flower stems an inch shorter, then refilled the vase, and handed it back to Max, all in the space of a minute.

"Any time you want to file a sexual harassment claim against him, don't let me stop you," Max said. "But he does pay half the rent and half of your salary."

"No, he does not pay half the rent. When I took the checks over to the realty office at the first of the month, the check for Derek's half was written by Ms. Lila Fortunato. I think our Derek is entering into that phase of masculine stupidity known as the post-divorce light sword display. Throw an aspirin in with these, and they'll last longer."

Unease joined the general tension of the day, which was tense enough. "Isn't Lila the admin at old man Hendershot's office who was—?"

"Named in Derek's divorce, much to her boss's dismay," Bonnie said. "Gotta love the gossip vine in a small town bar association."

Actually, Max did appreciate the gossip vine in a small town bar association, though he preferred to call it a network.

"I'm expecting a call from Valley bank," he said, peeling the coffee-making instructions from the bulletin board. "A very, extremely, sensitive call. It ought to come through on my cell, but if my line rings while I'm across the street, please pick up."

"I usually do," Bonnie said, unplugging the coffee maker. "Do I take a message or have the party call you back?" "The call will be from Ned Hirschman, and you will give him my cell number and tell him I'm waiting to hear from him." Max had made sure to give Hirschman his cell the last time they'd teed off in the same foursome, but that had been in the fall.

"Are we in trouble, Max?"

We? When it came to business, Max didn't deal in "we," and it took him a moment to realize Bonnie wasn't prying, exactly, she was concerned for him.

"I'm not applying for a line of credit, if that's what you're asking. Elias Brodie is meeting with the bank today. Could be he's opening a business office in the States, and simply wants the bank accounts under his cousin's watchful eye, or it could be something else altogether. Ned mentioned the meeting to me at the gym last night, and I asked for details."

Bonnie took the flowers from him and set them on the counter. "I thought a banker was supposed to be the soul of discretion."

Ned Hirschman's second wife was twenty years his junior, wanted another kid, and relished the pleasure of being Mrs. Big Fish in a Small Pond. Ned could not afford to be discreet when the largest construction project in the valley might be financed through his institution.

Or not.

"Ned is simply taking care of business, which I will also do, over a cup of coffee with Derek."

"Slip him some saltpeter, would you?"

Max did not slip Derek saltpeter. He instead took the chair opposite him in the coffee shop favored by most of the businesses centered around the courthouse. The bondsmen, private investigators, transcription services, and lawyers all ran on caffeine and carbs, and the Chat and Chew had thrived for decades as a result.

"You're not having anything to drink?" Derek asked.

"Had my two cups for the day." Rather than gag down the insult to the palate that was decaf, Max switched to water thereafter.

"You're not human," Derek said, sipping at something that left foam on his upper lip. He licked it off and set down his cup. "Bonnie will have that coffee pot plugged in and perking by lunchtime if she knows what's good for her. Speaking of perking, I did you a favor."

Derek Hendershot never did anybody any favors, though committing adultery had certainly allowed the former Mrs. Hendershot to depart for Scottish climes with her head held high.

"I don't ask for favors, Derek, and generally don't want them or reciprocate them when they come my way."

"That's what I mean about not being human, or maybe you were playing with your slide rule when the common sense was handed out. Business runs on favors. I know this because business is in my blood."

Nepotism was in his blood. Absent his father's influence, Derek would have little education and less revenue. Daddy Hender-bucks had taken a dim of view Derek fishing off the company dock, though, and Derek had been cut loose to stand on his own two Johnson-and-Murphy shod feet when the marriage had fallen apart.

"So what's this favor?" Max asked. "A first-rate single-serve coffee maker for the office might restore you to Bonnie's good graces."

Derek sneered, but with latte foam on his lip, the effect was comical. "Girl needs to get laid, not that I'm in the pity—"

"Bonnie is an adult, not a girl, and you don't talk that way about a co-worker in my hearing. I'm in a hurry, so listen up. I could well be moving my office. I'll know by next week, and the chances are, I'll turn in a 90-day notice at the end of the month. Plan accordingly, but plan quietly unless you want people to speculate that you're closing up shop."

The office lease was in Max's name, and had gone month-to-month at the first of the year. If the deal went through with Elias Brodie, a much larger space would be needed to serve as project headquarters.

Though no space Max chose would be large enough to include an office for Derek Hendershot.

"Remind me again why I do you favors," Derek said. "Your timing sucks, Max. I'm barely getting started as a solo, and you pull this shit? Are your boys in Baltimore ditching you?"

"No, as a matter of fact, and nothing's final yet. If this deal goes down, it could go down quickly, and you deserve notice."

"Notice," Derek said, draining his cup. "Notice that you're bailing on a guy who's made your life a lot easier in the past few months. Paid half of everything, no questions; put up with the legal assistant from hell, no complaints. I'm sorry for your troubles, man, but maybe now you'll see why favors are a good thing. I've pretty much guaranteed that Violet Hughes woman won't be a thorn in your side ever again."

Of all the grand pronouncements Derek might have made, that one hadn't been on the list of pronouncements Max might have predicted.

"Violet Hughes merely exercises her rights as a citizen." She did so at the worst possible times and places, hogging the mike at zoning hearings, rattling off facts and figures that by no means represented the whole land use debate fairly.

But Violet played by the rules, and Derek… Derek merely played.

"Violet Hughes would keep this valley sweating behind a team of stinking draft horses," Derek replied. "That's what you said after she trashed your last project at the public hearing stage. You're not the only person who feels that way."

Violet Hughes was a problem, of course. Max could and would buy the Hedstrom property, and then came the first major hurdle on the path to developing it: The land had to be rezoned to permit subdivision into residential lots. The risk of buying land speculatively was that the rezoning request could be denied, or take years to resolve.

Expensive, frustrating years while other developers went forward with their projects.

"Land use is always subject to debate," Max said, "and I have to get back to work. What favor have you done me?"

Derek crumpled up his coffee cup and lobbed it toward the trash receptacle. He missed, and the cup bounced to the floor.

Max waited a moment for Derek to get up and tend to the mess—the business owner hadn't been born who wasn't aware of the risks of a slip-and-fall hazard, even trash on the floor—but Derek stayed in his seat and waved to the barista on duty.

"I'll have another double sweet, double whip, large, babe."

Her smile should have had Derek backing slowly out the door. "Got it, Mr. Hendershot."

"I'm outside counsel for Brethren Amalgamated Insurance," Derek said, getting out his phone. "So happens I met with my clients last week. We came up with list."

Insurance companies were not among Max's favorite institutions. Many of them were in the something for nothing business—pay them exorbitant premiums for years on end, and when a claim was filed, they dithered around, denied coverage, or jerked the policy on a technicality.

"Did you check your list twice?"

"Yes, we did," Derek said. "If you were more of a businessman, you'd know that every prudent organization is always looking to keep itself in a lucrative posture. In a place like Damson Valley, for an insurance company, that means dumping high risk properties and keeping the low risk properties."

"I still think you should get Bonnie a new coffeemaker," Max said. "The single-serve version so nobody has to make a fresh pot."

"Fine. Don't listen to me, but when good luck comes your way, remember who sent it to you," Derek said.

Elias Brodie's late uncle was on the list of people sending good fortune Max's way—Max hoped—along with Ned Hirschman and a very few others.

"I'd rather earn my luck, Derek. You might give that approach a try yourself."

"Too much like hard work," Derek said. "I'd rather work smart."

The barrista suffered a coughing fit. Max winked at her, picked up Derek's discarded coffee cup, and tossed it in the trash. He was half-way across the street when his phone rang, the bank's main number beaming up at him from the screen.

* * *

"That went reasonably well," Dunstan said.

Elias walked along beside him, the morning sunshine and damned chirping birds adding insult to injury.

"I didn't resort to fisticuffs when you referred to my title, Dunstan, but that doesn't mean I've put the option entirely aside." The meeting had gone civilly, cordially even, on Mr. Hirschman's part. It had not gone *well.*

"Hirschman is a banker," Dunstan said, in the same tones he might have referred to a Scotsman who rooted for an English football team. "They are the most risk-averse species on the face of the earth, when it comes to their own interests, though it's not as if he'd be lending you his personal money."

"He's concerned with personal influence and with personal money," Elias said, stepping over a large crack in the sidewalk. "With the much greater money to be made on a hundred home mortgages rather than one farm mortgage. He's also concerned with his position, with the promotion he'll likely earn if the development is financed through his bank, and the mortgages are added to his portfolio too."

Why hadn't Elias seen this coming? Why had he assumed a small town bank would be interested in holding a relatively low risk note for a large farm? Low risk meant low return, in which few banks were interested anymore.

"He asked the right questions about lending to you," Dunstan said. "Turn right, if you're still intent on filing a police report."

"He was probably sniffing about in hopes of lending to my not-for-profit clients," Elias said, following the uneven sidewalk down another tree-lined street. "The clients I'm neglecting while I'm dodging kamikaze mosquitos in the jungles of Maryland."

"What sort of clients, Elias?"

What followed was an oddly comforting business discussion. Dunstan's law practice was general, though he and Jane each specialized somewhat. Divorces and wills made up a portion of the practice, but so did incorporations, contracts, and civil disputes.

"I had no idea you were even involved in such goings on," Dunstan said as they approached the police station. "Do you enjoy it?"

Interesting question, which nobody had asked Elias previously. "I enjoy when clients listen to me. They usually pay me exorbitant sums in exchange for what is mostly commonsense advice, then ignore the lot of it, and retain me again a year later to tell them why matters haven't improved."

Dunstan held the door to the police station. "Sounds a lot like being a lawyer. At least you're trying to build something up. We're often involved in tearing something down—a family, an estate, a business relationship. The criminal defense work is something of an exception, but I always feel as if a social worker on the case ten years previous to my involvement might have spared society and the client a lot of bother."

The police station had at one time apparently been a train station. The building was long and narrow with ornate plasterwork. After stating their business to a uniformed officer at the front window, Dunstan and Elias were ushered through a door with a coded lock, and then past a bullpen.

"They might have made that ticket area a bit homier," Elias said. "A potted palm or two, maybe a fern. The glass barriers are a bit off-putting."

"It's bullet proof glass, Elias."

The officer escorting them gave Elias a tolerant look.

The bullpen itself reminded Elias of a corner pub. Work progressed with a hum and bustle, the officers yelled to each other across desks and three-quarter height dividers, a copying machine of venerable size thumped out paper over in one corner.

Elias was unused to seeing guns on display even among law enforcement professionals, while Dunstan was not only at home in this environment, he was apparently welcome.

"Cromarty," said their escort, "next time you need to file a stolen property report, send Ms. De Luca with the client. She's good for morale, when we don't have to deal with her in court."

"She's good for my morale too," Dunstan said, "especially when she has a go at one of your rookies. Sergeant Detwiler, this is my cousin, Elias Brodie. He owns the Hedstrom farm, from which we believe livestock having substantial value has been taken."

Detwiler was a well-fed, graying specimen who nonetheless looked capable of handling himself well in dark alleys and dim bars. His smile was merry, his eyes watchful.

"You want forms, we got forms," Detwiler said, cracking a wad of gum. "What we don't got is a damned pen that works. MacHugh, lend me a pen!"

A pen came sailing through the air, which Detwiler caught with his left hand. "In here, gentlemen," he said, gesturing to a small conference room. "Make yourself at home and we'll get you squared away in no time."

The room was small, windowless, and devoid of decoration. "Do they interrogate suspects here?" Elias asked.

"Very likely," Dunstan said, taking a chair, "and probably play hearts at lunch time."

The form was simple to fill out, in part because Elias knew very little about the crime. Detwiler slid into a seat opposite Elias and glanced over the finished product.

"Frederick Mitchell," Detwiler muttered. "Name rings a bell. That could mean MacHugh dated his sister—MacHugh dates anybody who doesn't have pending solicitation charges—or it might mean my kid's third grade teacher was a Mitchell. Fred goddamned Mitchell. Wait here a minute."

"Uncle Donald would like him," Elias said, when Detwiler had left the room.

"I respect him," Dunstan said. "His job isn't easy, nor is it particularly safe or well paid."

Being a farmer was less safe. Elias had come across that statistic in his internet travels at some point. The frustration that had followed him from the meeting with the bank resurged, along with a sense of futility.

"They aren't likely to find my livestock, are they?"

"In all honesty, no. The trail is cold, and livestock are easily moved across state lines."

Now, Dunstan chose to be honest, now when Elias might have tolerated a ray of optimism in an otherwise rotten morning.

"Have you ever had to tell Jane you've failed her?" Too late, Elias realized that the plain, claustrophobic little room bore the quality of a confessional. Sound lay dead between these walls, and the only light was artificial. The day outside might turn to a raging storm, and in this interrogation room, nobody would know.

"Violet knew better than you what you were up against at the bank," Dunstan said. "I doubt she expected you to walk out with a mortgage closing on your schedule. Why not let the castle crumble to ruins?"

The notion was unthinkable and seductive, both. Elias rose from his chair—the legs of which had been uneven—but the room afforded nowhere to pace.

"Even if I halted work now, I'd owe a fortune in broken contracts, materials on order, permits, wages earned. Jeannie has uprooted her life and Henry's to manage the business in my absence. The only sensible path is forward."

"Forward, into enormous debt," Dunstan said. "What would you tell your clients, Elias? Would you tell them to cut their losses, regroup, and choose the farm over the castle, or to liquidate the farm, and along with it, ruin the hopes of the only woman who's caught your eye in years?"

"Are you trying to get your face rearranged, Dunstan?"

Dunstan was spared a reply by Detwiler's return. "I am not losing my marbles, contrary to Mrs. Detwiler's second worst fears. Fred Mitchell is wanted for non-support. Kid was born last summer, mama was in non-support court within 90 days, and our boy Freddy is racking up arrears. He failed to appear three times, and a bench warrant has been issued. Father of the year, he is not."

"Any priors?" Dunstan asked.

"DUI, a few years ago, a little too much weed, for which he was given probation. If you own the Hedstrom property, Mr. Brodie, you might want to take a close look around. Never know what might be growing on the back forty."

"The back forty acres," Dunstan translated. "Mr. Mitchell might have traded his alpacas for a crop of marijuana."

"*My* alpacas," Elias said, incredulity warring with indignation. "You're implying he might have grown an illegal crop on my land?"

"I wish I could talk like you guys," Detwiler said. "Mrs. Detwiler is always reading those books with the headless guys in a kilt on the cover. Don't go near 'em myself—my virgin eyes, you know?"

Detwiler wiggled his eyebrows, while Elias wanted to punch a hole in the wall. "Now I'm growing contraband somewhere on an 800-acre farm, which property I cannot mortgage even for pocket change. Perhaps I'll turn to a life of crime."

"I don't recommend it," Detwiler said as Dunstan stashed a copy of the police report into his brief case. "Decriminalization, you know. Takes all the fun and half the profit out of the business. Getting so an honest criminal can barely make a living."

Elias could not tell if this lament was in earnest or in jest. "Thank you for your time, officer, and your business advice."

Detwiler offered a brisk handshake. "Protecting and serving, that's me. Cromarty, say hi to the missus. We'll keep an eye out for Mr. Mitchell. FTA on a non-support for a baby less than a year old… guy is a goddamned dopehead sissy."

On that professional summation, Elias shouldered his backpack and followed Dunstan past the locked door, the bullet-proof glass, and out into the mid-day sun. Thank god for good sunglasses, and a slight breeze.

CHAPTER TWELVE

"What does it do to somebody, to work in environment like that?" Elias asked as he and Dunstan resumed their progress down the crooked, cracked sidewalk. "Interrogation chambers, combination locks on the doors, cameras in every corner, bullets a constant threat?" How much more gratifying, to stack a hay wagon under the blazing sun, than to endure the conditions the officers accepted as normal.

"They train for it, and those that can't take the stress often move on," Dunstan said. "The courthouse has many of the same security features, but you're the poor sod who's rebuilding an entire castle. Stone walls six feet thick are bullet proof, parapets give you the same advantage as surveillance cameras, a portcullis and drawbridge function as effectively as a combination lock."

"Remind me again why Zeb sent you to law school?"

"Because I enjoy analytical thinking, and I wanted to do good while doing well."

Modest ambitions, and honorable. Elias still wanted to hit something. "What's your point, Dunstan? I must somehow tell Violet that I've failed her, that the conservation easement is likely the only means of keeping the farm out of Maitland's hands. That approach will take cash flow miracles and a whisky auction to make workable."

"You can't auction the whisky," Dunstan said, coming to a halt on the sidewalk. "Every Cromarty on the face of the earth, every Brodie, would pillory you for auctioning that whisky. The ghost of William Wallace would haunt you, and Jane would be properly cheesed off too."

And in Dunstan's world, Jane's disfavor settled all bets. How enviable, to live such a simple, happy life.

"I have promised Violet I will not fail her. I have assets, I simply lack cash.

It's a common business problem."

Dunstan studied him for a moment, something about the angle of the sun, or the shade dappling his features, creating a resemblance to Elias's late father.

"You're daft, you know that?" Dunstan said. "You're still carrying your father's rucksack."

"It's the only thing I have of his that he made himself."

"Are those his sunglasses perched on your handsome beak?"

Elias and Dunstan both had their grandfather's nose. "They're good sunglasses and cost a pretty penny." Papa had also asked a pouting eleven-year-old Elias to keep them safe for him until he and mum got back from the islands.

"Elias, let the castle go, and build something here with Violet. She's in love with you, and that gift doesn't befall a man every day. She loves you, not your farm, not your title, not your sunglasses. You."

Dunstan spoke not with the ringing conviction of a barrister before the court, but with a cousin's heartfelt plea.

"I can't turn my back on the legacy I alone am in a position to protect, Dunstan. You're not wearing the title, you don't hold the keys to that castle. Zebedee claimed to have seen the ghosts of Auld Michael and his Brenna on those parapets. Those are our ghosts, our parapets. You'd let them crumble into the loch."

"I'd sooner see the stones crumble than your happiness thrown aside," Dunstan said, turning down the street that led to his office. "I expect Auld Michael *and* his Brenna would tell you the same."

"You and Jane are soon to start a family," Elias observed. "If you had to choose between your own happiness, and that of your children, which would you choose?"

Dunstan's steps slowed. "How do you know we're soon to start a family? Did Jane say something?"

"You're a Cromarty," Elias scoffed. "And Jane is enthusiastic about your company, for reasons known only to daft lady lawyers. I'll send along a Speyside for the christening."

"Come to the christening and keep your damned whisky. Bring Violet, too."

Violet, who was deadheading petunias or moving the fence that contained her sheep so their pasture rotated. How Elias would have preferred to spend the morning with her, doing hard, honest work, rather than flattering a greedy banker.

"I notice, Dunstan, you aren't admonishing Violet to sell her farm, as her mother wants her to, and fly away to Scotland with me."

"In the first place, you have doubtless been too pigheaded to ask the lady to come to Scotland with you. In the second, Violet appears to have nothing but that farm."

She had Elias's heart, did she but know it. "What do I have besides the damned castle and the earldom's assets?"

Jane was sitting on the front stoop outside the law office, reading some large brown book in the sunshine. She looked both prim and pretty, her hair up in a bun, her perch that of a school girl. Dunstan came to a halt, his gaze on his wife.

"Elias, you idiot, you have *us*. You have your family, you have a damned doctorate, and a beautiful farm. You have Violet's happiness in your keeping, and you're prepared to toss it all aside for a god-damned castle and a bunch of god-damned ghosts."

"Not for the castle itself," Elias retorted. "For the legacy I owe my children and yours, for the honor of paying debts incurred by the earldom in good faith, for the—you're not even listening."

Jane had caught sight of them and waved, her smile as radiant as summer sunshine off a still loch.

"Yes!" she said, springing off the steps. "The doctor's office called, Dunstan, and they said yes! Our due date is late November, and I am so happy—"

Dunstan caught her around the middle and spun her about, his brief case forgotten on the crooked sidewalk.

"Yes!" he roared, hugging her tightly. "Ah, wee Jane, such news, such happy, wonderful news! Elias, I'm to be a father, and Jane is to be a mother, and you're to be a cousin again of some degree. Yes!"

Kissing ensued, and hugging, and carrying on of a sort no mortal man could begrudge the happy couple. They disappeared into the office, arm in arm, and left Elias to retrieve Dunstan's briefcase. Rather than join the joyous—delirious—pair inside, Elias took the seat Jane has vacated on the stone steps.

The heat wasn't so oppressive to him anymore, the humidity not so cloying. Across the street, geraniums splashed bright red against a sky-blue exterior.

Dunstan and Jane were building something in Damson Valley, something as formidable as a castle, though on any day, their future could be snatched away. A plane crash, an illness, a drunk driver…

Tragedy could strike without warning.

Elias kept that gloomy reality to himself, as he had for years in the company of family, because another gloomy reality had arrived to push it aside. Tragedy could sunder a loving family without warning, and a castle could spend centuries crumbling into the loch.

While the castle stood, it was a symbol of safety and security, a fortress, much like the bustling hive of law enforcement in the made-over railroad station.

A castle could also, however, become a prison from which no escape was possible.

* * *

"You can't do this to me again," Violet muttered, hugging one upset, battered Rhode Island Red to her chest. "I spend all morning looking for you, and what do I find? A heap of bloody feathers where my Brunhilda should be."

Hildy remained quiet, though she was a voluble little clucker by nature.

"You two," Violet said, addressing Sarge and Murphy. "Go find the fox or coyote or varmint who did this to Hildy, and beat the crap out of them."

Murphy hopped around, Sarge looked puzzled.

"Fricassee of fox," Violet said, marching off toward the house. "Coyote casserole in a rattlesnake remoulade." Though if Hildy had tangled with a snake, she'd either gotten the better of the fight, or been spared a hunting bite.

The dogs trotted at Violet's heels, as did nagging worry. Scouring the property for Brunhilda this morning had been a distraction from a phone that hadn't rung, texts that hadn't arrived. Elias's meeting at the bank should have ended an hour ago, and—

The black pick-up came around the curve at the edge of Violet's property and turned into her drive. Violet waited on the porch, Hildy in her arms.

Elias emerged in jeans and a white button down shirt, his backpack over one shoulder, his sunglasses hiding any expression. Violet didn't need to see his eyes though. She could tell from his walk, from his posture, that no mortgage would be approved.

"You're housebreaking chickens now?" Elias said, prowling up the porch. He kept coming, until he kissed Violet on the mouth. "Hello, Brunhilda. I've seen you looking better."

Now, the damned bird cooed.

"She got loose last night and nearly came to a bad end," Violet said. "Is my valley coming to a bad end?"

"Let's sit," Elias said. "Mr. Hirschman was very pleased to make my acquaintance, full of bonhomie, and fascinated by what I had to say."

"He turned you down flat. I need to clean Hildy up." Violet also needed to cry, and say very, very bad words. Re-arranging several tons of hay might help, or driving her truck straight into Max Maitland's office.

"You suspected I'd fail," Elias said, tugging off his glasses, and hooking them on the collar of his shirt.

"You haven't failed, Elias, you've been out-maneuvered by the home team," Violet said, leading the way into the house, and down the hall to the laundry room. "You're on Maitland's turf, and Max is determined, not stupid. This is partly my fault because I got a development ten miles north of town stalled at the re-zoning phase a few years ago. Hold Hildy."

Violet shoved the hen at Elias. Hildy made happy-hen noises, though if the idiot chicken only knew how close she was to the stew pot, she'd have been flapping off to West Virginia at a dead run.

"Hirschman didn't say no," Elias replied, stroking the back of Hildy's neck with one finger. "He listened, he asked relevant though hardly brilliant questions, and he agreed to consider the mortgage application most carefully."

Violet retrieved an ancient, clean kitchen towel from the stack above the washing machine, got down triple anti-biotic, cotton balls, and a nifty veterinary scrub that was both anti-bacterial and anti-fungal.

"This stuff costs a fortune. Knock over the bottle and you'll owe me a mortgage." Violet spread the towel on the top of the dryer—upset chickens could be very untidy. "Put Hildy on the towel but keep hold of her too. Pet her, distract her, soothe her."

The next part went more quickly than many of Violet's chicken-doctoring encounters, simply because Elias was there to look after Hildy while Violet cleaned and disinfected various minor wounds.

"She likes you," Violet said, when Hildy was once again cradled in Elias's arms, and the medical supplies had been put away. "Chickens have a reputation for stupidity. They aren't stupid, but they can't fly to speak of, they aren't much for fighting, and they taste good. What's a girl to do when she's lost in the dark past her bedtime?"

Elias shifted the hen to one side and wrapped an arm around Violet's shoulders. "I hate to fly, but I'd love for you to fly to Scotland with me. Dunstan says I've been remiss—pigheaded—in not making that invitation explicit."

"That meeting must have gone really badly," Violet muttered against Elias's throat. He always smelled good—clean, spicy, alluring—even when he was holding a beat-up chicken, and bearing bad news.

"Hirschman implied that he doesn't lend vast sums to people who own farms they've no idea how to work, and his bank doesn't lend vast sums to Scotsmen who've no intention of investing the money here in Damson Valley."

Meaning Elias had made plain his intention to leave the area. "No doubt Hirschman will cheerfully lend a vast sum to Max Maitland, so that a gazillion mortgages, car loans, lines of credit, credit cards, savings accounts, and retirement plans come his way. I hope the bankers are the first to starve when we run out of arable land."

Hildy clucked, and Elias stepped back. "I should have reminded him of that," he said. "I was too eager to leave the man amid his pots of money. Dunstan and Jane are expecting. Jane confirmed the news when we got back from the bank."

Violet unhooked Elias's sunglasses from his collar, because they were tangling in her hair. "That pleases you?" she asked, setting the sunglasses on the dryer.

"This news pleases Dunstan and Jane. If they were obnoxious in their marital bliss before, they are transcendently unbearable now."

Elias looked pleased though. Pleased for his cousins, and pleased that he'd been with them when the news had been confirmed.

"You're a good guy, Elias. Let's get this hen confined to quarters."

As they returned Hildy to her sisters, and wedged straw bales behind the trough that had provided a means of escape from the chicken yard, Violet mustered her courage.

"What did you mean when you invited me to fly to Scotland with you?" she asked. "Did you mean, sell my farm, leave here, give up on Damson Valley and let Maitland and his McMansions have it all while I take up castle living in the wilds of bonnie Scotland?"

Elias kicked the last straw bale to jam it against the trough formed of a single hollowed-out tree trunk.

"You make coming to Scotland sound like a defeat," he said. "It's not as if"—another hard kick— "Scotland is some remote hinterland devoid of culture."

He was getting his manly ego into those kicks, and he was not making sense. Violet was gratified by both developments, because they confirmed that Elias was truly upset with the bank's refusal to mortgage the farm.

"Elias, I would love to see Scotland someday, but right now, I'm more interested in keeping your farm under cultivation. What do you say we print out the application forms for the conservation easement—unless you've decided to sell to Maitland?"

His sunglasses were back at the house, so Violet could see the determination in his gaze as he surveyed the property across the road and the view down the valley. The brilliant sun was chasing off the last lingering hints of spring, and bringing out the valley's summer plumage. Corn shot skyward on either side of the highway, trees were in full leaf, and the pastures were blankets of verdure.

The valley was beautiful. Elias, with straw on his jeans, and that look in his eyes, was beautiful too.

"I do not want to sell to Maitland," he said. "For many reasons, my castle among them, I do not want him to have this valley. I grasp the importance of maintaining what's good and deep-rooted, Violet. This valley is your castle. I take it you're not keen on moving to Scotland?"

Violet's heart gave a sad, silent lurch south. "That's complicated. I'm keen on you, Elias, but how well would I adjust to Scotland, knowing the price of my happiness was the ruin of a thousand acres of productive farmland? If your farm goes into development, and I give up at the same time, a half dozen of my neighbors will likely throw in the towel too. I can't have that on my conscience. I'd be no better than Hirschman."

Elias spoke of castles, but not of love, marriage, or a secure future. He and Violet had known each other only days, and Elias was still holding a return ticket to Scotland.

And that was fortunate, because if he had spoken of undying devotion, a shared future, and true love, Violet was nearly certain her already bruised heart would dissolve into a thousand, weeping pieces. Perhaps he'd spared her that speech out of kindness, for Elias was a kind man.

"To the computer, then," he said, laying an arm across Violet's shoulders. "I was in a hurry to discuss the meeting with you. I stopped to change but neglected my lunch. Can I beg a sandwich from you?"

Violet wished he'd beg an afternoon in bed from her, but understood his reticence in that regard as more kindness. The easement application was complicated, and a plate of sandwiches and two hours later, they still hadn't dotted every i or crossed every t. Frolics in bed—and further discussion of trips to Scotland—would have to wait.

"A wee dram might make this exercise less tedious," Elias said, pinching the bridge of his nose. "How does one go about creating a forestry plan?"

And certifying that the farm had no wetlands, and guaranteeing the soil types, and providing the metes and bound description of the property, procuring a title search, for starters. The list of to-do's was long and expensive.

"I'll start with my forestry plan," Violet said, "and see if I can adapt it for your property. We should probably nose around in your woods first, just to make sure your trees and my trees are more or less alike in species, age, and distribution."

Elias added something—perhaps a walk in the woods—to their list. "Can Maitland foil this application the way he ruined my chances at the bank?"

Well, damn. "I don't know. Maryland seems to have relatively ethical politics, but the tail wags the dog. Agriculture is the number one industry here, and yet, the population density around Baltimore and the Baltimore-Washington corridor means agricultural interests aren't well represented politically."

Elias tossed his pen onto the legal pad he'd been using to make notes. "Scotland faces similar challenges, complicated by questions of Gaelic cultural preservation, maritime interests involving hundreds of islands, environmental and energy concerns that don't always play nicely together. It seems as if politics attracts some of the very people least suited to holding the public's trust."

Violet put the computer into sleep mode. "In other words, does Max have enough pull at the Agricultural Land Preservation Foundation to deny you an easement? I want to say no, of course not."

"I've been here less than a week, and he's already cut off access to the largest bank," Elias said. "Dunstan and Jane think if the largest bank won't extend me credit, neither will the smaller institutions."

"We have only a couple other banks in the mortgage business out this way," Violet said. "You'll apply to both of them?"

"Dunstan will pick up the paperwork this afternoon, but I will still be a Scotsman who doesn't know how to farm and doesn't intend to invest in this valley."

Violet smacked him on the arm. "You discouraged?"

He kissed her. "I'm Scottish. We don't know the meaning of the word. Will you come to dinner tonight with me and the happy couple?"

Violet was tempted, but another friendly dinner, another evening spent getting to know Elias's family could go nowhere.

He'd invited Violet to dinner, he'd invited her to Scotland. Neither gesture changed the reality that, whether by selling development rights to the state, or selling land to Maitland, Elias would use that ticket home.

While Violet would stay in the valley she'd fought so hard to protect.

* * *

In the morning, Dunstan and Jane tooled off to work chatting happily about car seats, names, and which of the farmhouse's unfished rooms to turn into a nursery.

Elias completed the two remaining mortgage applications, but one required proof not of an American address—Dunstan and Jane's law office would have sufficed—but of an American *residence.*

Elias could claim he lived at the Hedstrom property, but that would be a lie. He finished the application using his Scottish residence, but his mood was soured to be once again defeated before he'd even toed the starting line.

His emails included word from Angus of pending appointments to three more charitable boards, though the organizations couldn't officially name Elias until their summer director's meetings, and the appointments would not take effect until the autumn quarter.

"Which means," Elias informed Wallace, "no director's fees until the new year. By which time, my masons will have walked off the job, grumbling to anybody who'll listen that Elias Brodie doesn't pay his crews."

Wallace had been occupying the sill of the study's open window, his bulk aligned along the screen. He stretched, righted himself, and would have walked across Elias's keyboard, except Elias caught the cat and rose with Wallace in his arms.

"I blew it," Elias said, settling into the recliner with the cat. "I asked Violet to come to Scotland, but I blew it. Bad timing, bad terms."

I'd love for you to fly to Scotland with me. Dunstan says I've been remiss—pigheaded—in not making that invitation explicit.

As if Elias had been inviting her to Aberdeen for a golf weekend. He was still remiss, but as he dozed off, with the cat purring on his chest, he couldn't put his finger on where, exactly, he'd come up short. Violet had asked for clarification—brave woman—but Elias hadn't obliged. He'd grumbled, he'd mumbled, he'd prevaricated, in other words.

A sandpapery tongue scraped across Elias's chin, just as his thoughts drifted to the castle as it would look when restored. Glamis was a larger edifice, but Brodie Castle was older. Blair Castle had larger grounds, but Brodie Castle stood in prettier surrounds.

The tongue scraped across his cheek this time.

"Stop that."

Elias had considered opening the castle and lodge to his charities for board meetings, but that would have meant hiring a caterer, finding help in the village to change the linens and clean. Jeannie, who managed a lovely little holiday cottage, had discouraged him.

A soft paw batted at Elias's lips.

Elias opened his eyes and found himself nose to nose with Wallace. "I'm occupying your throne, I take it. Enjoy your tyranny while you may, cat. By this time next year you'll be deposed by a wee prince or princess, and this will no longer be your castle."

The cat squinted, as if to say, he'd known a baby was on the way long before Elias had, and was in fact, responsible for wooing Jane into joining the household.

"I'm off to check on the chickens," Elias said. "And I'll try to un-bungle what I bungled yesterday. Guard the castle, cat, while it's still yours to guard."

He left Wallace curled in the recliner, and drove out to Violet's, stopping to pick up a six pack of heather ale from the bottle shop that ordered it for Dunstan at a scandalous price.

Violet was in her garden, Brunhilda scratching at the dirt beside her.

"Weeding again," Elias said, taking a cross-legged seat in the grass at the edge of the garden. "I see you have help today."

"I have company," Violet said, "which is almost the same thing." She used a tool with three curved prongs to hack at the soil, pitching weeds into her basket as she went. "I overslept, got a late start. We'll probably get rain this afternoon, and the weeds do love a good shower. What's in the bag?"

She sat back on her heels, wiping her brow with a forearm. The line of her throat was lovely, and the way her old T-shirt strained across her breasts riveting.

"Where is your hat, Violet Hughes?" Elias asked, extracting an ale from the brown paper bag at his side. "You will get a sunburn, and I can tell you from experience, sunburn is unpleasant. Try this." He twisted off the cap and passed her the bottle.

She took a sniff, then a cautious sip. "That's lovely," she said, examining the label. "If I drink one of those in this heat, I will soon be flat out in the glide-a-rocker. What brings you here, Elias?"

The question confirmed Elias's sense that on his last visit, he'd made a wrong turn.

"You do. You bring me out here. Give me one of those digging implements and I'll at least get as much done as Brunhilda."

"You eat bugs?" Violet asked, taking another sip of ale, then passing Elias the bottle.

"I eat crow, as you Americans would say. Will you marry me, Violet?"

She paused, the tool in her hand poised to strike at the earth. "Have you been drinking, Elias?"

"That is not among the usual replies to a marriage proposal," Elias said. "And no, I have not been drinking, though a wee dram or three never hurt a man's outlook. Yesterday, I invited you to come to Scotland, but I failed to make clear, that is, I neglected to…."

This was not going well. Elias carried the ale and his rucksack to the porch, returned to take the tool from Violet's hand, and scooped her up against his chest.

"Is this a Highlander thing, Elias? This hauling women around for no apparent reason? I'm capable of walking, and the beer will get hot if you leave it out for more than ten minutes."

"If I gave you two minutes, you'd hop on a tractor, or move sheep fences, or can dingleberries, or run off to whatever thousand other things you're intent on doing before I finish making a fool of myself. Besides, I'll take any excuse to hold you."

"Elias we need to talk."

No, they did not. Talk would be a somber undertaking, of which Elias had had a bellyful.

"We need to get married." Elias carried Violet up the porch steps, but she refused to open the door when he obligingly dipped at the knees. He compromised by settling with her on the glide-a-rocker, keeping her in his lap. "That came out wrong. Violet, will you please marry me? We'll get the conservation easement, hire managers, split our time between the crops and the castle. The renovations should only take a few years, and by then—"

She kissed him, though Elias didn't mistake the gesture for affection. He was babbling, and kissing him was a merciful gesture to shut him up. Bungling apparently grew easier with practice.

"I called the land preservation office," Violet said. "They know me there, because I'm such an advocate for the program."

Her tone was level, her gaze was sad. The orphan in Elias began to silently howl.

"Tell me," Elias said. "Whatever the news, just tell me."

"Maryland's fiscal year runs from July 1 through June 30."

Many business organizations used a date other than January 1 to start their accounting cycle.

"Why is that significant?"

"Because," Violet said, "the land preservation program has used up its purchasing funds for this fiscal year. They will accept new applications starting in September, and probably begin making awards around January. I knew how the program operated in theory, I'd just never acquainted myself with the actual schedule. Elias, I'm sorry."

She squirmed off his lap, and he let her go.

No mortgage, no easement, no hope, and Violet was *sorry*.

Elias rose and crossed the porch to where the ale and his rucksack sat at the top of the steps. He kicked the rucksack so hard it soared across the yard and landed immediately outside the sheep pen. The ewes startled, the chickens flapped, and Elias felt the smallest increment better.

"Does this mean," he said returning to Violet's side, "you're not interested in marrying me? You'd be a countess, for which I do apologize, but it can't be helped. Our daughters would carry the title lady, our oldest son would be a baron. There's nothing I can do about that, either."

Violet retrieved the open beer and resumed her place in his lap. "This is what it's like to be a farmer, Elias. You risk everything on a new hybrid strain of wheat, and a hailstorm knocks a bumper crop flat in thirty minutes. The most beautiful hay God ever grew springs up in your fields, but if the ground is too wet, you won't be able to cut it, much less bale it, until it's far past prime. Without farmers who can plow on through all those vicissitudes, nobody has anything to eat. You would have made a fine farmer."

She took a sip of the beer, and passed him the bottle.

"You are telling me, you can't abandon your post. This farm is a vocation, such that you can't sell it to one of your neighbors and take up the land preservation cause from another pulpit."

Elias was still searching for a solution, which suggested Dunstan's accusation of pigheadedness was spot on.

"Your castle is a vocation," Violet said, snuggling closer. "I know this farm, Elias. I know which fields dry out too fast, which stay boggy. I know which hollows will be nipped by an early frost, and where my dad buried my first dog. I could sell this property eventually, but because it's not in the preservation program, how do I know the buyer won't just flip it into Maitland's lap, and laugh all the way to the bank? People have to eat—they also have to learn to value our farmland—and I know how to grow crops on this patch of ground."

"So put your farm into the goddamned preservation program," Elias said. "You believe in the program, and even if you don't sell this land, someday, you will no longer be able to farm it."

Someday, she'd die, though hopefully not in a farming accident. Sitting on the porch, a part of Elias was dying, the part capable of enduring heartache on the strength of hope and sheer stubbornness.

"My mother would not agree to put her farm into the program," Violet said. "That leaves a very small acreage, Elias, and I'm not likely to be approved the first few times I apply."

Elias took another sip of cool, fragrant ale, though it did nothing to ease the ache in his throat. This must have been how his ancestors had felt, when their lands had been pried away by legal machinations, their cottages burned, their cows driven off so the landlords could raise the more profitable sheep. The only option for the tenants had been to accept defeat, and hope for the best in an unknown land.

"If there were no castle," Elias said, "I'd relocate here without a backward glance, Violet." Cousins, clients, aged single malts, a lifetime of memories—Elias would part from them, happily, and that realization brought a drop of comfort in a barrel of heartache.

Many of those memories were sad, and it was past time he let them rest in peace.

"If there were no farm, Elias, I'd be on the next plane to Scotland with you, but especially if you have to sell to Maitland, I can't turn my back on my property or my valley."

Elias loved this woman, for her integrity, for the ferocity of her passions, and for her honesty. He spared her a recitation of his sentiments, because like every Scotsman ever to pen a memorable ballad, he would apparently soon have to leave behind that which he treasured most.

CHAPTER THIRTEEN

Violet's guilty secret was a capacity for tears. She cried when the new lambs first went pronking across the barnyard on a sunny winter morning, she cried when the autumn light sharpened in anticipation of winter. She cried at falling leaves, and when she banged her thumb with a hammer. She cried at sappy movies, and sometimes, she cried after meeting with her accountant.

Cuddled in Elias's arms, she understood what it meant when a sorrow was too deep for tears.

If she left the valley, Max Maitland would snatch up every spare acre, and the families who'd been hanging on for the last ten years would take his coin with sigh of guilt and relief.

Once development began, it never stopped. It slowed, it even paused, but once it started, a region's quality of life was forever altered. Land ceased producing, and fell under the control of inane homeowner's policies intended to create homogeneity where life-sustaining purpose and diversity had been.

"Right now," Violet said, gazing out across the valley, "I hate Scotland. I hate your castle. I might even hate my life, and I surely do loathe Maxwell Moneybags Maitland, but I love you."

Violet felt the surprise of her words go through Elias. She'd surprised herself too, but what was the point of keeping silent about love?

"Thank you, but you're not... that doesn't...." Elias heaved a sigh, such that Violet's cheek rode the rise and fall of his chest. "I love you, too."

Never had a man sounded less happy to surrender such a declaration.

"Love is good, Elias. I love my farm, you love your castle. We make sacrifices for who and what we love."

They shared another sip of his flowery Scottish ale. A hawk took off from a leafy maple and soared over Elias's fields on a lazy thermal.

"The properties we love are on separate continents," he said. "Another item on the list of immutables that apparently cannot be helped. Will you at least visit me?"

He was so stubborn. "I'll want to." Every night for rest of her life, Violet would wish she was climbing into bed beside him.

"You'll want to, but a woman who can barely find three days to visit her own mother can't be nipping across the Atlantic to admire a castle that's only fit for weddings and *ceilidhs*. I'm good at missing people, Violet, and I will miss you terribly."

Violet did not invite him to visit her—what would be the point, when the Atlantic Ocean remained between them? She took the ale from him, finished it, and set the bottle aside. She'd keep it for a bud vase, and when the cat accidentally knocked it over, she'd glue the pieces back together.

Elias held her in an embrace at once secure and gentle, his gaze on the property across the road. Did he see houses there? Streets? A community center where his barn stood?

Violet would miss the quiet and the rural beauty of the property when his farm had been chopped into cul-de-sacs and jogging trails, but she'd miss Elias more. She'd miss his arms around her, his Scottish diction, the scent of him….

"Did you pitch the last condoms in captivity across the yard?" Violet asked.

"No," Elias said, lips against Violet's temple. "My wallet is in my pocket."

"So what do you keep in that knapsack?"

He was quiet for a moment. "I keep *things* in there—a clean shirt, toiletries, sometimes a book. Conveniences and comforts, not necessities. Anything irreplaceable, I carry on my person."

"You are irreplaceable. Let's go upstairs."

Making love with Elias would hurt like hell. Ignoring the opportunity to be close to him one last time would hurt worse even than that—and apparently, on this point only, he wasn't prepared to argue with her.

* * *

Elias wanted to carry Violet over the threshold of her home, but she denied him that pleasure by wandering across the yard to retrieve his backpack. He stole a photo of her, the sheep in the background and the mountains framing the barn and fields.

He had pictures of his parents, dear, somewhat artificial images of people trying to look happy. Violet looked strong, lovely, and absolutely, utterly, undeniably *at home*. She shouldered Elias's pack with lithe grace and rejoined him on the porch.

"Upstairs, you say?" Elias asked.

"Now would be good. If we're running out condoms, I will expect you to make our supply count."

"*We* will make it count," Elias retorted as she passed him the backpack.

"You'll want to put the ale in the fridge."

"You'll want to stop giving me orders," Violet said, snagging the remaining ale, and preceding him into the house. "At least until I have my clothes off. Then I might be more open to your suggestions."

Then Elias's wits would be too scrambled for coherent speech. Violet stashed the ale in the fridge, then led him up the steps. When Elias had stretched out on her bed between cool white sheets, Violet pulled her T-shirt over her head, stepped out of her sensible footwear, and shucked out of yoga capris that bore garden dirt on both knees.

She was naked, her braid trailing over her shoulder in an auburn rope, and she hesitated by the bed, her courage seeming to desert her. This intimacy had been her idea, but in her eyes, Elias saw the reality of what lay ahead.

This was not good-bye sex, of which they'd both probably had their share. This was not part romp, part relief, part friendly disengagement, a fond memory intended to spare both parties futile acrimony.

This was farewell forever sex.

The pain in Elias's heart as he watched Violet silently wrestle with their fate, was exquisite, different even from the resonating grief of losing both parents. Elias had been a mostly happy lad of eleven years one day, and a bewildered orphan the next. The lack of warning had been a mercy, for what boy could have borne the anticipation of such a loss? Now, Elias knew that in a few days, he'd leave behind hopes, dreams, most of his heart, and a woman worth treasuring.

"You come here to me, Violet Hughes," he said, holding out his arms. Not a suggestion or an order, but a plea.

In the next instant, she was bundled against him, bringing with her the scents of cut grass and lemons, sunshine and summer, and the taste of unshed tears in her every kiss.

If the pain of parting was exquisite, Elias was determined to make the loving exquisite too. He linked fingers with Violet as he slowly, slowly joined their bodies, holding her gaze as he brought more and more pleasure to her. Violet retaliated with kisses and sighs, with an embrace more intimate than ivy twining among ancient stones.

So much Elias wanted to give to her, so much he wanted to show her, but all he had was the next hour. He teased and tasted, dabbled and delighted, until Violet was a boneless heap of aroused female beneath him.

"Now, Elias," Violet said, stroking his chest. "Love me now."

"I will always love you."

He held back. He held back as if he could stop time, hold the sun to its position in the sky, and keep the moon from rising, but in the end, Violet's determination overcame his self-restraint. He followed her into exquisite pleasure, and then held her while her tears came at last.

* * *

"Have you a proper kilt?" Elias asked, tapping away at the computer keyboard.

Dunstan picked up Wallace and deposed him from the recliner. "I do. I was married in my kilt. Jane fancies me in it, and I've worn it to the occasional investiture of a judge or to a retirement dinner. I get a lot of looks and the usual questions."

"I am cursed," Elias said, staring at the computer screen.

Elias had been acting odd since he'd walked in the door shortly before dinner, but then, Elias *was* odd.

"You've an ancient title, good health, relatives who put up with you, an embarrassment of assets, a single-malt collection that's the envy of—Elias what the hell is wrong?"

Dunstan ceased lecturing because Elias's expression was stunned, disbelieving.

"Nick Aiken is my head mason, one of the best. Knows castles inside out, loves them the way Angus loves his pipe music, or wee Henry loves his mother. Nick claims the roof over the long hall isn't sound."

The roof over the castle's long hall was an enormous expanse of vaulted stonework, worthy of a cathedral, and probably centuries older than any cathedral in Scotland.

"Age takes a toll on us all, Elias."

Wallace hopped back up into the recliner.

"Just for that," Elias said, "I will not give you your pick of the single-malts before I auction them off."

"I want that bottle of 28-year-old Macallan, but you're not auctioning off the whisky. Did you expect the roof to be sound?"

Elias closed his document and turned so he straddled the chair before the computer and faced Dunstan. "Do you know how much it would cost to repair the roof of this house?"

Dunstan picked up the cat and settled into the recliner, because Jane had gone to bed early, and a considerate husband let his pregnant wife get some sleep. Then too, Jane was worried about Elias, and that meant Dunstan was obliged to worry about Elias.

"Roofs are a bloody pain in the arse," Dunstan said, as Wallace got settled on his lap. "If the wet gets in, the walls are soon the worse for it, and the whole structure is compro—shit. The long hall is enormous." It also ran between the two wings of the castle, connected the merely old with the ancient. If the long hall wasn't sound, the castle was essentially rotten in the middle.

"And that roof weighs tons upon tons," Elias said. "All of those tons will come crashing down at some point—probably in the middle of somebody's wedding—if I don't effect structural repairs, the cost of which, Nick can't even estimate until the work starts."

Wallace began to make odd noises, as if he had the hiccups.

"None of that," Dunstan said, scratching the cat under the chin. "The fat beggar's perfected the art of demanding attention. Is this why you're selling the whisky? Because the roof is about to cave in?"

Wallace subsided into purring, at which the cat excelled. He also, however, commenced kneading a delicate portion of Dunstan's anatomy, which necessitated picking the cat up.

"The roof might hold up another hundred years," Elias said. "It might collapse tomorrow. Nick is sending for an engineer he's worked with who has a way with old buildings."

And if master masons came dear, specialty engineers came astronomically dear. "How much are you prepared to invest in a building nobody has called home for decades, Elias? I understand that you're not a farmer, much less an American farmer, and that you don't care to become one. Seal off the long hall, take the money Maitland will pay for the farm, and enjoy yourself."

"Enjoy myself?"

The poor bastard looked perplexed, as if he were trying to make sense of Norse runes scratched on the wall of a tomb.

"You like fast cars, pretty women, fine whisky. Your lodge has art on nearly every wall and table, and you play polo. God's sake, *enjoy yourself*."

Elias plucked the cat from Dunstan's arms, leaving a shower of cat hair on Dunstan's clothing. "I consult to a number of automobile design shops, Dunstan, and cars are like whisky, like musical instruments. The more you grasp about their workings, the more you appreciate a well-made article. I honestly prefer blended whisky, but one doesn't blaspheme in the temple, and if you'd been dragged around behind Zebedee Brodie to every polo match on three continents, you'd have learned the rudiments of the game too."

"What about the women?" Dunstan said, as Wallace began to purr.

"I like women, and some of them have liked me back. When did that become suspect behavior?"

Valid point, so like a good litigator, Dunstan ignored it. "And the art?"

"Most of the art at the lodge belongs to Liam Cromarty, who rents art to corporations, some of whom I've introduced to his services. I don't own it, and I don't charge Liam rent to house it."

Liam was an art history professor, and also among the Cromarty cousins to recently marry.

"You're a complete fraud in other words," Dunstan said. "You have clients, you work, you don't even fuss when a cat gets hair all over your French shirts."

"English," Elias said, scratching Wallace's head. "I've held chickens while wearing this shirt."

This was apparently a fond memory. Globetrotting titled playboys didn't cherish memories involving chickens. Dunstan entertained the notion that he'd never really known his cousin, but he liked this stubborn fool who held Wallace and sat backward in the computer chair.

"Elias, what will you do about the castle?"

"Oh, I'll repair the castle. The alternative is to wait for the roof to cave in, and then it will be condemned, and I'll have to bulldoze it. I want your children to have the option to get married in that great hall. I want to see the ghosts of Auld Michael and his Brenna kissing on the parapets. Even if I can't finish the place out the way it deserves to be appointed, I'll get a good start on the job."

Dunstan rose, because the clock showed 11 p.m. and the day had been long. "I notice you don't mention your own wedding, Elias, or your own children. Will you let the castle cost you those dreams too?"

Elias stood with Wallace in his arms. "You'd make a lousy farmer, Dunstan Cromarty. A man contemplating fatherhood needs to develop some optimism about life, some philosophical resources."

"Have you children, then, Elias, to be explaining fatherhood to me?"

Elias followed him from the study, killing the lights and plunging the hallway into gloom. "I'm a man without parents or siblings, Dunstan, and that gives me insights that you have been spared. Dreams are expensive, and when they die, they take a piece of you with them. You don't get those pieces back. Not ever. If you find something solid to call your own, protect it while you can, but be prepared to part with that too."

Dunstan reacted with the instincts of a boy among his male cousins. He shoved Elias against the wall, pinning him by one shoulder. Not a fair attack, because Elias held the idiot cat.

"You did not die when that plane went down, Elias. Your heart broke, your life went to pieces, but I am damned glad you are alive. I hope you are too. Find new dreams, find new heart. Generations of Scots have had to do just that."

Elias petted the cat, who was glaring at Dunstan. "The state won't be buying my development rights, Dunstan. They have no money to spend and won't for months. Has to do with a fiscal year that's 180 degrees off the calendar year. Violet informed me of this cheery development when we said our farewells this afternoon."

The news about the easement might explain Elias's silence at dinner, his distracted air, but Dunstan suspected saying farewell to Violet Hughes played a part as well.

"The rotten ceiling is just another nail in the coffin, isn't it?"

"It's a castle, not a coffin, Dunstan," Elias said tiredly. "Sometimes, having no options makes life less complicated."

But seldom easier. "Can you make another option, Elias?"

Though what choices remained? Elias didn't know how to farm, farming was a difficult livelihood at best, and Max Maitland was offering a much needed pot of gold in exchange for the land.

"If you can think of another option, Dunstan, I'll consider it. More than the castle and the farm are at stake."

"That's two fortunes. What more could be at stake?"

"If I sell that farm to Maitland, I will break Violet's heart, and that is unacceptable." Elias leaned his head back against the wall and closed his eyes. "I've asked Jeannie to send me a few things. They should arrive to your office on Monday. We'll meet with Maitland on Tuesday, if you can spare me the time?"

"I can spare you the time. I hope you know what you're doing."

"I'm going up to bed, and if I haven't said it before, thank you, Dunstan."

For what? "You're welcome. Shall I put the cat out?"

"The Wallace sleeps in my bed now. I'm hoping his heroic nature might rub off on me along with his fur."

Dunstan declined to point out that William Wallace had been executed as a traitor and died a brutal death far from his home and his loved ones.

* * *

"Jane gave me your message." Elias stood outside the sheep pen, in jeans and a navy blue T-shirt, a blue and white plaid belt at his waist. Violet wished she dared take a picture of him.

She tipped up the metal tub she'd been scrubbing, watching the water run into the dirt. She and Elias had said their good-byes, and yet, Violet had chosen to invite—not force, but invite—one more encounter.

"Your sunglasses are on the kitchen counter," she said. "Give me a minute here, and I'll come with—"

Elias seized the empty tub, shook the last drops from it, then set it under the frost-free spigot. He flipped open the tap, the water hitting the empty tub in a gush.

"They'll drink more when the water's cold," he said. "You could have mailed my sunglasses, or dropped them by the law office. I left them here on purpose because I wanted you to have them."

"That never occurred—" Well, hell. Elias would not be extravagant about his gifts. His generosity would be subtle and discreet, a few beers left in the fridge, forgotten sunglasses. "They are nice sunglasses, Elias. Too nice to wear around a farm."

"You'll take good care of them because they are good quality," he said, flipping the tap off. "I've had them since I was a boy and never lost them. What's next?"

For an instant, Violet thought he was asking a philosophical question, about relationships foiled by thousands of miles of ocean, but as Brunhilda came clucking under the fence, Violet realized the question—like the man—was pragmatic.

"I was about to change the oil in the tractor," Violet said. "It's a messy job, and I've put it off for too long."

"I like anything to do with an engine," Elias said, squatting to pet the hen. "Let's have a look, shall we?"

Where was the harm in sharing a little more of the farm work? Where was the harm in listening to Elias hold a conversation with the underside of a geriatric tractor, watching his hands as he loosened bolts Violet would have been cursing at and kicking? He did in an hour what Violet would have spent all afternoon half-assing, and he seemed to enjoy the challenge.

Then came hanging a hammock between two maples—another job Violet had put off—followed by mucking out and rebedding the chicken coop, which Elias also dispatched more quickly than Violet could have. While Violet uploaded her latest blog post and made lunch, Elias hooked up the mower and scythed down the last field of hay for her, then got after a stretch of the sheep fence where the electric tape had come off its insulators.

Violet watched him through the window as he absently petted old Joan, the alpha ewe who occasionally put the ram in his place. Joan butted against Elias's work gloves, a gesture of affection she rarely showed Violet.

"I told him he'd make a good farmer," Violet muttered to the cat. "He would have made a great farmer. He probably makes a spectacular earl."

How she wished, just once, she could see him in all his kilted finery.

He could well have ignored Violet's message about the sunglasses, could have asked her to mail them, or sent her a note. Instead, he'd come to her door ready to put in a day's work. Even more than his tender loving, or his stubborn attempts to raise cash without selling to Maitland, his practical help stole Violet's heart.

The least she could do was feed him. By the time Elias sauntered in the back door, the dogs panting beside him, Violet had barley soup, ham and cheddar sandwiches, and brownies ready to go.

"You've cleaned off your kitchen table," Elias said.

"For special occasions, such as having a clean chicken coop at last, I will make a special effort. I hadn't realized the glads were blooming yet."

Elias passed her a long stem festooned with lavender blossoms. "I should have asked before I cut it, but my mother loved these. My father frequently brought them to her, and always with good effect. Yours appear to be thriving."

Violet fished under the sink for a vase, trimmed the stem, and put it in water. "Mine are odd. In this climate zone, glads aren't supposed to be hardy. My patch is on a southern wall, directly beneath a window. I think the house keeps them warm, and they keep coming up year after year. I periodically separate them, but only the ones I don't transplant survive without lifting."

Elias had filled one of the dog bowls with fresh water, and for a moment, the only sound was Murphy, lapping noisily. Sarge followed, after which Elias used paper towels to wipe up the mess, then washed his hands at the sink.

The domestic touches—consideration for the dogs, tidying up, taking on jobs Violet had put off—were breaking her heart. Of course this man would put to rights a castle that had been neglected for generations.

And he'd do it without complaining.

"Let's eat, shall we?" Violet suggested. "You've put me days ahead on my chores, and probably saved my tractor from blowing a head gasket."

"I have worked on my tan," Elias said, taking two of the heather ales from the fridge and setting one by each plate. "These taste better if they're not chilled, you know."

Violet took a seat while Elias opened both beers. "I'm in the company of a man who drinks beer for its flavor. Tell me about your castle, Elias."

They were pretending the day was normal, that Elias helped out around the farm occasionally, that Violet wouldn't miss the sight of him on her tractor, or treasure his sunglasses until she was a half-blind old woman.

In the spirit of the general prevarication, Elias told story after story about the Brodie family fortunes, which had taken a sharp turn for the better when Michael, the first earl, had come back from the Napoleonic wars and invested in the black Angus cattle that still featured heavily in the American beef industry.

"So you come from farming people," Violet said.

"Nobody dares attribute the Brodie fortunes to farming," Elias said, taking his empty dishes to the sink. "We claim that Auld Michael's ability to charm Queen Victoria is the foundation of our wealth. Where's your—?"

He knelt to peer under the sink, and came up holding a scrubber sponge. Violet finished clearing the table, put the dogs out, and let Elias do the dishes, while she watered the African violets on the window sills.

She should thank him kindly for his help and send him on his way. Instead Violet set aside her watering pitcher and embraced Elias from behind.

"Thank you, Elias."

He left off wiping out the sink, turned, and wrapped his arms around her. "I will worry about you, here by yourself, working around the livestock, the heavy equipment. I will worry a lot."

She should tell him not to worry, *then* thank him for his help, and send him on his way. "There is one more job I hate to do alone, so I usually put it off, and then it's cold weather, and that only makes it worse."

"Don't be proud," Elias said. "I meet with Maitland on Tuesday, and I'll fly back to Scotland on Wednesday."

Violet sagged against him, resting her forehead against his sternum. The knowledge of parting had been so carefully ignored all morning, and yet, that parting would come.

"If you could help me clean the chimney, I'd appreciate it. I don't mind heights, but I don't like to be up on a ladder when I'm here by myself. Bad things happen at the worst times."

Elias kissed her nose. "That they do. Let's be about it, and then you won't have to fret over the chimney until next spring."

Everything went more quickly when the job was shared. Elias was nimble as a monkey on the ladder, and had the spark catcher off and the long-handled brush down the chimney in no time. The mail truck came while Violet was holding the ladder, the letter carrier shoving bills and junk mail into each of the four mailboxes at the foot of her drive.

"I usually clean out your mail box when I'm getting my own," Violet said, when Elias was once again on the ground. "Even if you forward your mail, the junk keeps coming. I use it for kindling."

"I'll put the ladder away," Elias said, tugging off his gloves. "You'll want to fetch the mail."

Who wanted to collect another fistful of bills and shopping tabloids? Violet let Elias wrestle with the ladder though, because he was leaving on Wednesday and the ladder was heavy. The dogs followed her down to the mail boxes, and indeed, most of the mail was junk.

Her property insurance company had sent her an epistle of some sort, which was unusual because the premiums were paid out of the mortgage escrow funds. She slit the envelope open and read as she walked up the drive.

Disbelief, rage, and terror collided as she read the long list Brethren Amalgamated Insurance had sent her. When she looked up, Elias sat on the front porch steps, the dogs at his feet.

"Is something wrong, Violet?"

She shoved the letter at him. "That rat bastard Max Maitland thinks he's found a way to get me off this farm, but so help me, Elias, he will not succeed. Now more than ever, he and his low down, rotten, dirty, disgusting tricks will not succeed."

CHAPTER FOURTEEN

"It's legal," James Knightley said. "I'm sorry, Violet, but the fine print on the policy gives them a right of inspection, and you have a duty to maintain the premises in fit and habitable condition."

Elias had no fondness for lawyers, though Knightley had come on a weekend to sit at Violet's kitchen table and frighten her at her request.

"What does fit and habitable mean?" Elias said. "The house is entirely habitable, the barn is a dwelling for livestock, not the queen mum."

"I know what fit and habitable means," Violet said. "It means exactly what this letters says it means. If I don't do all of these repairs in the next sixty days, and have receipts to show the work is done, then they can terminate my policy or refuse to honor claims. If I can't find another insurance company to provide coverage for the farm, then the bank can accelerate my mortgage."

"I'd have to read the mortgage documents before I'd go that far," Knightley said. He was blond, lanky, and according to Violet, a competent farmer himself, but he was also a god-damned lawyer. His thorough reading of the mortgage documents would cost Violet as much as some of the "suggested" repairs.

"Is there anything on that list you were planning to do anyway?" Elias asked.

Violet held the letter by one corner, as if it were a filthy rag. "I clean the gutters and downspouts in the fall, after the leaves have come off the trees. I didn't get to it last year, but everything seems to be draining well enough. But the rest of this… I just repointed and parged the barn foundation four years ago and it cost an entire year's profit. The homestead cottage has never been painted, and the windows… They want me to replace nearly every window in the house, which is another fortune, and paint the barn, as well as replace damaged siding? There is no damaged siding. It's just old, and painting the wood will accelerate its deterioration."

While improving the property's curb appeal, of course. Far easier to sell a pretty foreclosure than a homely one.

Elias had been on the roof, and the gutters and downspouts could well use cleaning. Anybody could see that the shade trees had limbs overhanging the house, and the insurance company wanted all of those limbs cut down.

"I'd heard something about Brethren's hate mail campaign," Knightley said. "My guess is they're positioning themselves to be bought out by a larger firm, and any property with a policy more than a few years old is apparently getting the same sort of list."

"But no inspector came around," Violet said. "Aren't they supposed to send notice before they snoop on your property?"

"Notices get lost or tossed in the trash because they look like junk mail," Knightley said. "I can get after the hanging limbs, Violet."

"That's very kind of you, James, but—"

Elias put a hand on Violet's arm. The idea of her high up in a tree, wrestling a damned chainsaw with nobody else on the premises to know if she fell, suffered an injury, or got into difficulties made his blood run cold.

Violet looked at him for the first time since this impromptu kitchen conference had begun. Her gaze was devastated, broken, defeated.

"I'll take care of the gutters and downspouts this afternoon," Elias said. "Knightley can help with that, and I'll give him a hand with the tree limbs."

"But the windows, Elias, the masonry work, the painting—what is the point? Maitland will have my mortgage accelerated before my corn is ready to harvest."

Knightley rose and helped himself to a brownie from the pan on the counter. "I'd listen to Brodie, Violet. In the first place, the tree limbs are a safety hazard. They come down on your power lines, and it's bad news—expensive bad news. The gutters and downspouts prevent water damage, and as many storms as we get around here, you don't want to mess with water damage. That you take care of the obvious hazards makes it much harder for an insurance company to allege negligence if they want to refuse a claim. I'll get my saw, see if my brothers can spare a few hours."

"This inspector," Violet said, tossing the letter on the table. "I'm guessing he came on a farmers market day. I wouldn't have been here to keep an eye on him or chase him off. Maxwell Maitland had better hope I never come across him or his minions in a dark alley."

Elias would come across Maitland on Tuesday morning. "The idea," he said, "is for you to make a show of good faith. You do what you can immediately, taking pictures of the work before, during, and after. You pay Knightley for his time, and he gives you a receipt."

"And then I tear up your check," Knightley said, getting the milk out of the fridge. "Neils Haddonfield has done some masonry work for me. He'd probably take a look at your barn for a very reasonable sum. Nobody likes a bully, Violet, and Maitland is arguably bullying you."

Elias positively hated a bully. "Don't take the last of the milk, Knightley. Violet might want another brownie."

"I have plenty," Violet said, rising and wandering to the window sill. She tested the soil of the African violets she'd watered less than two hours ago, then tried to lower the sash, which resisted before screeching down two inches. "The window replacements will beggar me. Nobody does a good job on windows for less than a fortune."

"The windows don't leak," Elias said. "You show the insurance company all the work you've done, dab some paint on the window frames, and document that the windows are still quite functional. When was the last time you put in a claim against your policy, Violet?"

Her next task was to dump out the dog's water bowl that Elias had recently filled. "I've never put in a claim on the property policy. For decades, the premiums have been paid, as regular as clockwork, and now this."

Knightley downed a glass of milk, rinsed it out, and wiped his hands on the towel hanging over the oven handle.

"I'm off to get my tools, and round up a brother or two. Brodie, nice to meet you." Knightley's handshake was firm, but the look in his eyes was commiserating. He doubtless knew that Elias was doing business with the very devil threatening to see Violet evicted from her farm.

The quiet in Knightley's absence should have been peaceful. The occasional sheep baa'd out in the field, a confused cricket was chirping from the direction of the back porch.

"This is my fault," Elias said, taking Violet by the shoulders. "I'm sorry."

She was unresisting in his embrace, also un-reciprocating. "How do you figure that?"

"If your valley works anything like my glens and shires, Maitland knows I'm acquainted with you. Our properties adjoin, my cousin's truck has been seen sitting in your driveway for hours at a time since I arrived last weekend. I was supposed to cheerfully accept whatever offer Maitland made at our first meeting, a contingency contract, a pittance in earnest money, anything. I sent the negotiation in a different direction, and this is the result."

Violet slipped away and took the lid off the trash can, drawing out the plastic garbage bag inside.

"James says I'm not being singled out," Violet said, tying the trash bag closed. She extracted a fresh bag from a drawer, relined the trash container, and replaced the lid. "If this is a coincidence, though, it's the worst possible timing."

Elias took out the trash, when he wanted instead to deal Maitland the kind of physical blow that satisfied primitive impulses and solved nothing. When he returned to the kitchen, Violet was wiping down spotless counters.

She'd sweep next, or clean out the refrigerator. The impulse to restore order, to tidy and clean and assert control, was one Elias had learned early. When life went to hell, getting organized—

Insight clobbered him as he stood in the middle of Violet's kitchen.

He tidied up businesses in disarray. He tidied up familial situations that wanted resolution—Jeannie needing a job, Zebedee wanting company on his polo jaunts. Elias was hellbent on tidying up a castle that generations of Brodies had neglected.

"Violet, stop."

She straightened, folding the rag. "Is something wrong?"

Everything was wrong. Violet should sell her damned farm to Maitland for a huge sum, leave this valley behind, and set up a not-for-profit that advocated for family farms.

After she married Elias.

None of which was likely to happen, but he could at least open one door for her anyway.

"I want you to make a phone call for me," Elias said, getting out his cell. "I have a friend who took her blog from a casual set of personal observations to a paying website, to a thriving not-for-profit. Her issue is healthy food, healthy eating. You'd like her." Elias considered Lady Christina Decatur a dear friend, and had at one time been engaged to her. He scribbled her phone number on the tablet sitting on the table. "Promise me you'll talk to her."

Violet hung the rag over the spigot. "Farms are all about healthy food, especially family farms. Not that I'll have a farm much longer."

Elias hated it when Violet cried, even though he was probably among the privileged few to witness her tears.

"Give Christina my regards," Elias said. "And stop mourning a farm you haven't lost yet. I'm meeting with Maitland on Tuesday, and if he thinks this petty behavior will bring about the result he wants, he's in for a very rude awakening."

Violet stuffed the phone number in her pocket. "Elias, be careful. Maitland is tenacious, well funded, and well connected."

"I have been careful," Elias said. "For twenty goddamned years, I have been careful, and being careful won't make anybody's dreams come true. I'll be on the roof. Send Knightley up when he returns."

He kissed Violet passionately, then headed out the back door without another word.

* * *

Violet called Neils Haddonfield, who managed the therapeutic riding barn at the north end of the valley. His busy season would hit as soon as school let out, which was just weeks away, but he promised to take a look at Violet's barn in the next few days.

As for painting the barn, that wasn't going to happen. Violet would reconstruct her father's research regarding the durability of weathered wood. The window replacements would be exorbitant, but the boots tromping around on Violet's roof wouldn't let her dwell on that looming blow. Elias didn't know how to give up, and he had a point.

Three years ago, Violet had used every tool at her command to stop Max Maitland from turning one of the valley's largest hay farms into a subdivision. Why shouldn't she work equally hard to preserve her own property? Why had she been willing to accept defeat without throwing a single punch in her own defense?

"Because I am broke, tired, and already trying to wrap my aching head around the Hedstrom property being chopped into cul-de-sacs," she muttered.

Bruno hopped into her lap.

She put him down. "I have one more call to make. I promised Elias."

She had to call Christina Decatur, whom she hated sight unseen. Elias cared for this woman. She was probably skinny, blond, spoke eight languages, and looked more stylish in her jeans than Violet had ever looked in her life.

Violet punched in the numbers—a lot of them.

"Christina here," said a cheery British voice.

"Hello, Christina. My name is Violet Hughes, and Elias Brodie asked me to call you."

"Any friend of Elias's is a friend of mine. How is he?" No hesitation, no awkwardness, and the question was genuine.

"He's on my roof right now, cleaning out my gutters. I think he's angry. He suggested you know how to turn a blog into a business."

James was on the roof too, in the blazing sun. An occasional cascade of dead leaves and twigs would fall past Violet's kitchen windows, suggesting the gutters were badly in need of cleaning.

"Elias said that? He's an idiot. He's the one who gave me the idea. I was in-patient for the fifth time, and Elias was ready to kidnap me, he was so frustrated with my lack of—young man, what have I told you about when Mum's on the phone?"

The shift in Christina's tone was amazing. In the space of a breath, she went from Mary Poppins' bubbly younger sister to the Dowager Countess of Doom.

"Sorry," she said. "Three is such a determined age. What is your blog about?"

"Farming, specifically family farming and agricultural land preservation. What about yours?"

"How to not become a bulimic or fall back into it," Christina said. "Wretched business nearly killed me, and ruined my engagement to Elias. Is he in love with you?"

What had this to do with starting a business? And yet, anybody who could blithely announce a history of eating disorders would probably have an excellent bullshit—

"You were *engaged* to Elias?"

When Violet should have been jealous, she instead felt a pang of sorrow for her lover. Elias had hoped to build a future with Christina, and his hopes had not turned out as planned.

"It was years ago," Christina said, "but Elias wouldn't mention it, because he's such a gudgeon. Do you have a moment, because the story—if you do not get off that table this instant, I won't take you with me when I walk Pepper."

The conversation proceeded in the same vein, startlingly personal information interspersed with parenting directives, and then the sound of a child—possibly a child sitting in Christina's lap—humming softly.

Christina had nothing flattering to say about Elias's first fiancée, a mercenary trust fund princess who'd put on a grand show of charitable interests long enough to catch Elias's eye. He'd had a narrow escape, in Christina's opinion, but his relationship with Christina had been more rebound-driven than he'd been able to admit.

"Even after we became engaged, I held him at arm's length, so to speak," Christina said, "owing to body image issues the likes of which nobody ever talks about. Elias came upon me on my knees in the loo, and realized immediately what was afoot. It all came out, the previous hospitalizations, the failed therapies, my family's exasperation."

The boots on the roof had gone quiet. Violet had visions of James and Elias perched on the peak, having a guy talk about guy stuff, while she and Christina talked about sad stuff.

"What did Elias do?" Violet asked, because she couldn't imagine him turning his back on a fiancée when she'd most needed support.

"He found me a program I hadn't tried before, one with some history of actually providing treatment instead of 28 days of lecturing, shaming, and attractively disgusting meals. I didn't want my family to know, so Elias paid for it all, came to the family days, never breathed a word to anybody. I'd been there three weeks when he told me to stop blaming myself for a past that couldn't be changed, and instead to use my beautiful heart to help others. He said that—my beautiful heart."

"Elias says things other people don't have the courage to say."

"Elias knows that tomorrow isn't promised," Christina replied. "And he's a caretaker to his bones. Lovely, lovely man, though I couldn't marry him, not after that. He said he understood, but with him, one doesn't know. Tell me about your blog."

While somebody hummed an off-key version of *The Farmer in the Dell*, Violet described her blog, her audience, her plans and dreams for expanded content, newsletters, forums, and guest posts. Christina responded with observations about monetizing, ad revenue, grants, and products. When Elias and James came in the back door arguing about duct tape and baling twine, Violet had been on the phone for nearly an hour.

"Is that Christina?" Elias asked, passing James a heather ale.

Violet nodded.

Elias gestured for the phone, and Violet passed it over.

"Have you killed the boy yet?" Elias's question was rife with affection. He talked to the child—his godson, apparently—and asked after Christina's business, her husband, and her parents.

The conversation was so normal, so warm-hearted. Violet listened to the tone more than the content, her mind abuzz with the ideas she and Christina had discussed, the hopes and dreams that hadn't germinated even an hour ago.

And yet, as Elias rang off with a casual "give the boy a hug for me," Violet was equally aware of Christina's comment, about Elias being a caretaker to his bones. He was, though not in an unhealthy sense that Violet could see.

And yet, a question plagued Violet, as James and Elias switched to arguing about the best way to maintain a chainsaw.

Elias was a caretaker—of properties, charitable businesses, people, and entire family legacies.

But who looked after Elias?

* * *

"*Lady* Christina Decatur, your former fiancée?" Dunstan asked for the third time. "You put your current girlfriend on the phone with a former fiancée? Did you take a fall from Violet's roof?"

"It's not as if Christina and I were physically intimate," Elias said. The fireflies were out in greater numbers tonight, odd little lights glowing and fading in the gathering darkness of the hedgerow behind Dunstan's yard.

"Did you tell Violet that?"

"I suspect Christina did." Violet had been so animated when Elias had come upon her in the kitchen yesterday. She'd been pacing, the phone to her ear, her free hand waving about as she'd made some point about milkweeds and blueberries.

"I'm a deliriously happily married woman," Jane said from Dunstan's side, "but what sort of woman is engaged to *you* without taking the occasional test drive?"

Dunstan patted her hand. "Not every member of the family is as irresistible as your husband, wee Jane."

"I chose to be flattered that Christina—unlike her predecessor—would commit to me without sampling my charms," Elias said. "Christina was in significant difficulties and I barely noticed, which is apparently not unusual with the problem she battled. The simpler explanation is that I was an idiot." He was becoming proficient at idiocy. "Do you know what bothers me the most about this whole situation?"

"There's so much to choose from," Dunstan said. "Selling your land to a developer when you'd rather keep it in cultivation, leaving behind the first woman you've truly fallen for, imprisoning yourself in a tower of debt for the sake of a pile of rocks, ruining Violet's valley—"

Jane kissed Dunstan about two seconds before Elias would have smacked him. "Sweetie, Elias needs cheering up, not a litany of regrets."

"If he stays here and farms the land, he'll be a lot cheerier," Dunstan countered, kissing her back. "Though he might not smell as lovely. The castle isn't going anywhere, except possibly to the bottom of the loch."

The kissing and cuddling didn't bother Elias as they had a week ago. Dunstan had fallen, and Jane had caught him by the heart.

And Dunstan was, in his lawyerly, Scottish way, trying to cheer Elias up by inviting some friendly violence.

"What bothers me most," Elias said, "is that when I leave here, Violet will be working her farm, as her family always has, but Maitland will have an 800-acre toehold right across the road. Even if he doesn't go after Violet's farm next, he'll build up all around her, until she can't possibly qualify for the conservation easement."

The weekend had been spent sprucing up Violet's property in hopes the insurance company would be placated. The stonemason had said cosmetic effort alone would put the barn to rights, but replacing windows on an entire farmhouse would cost thousands.

"Violet will never sell to Maitland," Dunstan said.

The crickets chirped, the fireflies drifted, and Elias contemplated how much sorrow could fit into two syllables. He might well *never* see Violet again, never hold her again, never make love with her again.

All of that hurt like hell, but hurt was a fact of life. Worse than the hurt was the sense of abandoning Violet with the enemy setting up camp on her very door step—and at Elias's invitation. Come spring, Maitland might claim her gas tank had leaked into the soil, or her sheep had gotten loose on his property. Her dogs might turn up missing or injured.

If Maitland had committed arson, he had no scruples. Maitland didn't strike Elias as stupid enough to set a fire in broad daylight when anybody could have driven by, though.

"Elias, can't you commute from Scotland?" Jane asked. "Dulles Airport is handy, and Dunstan describes you a frequent traveler. Just pop over every couple months, beat Dunstan at chess, keep in touch with Violet? Even farmers get some down time over the winter. Maybe Violet could do New Year's in Scotland."

"Elias hates to fly over water," Dunstan said. "Not that anybody should blame him."

"I hate to fly, period," Elias said, "but one copes. Violet claims the last crops can come off as late as November, December is for accounting, and the lambs start coming in January. What she's not saying—what she doesn't have to say—is that a relationship with the man who betrayed her valley doesn't interest her."

"She's interested," Jane said, stifling a yawn. "She watches you the way I used to watch Dunstan when he had a case before mine. His closing arguments were… Well, I paid very close attention."

"Let's turn in," Dunstan said, rising and drawing Jane to her feet. "And you can hear a closing argument from me of a different sort."

In Scotland, the newly married cousins would never have flirted like this before Elias. His failed engagements, his upbringing in the home of a bachelor uncle, his history, his work, everything had set him apart. Odd, that Dunstan, the one who'd wandered the farthest, made Elias feel like a cousin again.

"You going to bed?" Jane asked.

"Soon," Elias replied. "I have some thinking to do."

Dunstan cuffed him on the back of the head. "Think all you like, and it won't change a thing. This is not a problem you can think your way through."

"Dunstan, leave him alone," Jane said, leading her husband by the hand.

"Yeah," Elias said, reciprocating the blow. "Leave me alone or wee Jane will turn you over her knee."

"You see before you a man sustained by hope." Dunstan saluted and let his wife lead him away.

The two of them wafted into the house on a cloud of marital bliss, while Elias shut off the porch light, and took up a seat at the top of the porch steps.

Summer nights in Damson Valley were alive in a way Elias hadn't experienced in Scotland. Night birds, bats, and droves of insects filled the air, while small animals skittered through the underbrush. The humidity lent every scent more weight, so that mown grass, woods, and baskets of petunias all perfumed the darkness.

Wallace butted his head against Elias's arm, then climbed into Elias's lap. The cat was a comfort, but no substitute for a hand to hold, or someone to love.

"Why is it, cat, that I feel more satisfaction from cleaning Violet's gutters than from saving a lovely old castle?"

The weekend had been educational, and gratifying. Mowing a field for Violet, changing the oil in her tractor, piling up the cut tree limbs for next year's firewood had felt relevant, real. Not like sitting around a conference table and brainstorming a new mission statement for an organization that needed a heart far more than it needed a catchy slogan.

"And I'll leave Violet here, with the worst possible threat building his empire directly across the road from her farm. Maitland is apparently well connected, determined, and ruthless."

Wallace dug his claws into Elias's thigh hard enough to hurt, just as Maitland would dig his claws into Violet's valley—if Elias gave him the opportunity.

CHAPTER FIFTEEN

"I should come out there, bring Ebersole and maybe Wainwright," Pete Sutherland said. "They've both played the course at St. Andrew's, you know. Eight-hundred acres is not something you want to negotiate on your own, Max. No offense, but we've been at this game a lot longer than you have."

Max was offended. Lately he was offended every time he talked with Sutherland or one of his investment buddies, who thought a grasp of civil engineering and complicated budgets resulted from walking manicured golf courses.

Sutherland and his usual gang of idiots were the primary reason Violet Hughes had been able to torpedo the Poplar Cove development three years ago. Sutherland had taken over the microphone at a public hearing, and good-old-boy condescended to a woman who'd rained down facts and figures like a Maryland thunderstorm.

The zoning board had listened, the locals had smirked all the way to the feed store, and Max had kept Sutherland at arms' length from any transaction of significance since.

"It's a simple deal," Max said, switching the phone to his other ear so he could use his mouse. "We're buying the land, straight up. The preliminary appraisals are done, the deed is clean, the only dickering to do is over the price. If you bring half your posse, you'll spook this guy."

A few hours of high-dollar cyber-research confirmed that Elias Brodie was what Max aspired to be—an international businessman. His origins might be Scottish, but his home turf was any conference table where assets and revenue were under discussion. Brodie had turned around more than a few not-for-profits, and his own resources included an earldom, an honest-to-God castle, some sort of baronial lodge, significant land, and an amazingly diverse and green portfolio.

"You sure we can't talk him into a contingency?" Sutherland asked. "A ninety-day exclusive? We're prepared to be generous with regard to earnest money."

A deluge of emails had assured Max just how generous, but Brodie wasn't a fool. Earnest money was spare change compared to the sale price. Max scrolled through a search of images from Aberdeenshire, Scotland, the terrain bearing a close resemblance to western Maryland.

Pretty, in other words. Low mountains, rolling fields, plenty of surface water, beautiful vistas. Some of the best salmon-fishing streams in the world flowed through Aberdeen. Too bad nobody had thought to develop that land.

"Max, are you listening to me? If you can't close this deal on Tuesday, the guys and I will have to look for another project elsewhere."

"Just printing out the last of the preliminary appraisals," Max said. "They all came in within a five percent range, which makes the pricing simple."

"You're offering too much," Sutherland said. "I'm telling you, Max, start out low. First rule of business. Start out low. Costs you nothing, earns you respect from your opponent. What time is this meeting?"

The meeting was tomorrow morning, which meant Max would endure at least three more calls from Sutherland, possibly some from his co-investors, none of whom knew how to use a nail gun, much less how to develop a piece of land without getting sued.

And Pete's threat—close tomorrow or the investors would walk—was anything but casual.

Down the hall, Bonnie and Derek were having their first argument of the week, and abruptly, Max had had enough. Enough micro-management from the privileged buffoons pulling his strings, enough putting up with bickering co-workers, enough balancing everybody's ego but his own.

Time for a little walk-away posturing. "I've been thinking, Pete."

"What have I told you about thinking?"

"Do we really want to get involved up to the neck with yet another residential development?"

A pause ensued, while Pete probably closed the game of solitaire he'd been losing. "What are you saying, Max?"

Get off my back. "We've done housing developments, nice ones, but this is the same old, same old. You wanted a project that would boot you into the big leagues. Is this it? Sediment and erosion control, curb and gutter, metes and bounds. It's the same drill, only larger, and we have no guarantee that the zoning board will play nice-nice come public meeting time. Maybe we should keep looking."

"I don't have time to keep looking," Sutherland retorted with gratifying alacrity. "The tax man cometh, Max, and that means the revenue has to be invested. Eight hundred acres is not the same drill. Nobody else has built anything that size that far out from D.C. and Baltimore, and I thought you said a strip mall was a possibility?"

"Be a lot of off-site road improvement," Max said, though every development of any size required modifying the highways and intersections in the immediate area.

"Like that has ever stopped us? You don't understand money, Max. You have to spend money to make money, and this deal has money written all over it."

"I always make you a healthy profit," Max replied, while the argument down the hallway escalated. "I'll make you a healthy profit on this project too, but next time around, let's think outside the box, Pete."

"As long as you bring in the money, you can think in a geosynchronous orbit over Disneyworld. Let me know how the meeting goes."

He hung up, and Max placed the receiver back on its cradle. The projects Max managed for Sutherland had been very profitable, because Max did not believe in building junk. Shoddy work cost a lot more to replace—or to litigate—than it did to get right the first time. His subcontractors either played by that rule or worked for somebody else, and the eventual buyers were willing to pay for value.

And yet, the notion of turning eight-hundred acres of farmland into yet another well laid out, pretty, inviting, instant neighborhood should have pleased Max more than it did—a lot more. Violet Hughes would dig in her heels as only Violet Hughes could, and she'd dog the construction phase like a bad rash. Telephoto lenses came to mind, and injunctions, and stop work orders.

"For God's sake, Derek it isn't your coffee maker. What part of asking permission don't you understand?"

Bonnie wasn't merely irritated. She was furious. Max shoved away from his desk and headed for the kitchen.

"What is wrong with you, Bonbon?" Derek held a cup of coffee in one hand, the scent suggesting he'd helped himself to the good stuff. "It's Monday. Mon-Day. A little joe to start the day is the American way, and the purpose of a coffee maker is to make coffee. I thought you wanted me to keep a fresh pot going for you?"

He imbued the last suggestion with lascivious intent, which was as disgusting as it was pathetic. Max got out his phone, and swiped it into video recording mode.

"This coffee maker was sitting underneath my desk," Bonnie spat. "The coffee was *in my shoulder bag*, and that means, you got into my personal space, and my personal effects to help yourself without permission. That's stealing, Derek."

Derek apparently hadn't sensed Max lurking behind him in the doorway, or

Derek was stupid enough not to care that he had an audience.

"You are the most uptight, controlling bitch," Derek retorted. "So I helped myself to your damned coffee without asking? Why don't you get laid and chill out? If you're that hard up, we can leave the lights out and I'll make an exception to my no pity-fucking rule. Either that, or find another job, Bonbon. I don't need your PMS on top of everything else I have going on."

He patted Bonnie's breast and took a sip of his coffee. *Patted her breast.*

The guy had a death wish. Max couldn't see Derek's expression, but he could see Bonnie's. He slipped his phone in his pocket, took three steps forward, and positioned himself between Derek and Bonnie.

"I'd set the coffee down," Max said. "You don't want to be holding anything hot when Bonnie slaps the shit out of you."

"She knows better than to assault a lawyer," Derek retorted.

Bonnie moved to stand by the door. If looks could kill, Derek would have been a scorched circle on the floor tiles.

"Bonnie," Max said, "may I see you in my office?"

"Sure, Max."

She left without a backward glance. Derek watched her go, his gaze fixed on her backside.

"Pack your desk," Max said. "Don't finish the coffee you stole, don't bother putting on your wounded-bro act, don't so much as sneer, or I will re-arrange your face and swear on a stack of Bibles you fell against the door. Bonnie will swear on a bigger stack of Bibles that I'm telling the truth too."

Derek took a slow sip of his contraband brew. "Max, the white hat just doesn't suit you, buddy. Wrong fashion accessory. If you want to suck up to a woman who thinks she runs a law office because she can type half-decently, that's your little-dick problem. What I'm going to need you to do, though, is explain to Bonnie that—"

Max took the coffee from him, held it long enough that even Derek understood he was at risk for a scalding, then dumped it in the sink.

"Pack. Your. Desk. Leave your keys in the mail tray. Your lease agreement provides that you can be evicted for moral turpitude at the sole discretion of the lessor, who would be me. Go, and go quietly, or you'll wish you had."

Derek leaned back against the counter and crossed his arms, the soul of nonchalance. "Are you threatening me, Max? Over a cup of coffee?"

A phrase Max's mother had used came to mind: *He's dead and he won't lie down.* "I'm evicting you, and if need be, I'll start the legal proceedings, and have the sheriff's deputies here putting your worldly goods in the street. Bonnie is taking the rest of the day off, recovering from a migraine. You are finding a new address."

Max left Derek slouched against the kitchen counter, trying to look sophisticated and amused, and failing.

"You OK?" Max asked, when he'd closed the door to his office. Bonnie sat at the table by the window, dry-eyed and composed, when she ought to be ranting and throwing things.

"I can't work here anymore," she said. "I'm sorry, Max, and I might need some unemployment and a reference, but you saw… I can't believe he did that. I can't—"

Her chin quivered, and Max wanted to throw something fragile. He got out his cell phone, and queued up the video.

"You are filing a sexual harassment claim, and you will sue for damages, Bonnie. I can't represent you because I'm a witness, should Hendershot be stupid enough not to settle. His father will likely pay any amount you name, but it won't be enough to save Derek's license to practice law."

Bonnie watched the vignette, her expression clearing. "Did I ever tell you that you are my favorite rat bastard lawyer in the world, Max Maitland?"

"Rat bastard lawyer is an oxymoron to some people. I'll file a complaint with the bar association, and by this time next month, Derek Hendershot will be in very, very hot water."

Bonnie reached for a tissue and replayed the video. "He really is awful. You're going after his license to practice law?"

Max watched the images of Derek petting Bonnie's breast. To create a stink like this in a rural jurisdiction now, when a major project was about to come to life, was bad timing. Max couldn't get the hell out of Dodge when he'd need to work closely with the zoning board and find office space here for his engineers and accountants.

"I won't have to go after his license to practice law. Bar counsel will investigate, interview us both, watch this video, and probably give Derek the option of surrendering his license voluntarily. I'm doing the citizens of Damson Valley a favor."

Which would earn him not one iota of support for his project.

Bonnie passed him back his phone. "Max, are you OK?"

Well, no, he wasn't. He was in the unenviable position of seeing his wishes fulfilled, and being less than impressed with the view. Damson Valley was crying out for development—beyond doubt—and the Hedstrom property was a terrific place to start the process, despite Violet Hughes's perch across the road.

But the project would take years to see through, the job would be uphill every inch of the way, and most of the money would go to a bunch of smug, lazy bastards whose idea of work was carving the Christmas roast. Max would get a good salary out of it, and another paragraph on his resume, and that would be…

Max emailed the video to himself and to Bonnie. "You ever get bored being a legal admin, Bonnie?"

"I've been bored for about twenty years, give or take, but I've also been able to pay my bills. That was the front door slamming."

"Derek has been evicted," Max said. "A moral turpitude clause comes in handy, even if it's largely unenforceable."

Bonnie's smile was downright diabolical. "You know what the best part is?"

The best part would be… Max wasn't sure what the best part would be. Hundreds of families would have beautiful homes in a beautiful setting, the local economy would grow significantly, job security would improve for the service sector, and tax revenues would give the local government options it couldn't dream of now.

And not one person would thank Max Maitland for making it happen, though like Bonnie, his bills would be paid, and that mattered a very, very great deal.

"The best part is my bills will be paid, too, Bonnie."

"Nope," Bonnie said, getting to her feet. "The best part is, if Derek wants to contest my complaint, or appeal the ethics findings, not a single attorney in this town will represent him."

"You're right," Max said. "That is a cheering thought. Can you call a locksmith or shall I?"

"I'll be happy to," Bonnie said. "As it happens, I know a guy with a lock and key service. He's kinda cute too, and a first rate dancer."

Bonnie sashayed out, ready to boot scoot new locks onto the premises, while Max surveyed his office. The flowers were all but shot, only the last blossom on each stem retaining its appearance. Tomorrow's meeting with Brodie called for fresh flowers but the farmers market wasn't open on Mondays.

"To hell with it," Max muttered, tossing the flowers into the trash. "Brodie will sell, for the next five years I'll work my ass off making Sutherland another few million, and Violet Hughes will hate me worse than ever. What's not to like?"

* * *

Monday arrived, and as the day wore on, Violet realized Elias would not be making an excuse to stop by. Over the weekend, Elias and various Knightley brothers had tended to all the repairs and maintenance that basic ability, power tools, and hard work could see to. Niels Haddonfield would get after the barn foundation over the next week.

Where Violet was supposed to get the money to replace windows she did not know, but that was the sole item remaining on the insurance company's list.

The little blue hybrid tooled around the bend, and Violet's heart leapt. What did it say about her, that she wanted to see Elias one more time, even if he sold his farm to Max Maitland, headed off to Scotland, and never set foot in Maryland again?

Which was exactly what he ought to do, from his perspective.

The compact turned up Violet's drive, bringing the dogs to attention. Both

Sarge and Murphy had started the day with a romp in the creek, and were consigned to the front porch until they dried.

Violet had joined them in their exile, to stare at the empty property across the road and wait for the phone to ring.

Jane de Luca got out of the car, looking professional and tidy in a forest green ensemble of slacks and a blazer. People who worked in offices dressed differently on weekdays. Farmers dressed for work every day.

"Good morning," Jane said, coming up the steps. "Do they bite?"

"They're wet," Violet replied. "They either shake all over your clean clothes, or stink you into submission. Sarge, Murphy, stay."

"I like dogs," Jane said. "I like cats too. That guy could be Wallace's brother."

Bruno sat on the porch railing, looking pleased with himself, as usual.

"He's an orphan from Elias's farm, abandoned by the caretaker. Is everything all right?" Jane was a lovely person, and family to Elias, but she was also a lawyer and making a house call in her lawyer finery.

"I wanted to ask you the same thing," Jane said. "Elias and Dunstan are supposed to meet with Maitland tomorrow. That has to be just about killing you."

"Have a seat," Violet said, because the thought of that meeting was killing her—forget just about—and Jane wasn't here in a lawyering capacity. "Can I get you some iced tea or lemonade?"

"How about half and half?"

"With or without ice?" Elias drank his cold beverages without ice, for no reason Violet could discern.

"Without," Jane said. "This valley is truly beautiful."

"Odd, how we notice what we care about only when it's slipping from our grasp." Violet went to the kitchen to pour the drinks, also to triple check her phone for missed calls. Jane was on the glide-a-rocker when Violet returned to the porch, Bruno sitting beside her.

"Thanks," Jane said. "So, you're OK with Elias selling his property to Max Maitland?"

What must it be like for Elias, to be bunking in with a pair of lawyers who were also family?

"I am not OK with it," Violet began, pacing the length of the porch. She'd repainted the porch herself two summers ago, a big, dirty job that had nonetheless improved the appearance of the house significantly.

"I'm here to buy eggs, by the way," Jane said. "Dunstan nearly decided to come along, but Elias is closeted with him this afternoon going over figures and contract language."

"Maitland sent a draft contract?" That would be like him, prepared down to the last detail. In anybody else, Violet might have admired such thoroughness.

"Violet, sit. Your wandering around is making me queasy, and you don't want to know what comes after queasy these days."

Violet sat, so Bruno was curled between her and Jane.

"Maitland did not send a draft contract," Jane said, holding the sweating glass against her cheek. "Elias has a zillion tradesmen swarming his castle, and some of them were already under contract to Zebedee. Dunstan has the contract law gene, so he's reviewing the documents with Elias, pointing out trouble spots and oversights. In at least two cases, Zebedee signed the tradesman's version of the contract with no modifications, and that's not good."

"When my dad died, we had the same sort of mess. What was the estate bound by, what was dischargeable due his having passed away? It was awful." And then the life insurance company had played games that only James Knightley at his most ruthless had been able to foil.

Now here was Elias, having to wade through a similar mess.

"Did Elias tell you about the roof over the long hall?" Jane asked.

"No, but I'm guessing it's not good news."

Bruno hopped down, sniffed each dog's nose, and then leapt from the porch to the grass. The day was slipping away, and still, Violet's phone hadn't rung.

"If I were a mouse," Jane said, "I'd hide but good. Dunstan claims if you have a cat preying on the mice, you're less likely to be troubled by snakes looking for the same—"

Now, when Jane de Luca sat two feet away, Violet's phone rang. She'd switched the ringtone to *The Farmer in the Dell*, after yesterday's discussion with Christina.

"Answer it," Jane said. "I'll just enjoy my drink and the lovely view."

Violet swiped into the call, cursing the timing. "Max, thanks for returning my call." She didn't bother sounding cordial. This was business, something at which Max Maitland excelled.

"Violet."

Good, nobody intended to indulge in farcical small talk. "You're meeting with Elias Brodie tomorrow regarding the sale of his property. I have a proposal for you."

Jane shot her a look worthy of Bruno when the dogs tried to steal his food dish. *What the hell?*

"I'm listening, Violet."

"You want to develop the Hedstrom property, and I hate the very idea. That farm is the largest agricultural parcel in the valley, with first rate soils, excellent topography, a clean environmental bill of health, and good surface water."

"All of which makes it well suited to development," Max countered. "People have to live somewhere, Violet. Why should your cows be the only ones to enjoy that view?"

Max's question was probably his idea of rational debate. It only sounded like baiting.

"I don't have cows. If you'd paid attention on your little fire-setting sortie, you'd know that."

"What fire-setting sortie?"

If he'd sounded indignant, Violet might have dismissed his query. He sounded cold—very, extremely, menacingly cold.

"This winter, somebody set my woodpile on fire, which could have easily sent my barn up in flames, and possibly spread from there. I happened to be home, and have frost free spigots in the barn yard. I was able to put out the fire. I know what you're capable of, hence my proposal."

"Somebody set a fire on your property? You're accusing me of *arson*?"

"I did not accuse you of arson because I didn't see the fire set," and Violet did not want to discuss past vandalism, no matter how vicious or dangerous. "You play dirty, I know that. You also build half-decent projects."

Jane rose and perched on the porch railing, as if she'd put distance between herself and the conversation. Would that Violet could do likewise.

"I build excellent projects, and I do not play dirty. If you called simply to antagonize me, then we're done talking, lady."

They weren't talking, they were negotiating. "So you didn't set the insurance dogs on me, demanding that I bankrupt myself doing five years of maintenance in sixty days—half that maintenance cosmetic rather than structural?"

The silence on the other end of the line was interesting. "Your policy is with Brethren?"

Why had she hoped Maitland had nothing to do with her problems? "Yes, unless they dump me for failure to turn this place into a family farm postcard. If I lose insurance coverage, I will be non-compliant with the terms of my mortgage. The bank will accelerate the loan, and I'll be out one farm. If that's not playing dirty, Max, I don't know what is."

Murphy rose and sniffed at Jane, who petted his mostly dry head gingerly. Because Murphy was a dog without shame, this encouraged him to wag his tail, and bump his nose against Jane's hand.

Antifreeze tasted good to dogs, though it also killed them. Anybody who'd set a fire, and see a mortgage unfairly accelerated would leave a dish of antifreeze out in a discreet location frequented only by farm dogs.

Violet could not best such an enemy.

"I play hardball," Max said. "I do not play dirty, and neither do you. Brethren, however, is apparently positioning itself to be bought, so they're harassing their policy holders into minimizing the risk of claims. If they jerk your policy, the mortgagor will put you into a forced coverage pool, which will probably result in reduced premiums."

"And?"Violet had forgotten that Maitland was a lawyer by training, but he wore the role well.

"And the forced coverage insurance will pay off your mortgage in the event of a catastrophe, but it won't do anything to help you rebuild. The mortgage companies have learned that too much foreclosure isn't a good thing, and the insurance companies feel the same way about making too many payouts. You won't lose your farm over Brethren's wish list."

Violet would ask James to verify that conclusion, though James would probably charge her for doing the research.

"Why would I believe you, when accelerating my mortgage would be a perfect way for you to add my farm to the Hedstrom development?"

"So don't believe me, but my grasp of Maryland property law is probably the best you'll find. Moreover, I don't want your farm, not right now."

Relief, cautious and pathetic, coursed through her. "What's wrong with my farm?"

"You are ornery," Maitland said. "I mean that as a compliment, though I don't expect you to believe a word out of my mouth. I don't want your farm, because buying eight hundred acres on spec is a big enough risk without adding your property to the pile. Every acre I buy is another acre that might have once been a dump, a colonial grave yard, a pit for tossing out old paint cans and weed killer. I also want to be able to sell these lots as having scenic views, and with you as a neighbor, I can be certain at least the eastern boundary of the property will never be developed. I do not want your farm, Violet."

"Good, because I'm not selling it to you." And according to Max, the bank wasn't foreclosing either.

"You won't sell to anybody else, which suits me fine. What's your proposal?"

"I hate that you're developing arable land, but that's what you people do."

"I hate that you people can't compromise, can't be reasonable. An awful lot of land is arable, given enough time and attention. The desert can bloom, Violet, and all it takes is some creativity and determination."

And money. Lots and lots of money.

"I can make your project wither," Violet said. "I've done it before, and I can do it again. I can muster the thousands of people who read my blog to join me. You've seen me motivated, Max. You haven't seen me dig in my heels, and put everything I have into wrecking your party."

"You're welcome to try. I'm making an offer on the Hedstrom property, Violet. I don't scare easily, and this is exactly the kind of project my investors are looking for."

Was it the kind of project Max Maitland was looking for? Violet hadn't the luxury of asking him.

Jane shifted again, this time perching at the top of the steps. Joan, the big alpha ewe, had gotten out somehow and was feasting on Violet's lawn. In about ten minutes, Joan would make her way to the garden.

"Sarge," Violet said, putting a hand over the phone's mike. "Take Joan home."

"I beg your pardon?" Maitland said.

"One of my sheep is loose, so I'll make this quick. You offer Elias Brodie top dollar for his property, and I will not oppose your development, absent environmental dirty tricks on your end."

"I do not play—" Another interesting pause. "Say that again."

"Offer Elias Brodie top dollar for his property, and I won't oppose your development, absent—"

"I got that part, and I'm the last guy to do anything shady, Violet. Shady only results in trouble, and my investors would be very certain I was the one doing the time, while they profited from the crime. What do you consider top dollar?"

Now they were truly negotiating, and Violet sensed victory within her grasp, which meant defeat was at hand too.

"I've got good friends in the agricultural preservation office, Max. They didn't violate any confidences, but they spent the morning sending me a lot of information about appraisals recently done on comparable properties. I know what the Hedstrom property is worth per acre to a developer, and you will pay that amount, and no less."

Jane was moving again—the woman could not keep still—down the steps, following Sarge in the direction of the fugitive ewe.

"I can offer a good price," Max said, "but why do you want Brodie to sell to me?"

"Oh, I don't. I want him to stay here and become a farmer, to attach himself to the land as firmly as I have, to keep you and all your kind out of my valley."

"And I want you to go back to Scotland with him, leaving me to bring civilization to the wilds of Maryland, free of your backward, obstructionist, manure-scented.... You were saying?"

"To a farmer, manure smells like prosperity. I hope my new neighbors get that. In any case, I want you to buy the property from Elias Brodie because you are the devil I know. Your developments win awards, the buyers aren't flipping their homes within two years of moving in because the roof leaks, the basement floods, and the appliances don't work."

"What is the rest of the reason? Why should I trust you to keep your word, Violet? Why not hold me up for every dime I can scrape together, then fight me every step of the way?"

Valid question. "Because I need Elias Brodie to go home to Scotland with enough money in his pocket to save at least one of our castles."

Violet should have conducted this negotiation face to face, because Max Maitland was given to silences. If he laughed at her, she'd at least be able to hate him in good conscience for the rest of her life, and she'd make good on her threats. To the best of her ability, she'd fight his project.

"Violet, if Brodie has in any way threatened or—"

Of all the men to turn up with a chivalrous streak. "*I'm* threatening, Max.

You either pay Elias Brodie what his farm is worth, or I'll wrap your project in so many hearings, injunctions, lawsuits, and investigations, it will be the last project you're hired to develop. I will delight in ruining your career."

Sarge was having a discussion with Joan, about moseying back toward the other sheep, who'd congregated along the fence. The dog put himself directly in front of Joan, sank his front half close to the grass, and yipped at the ewe.

She stomped a front hoof, and snatched another mouthful of grass, then retreated a few feet. Jane watched all this from a few yards off, as did Murphy, who'd bestirred himself to get off the porch.

"I will delight in opening Damson Valley to development," Max said. "If it's any comfort to you, the size of the project I have in mind should saturate demand in the area for at least the next ten years."

Violet rose, because the ewe would not hop back into the pen the way she'd got out. She was a sheep, and sheep logic required that somebody hold the gate for her.

"You don't get it, Max. I'm not in this fight for ten years, or twenty, or thirty. I'm in it for seven generations and beyond, and every one of those generations has to eat. Make Elias a decent, good faith offer, and I'll fight my battles elsewhere, while you destroy the garden in our mutual back yard."

Jane got the gate, Sarge escorted Joan back to the herd, and thus an ovine jail break ended.

"I will offer Brodie fair market value for his land, as is, where is. No contingencies other than a guarantee of clear title and an absence of toxic waste on the site. Certified funds payable upon signature."

That was more than Violet could have hoped for—no escrow, no waiting period, no inspections. Elias would have the money he needed virtually in hand when he got off the plane in Scotland.

"Then we have a deal."

Violet ended the call, then took a picture of Elias's property. The property was beautiful, and wanted only some love and attention to make it shine. Flowers on the porch, some yard work, a cat…

Jane approached, her expression severe. "Lucy, you got some splainin' to do. I don't know what you're up to, but if you intend to interfere with Elias's sale, then you will have two lawyers, one of them Scottish, the other Italian, making your life difficult. I don't think you want that."

Jane was so fierce, so loyal. Violet had been loyal too—to Elias.

"Will you attend the meeting with him?" Violet asked.

"Dunstan is going."

"Then let me explain what Dunstan should expect, and I want your promise that if Maitland gets at all weasely, Dunstan will grab Elias by the elbow and walk out of the meeting."

Sarge and Murphy trotted back to the shade of the porch. They were dry now, but they still stank like happy farm dogs.

"If anybody should be grabbing Elias Brodie by the elbow," Jane said, "it's you. Tell me what you've done, and don't bother prettying it up. You're a woman in love. That means you don't apologize to anybody for the choices you make. I'm a woman in love *and* expecting a baby. I don't make apologies either. I don't suppose you have any brownies?"

CHAPTER SIXTEEN

"You're screwed, laddie," Dunstan concluded, tossing his pen onto his legal pad. "Zebedee signed about the most lop-sided contracts I've seen this side of Maryland public procurements. You're bound hand and foot to the masonry crew, the landscape designer, the architect, and the carpenters. You haven't signed anything with Nick's hotshot castle engineer, so you can still dodge that bullet."

Dunstan apparently leapt into contract clauses with the same zeal Elias dug into corporate books, and yet, most of the contracts on the law office's conference table were simple enough. Zebedee Brodie, on behalf of his heirs, assigns, and successors in interest, agreed to pay for repairs further described as exorbitant, endless, and difficult.

"The castle engineer is the lynch pin that holds all the other repairs together," Elias said. "No point replacing the wainscoting if the rising damp is soon to take over the premises."

"If I had any money at all, Elias, I'd gladly give it to you."

Not lend, give. As bleak as the situation was, Dunstan's generosity warmed Elias's heart. A knock sounded on the conference room door.

"Dunstan, UPS wants me to sign for a package from Scotland," a small, graying woman said. "Are you expecting anything?"

"I am," Elias said. "I'll sign for it." He needed to get up and move, needed to check his phone on the off chance that Violet had called him.

Though what was there left to say? Think of me when you hear the bulldozers destroying that beautiful stone barn? Remember me when the traffic in front of your house becomes dangerously congested?

And Violet couldn't call him, because he'd never given her his phone number, his email, his anything.

Except his heart.

"I have one last client appointment today," Dunstan said, when Elias returned to the conference room. "Jane and I will drive home together, if you want to take the truck."

Jane had gone off on some errand at lunch time, and Elias hadn't heard her come back. "Are you trying to get rid of me?"

"You'll be gone soon enough, and I'll likely not see you until the child's old enough to travel. Jane wants to name a boy after you, though, and when Jane makes up her mind about something, the outcome is assured."

Dunstan ran a finger along the inlay edging the conference table. The piece was massive, elegant, and probably quite valuable, unlike the rest of the furniture in the law office, which was more utilitarian. His expression was fondly distracted, as if the conference table put him in mind of dear memories.

Which might well involve the wife with whom he shared a law practice.

"Are you and Jane managing?" Elias asked.

Dunstan picked up his pen. "Managing?"

"Financially. I know you've been remodeling your farmhouse, and that's expensive. You and Jane will need time off for the baby and children are not cheap."

"You know this, how?"

The fact that Dunstan didn't simply answer the question suggested Elias had been right to ask. "Zebedee never intended to have the raising of me. He made sure I knew at every turn what I cost him, to the point of keeping a ledger for me."

"That's awful," Dunstan said. "Even for a tight-fisted Scottish bachelor, that is inexcusable."

"Heidi and Helga told him as much, and he got out the ledger he'd kept on them. Keeping track of the pence and quid is a fine way to ensure a young man is responsible toward the ladies," Elias said, though he wasn't feeling very responsible toward his own lady right then. "Where do you suppose Jane has got off to?"

"Possibly shopping for maternity clothes."

"Jeannie said that's when Henry became real to her, when she couldn't fit into her clothes any more. Before that, he was a nice if somewhat worrisome and badly timed idea."

Dunstan tapped his pen on his yellow pad. "You'll not keep a ledger on that boy, Elias. I know you're the head of the family, and the earl, and all that rot, but children are for loving, not accounting."

Well, yes. Parents and cousins were for loving too. Castles were for… Elias wasn't sure what castles were for, though a week ago, he'd probably have spouted off knowledgeably if asked.

"Jeannie is earning a fine salary managing matters at the castle, and I've set up a trust for wee Henry. He'll have some options in life, no thanks to his useless father."

"So what's in the package Jeannie shipped to you?"

The package sitting out by the front door, so Elias would not forget it when he and Dunstan left for the day.

"A few items for tomorrow's meeting. I'll take you up on the loan of your truck. I need some fresh air."

"I'm chained to my oar here for another hour or two," Dunstan said. "About tomorrow's meeting?"

Elias closed his laptop and stashed it in his backpack. "I don't expect the meeting will take long. Maitland will offer a sum just above insulting. I'll mutter and dither for form's sake. You'll pretend I ought to refuse the offer. Then we'll grudgingly capitulate, provided Maitland is prepared to convey the funds immediately. He's already made the arrangements with his investors, because he's competent and his investors are greedy."

"You aren't a fool either, but I wish you had another option, Elias. I really do. Not for the sake of the local populace, or even for Violet Hughes, or the greater good of the greater number. I wish for your sake that you had another option besides selling your soul for a damned castle. The rest of the family goes there to get married, and that's about it."

Elias rose, because the whole topic was wearisome. "I live there, in case you'd forgotten."

"No, you don't. You live at the lodge outside the walls of the bailey, and the lodge is lovely. If the castle fell to pieces, wee Henry would just get married in the ballroom at the lodge. To you, it's a castle or a monument to your parents, or a symbol of Scotland's occasionally glorious past. To the rest of us, it's a cheap wedding venue."

Ouch. Though again, Dunstan was being kind, in his way. "Jane must be in love with you, if that's one of your scintillating closing arguments. I'll see you at dinner."

Dunstan tossed him the keys to the truck, and Elias left, making very certain to pick up his package on the way out.

* * *

"I don't understand," Jane said, pouring lemonade and cold tea into a glass, adding ice, and setting it before Violet at the kitchen table. They'd moved inside, both because the afternoon had grown oppressive, and because the stink of the dogs was upsetting Jane's stomach.

"Elias needs money to fix up the castle," Violet said, as if repeating a conclusion for her own benefit. "He's not playing high stakes poker, adding to his whisky collection, schmoozing politicians, or buying race cars. I understand that now."

Jane filled a glass from the tap, added ice cubes, and took the place at Violet's elbow. "You didn't understand that a week ago? I thought Elias was fairly forthcoming with you, for a guy."

"Elias is as honest as a farmer's day is long, Jane, but then I got that letter."

The water tasted different here—well water did that. Varied from property to property. Violet had good water, neither metallic nor sulfurous.

"The letter from the insurance company? I've heard something about this letter, but what can you expect from a company that hires Derek Hendershot as their outside counsel?"

Violet traced drops of condensation as they ran down the side of the glass. "Who's he?"

"The kind of lawyer who gives lawyers a bad name. Tell me about the letter."

"If I can believe Maitland, then the insurance company can't get me thrown off my property, but for a couple days, I walked around here feeling…"

"Like crap?"

"Like I was awaiting a sentence of transportation, like I was about to be banished from my own kingdom. If I couldn't get up the nerve to climb around on my own roof with no one to hold the ladder, use a chain saw thirty feet up a tree… I'm still not sure how I'll take care of what remains on that list, but I was a wreck, Jane."

Jane was hungry. She was always hungry lately, and she had to pee about every seven minutes too, but she also had to understand why two people who should be together were letting considerations as petty as an ocean, an eight-hundred-acre farm, a thousand-year-old castle, a social conscience, and family loyalty keep them apart.

"You look pretty good for a wreck," Jane said. "Do you mind if I make brownies?"

"It's too hot to bake, and you need protein. There are hard boiled eggs in the fridge, and sliced veggies with ranch dressing dip. That's my hot weather go-to combo."

Jane fetched the food, which appealed to her more than it should have. "So you were a wreck, and now you're only a heartbroken wretch?"

"I was terrified of being tossed off my own farm. My father died here, I grew up here, only here, nowhere else. My friends are in this valley, my past, my present, and I'd assumed my future. One letter shows up in the mailbox, and I'm homeless, with my cat, dogs, sheep and chickens."

"Is Maitland to blame? I might be able to get him disbarred if he broke the rules of professional conduct, which are quite strict."

Violet considered a stalk of celery. "That would be too easy. Max is the one who claims my mortgage can't be accelerated for lack of insurance. I believe him, oddly enough." She crunched the celery into oblivion, then went after a slice of green pepper.

Jane chose red pepper, no dressing. "Raw vegetables are fun because they're loud. I like loud food. If Max Maitland gave you an advisory opinion on property law, then you can rely on it. Everyone in the local bar association bounces commercial real estate questions off Max."

Violet winced at the half a green pepper slice remaining. "Max Maitland is the devil's cabana boy. Don't you be saying nice things about him or I'll sic my stink-bomb dogs on you."

"And people accuse lawyers of being sociopaths." Red peppers were also good, or this red pepper was. "You thought you were homeless, so now it's OK for Elias to dump a fortune into his castle?"

"I thought I was homeless, defenseless, friendless, broke, and blindsided. That's how Elias feels, only he's right and I was wrong. I don't hear anybody else from Clan Brodie rallying to the ramparts. He's on his own, and I hate that. If I can't be with him, he should at least have the castle of his dreams."

"You have it soooo bad," Jane said. "But you make a good point. Elias has a lot of family on his mother's side—I met them at the wedding—and yet, they haven't come to see Dunstan the whole time he's been in the States unless they had other business here. With the exception of Jeannie, they don't seem to be pitching in with the castle either."

"Jeannie needed a job and a place to raise her baby," Violet said. "The humidity's starting early this year."

"We say that every year. You should move to Scotland."

"I've caved on eight hundred acres of the best farmland this valley has, Jane. I can't go to Scotland and leave my own property for Max Maitland to snatch. He talks a good game about wanting me to stay where I am, but I don't trust that guy."

"You want to stay here to keep an eye on him," Jane said. "I want a pickle. Do you have any pickles? My sister warned me the cravings aren't just a cliché. I want a whole jar of pickles. I am at risk for swilling pickle juice, which is just disgusting."

Violet got up and fetched a jar of kosher dills out of the fridge, and Jane nearly caught a buzz from the smell.

"You know what the worst thing is about being pregnant?"

Violet's expression was forlorn as she helped herself to a pickle. "Haven't a clue."

"And I'm only in the warm up rounds. A lot of it's lovely, but this business of not being able to do proper justice to a bottle of wine is no damned fun. Somebody should get you tipsy, Violet. I cannot believe you just put ranch dressing on a perfectly respectable dill pickle."

"You want to drink the pickle juice, and you an officer of the court. If we got me tipsy, I might start to cry."

"If you start to cry, I'm likely to cry by association, another blessing of impending motherhood. I could just kick Elias Brodie. He's supposed to be a smart guy.

"Jane?"

"Violet?"

"I think I'm going to cry anyway, even without the wine."

"Me too."

* * *

"I have learned something," Dunstan said, as he and Elias marched down the bumpy sidewalk.

"Some of us are just a wee bit slow," Elias said. "Better late than never, though. What have you learned?"

"I have learned that one man in a kilt is an oddity, but two men in kilts are… I'm getting different looks when it's the two of us strutting around in plaid. When I wear my kilt to a retirement dinner, or an American wedding, I get odd looks. The looks we're getting now are…"

He fell silent as they passed two older women apparently coming from an exercise class.

"Stop smiling like that. You are happily married." Though Elias well knew what Dunstan meant. When he and his cousins turned out in their kilts for an occasion, all the men were a bit handsomer, a bit more charming.

A bit more of everything lovely about being Scottish, and today Elias needed that.

He'd awoken alone, from a dreamy memory of lovemaking with Violet. The contrast, between the warmth and pleasure of her beside him in bed, and the indifferent scrutiny of Dunstan's cat had been…

Rude and riveting. Wallace had perched on Elias's chest, regarding him as if he were a particularly large, lame mouse. In want of brains. In want of even common sense. Too dumb to deserve the mercy of being consumed.

The castle was a cheap wedding venue to the rest of the family.

"Where is your signature backpack?" Dunstan carried a briefcase, though it probably held only a yellow legal pad, some pens, and a bottle of water.

"I have everything I need in my sporran, and behind it."

"Feeling frisky? If you're planning some great blunder at this meeting, it's only courteous to tell your lawyer first."

"I left a suit of clothes at Violet's house," Elias said.

"That qualifies as a blunder. Your suits are worth nearly as much as my truck."

Violet would put much more value on a functional truck than on bespoke business clothes. "I left that suit there on purpose, in case I needed an excuse to stop back and see her one last time."

They'd arrived at Maitland's doorstep. In the few square yards of anemic grass that ran along the sidewalk, three dead gladioli lay in a sad tangle.

"I don't think Violet will pitch you off the property," Dunstan said.

"Though you might want to keep your lips to yourself. Jane stopped out to see her yesterday."

"Is Violet… she's not all right. I slept with the woman then turned around and broke her heart. I'm not all right." The words resonated with inner truth, for all Elias had spoken softly. "I woke up this morning, envisioning Violet in a wedding dress, the family surrounding her, the soaring vault of a medieval great hall rising around us. I can't have both—I can't have the woman and the castle."

"She can't have you and have her farm, that's the greater problem," Dunstan said. "You mention *a* medieval great hall, not *our* medieval great hall. Was it your own castle you saw, or perhaps one of the many castles littering the Scottish countryside?"

"There's no other castle so fine as ours, Dunstan, or so fine as ours will be. I've often thought of turning it into a wedding venue for hire. We'd get plenty of business from Aberdeen, family reunions, the occasional *ceilidh*. The fishing alone could bring in substantial revenue, and—"

The squirrel was traversing the telephone wire again, leisurely hopping across the road by a route mostly unseen, and for the squirrel, free of risk.

An idea wafted into Elias's mind, as a change of weather steals unseen across a valley, a trickle of cooler, dryer air in the middle of a steamy summer, a gradual shift from a white hot sky, to a clear blue. The idea was risky, different, and daring—but it coalesced in Elias's imagination like the squirrel's path across the road: To one with the requisite skill and perspective, the risks were minimal.

"Are we meeting with Maitland," Dunstan asked, "or standing about in our finery until somebody asks us what we're wearing beneath it?"

"Hush," Elias said, watching the squirrel leap into a venerable oak across the street. "I need to think." It could work. It could very possibly work. "We need to postpone this meeting. I've numbers to run, estimates to fine tune. I'll need to talk to Jeannie and Nick, and—"

The door opened, and Max Maitland stood on the threshold. "Gentlemen, if you've come to do business, then I suggest we use my conference room. Six other law offices have addresses on this street, and lawyers love to gossip."

He aimed a pointed stare at Elias's kilt.

"We've come to tell you that the meeting will have to be postponed," Elias said. "Apologies for the short notice."

"We either meet now, Mr. Brodie, or there will be no offer."

Dunstan propped a foot on the bottom stone step. "That's a bit unfriendly, Maitland. Elias has been in the country for less than ten days, and you want to snatch his land away with virtually no discussion."

"Come inside," Maitland said, stepping back. "If I had more time to give you, I would, but investors are a nervous bunch. I either get a handshake on this deal today, or they'll look elsewhere—elsewhere, very likely without me. And may I remind you, Cromarty, you and Mr. Brodie approached me, and this meeting was set up at Mr. Brodie's request."

Dunstan's silence left the decision to Elias. If the meeting went as expected, Elias would be on a plane for Scotland by this time tomorrow.

"Lead on, Mr. Maitland," Elias said. "We've much to discuss, and you're entirely correct. One does not conduct business in the street."

Maitland led them to the same conference room—no flowers today—and offered them coffee, which both Elias and Dunstan declined. The offer for the farm was fair, possibly even more than fair, and the terms were exactly what Elias had expected to have to bargain, wheedle, posture and negotiate for.

Cash in hand, or the next thing to it. A lot of desperately needed cash.

"That is a very reasonable and attractive offer," Elias said. "Dunstan, what are your thoughts?"

* * *

"Violet, hello," Jane said. "They've gone to their meeting. What is that?"

"A suit of very nice clothes," Violet said, knowing very well who *they* were. "May we talk in your office?"

A legal assistant had greeted Violet, the sort of compact, competent woman who was likely running the practice, did her employers but know it. She watched this exchange with a professionally unreadable expression.

"Come along," Jane said, taking the clothes from Violet. "You are a menace, did you know that? I've craved red peppers since I got up this morning. This is your fault."

"Red peppers are cheerful and bold, like you. They're good for us, and I like them."

Jane closed the door to her office, a tidy space sporting a bouquet of daisies next to a picture of Dunstan and Jane in their wedding attire. She hung the suit on a hook on the back of the door, and then stuck her head out the door.

"Kathy, please hold my calls."

"Got it, boss."

When the door was closed, Violet sniffed at the flowers, which was stupid. The scent of daisies was not pleasant.

"I kept Elias's shirt," she said. "He can come and get it if he needs it so badly. I wore it to bed last night—for the scent."

"Pathetic," Jane said. "Elias and Dunstan wore their kilts to this meeting. I have no idea why, but suspect it's a Scottish guy thing. Were you hanging on to the suit?"

"Nope," Violet said, taking a chair across from Jane's desk. "I needed something to do after you left yesterday and because the endless list of things I should be doing held no appeal, I decided to clean the powder room downstairs. I never use it myself, but Elias did the first day I met him. I wonder if he misses those clothes."

Or had he left them with Violet on purpose, like the sunglasses in her shoulder bag? Though what was she to do with a man's suit?

"You're sparing me a phone call," Jane said. "The cop shop called. They've picked up Elias's former caretaker on a non-support warrant. He was also charged with fleeing and eluding, which means trying to get away from the officer with the warrant. This guy thought they were after him for arson, which is a very bad felony."

"Arson?" Maitland had used that word, too.

"Seems he was stealing from your woodpile one fine and frosty morning, and the joint he was smoking dropped. Your woodpile is apparently surrounded by woodchips and tinder and this genius fled then too. He thought you'd seen him, and took off for the nearest girlfriend's couch."

Relief cut through Violet's upset. "What about Elias's alpacas?"

"He says Zeb told him to sell them, and he did—then sent the check to Zeb, who might have already expired."

"Elias will be pleased." Elias probably wouldn't much care, given the magnitude of the other problems he faced. "If he can find that check, it will help with immediate cash flow problems, assuming the check is still good. Did Elias say when he'd be back?"

And should Violet just go before he returned?

"Dunstan told me the meeting shouldn't take long," Jane replied, moving the flowers to the windowsill. "These things stink almost as badly as your dogs, at least to my pregnant nose. Did you want to wait until the guys are done with their meeting?"

What Violet wanted was impossible. "I did not. I wanted to drop off the clothes and run like a rabbit with two farm dogs in pursuit."

Jane opened a drawer and set two chocolate kisses on the desk blotter, then pushed one across the desk to Violet.

"No farm dogs here, Violet. Just us women in love, some chocolate, and a stash of peppermint tea."

And friendship, the most precious bloom to grow in any woman's garden.

"I'll wait then, if you don't mind. I want to say good-bye in person. Elias has done the best he could, the best anybody could. I'll have fond memories, and—"

Jane opened the drawer again and got out a whole bag of kisses. "People in love should stuff a lot of chocolate in their pieholes, so they don't say stupid things, about fond memories, and saying good-bye. I won't even charge you for that advice."

"Thanks. You mentioned peppermint tea?"

CHAPTER SEVENTEEN

"It's a more than reasonable and attractive offer," Max said, before Dunstan Cromarty could lawyer-piss on the parade. "It's my best offer, too, and the only one I'm prepared to make."

Take it or leave it in other words, because if Max didn't close this deal, at this meeting, on these terms, his investors would walk. His bills would not be paid, and that was unacceptable.

"I understand your position, and I have a counter-offer," Brodie said, which was not among the options Max had given him.

"Make it quick, Mr. Brodie, because this is not a complicated situation."

"Elias, might I have a word with you in the hallway?" Cromarty asked.

"Mr. Maitland, you'll excuse us?" Brodie said, rising. The inflection, even making allowances for a Scottish accent, was a question, but Max wasn't being given a choice—as usual. They went strutting out the door, leaving Max in a room without flowers.

At least Bonnie and Derek weren't arguing down the hall. The voices from the other side of the closed door were hushed, rapid, and… arguing? Maybe Brodie had committed that most frequent of client inconsiderations and failed to be straight with his lawyer.

Max gave them a very long five minutes, then opened the door. They stood nose to nose, fists on hips. Bonnie was goggle-eyed at her desk, and Max had the odd thought that he ought to get himself one of these kilt get-ups. His grandfather had been born in Scotland, and Max's mom had pictures of the old guy in a plaid skirt.

"I don't have all day, gentlemen. Are we doing this deal or not?"

Cromarty shoved Brodie on the shoulder—a good, hard shove, not exactly contemplated by the bar association's Rules of Professional Conduct concerning client contact.

"We are doing this deal," Brodie said. "It wants only an explanation, and your consent, Mr. Maitland."

"I'm all ears," Max said, gesturing back toward the conference room.

"Max?" Bonnie called. "You had a call from Mr. Sutherland. He'd like you to call him back as soon as your meeting is over."

Well, of course. And for the next few years, while Max shepherded the Hedstrom project through all manner of hazards and challenges, Sutherland would be demanding a call back at the most inconvenient times, creating artificial deadlines, and stomping all over schedules and budgets Max had lost sleep creating.

"Thanks, Bonnie, and if you go to lunch, please lock the front door behind you—though I don't think we'll be that long."

Brodie grasped Max by the arm, and hauled him into the conference room, while Cromarty closed the door.

"Are all Scots this physical?" Max asked, brushing out the wrinkle on his sleeve.

"Aye," Brodie said. "The ladies prefer us this way, just as they appreciate a man with the balls to wear a kilt. Sit down, Mr. Maitland, and pay attention, for I too have an offer I will only make this once. Do you happen to know which city has the dubious honor of being the oil capital of Europe?"

* * *

"They're back," Jane said, "letting the curtain fall into place. Put the chocolate away."

Violet did no such thing. She went to the window, and caught sight of two big, drop-dead gorgeous, dark-haired men, swinging along in their kilts and sporrans, arguing about something—or perhaps, given that it was Dunstan and Elias—having a friendly discussion.

"They don't look like a pair of guys who just committed treason against true love," Jane said.

They looked scrumptious. Dunstan wore his kilt well, with a certain confidence. It fit him beautifully, and he was entirely at ease in his Highland attire.

Elias, though, was breathtaking. The tassels of his sporran bounced with each step, the buttons on his coat winked in the mid-day sun. Whereas Dunstan was confident, Elias was *splendid.* Exuberantly male, uncaring what breeze might come along and tease at his pleated hem. He had places to strut, deeds to derring-do.

"They look fine," Violet said. "Elias did what he had to do, and I understand that."

"You're an idiot," Jane retorted, jamming the chocolate into the drawer. "Elias is a bigger idiot."

The men came into Jane's office a moment later, their expressions solemn. Gone was the animation Violet had observed through the window. Elias didn't, in fact, seem glad to see her.

"I wasn't expecting you," he said.

Dunstan back-handed him in the belly. "Tell her, ye daftie. Tell her, or I will."

"Tell me what?" Violet asked.

"He was brilliant," Dunstan said. "Damn near conjured the ghost of Rabbie Burns right there in the conference room. You'd think Maitland had never heard of Aberdeen, when half the Texas oil families have vacation homes there."

"What are you two talking about?" Jane demanded.

Elias crossed the room to stand very close to Violet. She caught his scent, a little floral, a little spice, blended with high quality wool.

"What bothered me most," he said, "was the idea of leaving you here, your sworn enemy in plain view across the road. Maitland has the entire world to develop, why should he choose your valley, right now, to build his little boxes?"

"It's a beautiful valley." Elias was a beautiful man too—also attractive as hell in his kilt.

Or out of it.

Jane drew Dunstan from the office, kissing his cheek as they went.

"I couldn't leave you here to contend with him, so I found a reason for him to go far, far away for at least the next few years." Elias's eyes were very blu, and very serious.

"You didn't sell your farm? What about the castle, Elias? The legacy, the family, the—*what have you done*?"

Violet had sat up half the night, wrapped in Elias's shirt, wracking her brain for fresh options, and coming up with only nightmares. Her valley turned into suburbia, her mortgage accelerated.

Her heart in Scotland.

"Maitland's people have money," Elias said. "I have a project requiring money. More to the point, I have a pressing need to get Maitland out of your valley. We negotiated a ninety-nine-year lease of the castle, and Maitland's people will take over the refurbishment at their expense. Brodie Castle will become a state of the art business conference destination, surrounded by scenery, history, sights to see, salmon rivers to fish, world-class golf courses, and locals needing decent employment.

"Jeannie will sit on the board of directors," he went on, "to deal with the local council, and to explain all things Scottish to Maitland and his investors. When she's had enough of that frolic, another family member will succeed her. She's pleased to be able to see the project through, in fact."

Elias was pleased with this arrangement too.

While Violet couldn't quite grasp what he'd done. "You let your castle go?"

"I still own that castle, but I found it a patron, so to speak, for my lifetime and beyond. A century is nothing in the life of a castle, and Maitland's people will make money on the arrangement. Aberdeen has a great deal of wealth, much of it American. Maitland will know how to finish out the castle so the Americans leave as much of their money in his hands as possible. Dunstan, for once, could find no fault with my plans."

"You like that too, having out-smarted your cousin." Violet liked this plan—liked it a lot.

Elias draped an arm across her shoulder. "I liked sending Maitland packing. I liked finding a means to fit out the castle that didn't deplete family resources. I love, however, being able to look you in the eye, and ask if you'd like to put our parcels of land together, and do some agricultural preservation with me."

Oh, that sounded wonderful, but not wonderful enough. "Are you hiring me to manage your farm, Elias?"

A second muscular arm draped itself across Violet's shoulders. "I offer no coin, though coin will come along. I offer myself, Violet, as a partner in all things. I love Scotland, and it will always be the land of my birth. I love you more. You are my home. There will be travel, and complications, and frustrations, I know, but if you marry me, no difficulty will be insurmountable, no problem too great."

Violet looped her arms around Elias's waist. The sporran prevented her from getting as close as she wanted to, so she pushed it aside.

"Yes, Elias Brodie. I will marry you. I will manage your farm—our farms—and travel with you, and face the difficulties. I would love to see your castle, meet your family, and invite them to come see us. I would love…" She swallowed past a lump bigger than all of Damson Valley. "I love you. I love you, I love you… Elias…"

They held each other for long, lovely minutes, until Jane came barging back in.

"I need my chocolate," she said, "and Dunstan was too polite to interrupt you. Elias, I hope you have honorable intentions toward Violet, or I'll have to ask Dunstan and his fists to have a word with you."

"We have honorable intentions toward each other," Violet said, remaining in Elias's embrace. "You'll be my maid of honor, right Jane?"

"Depends," Jane said, popping a chocolate kiss in her mouth as Dunstan joined them. "If you're getting married soon, then yes, because I won't be much farther along. If you're going to drag your feet and spend months planning the wedding, then no. Your godchild is on the way, in case you'd forgotten."

Elias kissed Violet, a question in his eyes.

"The wedding will be soon," Violet said. "The wedding will be very, very soon."

EPILOGUE

"If I weren't already married," Elias said, "this is exactly the sort of place I'd love to say my vows."

In fact, the image on the computer screen was where he and Violet had said theirs vows, but a version of Castle Brodie as it might have been in the first earl's day. Roses vined up the walls of the bailey, heather grew in thriving beds along the walks, windows sparkled in the Highland sun, and pots of blue and white pansies lined the front steps.

Elias had the odd thought that Auld Michael and his Brenna would have recognized this version of the castle as their own too.

"Maitland has a surprising eye for details," Violet said, peering over Elias's shoulder at the mock-up. "But then, he's a developer."

"Or he's listening to Jeannie," Elias suggested, pulling Violet into his lap. "Are you ready to argue with me about the bees and the lavender?"

"If you're ready to argue with me about the milkweed."

They argued a lot. Violet was cautious and practical, Elias had the exuberant creativity of the tyro. He understood business, and he understood hard work, but Violet understood the land. Learning how to put all that together would take them a lifetime, and the journey was off to a delightful start.

"We could compromise instead of arguing," Elias said. "We have more than a thousand acres to bargain with. You give me five acres for lavender, and I won't fuss over planting milkweed in all the hedgerows."

The milkweed was for the monarch butterflies, the lavender was for Zebedee, who'd been right about more than Elias had been willing to admit.

"Milkweed seeds are not cheap," Violet said.

"Neither will it be cheap to develop rain resistant lavender," Elias said, "but think of all the gardens and gardeners who will benefit. Think of the marvelous honey we can sell, and how happy the bees will be."

Elias still had corporate clients, but he cyber-consulted for the most part, and could see the day when his focus was entirely on the farms and his family. Violet's blog and website were growing, and within a year, they'd be selling honey, preserves, spices, and seeds from an online store.

"I'm happy," Violet said, kissing Elias's cheek. "Are you happy?"

She did this, periodically brought Elias back to earth with simple, direct questions. She also reminded Elias that they had decades to shape their property into the legacy Elias envisioned it becoming. No man knew for certain how long his time on earth would be, but increasingly, Elias was so pleased with his present, his future had ceased to worry him.

"I'm very happy," Elias said. "I think Dunstan and Jane are happy to have family in the area too, though if he doesn't stop introducing me as the resident earl, I will—"

"You will spoil our godchild rotten," Violet said. "Marriage must be agreeing with me, because I've even spared a thought for Max Maitland. I think he was relieved to get out of the business of ripping up farmland, not that he'll admit it."

Elias sent the computer to sleep and rose with his wife in his arms. "Maitland might have been relieved to get away from yet another housing development, but I don't think he's found his rhythm yet in Scotland. Jeannie's reports are interesting."

Wee Henry had taken a shine to Maitland, of all the curiosities.

"We might have to visit," Violet said as Elias carried her up the steps. "But only after Jane's baby has arrived, and the crops are off, and the—Mr. Brodie, where are you taking me?"

Elias could contemplate a transatlantic flight much more calmly than he had before his wedding. Violet was an intrepid traveler, having spent too many years in thrall to her farm. She'd even mentioned opening a distillery as part of the farm's five-year plan, and Cousin Magnus and his wife Bridget had all but threatened to back the venture.

"I'm taking you to bed," Elias said. "I wouldn't mind another trip to Scotland later in the year, but for now, the only place I want to be is in your arms and in our bed."

"Do you miss home, Elias?"

He set her on the bed, then lay down beside her. That particular question was one she hadn't put to him previously, but it was time to ask it of himself.

Violet crouched over him—no prevaricating or changing the subject allowed apparently. As usual.

"You would have made a good Scot," he said, wrapping his arms around her. "You have the perspective, the tenacity, the wiliness. I thought that Scottish legacy was my greatest asset."

"The past is important, and I love your Scottish legacy."

Elias had taken to wearing his work kilts around the farm, mostly to please his wife. "Important, yes, but I know better now. My greatest asset is your love, and the present and future I can share with you. The past has value, but to make a life's work out of enshrining the past would have been a mistake."

"And this way, nobody has to deal with Max Maitland or his big ideas. You are wearing too many clothes, Elias Brodie."

Violet set about remedying that situation with her customary dispatch, and soon Elias's clothing was heaped on the floor, along with his schedule for the afternoon, and the list of suggestions he'd intended to email to Jeannie.

Ah, well. Jeannie apparently had her hands full dealing with Maitland and his big ideas, a situation Elias would investigate when next he was in Scotland. For now, all he wanted was to please his wife, build their future, and guard their dreams as fiercely as he'd once guarded a certain Scottish castle.

As fiercely as he loved Violet and was loved by her in return. Elias's last thought as Violet commenced a kissing spree that went farther south on his person the longer she persisted, was that Auld Michael and his Brenna had founded an empire that had thrived for ten generations.

At the rate Elias and Violet were going, the eleventh generation would soon be making an appearance, and in all the ways that counted, the castle would still be there for them. The castle was not stones and bricks and parapets, any more than it was acres of crops or a weathered barn.

The best castles, the castles worth defending, were all built of love and always would be.

THE END

To my dear Readers,

I like to think that somewhere not far from my bide-o-wee in western Maryland, Elias and Violet are raising their rain-resistant lavender, as well as some really cool chickens, and a wee bairnie or two. Dunstan and Jane drop by for eggs, or just to visit on the front porch, and the relatives (Liam and Louise, Niall and Julie, Magnus and Bridget), take turns vacationing in Damson Valley too.

If you'd like to catch up with those fine people, Magnus Cromarty's story—Tartan Two-Step—is part of a two-novel ebook duet with ML Buchman, Big Sky Ever After. Dustan and Jane's RITA -nominated novella (Kiss and Tell) appears along with Liam's story (Dunroamin Holiday) in the novella duet Two Wee Drams of Love. Niall's story (Love on the Links) is paired with a tale for Scottish farmer Declan MacPherson (My Heartthrob's in the Highlands) in the novella duet Must Love Scotland, and all four novellas have been bundled into one volume (Four Wee Drams of Love), which is available exclusively on my website store (and is the best bargain, just sayin').

I love Scotland, and for the final story in the Trouble Wear Tartan series, you've probably guessed that Max Maitland will end up in Scotland, where he's managing restoration of Castle Brodie with the help of Jeannie Cromarty… or despite her help. I expect to have that story available for publication later this year or in early 2018.

You can keep up with all my new releases, sales, and illustrious doin's by signing up for the newsletter, following me on Bookbub, or catching up with me on social media. I've include an excerpt below from Tartan Two Step, and also a short scene from my June 2016 release, His Lordship's True Lady. Thanks for spending this time with Elias and Violet, and, as always…

Happy Reading!
Grace Burrowes

Follow me on Bookbub at
bookbub.com/search/authors?search=Grace burrowes
Sign up for my newsletter at
graceburrowes.com/contact/
Like my FB author page at
facebook.com/Grace-Burrowes-115039058572197/?fref=ts&ref=br_tf
Follow me on Twitter at
twitter.com/GraceBurrowes?lang=en

TARTAN TWO STEP

BY GRACE BURROWES

Magnus Cromarty and Bridget MacDeaver shared a lovely, unplanned encounter that neither of them thought could lead anywhere, but now they're finding that lovely, stolen pleasure has lead straight to trouble's doorstep….

Magnus's brain as he wrestled with the notion that the woman he'd glimpsed for half a second in the open doorway had borne a delightful resemblance to Bridget.

A girl had stood by her side. A little sprite with what looked like spaghetti sauce on her cheek and a crust of bread in her hand.

Then boom—literally—the enormous door had slammed shut.

It opened again. "Excuse my sister for her unique sense of humor," a tall blond man said. "You must be Mr. Cromarty. Welcome."

Bridget—*had* that been Bridget?—was nowhere to be seen, but two other tall blond men were in evidence, trying to smile.

"I am Magnus Cromarty. Have I found the Logan Bar ranch?" The turnoff to the drive was well marked, with a timber sign anchored in native stone, but that had been several miles ago.

"You have," the official greeter said. "I'm Luke Logan, and these are my brothers, Shamus and Patrick. I'll show you around your new home away from home, and if you have any luggage—"

"I'll show him around."

Bridget stood on a flight of steps leading from a truly impressive room. The American West was embodied in this room as a rugged, lovely, comfortable haven. The woman on the steps was furious, though, and nothing would protect Magnus from her wrath.

Which made no sense.

"Thank you," Magnus said. "I wouldn't want to put anybody to any bother."

Bridget descended the rest of the steps and clomped to the front door. "You won't be any bother at all, I can guarantee you that, mister. Luke, fetch his gear. Patrick, see to your daughter. Shamus, you can start cleaning up supper before the cats get after the pepperonis."

These must be the infamous brothers, though they scurried off at her command like chastened puppies.

"Bridget?" Magnus didn't dare touch her, though he wanted to. She had clearly added him to the list of men with whom she was furious, and he had no intention of remaining on that list.

"That would be me," she said, rounding on him. "What sick sense of humor inspires a man to charm his way right into the enemy's skivvies, Magnus? I don't expect much from the male of the species, but that's a new low in my experience."

"How did I become your enemy?"

"We'll discuss that later, when my brothers aren't lurking in the bushes, thinking up more inspired ways to ruin my life." She snatched a patchwork quilted jacket from a peg on the wall and flounced out the door.

A gentleman didn't argue with a lady, not when her expression promised to geld him at the first opportunity. Magnus followed Bridget across the driveway to a handsome stone and timber house with a roofed porch. Luke Logan followed with Magnus's suitcase and carry-on.

"Thank you," Magnus said.

"Your groceries got here a couple hours ago," Luke said. "If you need anything, we're just a—"

"Beat it, Luke," Bridget said. "Braveheart and I are due for a parley."

Luke's gaze skittered from his sister to Magnus. "You two know each other?"

"No," Bridget said, just as Magnus answered, "We're acquainted."

"That's… that's good, I hope," Luke said, taking himself down the steps. "Bridget, we'll save you a slice of pie."

That was a warning of some sort, obvious even to Magnus, who had no siblings.

"Inside," Bridget said, producing a key from the pocket of her jeans. "Get inside and prepare to explain why in the hell I should give you the time of day much less a tour of my distillery."

Her distillery? "Because," Magnus said, "if ever you should come to Scotland, I'd be happy to give you a tour of my facilities."

"I've seen your *facilities*, Magnus. I never want to tour them again."

* * *

Bridget's sense of betrayal was wonderfully righteous, and yet, a stupid corner of her heart hoped that Magnus hadn't spent the night with her in anticipation of stealing her distillery. Then too, her rage felt a little too good, a little too handy.

She had many, many reasons to be angry, and they weren't *all* Magnus's fault, even if he was in Montana to take her business from her.

He leaned against the guesthouse kitchen counter, looking windblown and wary in his jeans and a flannel shirt. He also looked tired.

"Are you hydrating?" Bridget asked.

"Bridget, I'm not a sot."

Did anybody sound as offended as an indignant Scot?

"The elevation here is nearly a mile above sea level," Bridget said, opening the fridge. "If you're used to living at lower altitudes, then you need time to adjust. You're also probably not accustomed to how dry it can be here."

She filled a glass half way with organic raspberry juice—he could afford organic raspberry juice, of course—and topped it off with seltzer water.

"Drink that."

He crossed his arms. "Not unless you join me, Bridget. You told your brother that you and I are due to parley. That means discussion, not you giving orders while the rest of the world scurries to do your bidding."

She took a sip of his drink, realized what she'd done—damn, it was good—then shoved it at him.

"Nobody scurries to do my bidding, Magnus. That's a problem I aim to fix. The Logan brothers suffer a deficit of scurry-ness, but they're educable, given enough patience and a cattle prod."

"Right now, one of them is cleaning up the kitchen; the other is seeing to the child. Luke is making sure there's a piece of pie waiting for you when you hop on your broomstick and rejoin them at the dinner table."

"You think so?"

"I think they scurry better than you notice. This drink is exquisite."

Real men didn't describe fruit drinks as exquisite, but Bridget had every reason to know that Magnus was a real man.

She fixed herself a glass and put the juice and fizzy water back in the fridge. Magnus had ordered a crisper full of fresh veggies, several different kinds of cheese, artisan bread, butter, eggs, and…

And Bridget was snooping, so she closed the door to the refrigerator and put on her trial-lawyer face.

"You want to talk," she said, "I'll listen." She'd hated the courtroom, but had found that out only after devoting three years of her life and all of her savings to law school.

Magnus held a chair for her at the small round table by the window. Bridget pulled the curtains closed, lest any nosy brothers get to spying, and took a seat. Magnus sat across from her, and for a moment, she battled with the pleasure of simply beholding him.

She'd parted from him yesterday morning, telling herself she'd stored up a fine little memory, but she'd also stored up a fine little heartache to go with it. She *liked* Magnus—or liked the Magnus she'd met at the Bar None—and had steeled herself against never seeing him again.

Now, she wanted to know if there was a way to keep liking him without losing her distillery or her pride.

Order your copy of Tartan Two-Step!

And read on for a sneak peek from my June release,
His Lordship's True Lady…

HIS LORDSHIP'S TRUE LADY

BY GRACE BURROWES

Lily Ferguson's finishing governess had warned her that a young lady must appear pleasantly fascinated with scandals and engagement announcements, no matter that they bored her silly.

"Aspic and small talk," Lily muttered.

They were equally disagreeable. Fortunately, the Earl of Grampion's dinner party was lively and the general conversation loud enough to hide Lily's grousing.

"I beg your pardon, my dear?" Neville, Lord Stemberger, asked. Because his lordship apparently longed for an early death, he leaned closer to Lily's bosom to pose his question.

At the head of the table, a footman whispered in Lord Grampion's ear. The earl was a titled bachelor with vast estates in the north. Thus, his invitations were coveted by the matchmakers.

Then too, he was attractive. On the tall side, blond hair with a tendency to wave, blue eyes worthy of a Yorkshire summer sky, and features reminiscent of a plundering Norseman. Strikingly masculine, rather than handsome.

Perhaps he had bad teeth, for the man never smiled. Lily would ask Tippy for details regarding the Kettering family, for Tippy studied both Debrett's and the tattlers religiously.

Lily had found Grampion a trifle disappointing when they'd been introduced. His bow had been correct, his civilities just that—not a spark of mischief, not a hint of warmth in his expression. Many handsome men were dull company, their looks excusing them from the effort to be interesting, much less charming.

Lily's musings were interrupted by the sensation of a bug crawling on her flesh. Lord Stemberger's pudgy fingers rested on her forearm, and he remained bent close to her as if entirely unaware of his own presumption.

At the head of the table, Grampion rose and bowed to the guests on either side of him, then withdrew.

Excellent suggestion.

Lily draped her serviette on the table. "If you'll excuse me, my lord. I'll return in a moment." Thirty minutes ought to suffice to fascinate Lord Stemberger with some other pair of breasts.

She pushed her chair back, and Lord Stemberger, as well as the fellow on her right, half rose as she departed. So polite of them, when they weren't ogling the nearest young lady or her settlements. Across the table and up several seats, Uncle Walter appeared engrossed in an anecdote told by the woman to his right.

Lily made her way down the corridor, intent on seeking refuge in the women's retiring room, but she must have taken a wrong turning, for a raised male voice stopped her.

"Where the devil can she have got off to?" a man asked.

A quieter voice, also male, replied briefly.

"Then search again and keep searching until—Miss Ferguson." The Earl of Grampion came around the corner and stopped one instant before knocking Lily off her feet. "I beg your pardon."

A footman hovered at his lordship's elbow—a worried footman.

"My lord," Lily said, dipping a curtsey. "Has somebody gone missing?"

"Excuse us," Grampion said to the footman, who scampered off as if he'd heard a rumor about free drinks at the nearest pub.

"No need for concern, Miss Ferguson, this has been a regular occurrence for the past week. My ward has decided to play hide-and-seek all on her own initiative, well past her bedtime, after promising me faithfully that she'd never, ever, not for any reason—I'm babbling." He ran a hand through his hair. "I beg your pardon. The child will be found, I've no doubt of it."

This was the polite, chilly host to whom Lily had been introduced two hours ago? "How old is she?"

"Almost seven, though she's clever beyond her years. I found her in the hayloft last time, and we'd been searching for hours. The nursery maids don't think she'd leave the house at night."

No wonder he was worried. Even Mayfair was no place for a lone six-year-old at night. "How long has she been missing?"

His lordship produced a gold pocket watch and opened it with a flick of his wrist. "Seventeen minutes. The senior nursery maid tucked the girl in at precisely nine of the clock—for the third time—and was certain the child had fallen asleep. She went back into Daisy's bedroom to retrieve her cap precisely at ten, and the little imp wasn't in the bed."

"You could set the guests to searching."

Grampion snapped the watch closed. "No, I could not. Do you know what sort of talk that would start? I'm supposed to be attracting a suitable match, and unless I want to go to the bother and expense of presenting my bachelor self in London for the next five Seasons, I cannot allow my tendency to misplace small children to become common knowledge."

Lily smoothed back the hair he'd mussed, then tidied the folds of his cravat, lest some gossip speculate that he'd been trysting rather than searching for this ward. He was genuinely distraught—why else would he be baldly reciting his marital aspirations?—and Lily approved of him for that.

For resenting the burden and expense of a London Season, she sympathized with him, and for his honesty, she was at risk for liking him.

And that he'd blame himself for misplacing the child… Lily peered up at him, for Grampion was a tall specimen.

"Where is your favorite place in the house?" she asked.

"I don't have a favorite place. I prefer to be in the stables, if you must know, or the garden. When the weather is inclement, or I have the luxury of idleness, I read or tend to correspondence in my study."

His complexion was a touch on the ruddy side, the contours of his features a trifle weathered now that Lily could study him from close range. As a result, his eyes were a brilliant blue and, at present, full of concern.

"Come with me," Lily said, taking him by the hand. "That you found your ward in the stable is no coincidence. You say she's been in your home for only a week?"

Grampion came along peacefully, suggesting he was possessed of sense, despite his upset. "She's an orphan, her parents having died earlier this year. The will named me as guardian, and so she was left almost literally upon my doorstep. The poor child was quite close to her mother and barely knows me from among a dozen other neighbors."

"What's her name?"

"Beelzebub, on her bad days. Her parents named her Amy Marguerite, her mother called her Daisy."

Lily dropped his lordship's hand outside the study, which was across the corridor from the formal parlor. "What do you call her?"

He focused on a spot above and to the left of Lily's left shoulder. "Sweetheart, poppet, my dear, or, when I can muster an iota of sternness, young lady."

Lily patted his lapel. "Refer to the child as Daisy, but do not acknowledge that she's in the room."

"You believe she's in the study?"

"I'm almost certain of it, if you frequent the study late at night. You will lament her absence, worry aloud at great length, and confirm to me that losing the child would devastate you."

He considered the door latch. "Devastate might be doing it a bit brown. With practice, I could endure to lose her for ten minutes here and there."

He'd be devastated if the child wasn't soon found. Lily was more than a little worried, and she hadn't even met the girl.

His lordship pushed open the door and gestured for Lily to precede him.

No wonder he preferred this chamber. Books rose to a height of two stories on shelves lining two sides of the room. The windows on the outside wall would look over the garden, and the furnishings were of the well-padded, sturdy variety that invited reading in unusual positions for long periods.

The wall sconces had been turned down, throwing soft shadows across thick carpets, and the hearth blazed with a merry warmth.

A pleasure dome, compared to small talk and aspic.

"We simply can't find her," Lord Grampion announced. "Daisy is very clever at choosing hiding places, and I despair of locating her when she doesn't want to be found."

"Where have you looked?" Lily asked as a curtain twitched in the absence of any breeze.

"We're searching the house from top to bottom, the maids are starting in the cellars, the footmen in the attics. Nobody will sleep a wink until Daisy is once again tucked safely in her bed."

Lily pointed to the curtain, and Grampion nodded.

"She must matter to you very much for you to leave your guests and set your entire staff to searching, my lord."

"Of course she matters to me. She's the dearest child, and I'm responsible for her happiness and well-being."

His lordship was clearly not playacting. In the space of a week, Daisy had captured his heart, or at least his sense of duty. Many daughters commanded less loyalty from their blood relatives, and nieces were fortunate to have a roof over their heads.

As Uncle Walter so kindly reminded Lily at every opportunity.

"Do you think she might be lost?" Lily asked as his lordship silently stalked across the room. "It's so very dark out tonight. Not a sliver of a moon in the sky."

"Daisy is too clever to be lost," Grampion said, pushing back the curtain. "But she's not too clever to be found."

A small blond child sat hunched on a window seat. She peered up at the earl, saying nothing. Most parents would have launched into a vociferous scold. Grampion instead sat beside the child. He said nothing and merely tucked her braid over her shoulder.

"I couldn't sleep," the girl said, ducking her head. "I miss home."

"So do I," the earl replied. "Are your feet cold?"

Bare toes peeked out from beneath the hem of a linen nightgown. "Yes."

The earl scooped her up and settled her in his lap. "You gave me a fright, Daisy. Another fright, and you promised not to do this again."

She sat stiffly in his arms, like a cat who had pressing business to be about in the pantry. "Will you beat me?"

"Never."

He should probably not have admitted that, and Lily should not be witnessing a moment both awkward and intimate. She took a step back, and the child's gaze swung to her.

"Who's she?"

Grampion rose with the girl in his arms. "Miss Lily Ferguson, may I make known to you Miss Daisy Evers, my ward. Daisy, this is Miss Lily."

He'd chosen informal address, and Lily was far more comfortable with it. "Hello, Daisy. The earl was beside himself with anxiety for you."

"Worried," Grampion said. "I was worried, and now I'm taking you up to bed, young lady."

"May I have a story, please?"

Grampion should refuse this request, because naughty behavior ought not to be rewarded.

"His lordship has many guests who will all remark his absence," Lily said, holding the door open. "I know a few good stories, though, and will stay with you until you fall asleep."

Grampion led the way up two flights of stairs, pausing only to ask a footman to call off the search. The nursery was lavishly comfortable, but all the furnishings looked new, the toys spotless and overly organized on the shelves.

Where were the girl's brothers, when her toys wanted a few dings and dents?

"You will behave for Miss Ferguson," his lordship said. "Do not interrupt to ask why nobody has ever seen a dragon, or how dragons breathe fire without getting burned."

"Yes, sir."

"Try to go to sleep," Grampion said, laying the child on her bed and brushing a hand over her brow. "Miss Ferguson, a word with you, please."

"I'll be right back," Lily told the girl.

His lordship plucked a paisley shawl from the back of a rocking chair and led Lily into the corridor.

"One story," he said, draping the shawl around Lily's shoulders. "No more, or you'll still be reading when the sun comes up. And you may slap me for asking, but are you enamored of Lord Stemberger?"

The shawl was silk, the feel of it lovely against Lily's skin. What sort of bachelor earl kept silk shawls for the nursery maids?

"I am in no fashion enamored of Lord Stemberger. Why?"

"He…" Grampion appeared to become fascinated with the gilt scrollery framing a pier-glass across the corridor. "He did not conduct himself as a gentleman ought at table. Sitting beside him, you might not have noticed where his gaze strayed, but I will not invite him back. He lacks couth."

Lily approved of Grampion very much for speaking up when many other men would have looked the other way or, more likely, guffawed in their clubs over Stemberger's coarse behavior.

Grampion lacked warmth, but he was honorable, and to an orphaned child, he'd been kind.

"See to your guests, my lord," Lily said. "I'll tend to the dragons and be down shortly."

"Miss Lily?" came a soft question from the child's bedroom. "Are you coming?"

Grampion bowed over Lily's hand, his grasp warm in the chilly corridor. "One story. Promise me. The child needs to know I mean what I say."

"One story," Lily said. "One happily ever after. I promise. Now be off with you."